LEND ME AN EAR

Jason heard the other pistol also fire wildly as its owner went down under a crush of assailants. Whatever implanted high-tech weapons the Transhumanists had, they dared not use them publicly. They were promptly overwhelmed by sheer numbers and held. The big man had pinned the Transhumanist leader face-down on the cobblestones, and had drawn his cutlass.

"God's holy shit!" he bellowed. "Try to shoot *me*, will you? What's this town coming to? I was telling Governor Modyford just the other day that we're starting to get a bad element in Port Royal. I ought to hand this cutlass to Zenobia and let her cut off your pox-rotten prick! But it happens I'm in a good mood today. So…"

He stood up, and brought his cutlass down with a whistle of cloven air. The Transhumanist screamed, and blood spurted from the right side of his head. The big man reathing up from beside him, The Transhumanist ga

"Like the taste   pper, unless you want   get out of here before I become annoyed and forget I'm a gentleman!" The big man gave a final kick to the ribs of the Transhumanist, who staggered to his feet

stanch
o's back
wn.

BAEN BOOKS by STEVE WHITE

To purchase these and all Baen Book titles in e-book format, please go to www.baen.com.

PIRATES
OF THE
TIMESTREAM

STEVE WHITE

A Baen Books Original

Baen Publishing Enterprises
P.O. Box 1403
Riverdale, NY 10471
www.baen.com

ISBN: 978-1-4767-3677-8

Cover art by Don Maitz
Map by Randy Asplund

First paperback printing, June 2014

Library of Congress Catalog Number: 2013005970

Distributed by Simon & Schuster
1230 Avenue of the Americas
New York, NY 10020

Pages by Joy Freeman (www.pagesbyjoy.com)
Printed in the United States of America

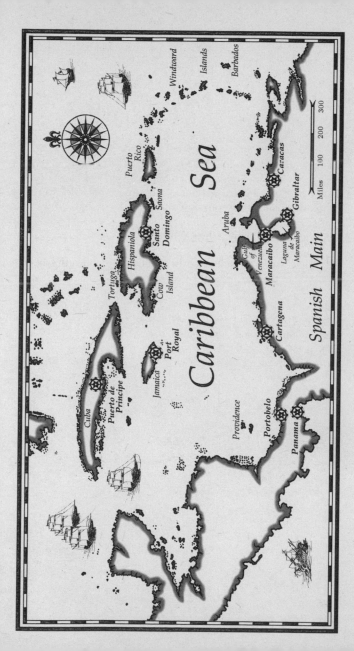

PIRATES
OF THE
TIMESTREAM

CHAPTER ONE

The immense dome rose above the center of a wide expanse of office buildings, machine shops, living quarters and other facilities—an area the size of a medium-sized town. Dwarfing even the dome was the antimatter power plant—the only one of its kind allowed on the surface of Earth or any other inhabited planet. Its presence was the reason the installation was located in Australia's Great Sandy Desert, northwest of Lake Mackay, a region that was practically uninhabited even in the late twenty-fourth century.

All this was what time travel required—or so the Temporal Regulatory Authority had believed until recently.

"I don't like it," muttered Alistair Kung nervously to his two companions, for at least the third time.

They stood in a glass-walled mezzanine, high up inside the dome and overlooking the circular thirty-foot platform that occupied the dome's center and was its reason for existence. Terraced concentric circles of instrument panels, control consoles and other devices of less obvious function surrounded the platform, giving it the aspect of the stage of a circular theater. Adding to that impression was the tense fixation with which the "audience" of technicians stared at the stage, even though it was pristinely empty of scenery and actors.

"I don't like it," Kung repeated. "It's been too long." With his portly figure and round Asian-featured face, he suggested an image of Buddha without the serenity; one had to somehow imagine a jittery Buddha. "Besides, I've *never* approved of this business of temporal retrieval devices that can be activated at the mission leader's discretion. It's dangerous! I ask you, what's wrong with the way things have always been done?"

Kyle Rutherford sighed, but kept his sigh inconspicuous. He himself was chief of operations for the Temporal Regulatory Authority, with broad powers. But Kung was a prominent member of the Authority's governing council. He had to be handled carefully.

"Nothing whatever, Alistair," he assured Kung smoothly. "And as you know, our normal research expeditions still use the traditional TRDs, set to activate at a prearranged time so we'll know precisely when to keep the stage clear." He permitted himself a frosty chuckle, stroking his equally frosty Vandyke. "Wouldn't do to have two objects occupying the same space at the same time, you know—least of all if one or both of them are living human bodies."

"Precisely my point! Now we seem to have thrown caution to the winds!"

"This has all been discussed exhaustively before the full council, Alistair," Rutherford reminded him. "In order for the Temporal Service's new Special Operations Section to function in its intended role, the mission leader must be given an unprecedented degree of latitude to make decisions on the basis of the actual situation in the field, which only he can know."

"Ah, yes...the Special Operations Section." This, clearly, was something else of which Kung did not approve. He had been a moving force behind the formation of a select committee of the council to oversee the Section's activities. "I've been meaning to speak to you, Kyle, about some of the people who've been recruited for it lately. Hooligans and roughnecks!"

"Isn't that a bit strong, Alistair?" Rutherford admonished mildly.

"By no means! Granted, our standards for Temporal Service personnel have always been, of necessity, somewhat elastic. But really—!"

"I grant you that the Special Operations Section's peculiar functions sometimes require blunt instruments," Rutherford conceded. "But remember, all personnel selections are subject to a veto by Jason Thanou, the head of the Section. And every Special Operations mission is under the strict control of a Service officer of proven experience and probity. In the case of this particular mission, whose return we are awaiting, the mission leader is Commander Thanou himself."

"Hmmm." Kung subsided somewhat, for this was a difficult argument to rebut. "Yes, I suppose Commander Thanou's record speaks for itself. And of *course* we *all* have utmost confidence in him, even though he *is*, after all, an outworlder." Kung suddenly and belatedly recalled that the third person present was from the colony world of Arcadia, Zeta Draconis A II. He turned to her with an agonizingly embarrassed smile. "Of course I did not mean to imply that—"

"Of course not, sir." Chantal Frey showed no signs of having taken offense at Kung's gaffe. She was a slender, youngish woman with straight, dark brown hair and pale, regular features. Her nondescript appearance was matched by a personality that was quiet to the point of diffidence. But she could be stubborn in her mild way. And she seemed undisturbed by—indeed, barely even conscious of—her somewhat ambivalent status as a returned defector.

She had been a member of an extratemporal expedition Jason Thanou had led to the Greece of 490 B.C. There they had made the shattering discovery that had led to the formation of the Special Operations Section: the Authority was not operating the only temporal displacer on Earth as it had always believed. There was another, using technology that allowed it to be small and energy-efficient enough to be concealable. Even worse, it was operated by a surviving cadre of the Transhuman movement which had been thought to have been extirpated over a century before.

The Transhumanist plot they had uncovered in connection with the Battle of Marathon had been a devious and clever one, and its leader—a certain Franco, Category Five, Seventy-Sixth Degree—had possessed a distinct Satanic charm. Chantal could testify to that, having been seduced by him.

"I understand your concerns, sir," she assured Kung. "But as you know, procedures have been put in place to minimize the risks. Our research expeditions still proceed as before, committed to the past for a set time, after which their TRDs return them to the displacer stage. But now when they uncover evidence of Transhumanist activity, they immediately inform the Authority via message drops." The leaving of written messages, on extremely durable media, in prearranged and out-of-the-way locations was the only way extratemporal travelers had to communicate with the era from which they had been displaced backward in time. "When such a message is received, a Special Operations unit using the new 'controllable' TRDs is sent back to that precise point in time to deal with the situation."

"At least," said Kung grudgingly, "it's not the *same* people you're sending back." One of the Authority's cardinal rules forbade sending time travelers back to overlapping time frames where they might possibly encounter their own slightly younger selves. He gave Rutherford a look of still-unappeased indignation over the one egregious violation of that rule Rutherford and Jason Thanou had engineered.

"No indeed," agreed Chantal. "Of course, they work with the academic expedition that is already in place in the milieu, but there can be no objection to that."

"Possibly not. But . . . blast it, Kyle, they're allowed to take modern weapons and equipment into the past! It's unprecedented!"

"Only very well-disguised weapons and equipment, Alistair, as you know. There's a workshop here that does nothing but produce such items. And we can hardly limit our people to in-period technology and expect them to go up against the Transhumanists, who have no scruples about such things."

"And," Chantal added, "these Special Operations missions, aimed at specific targets, can be accomplished in only a few hours or, at most, days. So they are given rigid time limits, which none of them have ever exceeded, and therefore it is not particularly burdensome to keep the displacer stage here open for their return. So you see, sir, all your concerns have been addressed." All at once, she allowed Kung a glimpse of her easily overlooked determination. "And at any rate, you may recall an old saying about desperate times calling for desperate measures. Remember, it is *Transhumanists* we are dealing with."

Kung said nothing, for what she was saying tapped into cultural imperatives so deep as to be beyond argument.

By the last years of the twenty-first century, genetic engineering, bionics, direct neural computer interfacing and nanotechnology had advanced to a level with potentialities that made those of atomic energy seem almost trivial by comparison, for they enabled the human race to transform itself into something other than human. Many in those confused times had reacted with avidity rather than revulsion. The upshot had been the Transhuman movement, which had seized power after a generation and then, for another three generations, made Earth a hell. Weird abominations had proliferated as the Tranhsumanist ruling elite had sought to transform themselves into supermen ruling an anthill society of specialized subhuman castes. The cleansing of Earth—sparked by extrasolar colonists whose ancestors had departed on slower-than-light ships to escape what they could see coming in the early days of the Transhumanist madness, and who now returned on the wings of the negative-mass drive invented on a colony world—had required a bloodbath beyond any in history. Afterwards, the Human Integrity Act had banned all tinkering with the human genotype, all bionic melding of human and machine, and all nanotechnology except for industrial uses, preferably in orbital factories. Never again would humanity listen to the siren song of "improving" itself. Man would remain Man.

Then Jason Thanou had returned from the fifth century B.C. with the news that had ended a century of complacency.

The Transhumanist time travelers could no more change history than anyone else—the poorly understood "Observer Effect" precluded that—but they could subvert it. The past could be changed in ways that created no paradoxes, as the "message drop" system demonstrated. This left the Transhumanists ample scope for the creation of a "secret history," as they filled the past's blank spaces with conspiratorial secret societies, genetic time bombs, and so forth—all very long-term, and all timed so as to come to fruition at a future date known as *The Day*, when it would become apparent that known history had never been anything all along but a façade behind which *real* history had been slowly and quietly building toward an inevitable Transhumanist triumph.

All this Jason Thanou and his expedition had learned. Chantal, in particular, had learned a great deal from Franco—more than she had thought she had, as it had turned out when professional debriefers had finished with her. Unfortunately, it was all of a general nature. Most unfortunately of all, she had not learned when *The Day* was scheduled to occur. Franco hadn't been about to reveal that to any Pug ("product of unregulated genetics," the scornful Transhumanist epithet for everyone but themselves), however infatuated she might seem.

Pondering the Transhumanists brought a new thought bubbling to the surface of Kung's mind. "See here, Kyle... if Transhumanist time travelers are operating from the present—"

"We don't absolutely know that," Rutherford cautioned. "The Transhumanist expedition Commander Thanou encountered came from slightly in our past... fortunately for him, if you think about it."

"Yes, yes. But why can't they go back in time a couple of centuries, to the era when their ideology ruled Earth, and make contact with those rulers, and... ?" Kung trailed to a halt, reduced to speechlessness by the implications.

"You forget, Alistair," said Rutherford in a calming tone, "temporal displacement of objects of significant mass is uncontrollable for a temporal 'distance' of three hundred years into the past." (*And only the past*, he did not need to add; even Kung understood that travel into one's own future was impossible, for reasons inherent in the fundamental nature of temporal energy potential.) "So, as a practical matter, no one can be displaced from the present to any date more recent than about 2080."

Kung looked relieved, but Chantal Frey looked thoughtful. "That," she mused, "was only a few years before the first recorded appearance of the Transhumanist movement. And there is much that is obscure about its origins. Assuming—and we dare not assume otherwise—that the surviving underground Transhumanists are still operating their displacer at the present time or a little in our future, then perhaps they founded their own movement."

Kung went pale, and Rutherford was heard to mutter what sounded like a literary quote—something about "that man's father is my father's son." It was the sort of thing that gave the Authority nightmares.

"And then, of course," Chantal continued even more thoughtfully, "assuming that they will continue to operate their displacer still further in our future..."

Kung shook himself with a force that set his wattles to jiggling. "Well, these speculations are all very interesting. But the point is that the Special Operations unit we are awaiting is late in returning."

"Not yet past its deadline," Rutherford admonished. But he sounded worried. It *was* getting close. And the rules were strict: after that deadline, it would be assumed that the unit had been lost, and the displacer stage would no longer be kept clear for them. If they should happen to return after that...

At that moment the display boards at the control consoles surrounding the central stage suddenly burst into a flashing light-show.

The Fujiwara-Weintraub Temporal Displacer could cancel the "temporal energy potential" that kept an object (living or otherwise) anchored in its own time—but only at the cost of a titanic energy surge, hence the huge and somewhat worrisome power plant in this (everyone hoped) safely remote location. The Authority's scientific staff was digging frantically for the flaw in Fujiwara's mathematics that the Transhumanist underground had discovered, enabling them to operate with far more energy efficiency. But however it was done, the restoration of temporal energy potential was almost incredibly easy, requiring a device—the "Temporal Retrieval Device," or TRD—barely larger than a ball bearing and drawing an undetectably tiny amount of energy.

Hence there was never any warning when a time traveler returned to the displacer stage at the time he had departed plus the time he had spent in the past—the "linear present," as it was called. At exactly the same instant the data displays awoke, five soldiers of the army of the Confederate States of America appeared on the stage. One of them, obviously wounded, was being supported by two of the others. All exhibited the disorientation of temporal transition . . . but only momentarily, for they were veterans.

Rutherford, followed by his two companions, hurried down to the main floor. The medical personnel who were kept continuously on alert while a Special Operations mission was in progress had already taken charge of the wounded man, whose injury was clearly not serious. They stepped up to greet a man with a Confederate captain's three bars on the collar of his gray coat.

"Welcome back . . . Captain Landrieu," said Rutherford with an ironic lift of one eyebrow. "You had us a bit worried."

"I think you look rather dashing in that uniform," said Chantal Frey, smiling at the man who had, uniquely in the annals of time travel, brought her back to her own time despite the loss of her TRD.

Jason Thanou smiled raffishly under his broad-brimmed slouch hat and stroked the mustache and goatee Rutherford had ordered him to grow for this mission. (Special Ops teams could spend as much time as they wanted preparing; it didn't matter when they departed from the present.) Then he took off the hat and wiped away the sweat of the humid Virginia April day from which he had departed mere moments before in his heavy wool uniform. It was the uniform of a

Louisiana regiment, which was appropriate to Jason's looks and those of his second-in-command Alexandre Mondrago. It had also helped account for any oddities in their pronunciation of neurally imprinted nineteenth-century American English, by the standards of the Virginians and North Carolinians they had found themselves among. All of which struck some Special Ops people as excessive caution for missions of such limited duration. But Rutherford, who had to deal with the council, would never yield an inch on such precautions. He was fussily insistent that they be able to blend, however brief their sojourns in the past were expected to be.

"All done," Jason reported. "That's just a scratch that Corbett has got, and it's from a local weapon—we did a clean job on the Transhumanists before they had a chance to use any of their out-of-period stuff. Pauline had done an outstanding job of getting all the relevant information into the message drop, and of course she was a great help after we made contact with her."

He was referring to Pauline da Cunha, one of the charter members of the Special Operations Section, who was now (in terms of the linear present, of course) leading a research expedition to Virginia, North America, in February through early April of 1865 to study the last days of the Confederacy. It was unusual for such an expedition to have a Special Ops officer as mission leader, but this one was out of the ordinary. In addition to its ostensible purpose, it was also charged with pursuing certain leads from certain sources (including Chantal Frey's debriefing) that pointed toward Transhumanist activity amid the collapsing South.

A short, dark, wiry man with sergeant's chevrons on his sleeve and an impressive nose on his face grinned wickedly. "Yeah. It was worth it just to see Pauline having to pass as a Creole belle!"

"You always did have a sadistic streak," Jason reproved, giving Alexandre Mondrago a look of bogus sternness. The Corsican-descended ex-mercenary had been with Jason in fifth century B.C. Greece, saving his life on one occasion. "And as I recall, she was some little help to you, getting across that bridge over the James River near the Tredegar Iron Works while Richmond burned." Mondrago had the grace to look abashed. "It's true, though, that after sustaining that role for two and a half months, I imagine she'll come back here in a *very* bad mood, even though she'll have gotten to witness Lincoln's visit to the ruins of Richmond." Abruptly, Jason sobered. "But the point is, she was absolutely right. What we found was worse than what we thought we were looking for. In fact, it was worse than *she* thought."

Rutherford went pale. They had believed the Transhumanists were planting the seeds of one of their secret societies—a kind of sociological supervirus developing undetectably within the relatively harmless (if repellent) historically attested Ku Klux Klan, much as they had attempted to plant one within the cult of Pan in ancient Greece. Da Cunha had thought they were really planting something far more insidious.

"I know what she thought," Rutherford said. "She thought they were planting one of their retroactive plagues." Now Kung also went pale, for he knew of the Transhumanist technique of spreading mutagens containing a genetic time clock over the plant life of an area they wished to turn toxic on or just before

The Day. The Authority's only countermeasure was the expensive one of sending an expedition back to spread anti-mutagens. "But . . . Jason, did I understand you to say *worse* than that?"

"You did. This was a *nanotechnological* time bomb. Nanobots in huge numbers, timed to begin corroding metal, turning plastics to goo, infecting computer systems, interfering with connections and whatever. Evidently, the Transhumanists' strategy calls for large expanses of North America to revert to a pretechnological level on The Day." Jason surveyed his listeners. Rutherford had gone an even paler shade. Kung seemed to be experiencing difficulty breathing. Chantal, who had heard of such things, simply looked grim. "Don't worry," he assured them hastily. "We were able to abort this at an early stage and destroy the stockpiles before the actual process had commenced."

Kung found his voice. "But how could you be so incompetent as to fail to bring any of these, er, nanobots back with you for study? Perhaps their time sequence could have led us to inferences concerning The Day!"

Rutherford held his breath. Jason Thanou's relationship with the Authority had always had its ups and downs, and more of the latter than of the former—unsurprisingly considering that he had never troubled to conceal his opinion of the governing council. But now he kept his face expressionless and spoke with a mildness Rutherford knew him well enough to recognize as deceptive.

"Aside from the dangers involved—built-in booby traps whose consequences wouldn't bear thinking about—there would be no point. We've learned of the extreme care the Transhumanists put into security. I assure you that any such attempt would have caused the nanobots to instantly go permanently inert."

"Er, yes, I seem to recall reading about this sort of thing. But surely—"

"The same philosophy extends even to their personnel, Alistair," Rutherford reminded him. "As you are aware, the few Transhumanists who have been apprehended in the present day have had implants which killed them—destroyed their brains, in fact—upon capture."

Kung subsided, for he was indeed aware of it. Law enforcement agencies were naturally engaged in a planetwide search for the Transhumanists and—especially—their temporal displacer. But the investigation was hampered by bureaucratic insistence that it be carried on in strict secrecy, to avoid alarming the populace, and the results had been disappointing. They would undoubtedly have been even more disappointing without the leads provided by Chantal Frey.

"Yes," she nodded. "After more than a century of operating underground, secrecy has become compulsive with them. You all know how little of any real value Franco revealed to me, not just while he was planning to let me return as a 'mole' but even afterwards, when my TRD was gone and he had absolutely no reason to think I would ever be able to return to the present."

"Well," Jason broke the gloomy silence that followed, "I'm going to check on Corbett in sick bay. Afterwards, Kyle, I'll give you my full report. And after that . . . I could use some R&R. And," he added, with a hard look at Rutherford, "I believe I've got quite a lot of unused leave accumulated."

CHAPTER TWO

The "negative mass drive" was actually something of a misnomer. What it really did was wrap a field of negative energy around a spaceship, creating an area of expanding spacetime which, by biasing the field, could be made to move faster than the rest of spacetime, thus enabling the ship within it to get around the lightspeed limit. (*Not* through it, as the theoretical physicists never tired of assuring themselves and anyone else who would listen.) It had once been believed that achieving this would require an energy expenditure equivalent to the total conversion of the mass of a gas-giant planet—or a planetary system, or a galaxy, depending on which theorist you asked. It was as though the door to the galaxy was unlocked, but no one had the strength to push it open. But then it had been discovered that the energy requirements could be reduced to practical levels by setting up controlled oscillations in the drive field.

Even so, the field could not form in a significant gravity field. Closer to Sol than just inside the region of the asteroid belt (the "Secondary Limit," as it was called), the drive could only alter the properties of space to reduce normal gravity on one side of the ship to produce thrust—a great deal of thrust, and with no sensible acceleration, but nonetheless subject to relativistic limitations. And deep in a gravity well— The "Primary Limit," closer to Earth than a little less than the distance of a geosynchronous orbit—the drive wouldn't function at all. So for some time after its invention a century and a half earlier there had been a rigid distinction between the interstellar ships, which never touched a planetary surface, and the surface-to-orbit shuttles powered by ordinary reaction drives. But then grav repulsion had effectively erased that inconvenient dichotomy.

Thus it was that Jason Thanou stood on the observation deck of the Pontic Spaceport's terminal building and looked out over a vast expanse of the steppes north of the Black Sea, dotted as far as the eye could see with interstellar ships, including the one that was to take him home to Hesperia.

There were, of course, spaceports far closer to Australia. But this was the only one from which transportation to the fairly out-of-the-way Psi 5 Aurigae system could be booked at a convenient time. So Jason had taken a suborbital transport from Australia over seas and lands with names out of Sinbad the Sailor and the Arabian Nights, and now he waited for his liner's departure, with time to contemplate the conscious archaism of those names and that of this spaceport.

It was typical of Old Earth, of course. Since saving its roots from being brutally torn up by the Transhuman movement, humanity had sought to nurture those injured roots in every possible way, including revival of arcane place-names. And, Jason reflected, nothing could be more appropriate for this world, where the memory of tens of thousands of years of human pain and pleasure, drama and farce, joy and despair, profundity and bathos, had seeped into the very soil, and layers of history lay in strata, as much a part of the planet's landscape as its geology. He had always found the pervasive aura of ancientness oppressive, for he came from a world with no past, only a future—a truly new world, not even one of the original colonies settled during the slower-than-light era that had commenced a little less than three centuries before. And now, for the renewal of his soul, he needed to return to that world and breathe air that was not thick with that psychic aura.

The public address system broke in on his thoughts, announcing the impending departure of the liner *Artemis*, of the Olympian Line. Jason took an instant to smile at the names Olympian gave its ships, for he had met the Teloi aliens who had been the *real* Olympian gods, and he had engineered their downfall. Then he turned away from the observation deck's railing and went to catch one of the grav buses that would take him and his fellow passengers across the miles of spacefield to their ship.

The drive's speed (or, rather, the elapsed transit time as experienced by the ship's occupants and also by observers at each end of the trip, as the theoretical physicists always insisted on painstakingly pointing out) was dependent on its power relative to the mass of the ship. At higher levels of power, there was a "diminishing marginal returns" effect due to unavoidable deformation of the drive field, suggesting that sooner or later a limiting factor would be reached at which more power would actually be counterproductive—at least until a new loophole in the math (or at least a way of tweaking the field's geometry) was found. But so far no one had been able to generate that much power. In the meantime, there was always a tradeoff between speed and payload capacity.

A liner like *Artemis* was built for comfort, not for speed. Nevertheless, little more than twenty days passed before Jason could look in the observation lounge's wraparound viewscreen and see the bluish dot of his homeworld in the light of what had swelled from a star into a sun.

Psi 5 Aurigae, a single G0V star not unlike Sol, had been recognized early as a likely hearth for a habitable planet. And so it had proved. No gas-giant planet had migrated insystem, becoming a "hot Jupiter" and wiping out any promising planets in the "Goldilocks zone" (not too hot and not too cold, but just right) where liquid water could exist—a zone that had proved to have more elastic boundaries than had once been believed by pessimists using overly simplistic models. But this was a younger sun than Sol, perhaps half a billion years younger, and its third planet reflected that stellar youth. It was remarkably Earthlike in mass and density, and even had a similar rotation period, and abundant life swarmed in its oceans, releasing by photosynthesis the oxygen that made its air breathable. But that life, excepting various local equivalents of seaweed and trilobites, was mostly microbial. Microorganisms had only recently (as such things went) begun to invade the land.

It was a common enough type of world. Fortunately, the task of terraforming it, which would have been daunting a couple of centuries earlier, had been rendered manageable by nanotechnology and genetic engineering, for both of which it was one of the clearly defined legitimate uses. Larger and larger areas of living soil spread from the original settlements, replacing barren rock and sand, expanding into Hesperia's often dramatic landscapes and supporting a carefully selected imported ecology. The fringes of the terraformed regions were a true frontier, complete with a degree of lawlessness. This was the jurisdiction of the Hesperian Colonial Rangers, in which Jason had risen to the rank of commander before being temporarily seconded to the Temporal Service. Or at least it was *supposed* to have been temporary....

Artemis landed at Port Marshak, and Jason emerged into the afternoon light of Psi 5 Aurigae, not unlike that of Sol but in some indefinable way brighter. It was a fine spring day here in the northern hemisphere. (The axial tilt was only slightly less than Earth's, resulting in similar seasons.) The gravity was almost exactly one Earth gee, but it seemed impossible not to walk with a jauntier step. He looked around. To the east, the plateau on which the spacefield was located fell away and the low light-tinted structures of Port Marshak could be seen beyond. To the west, the land rose in tree-clothed foothills beyond which the titanic Rampart Mountains piled range upon snow-capped range, the most distant of which were clearly visible in the atmosphere's preternatural clarity.

Jason took a deep breath of air that held none of the residual aroma of billions upon billions of humans and their byproducts. He closed his eyes, and a deep contentment suffused his entire being. *Home . . .*

"Commander Thanou?"

Jason's eyes snapped open at the sound of that nasal voice, and he stared at the slightly plump young man in Earthified clothes. "No," he moaned softly.

Irving Nesbit's face, with its puffy cheeks, receding chin and slightly buck teeth, had always reminded Jason, unpleasantly, of a rabbit's. His self-satisfied smile heightened the resemblance. "I'm *so* glad you've *finally* arrived, Commander. I departed Earth almost a week after you did, but I traveled in one of the new *Comet*-class courier vessels—not particularly comfortable, by the way—and I've been waiting in this, uh, city for three days." His tone said it had seemed longer. "I must say, I'm getting to be quite the old Hesperia hand by now!"

Jason forced himself to speak mildly. "So you are. After I'd quit the Temporal Service, Rutherford sent you here to inform me that I had been reactivated by virtue of some technicality." It had been the start of his expedition to the 1628 B.C. Aegean, whose purpose had been to observe the Santorini explosion but which had revealed the alien Teloi who had created *homo sapiens* to be their slaves and worshipers. Most of the Teloi had been permanently trapped in an extradimensnional cul-de-sac of their own creation, but some—the Indo-European pantheon of various myth-cycles—had remained abroad in the world. That, in turn, had prompted the 490 B.C. expedition which had stumbled onto the Transhumanist time-meddlers and the surviving Teloi who had become their allies, and resulted in the formation of the Special Operations

Section. In short, one thing had led to another and this was the first chance Jason had had to return to his homeworld since he'd last seen that rabbitoid face.

And now...

"Ah, yes," Nesbit's irritating voice disrupted his thoughts. "The 'technicality' in question was a clause in your early-retirement agreement with the Authority, which perhaps other demands on your time had prevented you from reading. As I recall it was Part VI, Article D, Paragraph 15, Subparagraph—"

"Yes, yes, I know!" With a physical effort, Jason forced his voice back down. "But the point is, what exactly are you doing here *now*? I happen to be on leave." Eagerly: "My leave papers are with my luggage, so let's go to the terminal and—"

"Oh, that won't be necessary. I have a copy here." Nesbit produced a sheaf of paper from his briefcase.

"Then you must know that everything's in order." Jason had made very sure of that.

"I invite your attention to the 'Recall' provision. It's right here in Section XVII, Item 8, line 31."

Jason clasped his hands tightly behind his back, to prevent himself from doing something with them that he knew he would regret later. "Are you telling me that Rutherford is canceling my leave?" he asked, quietly but in a tone and with a look in his eyes to which Nesbit seemed blissfully oblivious.

"In accordance with the 'Emergency' contingency." Nesbit nodded happily. "As you can see, that's a little further down, starting with line 37."

"I won't do it! This is too much! You get back in your fast but uncomfortable ship, go back to Earth, and tell Rutherford I said he can take his 'emergency contingency' and roll it up into a cylinder and shove it up his—"

"I am authorized to inform you that the contingency in question involves newly discovered evidence of illicit extratemporal activity by the Transhumanist underground."

All at once, Jason's expression went neutral and his eyes grew very focused. "What kind of evidence? What historical period?"

"I'm afraid I can't tell you that. In point of fact, I don't know. I believe I lack a 'need to know,' as it is called." Nesbit sniffed his disdain of such matters. "All I can say is that you are required to return to Earth immediately."

"'Immediately'? Can I stay here long enough to drop in on my family?"

"Director Rutherford indicated that your presence was required—"

"But did he specify a return time?" demanded Jason, who had learned that the way to deal with bureaucrats was to pin them down to specifics.

"Well, er, no. But he clearly indicated that the matter was urgent. And the courier ship that brought me here is required to return to Earth within a very tight schedule. If you do not come with me at once, you will miss the chance—"

—*To spend ten days in close quarters with Nesbit*, Jason thought with a shudder.

"Don't worry about a thing, Nesbit," he cut in with what certain late-twentieth-century acquaintances of his had called a shit-eating grin. "Go on back and assure Rutherford that I'll arrange my own transportation, as I did last time." *And, as I did last time,*

I'll do it by the most luxurious, expensive spaceline I can find, he mentally added. *And the Authority will have to reimburse me.* It was one of his few ways of exacting revenge.

"But," Nesbit expostulated, "it's urgent—!"

"Urgent? Hey, Nesbit, I've got all the time in the world. Don't you know? I'm a time traveler!"

He strode off toward the terminal building, leaving Nesbit spluttering. It undoubtedly added months to his life.

CHAPTER THREE

People stayed out of Jason's way as he stalked through the corridors of the displacer facility toward Rutherford's office. The look on his face was sufficient to convince even the most insensitive that now was not the time for banter. This, despite the fact that he had forgotten to change into his Hesperian Colonial Rangers uniform, as he usually did when he wanted to be assured of irritating Rutherford.

His expression was even enough to intimidate Rutherford's famously formidable secretary. She waved him through an outer office full of visibly resentful supplicants, and he entered the inner sanctum, surprisingly austere save for a display case containing items from the past, notably a certain medieval hand-and-a-half sword.

"Kyle," he began in ominous tones...then halted as he saw Rutherford already had another visitor: an early-middle-aged man, predominantly African by ancestry, with strong features and short hair turning gray at the temples. *The old bastard probably brought somebody else in here just to throw me off my stride*, he thought peevishly.

"Commander Thanou," said Rutherford with smiling urbanity, "allow me to introduce Dr. Henri Boyer." His use of Jason's rank-title in the Hesperian Colonial Rangers was scrupulously correct. Since it had become obvious that the Special Operations Section was going to have to function on at least a paramilitary basis, the council had grudgingly accepted the need for the kind of formalized rank structure the Temporal Service had never possessed. Casting about for an appropriate one, while continuing to shrink from anything with an overtly military sound to it, they had seized on something similar to the Rangers' very simplified version of the centuries-old British police system. (Jason had been amused to learn that the rank-titles had been adopted back in the days of Sir Robert Peel, founder of the London Metropolitan Police, for precisely the same reason: to quiet fears of a paramilitary force.) The Section was still so small that it only needed to go as high as "Commander" for its head man, working downward from there through "Superintendent," "Inspector," "Sergeant" and "Constable." As it grew, it would doubtless have to add "Commissioner" at the top.

"Commander Thanou," said the dark man in a deep, cultured voice, extending his hand.

With no other alternative but to appear churlish, Jason shook hands and made a vaguely courteous-sounding grunting noise.

"It is a pleasure to meet you, Commander," Boyer continued. "Director Rutherford and I were just discussing you."

"Oh?" Jason turned toward Rutherford with a

suspicious look rooted in long experience. This was all wrong. Rutherford should have been exuding supercilious disapproval of his tardiness in returning to Earth.

"Yes, Jason," Rutherford acknowledged smoothly. "You see, Dr. Boyer is also concerned with the same problem which occasioned your recall."

"Ah, yes: my recall," said Jason with a glare that had given pause to medieval men-at-arms and twentieth-century gangsters. "That's precisely what I'm here to talk to you about. As a matter of fact—"

"We've received a message drop from the expedition Asamoa has led to Haiti in 1791," Rutherford cut in.

"What?" said Jason, momentarily distracted from his own wrongs. "Is he all right?" Sam Asamoa was a veteran of the Temporal Service and an old friend of Jason's. And the message drop system had many limitations. The need for obtaining imperishable material for a message locally was the first. The location of the drop was the second; without being too inconvenient for the time travelers to reach, it had to be so out-of-the-way as to escape all notice for all of subsequent history, so as to avoid running afoul of the "Observer Effect." Even so, the fact that the technique could be used at all—and that the message was not there before the moment in the linear present when the time travelers left it there—had caused profound philosophical shock waves, for it had been the first incontrovertible proof that the past could be changed, with all the mind-destroying implications thereof. Even more disturbing was the way *something* had always seemed to prevent any attempt to observe the message drop location at that precise moment in the linear present. All such attempts had long since been abandoned, and Temporal Service personnel preferred not to dwell on it.

"Yes, he and the rest of his expedition are fine, as far as we know," Rutherford soothed. "As you are aware, their objective was to verify our received ideas about the origins of the Haitian revolution against the French, which resulted in the founding of the second independent nation in the Americas."

"I remember Sam Asamoa telling me about it before I left, but I was never entirely clear on it. Something about Voodoo, as I recall." Out of the corner of his eye, Jason saw Boyer wince.

"No doubt Dr. Boyer can clarify matters for you, as this involves his field of expertise. Indeed, he is of Haitian ancestry, and he was barely edged out for a position on Asamoa's expedition. Dr. Boyer, if you would be so kind?"

"The word *voodoo*," Boyer began, "has become a generic term for the Afro-Caribbean syncretic religions—and I can't deny that such an awkward name cries out for a convenience label, so we may as well go on using it. But it's an unfortunate one. For one thing, it has, over the centuries, acquired some unsavory connotations due to misconceptions and sensationalism. At the same time, it is too narrow and specific, being an Anglicized version of the Haitian manifestation of this religious impulse: *Vodou*." The difference in pronunciation was subtle but definite. "In fact, there are numerous manifestations, including Shango in Trinidad, Santería in Cuba and Puerto Rico, and others, wherever large numbers of African slaves were brought into Catholic colonial societies in the sixteenth through eighteenth centuries. You see, all those slaves came from Western and Central Africa—the Fon, Ewe and Yoruba peoples. They all shared the worship of a supreme creator-god named Damballah or Nana Buluku who did not intervene directly in human affairs but left the running of the world to a vast and complex pantheon of lesser spirits called *vodun*. In the New world, these religions blended with Roman Catholicism. In fact, Damballah is often called Bondye, a Creole form of the French *Bon Dieu*."

"I imagine the Catholic belief in intercession by saints and angels lent itself to that kind of syncretism," Jason opined.

"Very astute, Commander. There was also an element of sheer practicality: the only religious imagery the slaves could obtain was Catholic, so they tended to use the closest matches they could find. For example, Damballah was associated with the snake, so images of St. Patrick banishing the snakes from Ireland were used for him simply because those images had snakes in them—even though I assure you he was not in any degree Irish!" Boyer chuckled. "But as time went on, the syncretism went further. Biblical characters, historical figures and even popular-culture icons were incorporated as *loa*, spirits which can temporarily possess and speak through a worshiper—the 'horse'—who is deprived of free will. And unlike Catholic saints, the *loa* are morally neutral, with complex personalities that are neither entirely good nor entirely evil. A worshiper goes to a priest—called a *houngan* if male or a *mambo* if female—to obtain a spirit's help, whether for beneficent or malign ends. The spirit is appealed to by offerings of food or liquor or, sometimes, a ritually sacrificed animal. This latter aspect contributed to the negative reputation I mentioned earlier, as did the exploitation of Voodoo practices by various dictators in Haiti's depressing political history to intimidate and control the uneducated populace."

"I had the impression," said Jason carefully, "that it was believed that there was sometimes sacrifice not just of animals but of humans—especially in connection with turning people into zombies."

Boyer looked acutely uncomfortable. "There was, at one time, a secret society, the *Secte Rouge*, sometimes called the *Cochon Gris,* or 'Gray Pig,' that did indeed practice ritual murder—and possibly cannibalism, although this was never proved. As for zombies, I am sorry to say that they did indeed exist."

"I beg your pardon?" Jason was sure he must have misunderstood.

"Oh, not in the sense you're thinking. Of *course* people weren't actually brought back from the grave in an undead state and forced to do a *houngan*'s bidding, which was usually brutish manual labor. That was the terrifying illusion—even more terrifying for educated, upper-class Haitians, if you think about it. In reality, zombies were living people controlled by the use of drugs that robbed them of their will. The dictators I spoke of earlier were known to have corrupt *houngans* zombify political dissidents. But," he stated firmly, "these were aberrations. True Voodoo is simply a group of religions, eccentrically pagan in modern times but not devoid of ethical content, valuing virtues like generosity and social solidarity and condemning greed and dishonor. And these religions are still practiced today. Their very eclecticism has, I believe, given them a certain resilience."

"Yes," Jason nodded. "Sam Asamoa mentioned something of the sort." The mainstream religions had not fared well in the early centuries of the scientific revolution, either fraying out into bloodless "social gospel" or curdling up into the doomed rear-guard known as "fundamentalism." And then the Transhumanist regime had done its fanatical best to stamp out all religion. This, in turn, had sparked a counter-reaction. On today's Earth, *literal* belief in religion was virtually nonexistent, but there was more and more formal religious practice as part of the post-Transhumanist rediscovery of human cultural roots. "But I still don't quite understand the historical connection to the Haitian Revolution."

"After the French Revolution in 1789, the Haitians sent representatives to Paris to demand their rights from the National Assembly. But this meant rights only for the free *gens de couleur* or mulattoes, who included many large landowners who held scores of thousands of black slaves. The *real* revolution is traditionally held to have been sparked by a Voodoo—specifically Vodou—ceremony in August of 1791 at Bwa Kayiman, in which the *loa* Ezili Dantor was believed to have possessed a priestess and commanded the blacks to rise up. The situation was complex. The mulattoes had been scornfully rejected by the French, which drove them into the camp of the blacks, but after destroying the plantation system and massacring the whites, they both continued to recognize the nominal authority of France. Indeed, they joined with the French to repel—with the help of yellow fever—a British invasion from Jamaica in 1797. But then Napoleon, who had taken control of France, decided it was beneath him to bargain with black generals. He sent an army to reestablish absolute French rule and restore slavery. That army was decimated by yellow fever just as the British had been, and in 1804 a general named Dessalines declared Haiti independent and himself its 'Emperor.'"

"Thank you, Dr. Boyer," said Rutherford. "So you see, Jason, the confused nature of these events has left many unanswered questions—in particular, whether the Bwa Kayiman ceremony really marked the start of the revolution, or if the story was only a later embellishment of patriotic mythology representing the uprising as a kind of 'holy war.' Asamoa departed shortly after you left on your, ah, jaunt to your homeworld, leading an expedition which, of necessity, consisted entirely of persons of obviously African ancestry."

"Of necessity," Jason echoed with a nod. It was harder and harder, in today's cosmopolitan world, to find time travelers who could pass unnoticed among the less racially mixed peoples of the past. And in the wake of the Transhumanist madness it was unacceptable to use genetic manipulation to tailor appearances to order. Jason's variegated genes had happened to sort themselves out so that he could pass for a member of any of the Mediterranean ethnicities or their offshoots.

"They arrived in 1791 long enough before August to establish contacts among the communities of escaped slaves. In the course of their researches, they began to turn up disquieting hints of a dark, perverted cult that even the *houngans* feared."

"Like the *Secte Rouge* that Dr. Boyer mentioned?" Jason queried.

"No. For one thing, it had certain features which were foreign to Voodoo in any form but suggested

Transhumaist involvement—notably, a seemingly unaging supernatural figure who appeared from time to time at long intervals, each time uttering prophecies of the future that turned out to be accurate."

A tingling ran along Jason's spine.

"Furthermore," Rutherford continued, "there was a persistent tradition which traced the cult as far back as the 1660s and linked it with the pirates who operated out of Jamaica at that time. This, despite the fact that Voodoo, however defined, never became established in Jamaica." He looked for confirmation to Boyer, who nodded.

"That is correct. For one thing, the Catholic linkage Commander Thanou mentioned was absent there, and the Protestant denominations solidified their hold on the population by taking the lead in the abolition of slavery. But the pirate connection makes perfect sense. You must understand that this was at the same time that the French colony of St. Domingue, which was later to become Haiti, was first getting started. The entire island of Hispaniola was then nominally under Spanish control, although bands of buccaneers infested its coasts. In particular, the small island of Tortuga, off Hispaniola's northwestern tip, was a haven for French pirates, and became the nucleus of St. Domingue after the French crown took control of the island in 1660. The Spanish didn't officially cede the western half of Hispaniola to the French until 1697."

"I can see why Sam Asamoa used the message drop to inform us of this at once, instead of waiting until his expedition is scheduled to return. But," Jason continued, addressing Rutherford, "why the urgency? Admittedly, any evidence of Transhumanist activity is cause for concern. Still, you seem to be treating this like some kind of unique emergency."

"There's one other matter." Rutherford seemed to gather himself to repeat something he wished he had never heard. "In the course of following up the hints he had gotten, Asamoa stumbled onto wreckage on a mountainside in the Massif de la Selle in the southern peninsula of the island of Hispaniola where Haiti is located. Its condition, according to the expedition's archaeologist, suggested that it had been there for about a century and a quarter. And it had no business in that era." Rutherford paused again. "You'll recall, from your last expedition, that the Transhumanists used their superior technology to temporally displace an aircar."

"Vividly. What are you saying? Have they done it again? The seventeenth century would certainly be no problem for them, considering that they could take one back to the fifth century B.C."

"Not exactly. This was a good deal larger." Rutherford drew a deep breath. His gaze went to the sword in his display case—the sword that a French peasant girl had found behind the altar of the Church of Saint Catherine of Fierbois in 1429—as it often did when he needed to fortify himself with strength from sources beyond his own. "Now, you realize that neither Asamoa nor anyone on his team is an expert in such matters, which are irrelevant to their expedition's original purpose. But he thinks the wreckage is that of a small spaceship originating in our era."

"*What?*" Jason half shot up out of his chair before forcing his legs to lower him back down and his brain to stop swirling. "But that would have to be a colossal effort even for them. And what would be the point?"

"We have no idea," said Rutherford sadly. "We don't even have a theory. It seems to have no relevance to the creation of one of their secret societies or cults—certainly none that would justify the staggering expense it must have entailed."

"All right. Now I see what the excitement is about. But I still don't understand what you want *me* for. It doesn't sound like you have the kind of precise target date we require for Special Ops missions."

"No, we don't. And we need to ascertain one. I therefore want you to lead a research expedition, including Dr. Boyer, back to the late 1660s."

"Wait a minute, Kyle—!"

"This, of course, will be subject to the standard conditions under which such expeditions have always operated, such as the use of TRDs with an automatic, preset activation time, so that you can remain long enough for a thorough investigation. And the usual prohibitions on out-of-period articles, including weapons, will naturally—"

"Wait a minute! I thought we had an understanding, damn it! I don't do this kind of thing anymore, now that I'm heading Special Ops. It's no longer my job to—no offense, Dr. Boyer—try to keep parties of academics alive while they nose around in some of the most violent periods of Earth's history."

"This will hardly be one of your typical academic expeditions, Jason. It will be specifically targeted on detecting Transhumanist activity. Indeed, you may find that you have an opportunity to abort the problem yourself before your return. You will have full discretion in this matter."

"But," argued Jason, recalling the Observer Effect,

"if we already know that this cult or secret society or whatever still existed in 1791—"

"We don't know that for certain. All we have to go on are rumors of it, which may only reflect old fears. Besides, even if you can't actually scotch it in the seventeenth century, perhaps you can gather new intelligence on Transhumanist operations in general. And on further reflection I believe that, given the potential danger involved, we can allow certain compromises in the matter of high technology, as long as it is very subtle and well-concealed."

Jason's eyes narrowed. Rutherford was being suspiciously accommodating. "I still don't know why you want me. I can't exactly pass as an African."

"Nor will you need to. The pirates of the milieu in question were a remarkably heterogeneous group. Anyone whose ancestors came from anywhere around the Atlantic and Mediterranean basins will blend in with them easily. Which reminds me: since this will involve a displacement of only slightly over seven hundred years, you'll be able to take a larger group than was the case on your last two expeditions, which went back millennia." Jason nodded automatically; the highly expensive energy requirement for temporal displacement was a function of the total mass displaced and the span of time into the past it was to be sent. "Therefore," Rutherford continued, beaming, "in addition to Dr. Boyer and one other researcher, you can be allowed two Temporal Service personnel, whom you can choose yourself—from the Special Operations Section, if you like."

"Hmmm . . ." *Yes,* Jason thought darkly, *altogether too accommodating. Still . . .* "I'll want Mondrago. And Pauline Da Cunha is back by now, isn't she?"

"She is indeed. Excellent choices; you can have both of them."

"Well . . . All right. I'll do it."

"Splendid! Oh . . . by the way, Jason, there's just one small matter I neglected to mention."

All at once, Jason's suspicions came roaring back in full force. "Yes?"

"As you know, certain members of the governing council have expressed concern over the latitude the Special Operations Section has, of necessity, been granted—some of the departures from the Authority's traditional guidelines and procedures. Councilor Kung in particular—"

"Get to the point, Kyle!"

"Ahem! Well, the long and short of it is this. In order to obtain authorization for this expedition, I had to make one concession. Councilor Kung insisted that your group include a representative of the Authority, to exercise oversight and, ah, advise the mission leader on observance of, shall we say, the proprieties."

In short, a political commissar, thought Jason grimly, recalling the term from his experiences in the twentieth century. "And who might this individual be?"

"As it happens, he is here now." Rutherford touched a button on his desk. A side door opened and Jason looked up as the new arrival entered.

No, he thought, from the depths of a desolation too abysmal for mere despair. *No. This can't be happening. Please, God, tell me this isn't happening.*

"Hello, Commander Thanou," said Irving Nesbit, his rabbitlike face looking rather like he was anticipating a carrot. "We meet again!"

CHAPTER FOUR

Alexandre Mondrago stared at Jason aghast. "This is a joke, right?"

"No," Jason sighed. "Jokes are supposed to be funny."

They sat at a table in the station's rather nicely appointed lounge, which Jason had decided was the best place to break the news to the two Service people. He took another pull on his Scotch, *sans* his usual soda. It occurred to him that he ought to start getting used to rum. Mondrago, who was already doing so with enthusiasm, gulped some of his Appleton's and continued to stare. Pauline Da Cunha simply stared, visibly fuming. The intriguing mention of the possible spaceship wreck had been just barely enough to overcome her initial resentment at being tapped for this mission so soon after returning from the Confederate States of America's final cataclysm. And now this.

Chantal Frey hunched over and gazed miserably into her Chablis. "I swear I had nothing to do with it!"

"Of course you didn't. It's just council politics."

"How could you let them get away with it?" Mondrago demanded. "You could have protested, explained to them that—"

"Don't you think I did? I argued myself purple in the face. I told Rutherford that Nesbit isn't up to it. But, believe it or not, he's met all the health and fitness requirements, and passed the course in low-tech survival." Privately, Jason wondered if Kung's heavy finger might have tilted the scales of the test-scoring process just a bit despite the Authority's vaunted incorruptibility, but he saw no purpose to be served by sharing his suspicions with the others. "He was motivated, you see. It seems he has delusions of being a swashbuckling adventurer."

Mondrago and Da Cunha groaned loudly enough to draw glances from the other tables. Jason decided he'd better try to put the best possible face on things. "Hey, he probably won't be too much more useless than some of the academics we've had to deal with."

"Like me," Chantal put in ruefully.

"But," said Da Cunha with disagreeable realism, "in their case there's never been any question about who was in charge. The mission leader's authority has always been absolute."

"I was able to get a definite statement on that out of Rutherford," Jason hastened to reassure her. "The relevant provisions of the Temporal Precautionary Act are still good. As mission leader, I'll have the same legal powers as always."

"But," Da Cunha persisted, "this time you'll have to exercise those powers with someone looking over your shoulder. Someone who can come back and report over your head directly to Kung and the other fatheads on the council."

Jason made no reply, for he could think of none that wouldn't deepen the general gloom. Instead, he chugged what was left of his Scotch and stood up. "Well, it's time. Chantal, you'll have to excuse us. Let's drink up and head for the conference center."

Rutherford wouldn't approve of us getting oiled just before reporting for this meeting, he reflected. *To hell with him*.

Looking around the large oval table in the conference center, Jason reflected that if it hadn't been for Nesbit—who was looking insufferably, fatuously cheerful—he wouldn't have been unhappy with this expedition's personnel.

Dr. Henri Boyer was their expert on the Afro-Caribbean syncretic religions. He had already passed all the Authority's requirements to qualify for a position on Asamoa's expedition, before losing out to a slightly younger competitor for that position. He regarded this as a second chance, and Jason didn't anticipate any problems with him. And it had turned out he had a hobby of carpentry, which would stand him in very good stead where they were going.

Dr. Roderick Grenfell had, of course, also met the requirements. He was of nondescript predominantly European appearance, which as Rutherford had pointed out was all that was needed to fit into the target milieu. He was a specialist in Caribbean history, with an emphasis on the buccaneers of the seventeenth century. By birth, he was the only off-worlder present besides Jason himself, hailing from New Albion, Kappa

Reticuli II. In his youth on that frontier world, he had been exposed to some compulsory paramilitary basic training, which afforded Jason a degree of comfort.

"You've all been through the preliminary procedures," Jason began, "including the biological 'cleansing' procedure that is necessary to prevent you from endangering the peoples of the past by introducing more highly evolved disease microorganisms to which they would lack immunity."

"Rather like the natives of the Caribbean islands when the Europeans arrived," Grenfell remarked.

"That's the general idea," Jason nodded. "You have also had your TRDs implanted." Their expressions told him that they had found the operation distasteful, not because it was painful—which it wasn't, save for a slight sting on the inner side of the upper left arm—but because it violated their culture's taboo against implants in general, even passive ones. As usual, it had been explained to them that it made the tiny device impossible to lose. And—also as usual—this had helped, once they had grasped the fact that without the TRD to restore their temporal energy potential they would be stranded in the seventeenth century permanently. Jason saw no reason to go into the one exception he had engineered in the case of Chantal Frey, which was hardly likely to apply in their cases.

"As you have been told," Jason continued, "Your TRDs will activate at a preset moment, timed by atomic decay, at which you will return to the linear present, here at the displacer stage. This is always the case, except for Special Operations missions, which are brief and have very specific targets. You may have worried—people always do—that the sudden, unexpected transition will be a little disorienting. Don't be concerned. I'll give you warning. As mission leader I have, by grace of an exemption from the Human Integrity Act, a neurally interfaced brain implant which, among other things, will provide a digital countdown to the moment of activation." He observed, as always, the quickly smoothed-over shudders at a far more extreme taboo violation. "The countdown is projected directly onto my optic nerve. A map of our surroundings can be similarly projected. I'm sure you can all see how useful that can be."

Jason didn't add that their TRDs contained minute tracking devices that caused their locations to appear on that map. Mondrago and Da Cunha already knew it, of course. And as for the others—especially Nesbit— he didn't believe in upsetting people with things they didn't need to know.

He also didn't mention that Da Cunha had an identical computer implant, by virtue of having qualified as a mission leader. There was no point, inasmuch as hers had been temporarily deactivated. It was typical of the Authority's niggling adherence to the letter of the rules: only the *current* mission leader could make a case for such a flagrant violation of the letter and spirit of the Human Integrity Act.

"Another area in which the Authority has been able to make a case for a special exemption is that of language. There would be no point to sending people into the past unable to communicate. So we imprint the language of the target milieu onto the speech centers by direct neural induction. This time the process will be less lengthy and stressful than usual, because the language in question—seventeenth-century

English—is closely related to today's Standard International English."

"They could almost be regarded as different dialects of the same language," interjected Rutherford from his position at the opposite end of the conference table from Jason, "although our modern speech contains a multitude of loan words and neologisms which you will have to remember not to use."

"Furthermore," Jason resumed reassuringly, "the procedure will be done slowly and carefully, to avoid disorientation and other unpleasant mental side effects." A shadow crossed his mind as he recalled having the utterly alien Teloi language brutally rammed into his unprepared brain.

"But," said Grenfell, "surely this doesn't magically enable one to speak the language like a native."

"Of course not," Jason admitted. "The Service has a standard solution to that problem: no matter where you are, you always claim to be from somewhere *else*. Besides which, the piratical population of Jamaica in the 1660s was so polyglot that oddities of speech must have had to be pretty extreme to attract notice. And that brings me to the primary purpose of this meeting, which is to acquaint you with our 'cover story.'

"Our date of arrival will be December 20, 1668, and we will remain for five months. We will appear—just after dawn, as per standard procedure—near the eastern end of the harbor whose northern shore is now the site of Kingston, Jamaica but was pretty much uninhabited then." Jason manipulated a remote. The wall behind him flickered and became a screen displaying a map. "We will make our way westward along this narrow spit of land that encloses the harbor on the south—the

Palisadoes, it's called—to the town of Port Royal at the harbor's entrance. It was the capital of Jamaica at that time, and also the unofficial capital of the pirates, who poured their loot into its taverns and whorehouses like . . . well, like drunken sailors. It was known as the 'richest and wickedest city in the world.' We will be pirates down on their luck and looking to sign up for a new raid on the Spaniards." He smiled. "We'll even be able to use our own names and ethnicities, for a change. I'll be a renegade from Sicily, which was then a Spanish possession, part-Greek as were quite a few people there. Alexandre will be a Frenchman, of whom there were a lot in the pirates' ranks. Pauline will be from Brazil, and pose as my mistress." Jason's voice held no apology, and Da Cunha's expression held nothing but equanimity. She was used to this sort of thing. It was typical of the sort of dodges that had to be used to account for female members of extratemporal expeditions in the long ages of sexism. "This will not be incompatible with her being very handy in a fight; there were actually such cases in the history of piracy."

"Calico Jack Rackham and Anne Bonny," Grenfell murmured with a smile.

"Dr. Grenfell, you will be an English former merchant seaman whose ship was taken by pirates and who accepted their offer to join them—a common occurrence. Dr. Boyer, you will be a runaway slave from Saint Domingue, the new French colony on Hispaniola." Again, Jason's tone was expressionless, and Boyer did not react. "Your hobby will stand you in good stead, because carpenters were highly prized personnel among pirate crews—they got an extra share of the prize money. In fact, sometimes pirates would stop and board a merchant ship just to kidnap the carpenter and force him to join them! The carpenter and one other." Jason turned to Nesbit with a carefully neutral expression. "The only specialists more valued than carpenters were surgeons. You will be English, and a ship's surgeon's mate who was forced into piracy by the process I just described."

Nesbit looked panic-stricken. "But I'm not a doctor!"

"No, you're not. But you passed the first-aid portion of the survival course you took to qualify for this expedition. Believe me, that limited knowledge puts you at least on a par with most seventeenth-century physicians, especially nautical ones." *And it was the only thing we could think of that might possibly justify your presence,* Jason forced himself not to add.

"Thank you, Commander Thanou," Rutherford said with a nod, then addressed the meeting at large. "Over the next several days, you will receive instruction in the background of this historical milieu...by traditional teaching methods," he hastened to add. "Dr. Grenfell, who is one of the leading authorities on the subject, will naturally play an integral part in this. But at this time, I wonder if he might give us a brief overview of the piratical culture into which you will find yourselves."

"The Spaniards," Grenfell began, "really brought the problem on themselves. They were determined to maintain the monopoly on the Americas—exclusive of Portuguese Brazil—that the Pope had granted them. They tried to wipe out the English, French and Dutch settlements in the Lesser Antilles—tiny islands they themselves had never bothered with." Nesbit looked bewildered. Jason touched the controls, and the map changed to one of the entire Caribbean. He ran a cursor over the crescent of tiny islands curving southeastward from Puerto Rico to Trinidad just off the northern coast of South America.

"This caused refugees to follow the prevailing southeasterly trade winds from there to the Greater Antilles—Jamaica, Cuba, Puerto Rico and, especially, Hispaniola," Grenfell continued. "The Spanish settlements there were restricted to the areas around the port cities, so the newcomers—who also included runaway indentured servants and others—were able to settle on the wide stretches of unoccupied coast and live off the wild cattle and pigs, whose meat they smoked on a grill called a *boucan*, so they were known by the French word *boucaniers*, which came to be Anglicized as *buccaneers*. In addition to selling meat to passing ships, they also lived by raiding Spanish shipping. Here, again, the Spanish inflicted it on themselves. They refused to allow other nations' merchants free access to their colonies, which was really what the English and Dutch wanted. As a result many seamen, who would otherwise have been legitimately employed in a free-trade economy, joined the buccaneers and went into smuggling and piracy. By the 1640s they were calling themselves the 'Brethren of the Coast,' and they had a stronghold on Tortuga, of the northwest tip of Hispaniola, which came to be dominated by the French element.

"But they really came into their own after the English takeover of Jamaica in 1655. Oliver Cromwell, then Lord Protector, had sent a fleet to conquer Hispaniola. It was an ignominious fiasco. Cromwell was *not* a man to whom you wanted to go back and report failure! So Admiral Penn and General Venables, the leaders of the expedition, cast about for a consolation prize, as it were. Jamaica, which the Spaniards had never strongly held, was the obvious candidate. The conquest was easy, although a vicious guerilla war of extermination against Spanish holdouts and their surprisingly loyal former slaves went on for three years thereafter.

"The new English possession, lying across the southern approaches to the Windward Passage between Cuba and Hispaniola, was a perfect base for raids. And the colonial administrators and merchants actually welcomed the buccaneers as protectors, as the English crown was too cheap to provide adequate defense. In fact, in 1657, Governor Edward D'Oley invited the Brethren of the Coast to make Port Royal their home port."

"Sort of like townspeople in the nineteenth-century American West bringing in gunslingers to protect then," observed Da Cunha, who in the course of her last expedition had heard about what was happening on the frontier even as the Civil War raged in the East.

"Somewhat similar. And all they had to do to obtain this protection was issue letters of marque—or 'commissions,' as they were more commonly called in the seventeenth century—to legitimize piracy against the Spaniards, who were the buccaneers' mortal enemies." Grenfell chuckled. "And if England happened to be at peace with Spain, all the buccaneers had to do was sail off to the nearest French or Dutch island and get commissions there. *Somebody* was always at war with Spain."

"Thank you, Dr. Grenfell," said Rutherford. "You will, of course, get a much more detailed historical orientation over the course of the next week or so, but that will suffice for now. Commander Thanou, would you like to add any closing remarks?"

"Just a couple of points that can't be emphasized enough. One is that this expedition is somewhat more narrowly focused than has normally been the case in the past. We certainly welcome any historical enlightenment that you two gentlemen's research can provide. But our primary objective is to obtain evidence of illicit extratemporal activity by the Transhumanist underground we now know continues to exist. This is why we have been granted certain limited exemptions from the usual prohibition on taking advanced technology into the past. It also means you will potentially be facing extraordinary hazards. You already know this from your preliminary briefings, and have signed the Articles of Agreement releasing the Authority from liability. I merely reiterate it now.

"The second point is that we are going into a milieu which was, by the standards of our modern civilization, an almost grotesquely violent and brutal one. Actually, quite a lot of human history was like that, but the seventeenth-century Spanish Main was exceptional for a couple of reasons. For one thing, that century was a period of genocidal religious warfare, which tends to be sort of desensitizing. Some rules of civilized warfare still obtained in Europe, but in the New World—'beyond the line' as they called it— even those went by the boards. The Spaniards were justly notorious for ruthlessness and cruelty, and their buccaneer enemies reciprocated with interest. Now, if things go according to plan, you won't actually be exposed to the more extreme manifestations of this sort of thing. In other words, we're not expected to *be* pirates; that's just our cover story. But you may find the small, everyday things difficult to adjust to . . . the absence of a great deal that we take for granted in the way of amenities."

"Oh, surely, Commander," said Nesbit brightly, "it can't be all *that* bad. After all, those were *people* then, just like ourselves, so *surely* the basic fundamental must be essentially—"

"Toilet paper," Jason cut in succinctly.

"I beg your pardon."

"Just a very minor example. Toilet paper, like so many things, was a Chinese invention. It wasn't introduced into the West until the nineteenth century." Seeing Nesbit's blank look, Jason explained patiently. "We're going to be in the seventeenth century."

"But . . . er, that is . . . what does one, well, *do*?"

"One does without," said Mondrago with a grin that was wicked even for him.

"Thank you, Commander Thanou," said Rutherford firmly. "I believe that's all the orientation we need for now."

CHAPTER FIVE

"Now this," said Alexandre Mondrago admiringly, "is one *good-looking* gun!"

"Somewhat more to the point, it was a state-of-the-art firearm for its time," said Grenfell rather didactically. "One of the reasons why the buccaneers were so successful against the Spaniards was that they were, quite simply, better armed." His expression softened a trifle. "But there is no denying that it is almost a Baroque work of art, in its way."

They all stood in the armory, just inside the wide doors that led to the firing range, and admired the five-foot-long, broad-butted musket Mondrago held. It had been produced by the Authority's workshops to the exacting standard of authenticity time travel required. In this case, that had been harder than usual. Grenfell was explaining why.

"Each of these muskets was one of a kind. Remember, mass production of firearms using interchangeable parts didn't come in until the mid-eighteenth century. This is a reproduction of the kind of musket crafted by the great French gunsmiths of Normandy like Brachere of Dieppe and Galin of Nantes—the best in the world. Each one required a whole staff in addition to the designer: specialists in stockmaking, barrelsmithing, metal carving, engraving and inlaying."

"I believe it," said Jason. The four-foot-long blued barrel had an almost porcelainlike gleam, and was decorated with mythological scenes. "Did they work all this artwork into the cold metal?"

"Yes. The craftsman was also a metallurgist."

"Again, I believe it." Jason took the weapon from Mondrago and hefted it. It had an odd look, with its spade-shaped stock, but it balanced beautifully. "It's a lot lighter than it looks."

"The French gunsmiths were able to achieve that lightness by a combination of superb metallurgy and certain design innovations. It was one of the things that gave them an edge over their competitors and enabled them to charge the high prices they commanded. This particular example is—or, to be precise, would have been—even more expensive than average. Most of the muskets were still matchlocks, in which a moveable clamp called a serpentine connected to the trigger held a burning taper, which was dipped into a tiny pan of gunpowder. It was old technology—it had been around for more than two and a half centuries before our target date—and was not noted for either convenience or reliability."

"That's one way to put it," said Jason, recalling his experiences in the Thirty Years' War.

"But it was cheap, which was why it was still the standard ignition system for infantry weapons. This one, on the other hand, is a wheel lock." Grenfell pointed at the little roughened steel wheel set just under the pan. In front of it was a serpentine, crafted to resemble a leaping dolphin, whose clamp held an iron pyrites, resting against the pan cover. "When the trigger is pressed," he explained, "it sets the wheel spinning and also pushes back the pan cover and allows the pyrites to come in contact with it, causing sparks to fly. This system was superbly reliable, but its complex clockwork mechanism made it very expensive."

Jason held the stock against his right shoulder and sighted along the barrel. "It isn't rifled, of course."

"No. Rifling had been known for some time, and was used for some specialized hunting weapons. But aside from the added expense, it was hard to get a ball down the barrel of a muzzle-loader when the inside of the barrel was grooved."

"But how accurate was a smoothbore musket like this? I seem to recall reading that the flintlock versions of the following century—the 'Brown Bess' type muskets—could consistently hit a foot-square target at up to forty yards but fell off drastically beyond that and couldn't hit anything much smaller than an elephant at a hundred yards."

"Which was why the tactics of that era emphasized massed volley fire by dense formations of infantry," Grenfell nodded. "No individual soldier was expected to hit an individual target. But the tests we've performed indicate that the kind of musket you're holding, although of earlier vintage, could do considerably better. For one thing, it has a somewhat longer barrel, always an aid to range and accuracy. For another, compared to standard infantry weapons it is, as you will have gathered, *very* well-made."

Jason passed the musket around. When it came to Nesbit, he handled it as he might have a dead animal. "Dr. Grenfell, I don't understand. You've intimated that one of these guns cost a small fortune. And in our history orientation you explained that, in terms of their social origins, most of the pirates could best be described as . . . well . . ."

"Lowlifes," Mondrago suggested helpfully.

"That's one way to put it," Grenfell nodded.

"Then how on Earth did they afford these very high-priced weapons?"

"Any way it took," stated Grenfell succinctly. "When someone went into piracy, his first order of business was to obtain a good musket from the Dutch traders who handled their distribution. The original buccaneers in Hispaniola had traded hides for them—twenty hides per musket—because they needed them to bring down the wild pigs and cattle. And they needed to do so without ruining the hides, so they became crack shots. In our target period, aspiring pirates would either use whatever they had saved from their wages as indentured servants—if that was what they had been, as was often the case—or else borrow the money against their future shares of loot. It was an essential initial investment, because of the advantage it gave them over the Spaniards."

"Who were armed with what?" Pauline Da Cunha inquired.

"Arquebuses, for the most part. They were the earliest kind of practical matchlock shoulder-fired arms, and had been around for almost two hundred years by the 1660s. They were obsolete, and inferior in every way. But they were cheap, which was why the Spanish government still equipped its solders with them—often shoddy ones."

"Typical!" sniffed Mondrago.

"Then why didn't the Spanish colonials buy good weapons from the Dutch traders for themselves, like the pirates did?" Da Cunha persisted.

"They couldn't, without dealing with smugglers—a serious offense. Remember, trade with the Spanish colonies was a royal monopoly. Neither the Dutch nor any other foreign merchants were allowed in. And the Spanish mercantile network, if you could call it that, was hopeless. The colonials had a saying: 'If death came from Madrid, we would all live to a great age.'"

"I'm beginning to understand," said Boyer after the chuckles had subsided, "why the Spanish empire, which looks so vast and mighty on a map, was so unsuccessful in coping with a relative handful of . . . lowlifes."

"Actually, there were a lot of reasons. The stultifying centralized bureaucracy made flexible response impossible. The outdated arquebuses were largely wielded by amateur militia, who were up against hardened killers. Those Spaniards who *were* professional soldiers had little incentive to fight for a government that was often as much a year late in paying them—in fact, they often reverted to the level of part-time militia themselves as they did other jobs to keep body and soul together. Speaking of lack of incentive to fight, remember that the pirates weren't conquerors who permanently occupied the land and enslaved the inhabitants; they came, plundered, and went away. Under those circumstances, flight was often a more attractive option than fight, especially if you had some advance warning and could hide your valuables.

"But more fundamental than any of that was the empire's innate vulnerability. It was totally dependent on the flow of precious metals from the New World to Spain, especially the silver mined at Potosí in Peru and Zacatecas in Mexico. The amounts were fabulous, and the kings of Spain could never understand why they were chronically on the brink of bankruptcy and, in fact, went over the brink numerous times. Nobody in those days, you see, had any concept of inflation. By constantly increasing the quantities of monetary metals they were causing the 'Price Revolution' of early-modern Europe and inflating their wealth away. The only solution they could imagine was to bring in still more gold and silver, which of course only perpetuated the vicious cycle."

"Junkie behavior," Mondrago stated shortly.

"Hmm!" Grenfell gave the Corsican a look of hitherto well-concealed appreciation. "I'd never thought of it in exactly those terms. But that's not a bad way of looking at it." Jason suspected he was looking forward to springing Mondrago's insight on some of his earnest academic colleagues. "The empire was living on borrowed time until someone saw past its imposing façade and realized how vulnerable its lifeline was, how dependent it was on the steady supply of silver that enabled it to . . . support its habit. At the time we're going to be visiting, that someone had appeared: Henry Morgan."

"Yes," Jason nodded. "You've mentioned him several times in the orientation lectures."

"The most successful pirate who ever lived. In fact, he was so successful that he ceased to be a pirate. Eventually King Charles II knighted him and appointed him lieutenant governor of Jamaica, with instructions to hunt down his former cronies and suppress piracy—which he did with great efficiency. He died in bed, honored and filthy rich—practically a unique event in the annals of piracy. When they buried someone who had served in a gubernatorial office, it was customary for the Royal Navy ships in port to fire a twenty-one gun salute. They gave Morgan twenty-two."

"But all of that still lay well in the future in our target year, right?" asked Jason after a pause.

"Oh, yes. In late 1668 he was gathering recruits for his greatest raid up to that time. His reputation was already such that buccaneers were swarming in to join him. I think we'll find Port Royal to be even fuller than usual of, ah, ahem, colorful characters."

"Some of us," Da Cunha commented archly with a sidelong glance at Mondrago, "ought to fit right in."

"Well," said Jason, "let's get out there on the target range and get some practice, so we can *all* fit in."

The muskets did turn out to be more accurate than expected. Of course, it helped that the Authority's artisans had been able to embed very tiny laser target designators in the end of the stock just to the rear of the muzzle, activated by a partial squeezing of the trigger. It was one of the concessions Jason had been able to extort from Rutherford, using the argument that they might—perish the thought!—find themselves in a position where they needed to display the level of marksmanship for which the buccaneers were renowned. He had no real worries in the case of himself and the other two Service people, and Grenfell's training, however rusty, should help. As for Boyer and Nesbit, the target designators should enable them to perform as well as a carpenter and a doctor were expected to.

"What if somebody notices a tiny little dot of light on someone else just before that person gets shot?" asked Da Cunha dubiously.

"He'll blink, feel slightly puzzled for a moment, then shake his head and forget it," Grenfell asserted confidently. "It simply isn't part of his reality structure."

On Nesbit's first try, the target designator did him no good. Unprepared for the musket's kick, he almost fell over backwards and sent the ball flying over the target. Afterwards, he gradually improved, and when he finally managed to put a ball through the target board (though not in the circle) he looked fit to burst with pride. Jason sighed. A surgeon's mate wouldn't be expected to be a crack shot, and at any rate the chief concern at the moment was to familiarize everyone with the mechanics of loading and firing: the pouring of the powder down the muzzle, followed by the lead ball with its rammed-in wad of rag. Everyone bitched about the awkwardness and inconvenience, but Grenfell assured them that matchlocks were a lot worse.

Naturally, single-shot muzzle-loading longarms were no good for boarding actions involving fast and furious close combat. They went back inside the armory to see what a buccaneer typically used for that: a brace of pistols—flintlocks, which for reasons Grenfell was unable to explain, had caught on for handguns before they did for muskets—and a cutlass. The latter was a short, slightly curved sword with a wide single-edged blade and a crude basket hilt like a metal shell protecting the whole sword hand. Mondrago, whose real forte was edged weapons, looked at it somewhat askance.

"The workshop deliberately made it look crude," Grenfell explained. "The original ones were pretty low-quality. These, on the other hand, are better than they look, thanks to modern metallurgy."

Jason hefted his pistols. One of them differed from all the others, for it incorporated another of the devices that Rutherford had grudgingly allowed. The handgrip concealed a very small sensor whose only function was the short-range detection of active bionic body parts. It was connected with Jason's brain implant via a hookup the latter possessed for remote linkage with such devices, so its findings automatically appeared on his neural heads-up display—a useful capability whether the hat he was currently wearing was that of the Hesperian Colonial Rangers or the Temporal Service Special Operations Section. He had been able to overcome Rutherford's jitters by pointing out that they needed a means of recognizing enhanced Transhumanists for what they were.

They had a few days to practice with the various weapons. They were also issued their clothing: tuniclike shirts of coarse cotton, rawhide breeches, pigskin boots, and the broad-brimmed hats that were a necessity in the tropical sun. Da Cunha was dressed pretty much the same as the men, albeit with a shirt of somewhat better quality and even slightly frilly; any unmarried woman in Port Royal's pirate quarter who dressed in the era's full-skirted feminine styles was presumed to be a whore. They all acquired the tattoos without which seafarers of the period would have seemed naked—or at least the semblance of such tattoos, by grace of dermal imprint circuitry.

Nesbit was disappointed in the outfits, having

expected something more colorful and flamboyant. It was explained to him that pirates only decked themselves out in gaudy silks, damasks and velvets after plundering a merchant ship laden with such fripperies, which never lasted long. He had other disappointments in store. One was the fact that black flags (with skulls and crossed bones, or full skeletons, or bleeding hearts, or whatever), while not unknown, were not the pirate flags that were truly feared. Such a flag meant that quarter would be given to those who surrendered; a red flag meant no quarter, period.

Practice in seamanship was—and had to be, considering that they were in the middle of a desert—done by means of virtual-reality technology. Going into it, Nesbit recovered some of his animation. "Will I get to, ah, man the steering wheel?"

Grenfell rolled his eyes but explained with his usual patience. "The steering wheel was an early eighteenth-century invention. Before that, they used what was called a whipstaff, attached to the tiller, which moved the rudder." He used a remote control unit to activate a cursor on the holographic ship-image they were studying. "As you can see, it's below the quarterdeck. The steersman, unable to see outside, was dependent on commands from above."

"And at any rate," Jason added firmly, "that isn't going to be your job. In fact, while we're having to acquire certain basic skills, I have no intention of *unnecessarily* putting us in positions where we'll have to use those skills. Our guiding principle is going to be *just enough to get by*."

Nesbit looked slightly deflated. Jason had a feeling that his disappointment, and his fantasies, would vanish once he saw the seventeenth-century Caribbean at first hand. At least he devoutly hoped they would.

"I wish I could have been more help," said Chantal Frey as they walked toward the displacer stage. "But Franco never said anything about any scheme resembling this one—and certainly nothing about temporally displacing a spacecraft!"

"Which, given his propensity for boasting, suggests that this Transhumanist operation originates in his future...and perhaps our own," said Rutherford, who was also accompanying them. His brow was furrowed with worry as he mulled over the implications.

"You've been a lot of help," Jason assured Chantal, "with general background information about Transhumanist organization and procedures and ways of thinking. You never know when that kind of thing is going is going to come in handy."

"I hope so." She hesitated. "There was just one thing. It probably has nothing to do with this. But one time Franco said, while we were...well..."

"Yes?" Jason prompted, helping her past her embarrassment.

"He mentioned that he had left a message drop—they use the same technique as we do—letting his superiors uptime know about something he had learned from his Teloi allies. He didn't say anything specific, you realize; he never did really trust me. But he was even more self-satisfied than usual about it. He bragged that it would cause the Transhumanist underground to make their biggest investment in time travel yet, and that he would be remembered as the Transhuman Movement's greatest hero. He went on like that a lot, you know." All at once, her face took on an expression not at all like its usual shy diffidence. "Give them one in the eye for me, will you?"

"At every opportunity," Jason promised her.

The six members of the expedition received the traditional handshake from Rutherford and stepped up onto the stage. Nesbit spoiled the solemnity of the moment by tripping over his musket and almost falling on his face. Jason gave Mondrago and Da Cunha a stern look, and they kept their features expressionless. Then Rutherford and Chantal turned away, and the displacer began to power up.

"Hey, Chantal," Jason called out, remembering his last retrieval, "do you think I look 'dashing' in *this* getup?"

She turned and gave him a cool once-over. "I think the word I'd use is 'piratical.'"

"Yo-ho-ho and a bottle of rum!" he intoned.

Her smile was the last thing he saw before the indescribable dissolution of reality that was temporal displacement took him.

CHAPTER SIX

For an experienced hand like Jason, the disorientation of temporal displacement only lasted a few moments. But not even he had ever entirely gotten over it. No one ever did.

An instant before, they had been standing on the displacer stage. Then the brightly lit dome, with its concentric tiers of instrument consoles and its overhanging glassed-in control center, was no longer there. It had vanished like a dream, with no recollection of it having vanished and no sensation of time having passed. Sweat popped out on them, for the dry, conditioned air of the dome had abruptly been replaced by the moist warmth of a tropical dawn.

They were standing on a narrow beach where the town of Harbour View would one day arise, and the rising sun was just peeking over the jungle close behind them, sending multitudes of land crabs scuttling away into the forest after their nighttime feeding. Before them to the west stretched one of the most magnificent natural harbors in the world, the sun just beginning to glisten on its wavelets.

To their right, the beach curved away, stretching into the semi-darkness, with mountains dimly outlined in the far distance. On that northern shore, Grenfell had explained, a camp would be established in 1692 for refugees from Port Royal after that town's destruction by an earthquake—or by the hand of God, according to contemporary clergymen, as a punishment for its wickedness. From that camp would grow the city of Kingston. Now only thick jungle fringed the shore, although Grenfell had mentioned that there were ever-growing sugar plantations further inland on the alluvial plains. Those hellish plantations acted as breeding grounds for pirates, as indentured servants and slaves, surfeited with the brutality of their lives, ran away to Port Royal.

To the left, the curving beach merged with the base of the long, narrow peninsula known as the Palisadoes, which enclosed the harbor to the south. At its far western end was Port Royal.

"All right," said Jason after all of them—even Nesbit—had recovered their equilibrium. "Let's get going. It's about eight miles along the Palisadoes, and we'll want to cover as much of that as possible before it gets too hot. Even in late December it can get into the upper eighties."

As they walked, they all began to understand his impatience. The temperature rose rapidly, and even the sea-breeze that sprung up around ten o'clock did little to relieve the discomfort. With the heat came the insects. The clouds of malarial mosquitoes grew less as they proceeded along the Palisadoes and left the jungle behind, but the sandflies increased. Jason had tried, without success, to talk Rutherford into letting them bring insect repellant in containers disguised as in-period canteens.

"Was it really necessary for us to arrive so far from Port Royal, Commander?" whined Nesbit as he trudged along, wiping sweat from his brow and attempting to shoo away insects. He sounded as though romantic high adventure was already starting to pall.

"It's because of the paramount importance of not having any of the locals see us pop into existence out of thin air, Irving," said Jason with a painstaking care that would have been insulting had Nesbit been discerning enough to recognize it as such. "That's why we always pick an out-of-the-way location, and time it for dawn. Actually, that timing is a compromise; we'd prefer the middle of the night, but for some reason transition in complete darkness has proven to have undesirable psychological effects."

Mondrago, who had never ceased to marvel at past ages' rudimentary notions of security, seemed to have a sudden thought. "I understand why we couldn't simply materialize in Port Royal. But are we really going to be able to just *walk* into it?"

Grenfell answered that one. "I think you'll find that no one pays much attention to the landward approach. All of Port Royal's connections with the rest of the island are by boat." He gestured at the cactus-fringed path—there was nothing really describable as a "trail"—they had been following along the Palisadoes, with the water visible on both sides. "No one comes this way."

"They've got better sense," grumbled Da Cunha in the steadily rising heat.

More people were in evidence as they approached the town, but it was obvious that all the fortifications—most notably the massive Fort Charles at the entrance to the harbor—were oriented toward the sea. Mingling inconspicuously with the crowds, they entered the sweaty bustle of what would have been instantly recognizable in any era as a boom town.

It was only early afternoon, but as they passed through the packed, raucous streets it was clear that the drinking establishments were already doing a healthy business, and had been for a while. And there were a *lot* of them. Jason commented on it to Grenfell, who chuckled.

"By actual count, there was one grog shop for every ten residents—although it was hard to keep track of the residents, as more and more of them were coming in all the time. Right now, the population is probably between sixty-five hundred and eight thousand, depending on which estimate you accept. This had become the largest English-speaking city in the Western Hemisphere, as well as the richest—by far the richest and, by general consensus, the wickedest." Grenfell seemed about to say more, but three men came staggering out of a tavern in front of them, dressed much as themselves but even dirtier and—Jason felt he could claim without fear of successful contradiction—uglier. The one who seemed to be the leader glared about him with his one eye—a patch covered the other eye-hole—out of a face that was largely a pattern of scars. The trio did not exactly look like convivial drunks, and Jason led his followers carefully around them. The detour took them past an alley between the tavern and what seemed to be an inn. Another tavern patron had taken a woman dressed in a style of scanty and filthy gaudiness halfway down that alley before overcoming her patently bogus resistance and lifting her skirts. Jason had to drag Nesbit away lest he stand and stare, goggle-eyed, at what the two were doing. No one else on the street seemed to paying any particular attention. As they hastened past the inn, Jason had to do a quick sidestep to avoid a warm spatter as one of the inn's guests urinated out his second-story window into the street. Nesbit wasn't quite quick enough.

They entered the dockside area, lined with huge warehouses and bristling with wharves, and walked along a cobblestoned street under the jutting bowsprits of dozens of ships. Here ship chandlers' offices, sail lofts, carpentry stalls and other such establishments alternated with the ubiquitous grog shops, gaming houses and brothels. There were also meat markets where the slaughtering took place on the spot so that the customer could watch and be sure his purchase hadn't spoiled in the tropical heat. The Bear Garden wasn't in use yet, as it was too early in the day for the "sport" of bear baiting—which was just as well, as far as Jason was concerned. Outside it, some fun-loving types whose typical pirate garb was bedizened with soiled tatters of looted Spanish finery had smashed a hole in a wine cask, and laughing whores were dancing through the spraying gusher before putting their mouths to it.

Further back from the waterfront could be heard the clip-clop of hooves, as six-horse teams pulled the carriages of the wealthy, well-dressed merchants. In that direction were houses, some as much as three or four stories high and many of them still under construction, interspersed with the remaining huts of the colony's earlier years. Here also were the grocers and bakers, the goldsmiths and blacksmiths, and the few reputable inns, as was the stone cathedral that was the pride and joy of Port Royal's respectable element. What was striking about it all was its *English* look. The houses were gambrel-roofed, and both they and the warehouses were stone and brick. Jason commented to Grenfell on it.

Grenfell shook his head sadly. "The Spanish colonists had, by this time, evolved a relatively earthquake-proof style of low-slung architecture anchored to the Earth with thick, deeply-driven wooden posts. The English wouldn't hear of it. They wanted to recreate England here in the tropics. All this massive construction is standing on a thirty- to sixty-foot layer of loose sand resting on coralline limestone and loose gravel. The great earthquake of June 7, 1692 and its accompanying tsunami will result in liquefaction of the sand and cause the entire northern part of the town—that's where we're standing now—to simply sink into the sea. Nearly half the population will be killed outright, and another two thousand of the homeless survivors will subsequently die of disease among the thousands of decomposing bodies."

Jason looked around him with new eyes. The solidity of Port Royal suddenly seemed an illusion. He had forgotten that only twenty-four years from now all of this was going to vanish into the sea with Atlantis-like thoroughness, providing clergymen as far away as Cotton Mather in Boston with material for sermons on the wages of sin.

"For now, though, Port Royal seems to be going full bore," he observed.

It certainly was. They continued past warehouses stuffed with the island's exports: animal skins, logwood, tortoiseshell, spices, dyes and the up-and-coming product: sugar. Other warehouses were receiving ironwork, clothing and assorted luxuries from England. Still others took in goods from elsewhere in the Caribbean for transshipment. All of the great buildings were beehives of activity, with slaves and indentured servants hauling on ropes to hoist the cargo up to large windows where other laborers grappled and pulled it inside. They passed merchants' establishments where gold and jewelry brought back by buccaneers was being weighed on scales, which archaeologists centuries later would find to have been discreetly weighted in the merchants' favor. Everywhere, money was changing hands—all sorts of money, from the floods of pirate plunder that flowed through Port Royal, including doubloons, piastres, golden moidores and especially Spanish pieces of eight.

"They've recently declared pieces of eight to be legal tender here in Jamaica," Grenfell remarked. "They practically had to, after Morgan's sack of Portobello earlier this year, which brought in a haul of seventy-five thousand pounds, as compared to a total annual value of ten thousand pounds for the entire island's sugar exports. Ordinary seamen each had sixty pounds or more to squander on rum and whores. That was what an average worker earned in three years!"

"I'm beginning to see why this town is the way it is," said Jason.

"For now. But the sugar industry—including the

production of rum—is the wave of the future. Henry Morgan himself understood this. In the end, he plowed his loot into his vast plantations and made far more money that way than he had ever pillaged. A remarkable man all around. At present, though, sugar cultivation is still getting started. The first shipment to England was only eight years ago, in 1660. But exports are now in the hundreds of tons. In a few years, they'll outstrip plundering as a source of wealth."

"Which," Boyer said tonelessly, "accounts for *that*." He pointed ahead at a wharf where a line of bound blacks were being led down a gangplank under the watchful eyes of guards with short, vicious-looking whips. They had all thought they had adjusted to the aromas of a seventeenth-century port city. But the ship from which the blacks were emerging gave off a stench that almost bowled Jason over, accustomed though he was to the smells of earlier and less delicate ages. Nesbit scurried into concealment behind a large packing crate and was violently sick.

Grenfell nodded. "Yes. Sugar is a crop that requires backbreaking work, especially when the plantations are just getting started and need to be cleared, degrubbed and dewormed even before the planting. At first, most of that work was done by white indentured servants or 'buckras.' These men lived a hellish life—packed into tiny shacks, subject to beatings and floggings for any reason or no reason—which between a third and a half of them did not survive. But at least in their case there was light at the end of the tunnel. Indentured servitude was for a fixed term, typically seven years. Slavery was forever. And by this time, the indentured servants are starting to be replaced by the African slaves who will form the basis of the future population. In just a few years, Jamaica will be importing fifteen hundred of them annually."

As they watched, one of the slaves stumbled and fell, dragging down the nearby ones to whom he was roped. One of the guards sprang forward and brought his whip down across a back already crisscrossed with welts and running with pus. The slave gasped with pain and staggered desperately to his feet to avoid more blows. The line resumed shuffling forward.

Jason watched Boyer closely. They had all been warned to expect this, and cautioned that they must react—or appear to react—with the same indifference any other seventeenth-century pirates would have displayed. But such instructions were sometimes very difficult to follow. A mission leader always had to be alert to the possibility that emotions might grow too intense for some people when they came face to face with the various horrors of the human past, and stand ready to take whatever preventative action was necessary. But Boyer's dark face remained carefully expressionless.

"It's easy to understand why slaves and indentured servants often ran away and became pirates," Mondrago commented. "The planters must have just loved that!"

"They were always complaining about it," Grenfell nodded. "But not very loudly, even though they technically had the law on their side. They could never forget that the buccaneers were the only defense they had against the Spaniards. And besides, any slave-catcher who came aboard a pirate ship demanding the return of a runaway would have been pitched over the side to feed the sharks."

"Good enough for him," Da Cunha opined coldly.

"But a rotten thing to do to the sharks," Mondrago added. Boyer continued to maintain a silence that Jason thought might be a little too tightly controlled.

Nesbit rejoined them, wiping his chin, his complexion pale green. Jason motioned them onward, past the slave ship and its cargo of misery. They had gone a short way before a commotion—noisy even by the raucous standards of Port Royal—erupted from an alley to the left, a short distance ahead of them.

A figure came running from the alley into the dockside area, with four men in pursuit.

She was female but clearly no whore, and black but clearly no slave, for she wore garments similar to their own and had a brace of pistols thrust through her rope belt. Jason barely took all this in, so stunning was her appearance.

She was tall even for Jason's era, which made her towering for this one, and her body was that of a warrior goddess: slim-waisted, full-breasted and leanly muscular. She was ebon-dark, but her features suggested mixed race, for her lips were full without being thick and her nose had a narrow and slightly curved bridge, although the nostrils flared. It was a striking face, and one of the most beautiful Jason had ever seen.

One of her pursuers sprinted ahead of the other three and was almost within reach of her. With a motion of almost invisible quickness she turned toward him, whipped off the broad-brimmed, feather-plumed hat that crowned her tightly curled black hair, and sent it spinning into the man's face. It threw him off his stride, and as he tried to regain his balance her booted left foot shot out in a powerful kick that caught him between the legs. With a whistling shriek, he doubled over.

"What a woman!" Mondrago gasped admiringly. Equally admiring, in its own way, was the laughter from the crowd that had already begun gathering to watch the fun. Evidently this sort of thing was considered a form of free public entertainment in the Port Royal waterfront district.

But the kick caused the woman to lose her own balance. She staggered against a pile of coiled rope and fell over. The other three men caught up and were almost atop her.

With a non-verbal roar, Boyer plunged forward past Jason's right.

I knew he had been holding too much in, flashed through Jason's mind in a tiny fraction of a second. *I've got to stop him!*

Even as he thought, he bunched his leg muscles for a lunge.

But at the same moment he became aware that, at the lower left of his field of vision, a group of tiny blue lights were blinking for attention.

Without time to consciously analyze his change of plans, he shouted, "Follow him!" to the others.

"What?" Mondrago and Da Cunha blurted as one, as Grenfell gawked and Nesbit dithered.

"No time to explain!" Jason snapped, as he launched himself after Boyer.

There definitely wasn't time. There were active bionics up ahead, here in this time and place where they did not belong.

Which could only mean one thing.

CHAPTER SEVEN

One of the three pursuers was a length ahead of the others. Jason rushed in front of him, to Boyer's left, and as he moved he unslung his musket. Gripping it like a quarterstaff, he brought it around and slammed the butt into the man's midriff, doubling him over.

"Get her out of here, Henri!" he shouted at Boyer. Not daring to turn and see if he was being obeyed, he brought the musket back up and backed off a step, as the other two men approached more cautiously, drawing their cutlasses. Off to the side, the man the black woman had kicked was getting to his feet, sooner than Jason would ordinarily have thought possible. But then, looking into their faces, he recognized some of the indicia of the Transhumanist strong-arm castes—"goons" as Special Ops people called them. It was nothing blatant—the Transhumanist underground naturally couldn't send any of their grotesquely gene-modified varieties, or obvious cyborgs, back in time to milieus in which they would have stood out. But you could always tell if you knew what to look for in those mass-produced faces. Jason had no idea of the nature of their concealed bionics—his sensor couldn't tell him that, only that they were present—but they wouldn't be able to openly use anything too flashy.

Mondrago, Da Cunha and Grenfell had now joined him, cutlasses in hand. The Transhumanists hesitated, seeing themselves outnumbered as Nesbit took his place with the others. (*If only they knew!* he gibed to himself.) It was a tense momentary standoff, and he risked a glance over his shoulder at the woman. "Stay there!" he told her.

"I don't want your help!" she snarled in an accent he couldn't place. She was still trying to get up, her feet tangled in the rope. Boyer extended a hand to help her up. She angrily struck it away. Then her eyes met his for an instant, and she took his hand. He hauled her up. Then, with a swift judo-like motion, she swung his arm back around behind him and sent him sprawling face-down. Before Jason had time to react, she had burst through the ring of spectators and was sprinting along the dock.

For a fractional second, Jason stood frozen in unaccustomed indecision. Then he saw two more men emerge from the alley, holding pistols as though they were already loaded. He couldn't be sure these were more Transhumanists, but if they were the balance had suddenly shifted.

And he badly wanted to know why Transhumanists were in pursuit of that spectacular-looking black woman. The first step was to find out who she was. And she was getting further away every second.

Then the two new arrivals took their place with

the Transhumanists. The standoff clearly couldn't last more than another couple of heartbeats.

"After her!" Jason yelled. He turned and broke through the crowd, eliciting bellows of outrage.

Before the Transhumanists could recover from their surprise, the others followed him, with Mondrago in the lead. Da Cunha grasped the arm of Nesbit, who stood gaping, and yanked him along. They all set out at a run, in the direction the black woman had taken.

The Transhumanists broke free of their paralysis and started out in pursuit. But the spectators had also recovered, and with Jason and his followers now gone they vented their indignation on the Transhumanists trying to break through the press. Glancing back over his shoulder, Jason saw that a full-fledged brawl had erupted. It would doubtless take the Transhumanists time to break free of it, time on which Jason was counting.

"Up ahead!" he shouted as he saw the woman turn left into another of the alleys leading south, away from the waterfront. They pounded after her, emerging from the vile-smelling mud alley onto a street running parallel with the water. At the intersection the street widened into a kind of square.

In the middle of the square sat a large cask. It had been broached, and gathered around it were a group of obvious buccaneers, holding out drinking jacks for refills from a man who was haranguing them in a booming voice as he passed out drinks, pausing only to take deep gulps of his own.

Jason didn't immediately take all of it in, for at first he could only stare at that man.

He was sweating freely under the kind of three-piece suit that, thanks to the influence of King Charles II, had begun to replace the older jerkin-and-doublet as the dress of a gentleman. But around his waist was a wide, flamboyant scarlet sash, and over his right shoulder was a baldric from which a cutlass hung. An equally scarlet kerchief was tied around his head, and a purple plume was stuck in the cocked hat he wore over it. But Jason noticed none of this. It was the man himself he stared at. He had encountered a very few men who, for no reason that could be put into words, made it impossible to look anywhere else when they were present. This man was one.

He was moderately tall for this milieu, but one couldn't help thinking of him as a very big man because the overwhelming impression was one of broad-shouldered, stocky power. One also got the impression, looking at the waist his red sash encompassed, that as he got older—he appeared to be in his mid-thirties—he might well develop a weight problem if he didn't exercise a moderation which, Jason strongly suspected, was foreign to his nature.

But it was his face that really held the attention: broad, sun-bronzed to a shade even darker than its normal swarthiness. He sported a short, pointed beard, neatly shaped but merging into a dense dark shadowing, for he was overdue for a shave. Under level black brows, his large, dark brown eyes twinkled and, Jason thought, missed very little. It was a mobile, expressive face, and, underneath the roistering, gargantuan laughter, an almost frighteningly intelligent one. Above all, it was a face that was full of life . . . more life, it seemed, than a single body ought to hold. This, Jason was sure, was a man who would not reach a great age; he would die early from having lived too much.

The black woman caught the man's attention as she ran across the square. "Zenobia!" he bellowed. "Haven't seen you in much too long. Here, have some rum! All who pass here must pause for a drink while I tell them of the expedition I'm planning—one that'll make Portobello look like nothing, by God!" His deep voice held a kind of lilt that Jason, from various experiences in the past, recognized as the worn-down remnants of a Welsh accent.

The woman skidded to a halt. She looked back over her shoulder at Jason and his following. Then, coming to a sudden decision, she turned to the big, flamboyantly dressed man. "Aye, Captain, so I've heard. That's why I'm here. I've come to sign on with you." He gave Jason another look, this time one of mocking triumph.

"Then come here and drink, girl!" The big man thrust a brimming jack into her hands. "Glad I am to have you and your crew of Maroon throat-cutters. And," he added with a significant glance around, "if I hear any old women in breeks repeating any of those silly stories about you, I'll hand them their balls, if they've got any."

Mondrago came up alongside Jason. "What now, sir?" he muttered. "We're following her because those were Transhumanists chasing her, right?"

"Right. And I want to know why they were. But we'd better play it cautiously for now. She's obviously among friends."

At that moment, the six Transhumanists burst into the square and headed toward Zenobia. She immediately flung aside her half-full drinking jack and turned to face them with a glare.

"What's this?" demanded the big man, clearly appalled at the waste of rum.

"Ahoy, Captain!" The Transhumanist who seemed to be the leader swaggered forward and pointed theatrically at Zenobia. Jason felt the man was slightly overplaying the pirate role, but on further reflection he decided that such a thing was probably impossible. "We want this black-assed bitch. She cheated us of part of our shares on our last voyage."

"He's a lying bastard, Captain," she snapped.

"Shut up, you stinking nigger cunt!" The Transhumanist grabbed at her again. She struck his hand aside.

The big man thrust himself forward, in front of Zenobia, seeming to expand beyond his natural size. "She's just become part of my company," he said in what Jason imagined passed for a mild tone of voice with him. "If you want her, you'll have to take it up with me."

"This is none of your affair, Captain." The Transhumanist shifted his tone to one of bogus reasonableness. "Just turn her over to us and we'll settle this nice and peaceably. After all, why should a black gash come between two gentlemen, eh?"

"Two gentlemen?" the big man purred, and his eyes narrowed. "It seems we're short one of those!" All at once his voice rose to a roar that could have been heard over a storm at sea. "Get out of my sight, you sons of worm-eaten whores!"

"Then we'll take her, damn you!" snapped the Transhumanist. At the same time, he gave what Jason recognized as a hand-signal to one of his men—one of the two with loaded pistols. He inconspicuously cocked the pistol and moved toward the big man's side where he would have an unobstructed shot.

Jason lunged forward, but Mondrago was ahead of him. The Corsican dropped to his hands and brought his legs around in the sweeping *savate* move Jason knew all too well from practice sessions, and knocked the Transhumanist's feet out from under him. The pistol went off, firing into the air. Jason landed on top of the prone figure, grasped his right wrist, and yanked the arm up behind him, forcing the pistol from his fingers.

It was the signal for a general brawl. Evidently the discharge of a firearm in the streets in broad daylight got attention even in Port Royal. The big man's adherents, enraged, surged from around the rum cask faster than Jason would have imagined, given their condition. Jason heard the other pistol also fire wildly as its owner went down under a crush of assailants. Whatever implanted high-tech weapons the Transhumanists had, they dared not use them publicly, nor did they dare openly display the full capabilities of their genetic upgrades. They were promptly overwhelmed by sheer numbers and held. The big man had pinned the Transhumanist leader face-down on the cobblestones, and had drawn his cutlass.

"God's holy shit!" he bellowed. "Try to shoot me, will you? What's this town coming to? I was telling Governor Modyford just the other day that we're starting to get a bad element in Port Royal. I ought to hand this cutlass to Zenobia and let her cut off your pox-rotten prick! But it happens I'm in a good mood today. So . . ." He stood up, and brought his cutlass down with a whistle of cloven air. The Transhumanist screamed, and blood spurted from the right side of his head. The big man reached down, picked something up from beside him, and shoved it into his mouth. The Transhumanist gagged and spat blood.

"Like the taste, do you? Now take it with you and fry it for your supper, unless you want me to feed it to the pigs. And get out of here before I become annoyed and forget I'm a gentleman!" The big man gave a final kick to the ribs of the Transhumanist, who staggered to his feet and scrambled away at best speed, trying to stanch the flow of blood. Jason got off the pistolero's back and sent him on his way with a kick of his own. The rest of the Transhumanist underlings were likewise released and fled after their leader, to the profane jeers of the crowd. Jason wondered if they had brought any twenty-fourth-century tissue-regeneration equipment with them...and if so, how long it would take to regrow an ear. Nesbit looked as though it was just as well that he had recently emptied his stomach.

The big man turned to Jason with an affable smile, as though nothing particularly out of the ordinary had occurred—as, indeed, it might not have, from his perspective. "You and your mate here did me a good turn. Here, have a drink." He filled another jack with rum and thrust it into Jason's hands. "What's your name?"

"Jason, Captain. And this is Alexandre. And many thanks. Fighting's thirsty work." Suspecting that sipping and savoring was not the approved drinking style in this social milieu, Jason took a fairly substantial swallow. The top of his head came off and a stream of molten lava flowed down his throat to his stomach, where it caused a small boiler explosion. He managed to suppress a choke. *Now I see why this kind of rum was called "kill-devil,"* he thought as he gasped for breath, shivering. *It's strong enough to do precisely that.* He handed the jack to Mondrago, who read the signs and drank cautiously. Meanwhile, the big man finished his at one swallow, letting it gurgle. Then he got a refill.

How in God's name can he still be on his feet? Jason wondered, as Mondrago passed the jack along to the others, who handled it with varying degrees of success. Nesbit's eyes turned red, and he emitted a high-pitched wheeze. Jason fancied he could see steam escaping from his ears.

"I don't recall seeing you and your crew before, Jason," said the big man. His eyes narrowed shrewdly. "You talk like an educated man. And you look almost Spanish, though somehow not quite."

"I was born in Sicily, a subject of the King of Spain," said Jason. "I deserted the god-damned Spaniards, who threw dung in my face because I'm half Greek."

"What better can you expect of the Dons?" the big man commiserated, to a general chorus of growled agreement.

Jason briefly recounted their cover story and introduced the others. The big man took Da Cunha's presence in stride. But his eyes lit up at Nesbit and Boyer. "A surgeon's mate and a carpenter, eh? Well, it's a shame your last ship was lost, but I can offer you a place on mine—the *Oxford*, greatest ship in these waters!"

Off to one side, Grenfell seemed to stiffen at the name of that ship. But Jason barely noticed, for his attention was riveted on something else. He had forgotten about his heads-up display when the Transhumanists had fled, assuming that the sensor in the pistol-butt would no longer be of any use. But now he saw that one of the little blue dots was still there. It seemed to be slightly off to the side...

He glanced in that direction, and found himself looking into the suspicious, hostile coal-black eyes of the woman named Zenobia.

I didn't understand why the Transhumanists were chasing her. And now I understand it even less, for she must be one of their own.

And what, I wonder, was that about "silly stories" concerning her?

I've got to get to the bottom of this, whatever it takes. Which means we have to stay with her, even if it involves following this character wherever he leads.

"Aye, Captain!" he exclaimed without another instant's hesitation. "In fact, it was to join you that we came here, as soon as we heard you were planning a new venture and had put out a call." Out of the corner of his eye, he saw Zenobia's disgusted look. But then her eyes met Boyer's, and her expression seemed to soften just a trifle.

"Splendid!" The big man slapped Jason on the back, nearly sending him sprawling, and quaffed the last of his rum in a gulp the very sight of which made Jason's hair stand on end. Then he thrust his jack back into the cask and brought it up brimming. "Let's drink to that! And you won't regret it, by God! I'll show you treasure such as you've never dreamed existed in all of the Main, or my name's not Henry Morgan!"

Grenfell stared, goggle-eyed, and then tossed back a slug of kill-devil that Jason doubted he himself could have survived.

CHAPTER EIGHT

"All right, Roderick," said Jason. "Let's have the full background on Henry Morgan."

They sat in the main room of the inn where they had found what courtesy dictated must be called "lodgings." Their rooms were too small and cramped for six people to squeeze in, so they had appropriated one of the heavy wooden tables on the main room's dirt floor and paid the landlord a coin for privacy. Now they huddled together and spoke in low tones—except Nesbit, who had passed out from the effects of the rum he had consumed and was snoring face-down on the table. Boyer looked to be in very little better case. Jason and the other two Service people had more resistance, for they were used to those past eras—most past eras, actually—when failure to drink heavily was considered unsociable. Their current setting was an extreme example. Centuries before W. C. Fields, the buccaneers were firmly convinced that one should never trust a man who didn't drink. Jason hoped Boyer and Nesbit would develop a higher tolerance.

As for Grenfell, he was too excited to show the effects of alcohol.

"Well, to begin with, by strict legal definition he isn't a pirate at all, but rather a privateer; he's always careful to have commissions from Sir Thomas Modyford, the royal governor of Jamaica. Modyford, you see, is a good bureaucrat."

"Isn't that an oxymoron?" asked Mondrago skeptically.

"Not always. Modyford works tirelessly to get the privateers all the latitude he can, using them to keep Jamaica from being reconquered by Spain while navigating a path through the constantly changing game of war and diplomacy in Europe. Remember an enemy whose cities you've been looting can become an ally months before anybody on this side of the Atlantic heard about it. That will get Morgan in trouble later. But to the extent he can be, he's scrupulous about observing the legal niceties.

"Nor does he think of himself as a pirate. In fact he *hates* being called one, and I earnestly advise everyone not to do so in his hearing. As far as he's concerned, he's a patriotic soldier of the king. No, really," Grenfell insisted, seeing the looks on his listeners' faces. "He's a sincere royalist. He just sees no incompatibility between that and gaining what he most wants—riches and respect—by grabbing anything that's loose at one end. The Morgans are an old Welsh military family of the so-called *uchelwyr* class. He was only seven when the first English Civil War began in 1642, and it split the family. He had two favorite uncles, one of whom, Thomas, joined the Parliamentary side while the other, Edward, remained loyal to Charles I. It's pretty clear which side young Henry came down on. He was sixteen when the Civil Wars ended and Cromwell's Commonwealth was established, and what he was up to for the next four years is a mystery I hope we can solve. But, one way or another, he ended up signing on with the expedition Penn and Venables led to Jamaica—the exact circumstances are something else I'd like to clear up.

"Again, there's a gap of a few years. But in 1559 he was with Christopher Mings, the Port Royal buccaneers' first great leader, on an expedition that pillaged one Spanish town after another on the mainland of Venezuela. By 1661, at the age of twenty-six, he was a captain of one of Mings's ships when they took Santiago de Cuba, which was supposed to be impregnable, and Campeche in Yucatan.

"Afterwards, Mings went respectable—he was knighted and became an admiral in the Royal Navy, and was killed fighting the Dutch. In the meantime, Morgan came into his own. He led a small fleet that, from 1663 to 1665, ravaged Yucatan and Central America. It was an adventure no novelist would dare make up; they traveled over thirty-seven hundred miles in the space of eighteen months before returning to Port Royal laden with plunder. By that time, his old uncle Edward—the royalist—had been appointed Lieutenant Governor of Jamaica under Modyford. He had brought his daughters over with him, and Morgan proceeded to marry the eldest, Mary Elizabeth."

"Uh . . ." Da Cunha's brow furrowed with thought. "Wouldn't that have made her his—"

"—First cousin," Grenfell nodded. "That sort of thing is considered acceptable in this era. And even though she never gave him the heir he wanted, it seems to have been a happy marriage. Morgan's worst enemies never accused him of cheating on her...at least not as cheating on your wife is defined in this era."

"What does that mean?" Da Cunha wanted to know.

"Well, it doesn't include raping female enemy captives—"

"—And it definitely doesn't include sex with one's own female slaves," Boyer finished for Grenfell. "That's just making legitimate use of one's property."

"Yes," Grenfell confirmed. "Quite a few Jamaicans in our era claim descent from him. In the meantime, he was appointed head of Port Royal's militia—he supervised the building of Fort Charles—and also elected their admiral by the Brethren of the Coast. Then, early this year after a not very lucrative raid on El Puerto del Principe, Cuba, the French contingent of the Brethren deserted him and followed one of their own: Francois L'Ollonais, one of the most bloodthirsty psychopaths in the history of piracy, which is saying a great deal. Far from being discouraged, Morgan talked his remaining men into following him against an unknown target—quite a deviation from buccaneer custom—which turned out to be Portobello on the Isthmus of Panama, whose defenses had defeated Sir Francis Drake. Morgan took it. It was his most brilliant—and profitable—stroke to date." Grenfell hesitated. "It also established his reputation as a ruthless bastard. There's no reasonable doubt that he used some, ah, controversial methods there."

"Such as...?" Mondrago sounded intrigued.

"Such as using monks and nuns as human shields, driving them in front of his men so that the Spaniards, good Catholics all, would hesitate just long enough before opening fire. But some of the lurid stories of grotesque tortures used to extract ransom from the townspeople are almost certainly exaggerated. They derive from a bestselling book entitled *The Buccaneers of America,* which a former Dutch or French buccaneer named John Esquemeling will write in 1678." Grenfell chuckled. "Morgan will sue the publishers for libel, and win an out-of-court settlement. But some of the mud will stick. Perhaps we'll be in a position find out how much of what Esquemeling said about Morgan was deserved."

"Are you sure you *want* to be in that position?" inquired Da Cunha. Grenfell's expression changed abruptly. Evidently he hadn't thought through the implications.

"Anyway," Jason prompted him, "what about Morgan's current plans? What are we getting ourselves into?"

"Oh, yes. Remember what he said about the *Oxford*? She's a thirty-four gun frigate which the English government recently sent to Governor Modyford with tongue-in-cheek instructions that she was to be used to suppress piracy. Naturally, she's ended up as Morgan's flagship. He's going to assemble his fleet off Cow Island, just southwest of Hispaniola, and talk the captains into taking advantage of the *Oxford*'s firepower to attack Cartagena, in what was later to become Colombia, the greatest port in the Spanish empire. But then a somewhat mysterious event will occur." Grenfell frowned. "As they're drinking toasts—lots of toasts—to the success of their venture, the *Oxford* will blow up with a loss of about two hundred men. There'll be only ten survivors, including Morgan."

"It doesn't sound so mysterious to me," Mondrago opined. "A bunch of armed drunks running around on a ship made out of flammable materials and loaded with black powder..."

"It does seem that way, doesn't it? But nobody will be sure afterwards. There will be a lot of theories—including sabotage by malcontents, which doesn't seem too plausible, since they would have gone down with the ship. Maybe that's something else we can clear up."

"But let's try to not be aboard the *Oxford* when she's due to go up," Mondrago cautioned anxiously.

Grenfell looked sheepish. "Yes, intellectual curiosity *does* have its limits. At any rate, after that Morgan will—"

"That's fine for now, Roderick," Jason cut in. "I think you've given us an idea of what's coming next. Now let's talk about that woman, Zenobia."

Boyer looked troubled. "You've told us she's a Transhumanist, Commander. But how can you be sure? Yes, I know, you said she has bionics of some kind. But couldn't she be one of our own, from further in the future than ourselves?"

"I can't believe that. The Authority will know, from its own records, of our presence here. Even if they violate their own rules by sending someone else back to the same time and place, she wouldn't be trying to avoid us. No, she's got to be a Transhumanist—with other Transhumanists chasing her."

Da Cunha looked grim. "Are those the only possibilities? What if, at some point in our future, there's a *third* group practicing time travel?"

For an instant, silence held them. Nesbit had awakened to bleary, head-splitting consciousness, but he was as silent as the rest of them in the face of Da Cunha's highly unwelcome thought.

"For the present," said Jason firmly, "I refuse to speculate about that. We've got enough problems already. Let's try to deduce as much as we can from what little we know of her. I heard Morgan say something about her having a crew of 'Maroons.'" He turned to Grenfell and Boyer. "Does anyone know what those would be?"

"My field," said Boyer. "When the English conquered this island in 1655, the black slaves of the Spaniards, having no wish to be re-enslaved, fought an unsuccessful guerilla campaign against them and then fled into the mountainous interior of the island, where they amalgamated with the few remaining native Taino people to form the population known as the Jamaican Maroons. They were subsequently reinforced by escaped slaves of the English, mostly of the Akan people of Ghana, who would eventually become the predominant cultural element, a process which I imagine has begun even now. Much later, they will maintain their independence through a series of wars in the eighteenth century, despite mass deportations to Sierra Leone and—of all places—Nova Scotia."

"Br-r-r-r!" said Mondrago with a mock shiver.

"Finally, they will sign treaties with the British—confirmed later by the national government of Jamaica—granting them self-government in certain locales. But of course all that lies far in the future. At the present time they are surviving by subsistence farming and raiding plantations."

"Both of which occupations seem to have worn thin for some of them," Grenfell pointed out. "At least one crew has taken to piracy."

"Under the command of a woman," Da Cunha added.

"Well," Boyer smiled, "there's a precedent for that—or *will be* a precedent. . . ." He trailed to a perplexed halt.

"Tenses are a problem for all of us in the time travel business," Jason assured him.

"Thank you. One of the greatest Maroon leaders in the early eighteenth-century wars against the British will be a certain Queen Nanny, a renowned guerilla fighter. She'll be remembered as one of Jamaica's national heroes . . . the only female one."

"The pieces are beginning to fit together," Jason mused. "Remember, the cult Sam Asamoa's expedition learned of in 1791 Haiti was supposed to have dated back to the 1660s and been somehow linked with Jamaica."

"One piece that still doesn't fit," said Mondrago dourly, "is that crashed spacecraft Asamoa found in Haiti."

"We'll have to leave that for later. We don't have enough data to even speculate. All we know for certain is that there are Transhumanists operating here and now—which was fairly certain anyway, given the spacecraft wreck. The only real lead we have is this Zenobia."

"Who doesn't exactly seem well-disposed toward us," observed Grenfell.

"No, she doesn't. Which is where you come in, Henri." Jason turned to Boyer. "Whenever an opportunity presents itself, I want you to try to approach her and see what you can learn."

Boyer looked slightly alarmed. "But I'm not a trained police investigator."

"Of course you're not. But a couple of times, I've

gotten the impression that she's a little more open to you than to the rest of us. I think you'd have a better chance of establishing some kind of relationship with her and obtaining information."

"Tell me one thing, Commander: we know she's from the future, but does *she* know that *we* are?"

"I can't be certain, but I doubt it. Granted, if she has a sensor like mine, she knows about my brain implant. But my guess is that she doesn't have one. Why should she? There aren't supposed to be any bionics in the sixteenth century for her to detect. You're just going to have to stick to our cover story, not reveal what we know about her, and play it by ear. I know it's not supposed to be your job. But can you do it?"

"I'll do my best."

"I'm sure you will. And while you're at it . . . try to find out what Morgan meant when he mentioned 'silly stories' about her."

CHAPTER NINE

Morgan wanted, at least for the present, to restrict access to the ship that was his pride and joy. So HMS *Oxford* rode at anchor out in Port Royal harbor.

Grenfell had been fascinated by the seventy-two-foot frigate. The system of classifying warships into six "rates" would not assume its definitive form, based on the number of guns they carried, until 1746. Currently, the English navy used the much less satisfactory basis of number of crew, introduced during Cromwell's Commonwealth in 1653. But *Oxford* was what would later be called a "fifth rate"—a frigate too light to stand in the line of battle but ideal for commerce raiding or hunting down the other side's commerce raiders. In the epic fleet actions of the European wars, she would have been a marginal player. Here, "beyond the line," she was a game-changer. Never before had the famously parsimonious English crown committed so formidable a warship to the defense of its colony of Jamaica.

Morgan had mentioned she was twelve years old, and according to Grenfell this meant she had come in after the revolution in design philosophy that would establish the basic look of warships until the advent of steam propulsion in the nineteenth century. That revolution had begun in Tudor times, when the English had abandoned the old high forecastles that had looked impressive and provided a "high ground" for boarding actions but had ruined the sailing qualities of the ships, causing their bows to be blown down to leeward. The high poops had also gone, resulting in the "race-built" ship intended primarily as a gun platform. *Oxford* was typical in still having a quarterdeck and forecastle, but an open rail was used for these higher parts, allowing a sweep of sheer line, albeit not quite as straight a sheer line as it would become in the next century. These ships had also acquired finer configurations, being almost three times as long as their beam. And most recently they had gone to three masts rather than four, eliminating the bonaventure mizzen, while adding a topsail on the bowsprit and "top gallant" sails above the topsails. All of which had made them faster—twelve knots maximum, although five or six usually—and easier to handle.

Grenfell had enthusiastically explained all this to them. It wasn't Henri Boyer's field. But now, walking along the dockside and looking out at *Oxford*, he first began to feel something of the enduring appeal of sailing ships, the romance that the passage of centuries had been powerless to entirely dispel.

The ships tied up to the dock as he walked past were more typical pirate craft: former merchantmen, most of them small. Some, indeed, were little more than large open boats with a single mast and some shelter for provisions and men. None but the largest had any more armament than a few light cannon, often mounted fore and aft as "chasers," and swivel guns to repel boarders. From Grenfell's description, Boyer decided he could recognize some of the modifications the pirates typically made to their captured vessels, like stepping the mainmast aft for increased speed in the wind. It made him feel quite the old salt.

Up ahead he saw the vessel he was looking for. Across her stern was painted the name *Rolling-Calf.* He assumed a casual air as he walked past under the eyes of its crew, who looked over the railing with expressions ranging from indifference to suspicion. They were mostly black, but included a few with the Native American features and coloring of Jamaica's native Taino people, a branch of the Arawaks who had been in the process of being pushed out of the Antilles by the cannibalistic Caribs from South America at the time Columbus had arrived. In short, it was a typical assemblage of Jamaican Maroons of this period. The process of amalgamation between the escaped slaves and the Tainos hadn't been going on long enough to have produced any mixed offspring who would have reached adulthood. Boyer nodded to them without receiving any response, and sauntered on. He had almost passed by when that which he had hoped for happened.

Zenobia emerged from below decks and looked around, enabling him to catch her eye. He gave her what he hoped was an appropriately jaunty wave.

"Ahoy!" he called out. "I already know your name. I'm Henri." Slaves didn't have last names, for they could not contract legal marriages.

"So it's you." Her voice did not overflow with

friendliness, but she didn't turn disdainfully away. In fact she leaned on the rail and looked him over. His mind automatically processed her speech into Standard International English. In fact, it was an odd-sounding form of this century's English, not quite like what had been neutrally imprinted on his brain. It held a very vague suggestion of a French accent, although with a lilt in which he thought to detect the distant ancestry of the Jamaican patois of later centuries. "I'd hoped to have seen the last of that crew you're with."

Not, specifically, "*The last of* you," Boyer noted optimistically. He decided that a little truculence of his own might be the best approach. "What are you complaining about? I'm the one who ought to be angry. You sent me sprawling, wench! My mates still haven't let me live that down."

"Nor should they," she said with a smile of catlike complacency.

"And besides, what were you being so disagreeable for? We were just trying to save you from those swabs who were chasing you."

"I didn't ask for your help!" she flared. "I take care of myself—and of my men."

"Well, anyway, we're going to be seeing some of each other starting a few days from now when the fleet rendezvous at Île-à-Vache." He was careful to call Cow Island by its French name. She seemed to notice.

"I knew you weren't from Jamaica—something about the way you look and sound. You must be from Saint Domingue. Runaway?"

"Yes." Boyer put bitterness into his voice. "I'd seen enough of our men being whipped—and enough of our women being raped."

"Then you've seen nothing! Do you know what they do to a disobedient slave on Barbados—and have started doing here on Jamaica? They chain him down, flat on his belly, and burn him to death little by little, starting at the soles of his feet. Sometimes they can make it last so long that a good part of him is ashes by the time he finally dies. Or sometimes they'll starve him to death with a loaf of bread hanging just outside his reach. That *really* takes a long time." Her voice remained level, but her eyes burned. She gestured at her crewmen. "Is it any wonder that they run away when they think they see a chance? Or that the penalties for piracy hold no particular terrors for them?"

"Yes, I've spent enough time here in Jamaica to know about these things. And I certainly know about that last part."

"I suppose you do," she admitted, softening a trifle. "You turned bucaneer yourself after running away."

"But what about you? You're no runaway. And," Boyer ventured, "from some of the stories I've heard about you, I can understand your ship's name. After all, the Rolling-Calf has no fixed abode but wanders where he will, moving like lightning...and is put on Earth to cause trouble." He could see her surprise at his knowledge of the Jamaican legend. It encouraged him to push a little harder. "It makes me wonder if there might be some truth to those stories. Where do you come from?"

"Where I come from is none of your damned business!" she flared. She seemed to feel she had somehow lost ground by letting her hostility slip momentarily. "Now get out of here! We've got preparations to make. One of our crew has died of dysentery, and before we leave for Cow Island there are certain things we must do, and do ashore."

"Of course there are," said Boyer, glimpsing an opening. "His duppy must be appeased lest it do harm to the living. But must you drive me away? After all, is it not a rule that all bad feelings must be suspended so that all can sing together with the dead?"

It was a shot in the dark. Boyer's knowledge of the Jamaican ceremony known as "The Nine Night" was based on accounts going back no further than the early twentieth century, when anthropologists and folklorists had first begun to record such things. But he knew the ceremony was one of great antiquity, with roots reaching back to Africa, and he dared hope that his knowledge might not be entirely irrelevant even in 1668. From the look on Zenobia's face, he knew he had guessed right.

"You *have* spent some time in Jamaica," she said slowly. "Yes. This man was a hot-headed man, and his duppy could do a lot of mischief. Of course, since we're about to leave for Cow Island we're not going to have time to do all that is needful. But we'll do as much of a *Koo-min-ah* as we can in the time we have tonight. The preparations are made."

"May I be of help?"

"You're not one of us," she said suspiciously.

"No. But we're going to be part of the same fleet, and the duppy could work ill on all of us."

"Maybe." She cocked her head and gave him a challenging smile. "Are you sure you want to? This isn't going to be exactly like what you may have seen before. You see . . . those stories you say you've heard about me . . ."

"I don't believe everything I hear."

"Maybe sometimes you should." She held his eyes with hers for a moment. "All right. Be here just after dark...if you dare."

"Er...a 'duppy'?" Jason Thanou wore a blank look.

"Sometimes equated with a 'ghost,' but that's not really correct," Boyer explained. They sat in Jason's room in the inn, which was barely large enough for the two of them, in the stifling late afternoon heat.

"What's the difference?" Jason asked.

"The belief goes more or less like this, although there are many local variations: the duppy is that which gives a body the power to function as a living body. It is the most powerful part of a person, and it can work much evil. When a person is alive, the heart and the brain control him and he won't abandon himself to this evil—or," Boyer added with a grimace, "at least that's the way it's supposed to work. But some people have more powerful duppies than others. And when a person dies, the duppy no longer has anything to restrain it. It can do much harm if it is let loose among the living. So there are rituals—the *Koo-min-ah*—to force the duppy to stay in the grave."

"Hmm. And you've been invited to join in. At least you know what to expect."

"Not necessarily. I do know something of the 'Nine Night' ceremonies that were later common in Jamaica. But my information dates from centuries in this period's future. And Zenobia admitted that our impending departure for Cow Island is forcing her to settle for an abbreviated version. And besides...she dropped some hints about those 'stories' concerning her, as though warning me to expect something out of the ordinary."

"So maybe you'll get to see the basis of those stories."

"Maybe. But I couldn't get anything out of her about her origin. She's very reticent about that."

"Understandable." Jason reflected a moment. "Has she given any indication that she knows you're a time traveler?"

"None. I'm not sure exactly what she thinks of me, or why she consented to let me participate in whatever is planned for tonight. I get the impression that she thinks of me as a kind of...potential convert."

"Why fight it?" Jason grinned. "She likes you."

"You're almost late," snapped Zenobia irritably as Boyer came aboard.

The tropical night had fallen with its usual suddenness, and the shapes of the crew were only dimly visible around him. There didn't seem to be many of them. And... "I don't see the body."

"Of course not. It's already been taken ashore so the rest of us can meet it halfway."

Boyer mentally kicked himself for not recalling this aspect of the ritual. "But where are we going to meet it?"

"We have a place west of the harbor-mouth, where nobody ever goes. Now come on! We've got almost a two-mile row."

They clambered over the side into a small boat which rocked alarmingly under the weight of a chest that had already been lowered into it. Boyer manned an oar, and with Zenobia sitting in the stern and steering they pushed off and rowed west by northwest. The dim lights and raucous sounds of Port Royal's nocturnal revelry dwindled astern. Ahead was only blackness, although overhead were the myriad stars of Earth's pre-electric-lighting night sky.

Boyer wondered how Zenobia was going to locate a particular point on the shore in the dark. But after a long while, she began making purposeful course corrections. He glanced over his shoulder toward their destination and saw the tiny light of a torch dead ahead.

They pulled up onto a narrow beach—not far, Boyer calculated, from the future site of the town of Portmore—where the torch was embedded in the sand, revealing the scuttling crabs emerging from the water. Another boat like theirs was already there, unattended. They tied up beside it and, with one man bearing the torch ahead of them and two others carrying the chest, they silently set out along a very rudimentary trail into the jungle. They soon came to a clearing and simply stopped. No one spoke.

Boyer was aching in various places, and his hands were blistered from the unaccustomed labor of rowing. But he hardly noticed, for it was as though he had entered a dreamlike realm of unreality. He was a child of twenty-fourth-century Earth, where ancient ethnic and cultural identities were rapidly dissolving despite all self-conscious efforts to preserve them. Doubtless as a result of those efforts, he had been drawn to the study of his own Haitian origins. But realistically speaking, he had never felt any particular identification with them. He had, in fact, consciously resisted any such identification, which would almost have seemed a betrayal of the ideal of academic objectivity to which he had always subscribed. And still less had he felt any identification with the folkways of the Jamaicans, with whom he had nothing in common save remote

African roots. But here, in this jungle clearing in the firefly-flashing darkness with the Blue Mountains to the northeast rearing up darkly against the blazing star-fields and these people around him awaiting the body in soundless stillness—or what somehow seemed that way despite the din of birdcalls and monkey-jabbering—he felt something within him he had never known was there.

They had not long to wait. Soon—and afterwards Boyer suspected it was sooner than it seemed—a distant whisper of sound was heard, and the flicker of approaching torches could be seen. Someone had brought out additional torches from the chest, and now these were ignited.

The sound became a hum, and then became singing, rising to a keening harmony. With Zenobia in the lead, they joined in the singing, to welcome the dead. And a line of men brought the dead man into the circle of torchlight, borne on a kind of hammock.

Now, in the light of the torches, Boyer could see that a grave had already been dug, and that a very crude coffin lay beside it. He tried to follow along in the singing, whose words he could not comprehend.

They laid the dead man down. He was wearing a shirt, and—unusually for a seaman of this era—a pair of crude socks. Boyer refrained asking Zenobia about that shirt, for there were no nanas, or old women of the village, available here to make it as was proper. But that, like so much else, might well be an accretion of later times. And besides, this was no time to speak to Zenobia. By some silent transformation, she had ceased to be a she-pirate and become a high priestess.

Some of the precautions for keeping the duppy in

the grave were already more or less as he knew them, even this far back in time. This became apparent as various items were removed from the chest and used. The dead man's nose, mouth, underarms and crotch area were rubbed with lime and nutmeg. After he was lowered into the coffin, a pillow stuffed with parched peas and corn—but not coffee beans, which were doubtless unavailable—was placed under his head. Then the socks and the cuffs of the shirt were nailed down. Zenobia stepped forward and spoke to the dead.

"We nail you down hand and foot. You must stay there. If we want you we come and wake you."

A low chanting began in response. Boyer joined in. He suddenly felt more relaxed, and agreeable to whatever Zenobia might say. . . .

With a sudden shock, he remembered reading of an implant the Transhumanists had used, causing the voice to emit a subsonic wave that reduced its hearers to docile acceptance. This, he was coldly certain, was what he was now experiencing. But it was only effective with those who were not aware it was being used on them. He grimly concentrated on retaining control of his own will.

Now the coffin was closed and nailed shut. Bottles of rum were handed out. As they were opened, the first drink out of each was poured into the grave for the dead. Then more parched corn and peas were thrown in. Finally, the coffin was lowered in. As the rum was drunk, some of the men began to recount Anansi stories from Africa—the germ of the later "Uncle Remus" tales of the North American plantation states, although with somewhat different animals—because duppies were believed to find them entertaining.

Zenobia turned to face her crew...and a low moan went up. Boyer could see why. In the dim light of the torches, her eyes now glowed with a fluorescent yellow-white light that was clearly supernatural.

Clearly, at least, to anyone who doesn't know about bionic eyes, and some of the features that can be built into them, thought Boyer, who now knew that Zenobia's large, finely shaped black eyes were not her own. He wondered what other special capabilities, besides that of lighting up, they might possess. Infrared vision, perhaps, or microscopic or telescopic focusing...?

First the vocal implant, and now this. What else, I wonder? Clearly, this woman was a cyborg designed for one purpose: the founding of a cult of the sort the Transhumanist underground used to subvert history.

So we keep coming back to the question of why they were chasing her, and why she was so desperate to keep away from them.

Boyer had no chance for further reflection, because Zenobia began singing and he had to concentrate on resisting that which vibrated below the level of sound in her voice. The men also sang, in response to her, and as they did their bodies began to sway in a kind of dance in the flickering torchlight.

"Ah Minnie wah oh, Ah Minnie wah oh!" crooned Zenobia.

"Saykay ah brah ay," responded the men.

"Yekko tekko, yekko tekko, Yahm pahn sah ay!" Zenobia cried.

"Ah yah yee-ai, Ah yah yee-ai, ah say oh," the men replied.

Zenobia put her splendid body through a violent dance movement and cried out again:

"Yekko tekko, ah pah ahah ai!"

And then the whole thing was repeated, the dance movements growing more furious with each repetition.

Boyer did his best to follow along, with more success than he would have dreamed possible. Maybe it was that which underlay Zenobia's voice. More likely, it was the fact that he knew much of this already, for the traditions of the *Koo-min-ah* evidently were very persistent across the centuries.

But then, abruptly, Zenobia halted and fell down into a crouch, and as she did all motion and all sound instantly ceased. Then she raised her head, and the light in her artificial eyes was extinguished. When she stood up and spoke, her words were relatively matter-of-fact.

"We have not been able to do everything we should for the duppy. We cannot remain here for the Nine Night. And we have no goat to sacrifice and drink its blood." (Boyer was just as glad for that omission.) "But we have done all we could, and the duppy must go on to his rest and do the living no harm." An affirmative-sounding murmur arose from the men. "And most of all, the duppy knows he must stay away from the demons. We all know this. And we all know that the living must avoid them as well."

The murmur of agreement rose a notch, almost to the level of frantic affirmation, and a shudder of fear and revulsion ran through the group.

What's this? thought Boyer, suddenly jolted out of his comfortable feeling of familiarity. *There's not supposed to be anything about "demons" in this kind of ritual.*

"Yes," Zenobia continued, her words reinforced by the subsonic siren song of her vocal implant. "You all know that demons can do only ill. And I have taught you how to recognize them. They wear flesh—paler flesh than that of the white men—and they walk on two legs like men. But they are not men. Their flesh is a *different* flesh, not that of men, for they are of star-stuff. They are taller than men by two heads. Their hair is pale, and gleams of silver and gold. Their faces are long and thin and sharp and cruel—worse than those of the white men. And their ears are not as those of men. And their huge eyes are blue . . . but not like the blue eyes of some of the white men. No, they are blue throughout, with no whites, as though the blue has seeped out into the whites. All of this you know, for I have told you many times so you will recognize them for what they are if you ever see them—and know them for the enemies of man."

"We know, we know," came a general murmur, like distant surf.

This isn't right, thought Boyer. *What's she talking about?*

But then the murmuring gradually subsided, and there was silence. The African magic had departed from the clearing. There were only ragged men in torchlight, and a fresh grave.

"Let's be going," said Zenobia, her vocal implant no longer activated. "It's a long row back."

"Well," breathed Jason after hearing Boyer's description of Zenobia's bionics. "Now we know how she dominates her crew."

"That, and the fact that she's obviously a product of genetic upgrade," added Mondrago. "She can probably beat most of them at arm wrestling!"

Boyer struggled to stay awake. It had been well into the small hours by the time the boats had returned to Zenobia's ship, after another row that had given him no opportunities to sound her out, and still later when he had made his way back to the inn and awakened Jason and Mondrago. Now it was almost dawn, and he was fending off the enveloping dark arms of exhaustion. But a thought shook loose.

"There's just one more thing. Almost everything about the ceremony was recognizably part of the origins of Jamaican folklore. But when it was over, Zenobia said some things that simply didn't fit in. She started talking about some kind of demons that duppies have to be persuaded to have nothing to do with, and that the living should avoid and oppose at every turn. She even launched into a physical description of them so they'll be easy to recognize. It was obvious that they had heard it from her many times before. She was just reinforcing it."

"A physical description?"

"Yes. And it was like nothing I've ever heard of in any Jamaican legends." Boyer repeated what Zenobia had said, as nearly as his fatigue-deadened brain could recall it. By the end, he was almost dozing off. "As I say, this really doesn't mesh with . . ." His voice trailed off and he snapped back to alertness as he saw the haunted looks in his listeners' faces.

"Henri," said Jason slowly, "you have just described a Teloi."

CHAPTER TEN

"But the Teloi are all supposed to be dead!" bleated Irving Nesbit. "You said—"

"I never said anything of the kind, Irving," sighed Jason. Out of the corner of his eye he saw Mondrago glance first at Nesbit's back, then over *Oxford*'s rail and down at the Caribbean waters, and finally at Jason with an urging, almost pleading look. He gave the Corsican a quelling glare and then turned back to Nesbit.

"Let me explain it one more time, Irving. I said I was as sure that all the Teloi on Earth have died out a long time ago as I could be of anything that can't be proved. I gave no guarantees."

"But I've heard the stories of your last two expeditions!"

"Then you must have misconstrued them. Let me go over it again. In 1628 B.C. we discovered the truth behind the Greek myths and other similar bodies of legend: that a group of Teloi had established themselves on Earth a hundred thousand years ago, setting

111

up shop as gods. They genetically engineered *homo erectus* into *homo sapiens* in the northeast African and southwest Asian region, to be their slaves and worshippers. We were able to permanently strand most of them—their older generation, the ones known then as the 'Old Gods' and remembered in the Greek legends as the Titans—in their private extradimensional 'pocket universe' by arranging for its only interface portal to be obliterated by the volcanic explosion of Santorini." A shadow crossed Jason's mind as he recalled the sacrifices that outcome had required. A human, Sidney Nagel, had given his life. So had Oannes, the last of the Nagommo, the amphibious race that had been the Teloi's inveterate enemies. "We did it with the tacit cooperation of the Teloi's own younger generation—the ones known at the time as the 'New Gods.' They were not trapped. They are remembered as the Olympian gods and also as various other pantheons across the Indo-European zone. But they had lost most of their self-repairing high-tech paraphernalia, and they belonged to the last Earth-born generation, whose life expectancy had declined greatly from the near-immortality of the earliest arrivals. In addition, they had become infertile. Essentially, they were running a bluff after that.

"Nevertheless, on our subsequent expedition to 490 B.C. we found they were still alive, although even less sane than ever by our standards. That last, plus their ignorance concerning time travel, was why the Transhumanists had been able to trick them into an alliance by promising to change history so as to restore their worship. When they found out they had been made fools of, they went mad with rage—even madder than their norm, not that the change was especially noticeable. They and the Transhumanists mostly killed each other off. I listened to Zeus' last words," Jason added with a reminiscent smile, recalling that day on a mountain overlooking the battlefield of Marathon. "But," he concluded firmly, "they weren't all killed. The one known to the Greeks as Aphrodite definitely survived, and there were several others about whom I couldn't be sure."

"But," Nesbit protested, "that was well over two thousand years ago! And you said their lifespans were greatly reduced. How can any of them still be alive now?"

"I didn't expect them to be," Jason was forced to admit. "The possibility of encountering them on this expedition never even entered my mind."

"Another point," said Grenfell, who had been listening thoughtfully. "From what you've told us, the area of operation of the 'New Gods' stretched roughly from Ireland to northern India. They certainly never established their worship in the Western Hemisphere. So even granting that they are present *now*, what are they doing *here*?"

"I don't know. I don't even have a theory. Actually, there are only two things we *do* know for certain. The first is that some Teloi are still around; Zenobia's description, as repeated by Henri, is too exact for coincidence. The second is that Zenobia is aware of them and regards them as her enemies. From Henri's account, she uses even a funeral as an excuse for a kind of sermon warning her followers to watch out for them."

Da Cunha's brow furrowed with thought. "And

when we first saw her, she was fleeing from the Transhumanists—of whom we seem to be assuming she's one. And the last time you saw *them*, they were having a falling out with the Teloi, who had been their allies. . . ." Her brow furrowed even more intensely. "Of course, we have no idea what point in the future she—or the Transhumanists who were chasing her, or both—come from."

"I'm getting a headache," Mondrago complained.

"This is *terrible!*" Nesbit exclaimed. "Commander, you *must* use a message drop to inform the Authority of this appalling new development!"

Jason expelled a long, exasperated sigh. He swept his arm out in a gesture that encompassed the ship and the Caribbean all around it. "How, precisely, do you suggest I do that, Irving?"

Even Nesbit seemed to understand.

The message drop system was subject to almost crippling limitations. First of all, it required a site that was sufficiently geologically stable and out-of-the-way to remain fairly unchanged until the twenty-fourth century. Port Royal itself was out of the question for obvious reasons, and the Palisadoes were subjected to repeated change over the centuries under the lash of earthquake and hurricane, while the shores of Kingston Harbor would be overrun by construction. So a spot a few miles northeast of the harbor, in the foothills of the Blue Mountains, had been selected. But that ran headlong into the *other* requirement for a message drop site: accessibility. No one had pretended to have any clear idea how Jason was going to have an opportunity or an excuse to struggle up there.

Now, of course, the question was academic, for they

were en route to Cow Island where Morgan's fleet was to rendezvous, aboard HMS *Oxford*. (The "HMS" was still appropriate, Grenfell had quipped, although now it should be interpreted as standing for "Henry Morgan's Ship.") The frigate's original hundred-and-sixty-man crew had been augmented up to about two hundred and fifty, including Jason and his party. This was the usual way of pirate ships, which carried large numbers of men to provide overwhelming boarding or landing parties, not to mention prize crews. The practice had persisted aboard *Oxford* even though the frigate, unlike the usual pirate ship, was primarily intended as a formidable gun platform. It didn't exactly make for privacy, especially below decks. They were carrying on this conclave amidships on the spar deck, but Jason knew they'd have to break it up soon, for they were already drawing the kind of glances that indicated suspicion of "being in a plot against the Brethren."

A sound from abaft caught Jason's attention. The quarterdeck hatch leading down a short ladder to the captain's cabin had opened, and Henry Morgan had emerged.

The very fact that he had a cabin spoke eloquently of this expedition's uniqueness, and of his. Typically, the pirates took one of their captured merchant ships and ripped out all below-decks bulkheads, whether used for cargo storage or for individual cabins. The resulting open space belowdecks had a practical function—to accommodate the excessive number of men these ships carried—but it went deeper than that. The buccaneers had never heard of any such word, or concept, as "ideology," but theirs was still the very basic democracy of the original *boucaniers* of the Antillean coasts: no man had any special right to a greater share of anything than any other. This extended to quarters aboard ships. And among them the captain was not the absolute despot he was to become in naval tradition. He was only in command during battle or when pursuing or being pursued—during which periods his word was law. Otherwise, he was just one among peers, and the most important man was the elected quartermaster who was the "business manager."

Looking out over the billow toward the accompanying ships, Jason saw Zenobia's *Rolling-Calf*, and knew from Boyer's description that she was typical in all these respects. And it worked even though she was a woman. She slept in the common space, and no one dared molest her, for all knew her to be uncanny.

Morgan, in his own way, was also special. Partly it was the nature of the ship. No one would have dreamed of performing upon this specialized fighting machine the kind of radical surgery practiced on ordinary merchantmen. And Morgan himself, although everyone still addressed him as "captain," was the elected admiral of the buccaneers, and had been even before his fabulously lucrative sack of Portobello. The ordinary rules didn't apply to him.

Not that he was dressed exceptionally at the moment. At sea, he wore shirt, breeches and boots like everyone else, with his usual scarlet kerchief tied around his head. He looked about him and began sauntering in their direction.

"Let's break it up, people," said Jason in a low voice. Then, as an afterthought: "Except you, Roderick. Stay with me."

Morgan paused and spoke to various crewmen as

he walked, laughing and joking in his deep, resonant voice. But always, in some indefinable way, there was a certain intangible distance, an unspoken consciousness of command. Morgan was one of these men, able to match them drink for drink and violent act for violent act . . . but not quite one of them. It might, Jason thought, have something to do with the fact that Morgan, aside from his eloquence and assurance, spoke in the accents of an educated man—the gentleman he insisted he was. These men might have turned their backs on this century's deeply class-conscious society, but they were inescapably products of it.

Or, just as likely, it was something about the man himself.

"Jason!" he greeted. "We've a fair wind. It shouldn't be too long before we raise Cow Island."

"Aye, Captain. Think you the rest of the ships will be there?"

"The Frogs? Oh, they'll be there, most of them. What they've heard about our haul from Portobello caused them to have a change of heart about me. And besides, they no longer have that lunatic Francois L'Ollonais to follow." Morgan chuckled. "Have you heard the story of how he died?"

Jason did know, from Grenfell's background lectures, how the appalling French sadist had met his richly deserved end. But he wondered if Morgan would tell a different version. "No, Captain."

"In Nicaragua, he managed to make the Darien Indians his enemies, by his mad cruelties and slaughters." Morgan shook his head and looked disdainful. One of the secrets of his own success in his eighteen-month rampage through Central America had been his ability to forge alliances of convenience with the local Indians, who had excellent reasons for hating the Spaniards. "They captured him and tore him to pieces while he was still alive, burning each part as soon as it came off and scattering the ashes into the winds to make absolutely sure no trace remained of such a creature." Morgan chuckled grimly. "They're cannibals, but they must have lacked all appetite for *him*."

"We *have* heard a lot of stories about L'Ollonais," Grenfell prompted.

"They probably fell short of the truth. He particularly enjoyed pulling out men's tongues. But when he'd *really* fly into one of his wild rages he'd cut a prisoner's chest open, reach in, and pull out the heart. Then he'd take a bite out of the heart himself before making another prisoner finish it off. He boasted that he never let a Spaniard live."

"We've also heard a few stories about what went on at Portobello when you took it, Captain," said Grenfell. Jason held his breath, fearing that Grenfell might have gone too far. But Morgan showed no sign of taking offense. Instead, he turned discursive.

"As you know, persuading people to reveal where they've hidden their valuables often requires questioning with the usual ceremonies." The last five words, as Jason knew, meant *torture* in piratical argot. "And having a reputation for doing it works wonders—saves you no end of trouble. I learned my lesson at Puerto Principe." Morgan scowled at the recollection of the one time he had, in spite of taking a Spanish town, come away with too little booty to secure the enthusiastic loyalty of his men. "I was too soft. I didn't make that mistake again at Portobello. I had an obligation to my men, who had a right to expect healthy shares, and I did what was needed to fulfill it. That's the difference between me and L'Ollonais: purpose. For him, slashing people to ribbons and racking them and woolding them were simply *fun*."

It took Jason a moment to recall that "woolding" meant tying a rope around a prisoner's head and tightening it, tourniquetlike with turns of a stick, until the eyeballs popped out of their sockets. It was standard procedure on both sides of the ongoing war between the buccaneers and Spain. He began to understand. Morgan sincerely disapproved of L'Ollonais, but his disapproval was rooted in the Frenchman's lack of *professionalism*.

"You must have also learned something of that kind of thing when you first arrived in Jamaica, in the fighting against the escaped slaves," he ventured.

"Yes, we've heard various different stories about how you happened to be there," said Grenfell, a little too eagerly. Jason gave him a cautioning look. But once again, Morgan proved to be in an expansive mood.

"I was 'Barbadosed,' as people say: thumped on the head and shipped off to Barbados as an indentured servant. To get away from that, I ran off and joined Penn and Venables when they put in at Barbados on their way to Hispaniola—even though they were damned Parliamentarians! God's blood, how could that canting bastard Cromwell have found such a pair of incompetent buffoons in all of England? But I must admit I learned a lot from them: how *not* to organize an expedition, how *not* to deal with the Indians, how *not* to fight the Spaniards, and above all how *not* to lead men."

Jason saw Grenfell's eyes light up at the resolution of the long-standing controversy over how Morgan had gotten to the New World. The other theory—the more respectable one—was that he had been with the Penn/Venables expedition all the way from England, as a junior officer. In fact, it seemed he really had come up from nothing. Esquemeling would write as much in 1678, which was one of the things for which Morgan would sue his publishers, for by that time he would be Lieutenant Governor Sir Henry Morgan and would require a more high-toned background. At the present time, he could still afford to be honest.

"Taking Jamaica from the Dons was so easy even that pair could manage it," Morgan continued. "But afterwards . . . those of us that the diseases and starvation didn't carry away were lucky not to be chopped up by the runaways. And believe me, dysentery and plague were better! All in all, less than half of us survived. Those were fighters I'd not want to face again!"

"Like Zenobia's crew of Maroons," Jason suggested, pointing over the rail and across the water at *Rolling-Calf.* "It seems you don't hold a grudge where they're concerned."

For an instant, Morgan looked blank, as though he didn't even understand the last sentence. "Oh, aye, I'm damned glad we've got them with us. And Zenobia herself . . . By God, she's worth any two men in a fight. Cut! Slash! That's her way!" His voice dropped. "Since you're new, there's something I ought to tell you. Tongues will always flap at anything out of the ordinary—and God knows Zenobia's out of the ordinary! You may hear some idiots among the crews telling stories about her . . . as though she was some kind of, well, witch." Morgan looked grim—as well he might, Jason reflected, for such accusations could have grim consequences in this century. Certain female residents of Salem, Massachusetts would learn that in 1692, the same year Port Royal would vanish beneath the sea. "But don't listen to them. It's just ignorant sailors' foolishness. She may be a devil of a fighter, but there's nothing really unnatural about her."

You might be surprised, thought Jason.

"So, how did it go?" asked Mondrago later.

"Well, Roderick got a couple of historical mysteries solved," said Jason.

"That's nice." Mondrago did an admirable job of containing his excitement. "I've got some news that isn't quite so good."

"What?"

"Remember that last batch of men that came aboard before we set sail? I've tried to check them out without being noticed. Nothing special about most of the ones I've been able to get close to. But one...well, he wasn't one of those we saw in Port Royal the day we arrived. But I got a good look at him, and I think I know the signs. He's one of the Transhumanist goon-caste types."

CHAPTER ELEVEN

As Morgan had predicted, the voyage to Cow Island was not a long one. But brief as it was, it served to complete the time travelers' off-the-deep-end acculturation.

It was easier for the Service people, of course, inured to culture shock as they had long since become. And even the academics and Nesbit had learned while in Port Royal to adapt to seventeenth-century standards of sanitation and personal hygiene. But none of them had ever experienced the hellish conditions below decks on really overcrowded sailing ships.

Aboard *Oxford* they were better off than most of the fleet, for accommodations aboard the frigate were a good deal roomier than those being endured by the crews of the smaller vessels. Nevertheless, at sea the gun ports were closed and the hatches battened down, so they existed in stifling, rancid-smelling darkness as the ship rolled and lurched and creaked without letup. And aside from the ship's head—the platform jutting forward from the bow, which was to give its name to all latter-day maritime toilet facilities—the only places to answer calls of nature were the corners of the decks on which they slept. Jason could only imagine what it was like in really heavy seas, with even salted seamen vomiting, or when intestinal ailments stuck (as they invariably did, due to the abominable quality of the drinking water) and diarrhea became widespread.

It didn't help that they had to keep their twenty-fourth-century fastidiousness strictly to themselves. Given the absolute lack of privacy, any squeamish reactions to conditions everyone else took for granted would have drawn attention. But the point had been emphasized in their orientation, and even Nesbit only gave Jason a couple of anxious moments. Still, the group couldn't help acquiring a certain reputation for keeping to themselves.

Needless to say, they went topside at every opportunity. One afternoon, Jason did so, to find Henri Boyer already there, leaning over the port rail. It was a clear day, and off the port bow, to the northeast, it was now just possible to glimpse the Massif de la Hotte, the mountainous western tip of Hispaniola's southern peninsula. But Boyer was gazing aft. Quite a few others were doing the same, including Morgan.

"Look," said Boyer, pointing. In the far distance was *Rolling-Calf*, her sails furled, dead in the water and falling further and further behind the others. Morgan turned, muttering an oath.

"What's the matter, Captain?" Jason inquired.

"Arrgh, it's what I was telling you about before. I'm having trouble finding anyone to send over there to Zenobia to find out what's wrong. None of these ignorant fools want to set foot aboard *Rolling-Calf*.

They're all pissing in their breeks with fear of witch-craft and black magic. But I can't afford to bring the whole fleet about, although I'll have everyone take in sail."

Abruptly, Boyer stepped forward. "Send me, Captain. She knows me—I met her back in Port Royal."

Morgan's scowl vanished. "Well, thank God there's one *man* aboard this ship!" he roared, loudly enough to be heard by the generality. "I'll have a boat readied."

"Good work, Henri," Jason murmured. "Maybe you'll have a chance to get some questions answered. And by the way . . . take your musket with you as well as your cutlass."

"Why?"

"Oh . . . just a feeling I have."

By now, Boyer had listened to enough of Grenfell's lectures about this era's sailing vessels to identify *Rolling-Calf* with some confidence as what was called a "ketch"—two-masted, armed only with a few small guns, and with a tiny poop. (Only landlubbers called it a "poop *deck*," he recalled with the smugness of the nautical neophyte.) Zenobia stood on that poop, looking down at a small boat being towed just astern, from which a diver was just slipping into the water. Boyer's two rowers brought their boat up alongside, and a line was cast to them.

"Ahoy!" Boyer called up to Zenobia. "Captain Morgan wants to know if you need assistance."

"Our rudder is fouled. But we can fix it ourselves. We don't need anybody's help!" Having gotten that out of her system, Zenobia allowed her truculence to soften a trifle. She even smiled down at him. "But since you're here anyway, I suppose you may as well come aboard."

"Thanks." Boyer did so, somewhat awkwardly with the heavy musket strapped to his back.

"That looks like a good-quality piece," Zenobia commented approvingly.

You'd be surprised, thought Boyer. He changed the subject. "I haven't seen you since...that night before we left Port Royal. I never got a chance to ask you—"

"Sail ho!" came a lookout's shout.

From almost due north, a ship was sailing about sixty degrees into the wind, coming straight for the immobilized *Rolling-Calf*.

With a curse, Zenobia took up a spyglass. "It's *L'Enfer*," she said, in a tone of voice that did not conduce to Boyer's peace of mind.

"You know her?" he asked.

"Aye. She's one of the French ships that *haven't* rejoined Captain Morgan. No surprise there. Her master—he's known only as 'Captain Gaspard'—was a crony of L'Ollonais. For some reason, he wasn't along on L'Ollonais' final expedition, so he unfortunately didn't get chopped up by the Darien Indians like the rest of them. Instead he's gone rogue. He operates out of Tortuga, but even the other French don't much like him. He plunders his fellow buccaneers."

Like this one, thought Boyer with a heavy feeling in the pit of his stomach as *L'Enfer* drew closer. *The sick or crippled animal that's fallen out of the herd and become a straggler.*

But in any ecosystem, predators don't normally prey on each other.

"I thought the Brethren of the Coast didn't do that," he protested aloud.

"They don't," said Zenobia grimly. "Not even L'Ollonais did. But Gaspard is a mad dog."

Before either of them could speak further, a twin report crashed out from across the water and a cloud of smoke rose from *L'Enfer* as her bow chasers fired. There was a whistling *whoosh* and two geysers of water erupted ahead of *Rolling-Calf.*

"That's just to frighten us," said Zenobia with a calmness Boyer wished he could share. "He doesn't want to sink us. He wants to strip us bare of everything—including the crew, to sell back into slavery."

Boyer involuntarily glanced down at the African-dark skin of his forearms, and felt clammy sweat begin to break out. He forced steadiness on his voice. "But without our rudder we can't maneuver. He can approach us from a direction where our guns can't bear." *Rolling-Calf* had only four small guns, mounted in the waist two to a side, besides the little swivel guns on the rail, which crewmen were already loading with a crude grapeshot of musket balls and scrap. Boyer decided they had the right idea, and hastily loaded his musket.

"Maybe that's what he thinks." Zenobia studied the attacker's course and seemed to do some mental calculations. Then she leaned over the taffrail and shouted orders to the men in the boat. "Will your boat help?" she demanded of Boyer.

"Of course. You men," Boyer called out to his rowers, "take your orders from her."

The two *Oxford* crewmen looked dubious, but only for a moment, for *L'Enfer* was getting closer and the sound of Gallic taunts could now be heard. They put out their oars and joined with Zenobia's Maroon boatmen in towing *Rolling-Calf*'s stern to port.

L'Enfer was closing rapidly now. She was a two-master like *Rolling-Calf*, but obviously bigger. Boyer, from his limited knowledge of ships' rigging, thought to classify her as a small brig. Typically, she was overcrowded with men. Their jeering was starting to take on an ugly undercurrent as they saw what Zenobia was up to, for *Rolling-Calf*'s stern was starting to swing perceptibly, bringing her portside guns into line. One of them, a powerfully built man dressed more flamboyantly than his fellows, waved his cutlass and screamed an order.

"*Down!*" yelled Zenobia.

Boyer had barely obeyed when *L'Enfer*'s starboard guns thundered and sent iron balls crashing through *Rolling-Calf*'s upperworks. He heard a scream as a crewman was lacerated by the large splinters that Grenfell had mentioned were among the chief terrors of battles like this between wooden ships.

"Still avoiding hitting us below the waterline," observed Zenobia with inhuman calmness, just as *Rolling-Calf* shuddered to the discharge of her two portside guns. They smashed into *L'Enfer*'s side, rocking the larger ship and sending some of her men who had been clinging to the rails toppling over into the water. The rotten-eggs smell of burning black powder filled the air.

But then the big, gaudily dressed man who had to be Captain Gaspard shouted another order, and a series of grappling hooks were thrown out to entangle *Rolling-Calf*'s rigging. Men hauled on their lines, and the two ships began to draw together.

Boyer got to his feet and hefted his musket. Zenobia gave him a sharp glance, for it was unusual for anyone to try sharpshooting from a rolling deck. Ignoring her, he activated the laser target designator as he drew a bead on one of the men holding a grappling line. Squinting through the inconspicuously tiny sight at the pirate's magnified image, he gave the trigger a half-squeeze and saw a red dot appear on the man's chest. He completed the squeeze, the musket barked and recoiled bruisingly against his right shoulder, and through the smoke he could see his target fall. Only later would he have the leisure to reflect that he had, for the first time in his life, killed a human being.

"Good shot!" exclaimed Zenobia. Then she gave a puzzled frown, as though thinking it had been a little *too* good, and for an instant Boyer wondered if he had made a mistake. But then the two hulls ground together, the screaming French pirates came swinging across the gap on ropes, and they both had other things to occupy their minds.

Zenobia fired two flintlock pistols at once into a Frenchman who was still in midair. As he dropped, squalling, she threw the pistols into another man's face and whipped out her cutlass. Then Boyer could no longer see her, for the deck became a maelstrom of brutal hand-to-hand combat as more Frenchmen swarmed aboard. One of them crashed against a Maroon who was about to discharge a swivel gun into the mass of boarders, knocking him aside and slashing him across the belly with a cutlass. As the Maroon fell with a scream, doubled over and trying to hold in his spilling guts, the Frenchman turned on Boyer, who had dropped his musket and now had his own cutlass out.

He immediately found that his limited orientation with the weapon was no match for his opponent's experience and sheer, mad ferocity. With a series of artless but powerful swings, the pirate beat down his desperate defense. Then Boyer's feet slipped in the blood that was rapidly covering the deck, and he fell over backwards. With a yell, the pirate gripped his cutlass two-handed over his head and brought it down.

Before Boyer even had time to despair, Zenobia appeared and, with a single slash of her cutlass, severed both the Frenchman's hands. For a split second he stared stupidly at the blood-spurting stumps. Then Zenobia's sea-booted foot shot out and kicked him backwards, to topple over the gunwale.

"Thanks!" gasped Boyer as he tried to scramble to his feet. But then Captain Gaspard, his finery begrimed with blood and smoke and his bearded face a mask of fury, appeared out of the melee, swinging a cutlass. Zenobia, still off-balance, grasped his sword-arm. But not even her genetically enhanced strength was a match for the Frenchman's gorillalike arms, and he flung her away. Her back slammed into a mast, knocking the wind out of her, and as she slumped to the deck Gaspard raised his cutlass.

It was as though Boyer existed in a state of accelerated time, with the din of battle a faint roar and the combatants moving with dreamlike slowness. Without thought, he lunged for the unfired swivel gun behind Captain Gaspard. Grasping the little artillery piece by the ball-shaped cascabel at its breech, he swung it sharply around on its stirrup mounting. With a *clunk* audible even above the general noise, the cast-iron barrel connected with the back of the Frenchman's head, sending him staggering forward.

He must, Boyer thought, have had a very hard head. He quickly regained his balance and turned around. His face—ugly at its best—was now contorted beyond all human semblance, and his eyes held nothing but insane rage. He gathered himself and lunged, roaring his hate.

But Boyer had taken up the match and thrust it into the small brazier mounted on the inner surface of the gunwale. Now he pointed the swivel gun and inserted the glowing match into its touch-hole.

The swivel gun crashed out and belched fire. Captain Gaspard's head burst backward like an overripe melon, spattering blood and brains and bone fragments across Zenobia even as she reared to her feet with a cry of triumph. At that moment, Boyer's time-sense came by into synchronization with the rest of the universe.

The ear-shattering blast of the swivel gun had brought the battle to an abrupt pause. But only for an instant, for the Maroons took heart and began to drive the now-dispirited boarders back. Boyer, suddenly in the grip of reaction, sank to the deck. But Zenobia plunged back into the battle with the superhuman quickness of her heritage, her cutlass singing a whining song of death as it cut through the air and men's limbs.

Then, all at once, the French pirates broke off the fight and scrambled back aboard their own ship. As the wind blew the smoke away, Boyer looked forward and saw why. In the distance, *Oxford* and her consorts were coming about. The French renegades might be crazy, but they weren't stupid. They cut the cables of the grappling hooks and pushed off, making no attempt to sink *Rolling-Calf* in a fit of pique, for without their captain they weren't about to risk getting Henry Morgan sufficiently annoyed with them to spend time on a stern chase. Nor did the Maroons provoke them into doing so by firing their own guns. The two ships parted with nothing more than an exchange of obscene insults and gestures.

Now Boyer had a chance to look around him, and recollections came crowding back. He felt his gorge begin to rise.

"Come on!" He felt a hand grip his upper arm, and Zenobia hauled him to his feet. She wiped blood from her eyes and spat out a bit of gray matter. "What's the matter? It's over now. And it looks like your boat is all right, as is ours; they didn't bother with those. So," she finished matter-of-factly, "now we can finish fixing our rudder."

"But . . . but . . ." He gestured vaguely around, and once again thought he was going to be sick.

She grinned—the first time he had seen her do that. "And besides, I think we're even now." She indicated the practically headless horror that had been Captain Gaspard, and then the two severed hands on the deck that still convulsively clutched a cutlass. "See what I mean?"

"I suppose I do." Boyer found he couldn't hold back a shaky laugh, and the wave of nausea retreated.

Still, he didn't feel up to trying to press Zenobia with any questions before returning to *Oxford*.

CHAPTER TWELVE

As expected, Morgan didn't bother pursuing *L'Enfer* and her now leaderless crew. The fleet proceeded to the rendezvous point with only a slight delay.

Most of the French buccaneers (none of whom seemed to be wasting any tears on Captain Gaspard) were already at Cow Island—including one ship, *Le Cerf Volant*, whose presence not only delayed the rendezvous but almost disrupted the fragile alliance of English and French privateers. A captain from Virginia accused her of robbery and piracy, which was something that had to be settled before matters could proceed further. So Morgan and HMS *Oxford* took her back to Port Royal—a particularly easy run given the prevailing winds—where the Court of Admiralty promptly condemned her as a prize and sentenced her captain to hang. The latter was commuted, which smoothed ruffled Gallic feathers somewhat, and Morgan returned to Cow Island with *Oxford* and the former *Cerf Volant*, now renamed *Satisfaction*.

All of which comings and goings kept them away

from *Rolling-Calf*, with no opportunities to try to unravel the multiple mysteries surrounding Zenobia. They did have the chance to scour *Oxford* for other Transhumanists, but discovered none except the one Mondrago had already spotted (and Jason's sensor now confirmed), and he kept to himself as much as was possible on this ship.

Now, on the first day of 1669, they finally lay at anchor at the rendezvous point, just off the tiny speck of land that was Cow Island. And Morgan was sending out word to the captains to meet aboard *Oxford* the next day for the traditional war council that would choose a target.

Jason stood by the rail, looking northward. Across a channel to the north, the mountainous spine of Hispaniola's southwestern peninsula loomed: the Massif de la Selle to the east and the Massif de la Hotte to the west. With *Oxford* was a multinational fleet of twelve other ships and over nine hundred men, which Jason doubted would have held together for anyone but Morgan, the conqueror of Portobello. He picked out *Rolling-Calf*, which was somewhat farther away than most. Then he looked around the deck. Morgan was in the process of dispatching boats to the other ships.

Boyer joined him and looked across the water at *Rolling-Calf*. "So near and yet so far," he philosophized. "I'm sorry I haven't been more help with her."

"Not your fault," Jason replied absently. "You had other things to occupy your mind last time you saw her."

Morgan stepped up to Boyer. "As usual," he growled, "I can't find anyone who wants to set foot on *Rolling-Calf*. Henri, take a boat over there and tell Zenobia about the captains' council. I know *you* don't mind—especially after that fight the other day! Come on, your boat is waiting."

"Aye aye, Captain," said Boyer. And, in an aside to Jason: "Maybe this time I'll get lucky."

"Well, well!" greeted Zenobia as Boyer clambered aboard *Rolling-Calf.* "It's you again. And with a message from Morgan?"

"Yes." Boyer delivered the news of the next day's captain's council. "Besides, I wanted to pay my respects. We never got to talk very much in the course of our unpleasant encounter with the late unlamented Captain Gaspard. For that matter, I also never had a chance to talk to you that night, on the way back to Port Royal, after the *Koo-min-ah.*"

"Well, here I am now," she said with a lazy smile, leaning back with her elbows on the taffrail, up on the poop and therefore looking slightly down at him. "What did you think of what you saw that night?"

"I don't know what to think."

"You don't think I'm a witch?" she asked boldly.

"No. I saw some things I can't explain, but I don't believe that."

"You wouldn't." She cocked her head and looked him over. "You're not like the others. There's something odd about you . . . you're not just an ordinary runaway slave, whatever you may claim. I don't know what to make of you."

Does she suspect? Boyer wondered. *But of course if she does she can't say so outright. And I'm not supposed to state outright what I know about her.* He noticed that the Maroons had all moved forward and busied themselves with various tasks, as though sensing that Zenobia wanted to have a private conversation. He cautiously stepped up onto the poop with her. It was barely large enough to accommodate two. She made no objection.

"You puzzle me a lot more than I do you. In fact, you'd be a mystery even without . . . what I saw and heard that night ashore."

"Why?"

"You're no simple runaway either." Boyer decided to risk the *either*, even though he was tacitly confirming that there was more to him than he had admitted. "Where *do* you come from anyway?"

"I've told you before, that's none of your business!" All at once, the fire in her eyes died down to something resembling warmth, with underlying flickers of amusement. "If you don't believe I'm what I seem to be, then just where do you think I *do* come from?"

He held her eyes and would not let go. "Even though you aren't a runaway slave, I think you come from a place where you were never treated as a full human being."

For a long moment, the creaking of a wooden ship swinging at anchor seemed unnaturally loud.

Her eyes slid aside and would no longer meet his. "What are you talking about?" she muttered in a surly voice . . . and then stopped short. Her head swung around and she stared at him with eyes that were wide with sudden realization.

He had spoken in twenty-fourth-century Standard International English.

He smiled, and continued in the same language. "I got tired of fencing. It's contrary to my orders, but I think we ought to start being honest with each other. I'm a time traveler—like you."

"What babble is this?" she demanded with an attempt at bluster.

"It's no use. Our mission leader has a sensor that detected your bionics—and, of course, I saw them in action. You don't belong in this century any more than I do. By the way, don't bother trying that vocal enhancement implant of yours on me. As you're probably aware, it's ineffective against someone who is alert to it and is consciously resisting."

Her eyes turned to black ice. "If I say the word," she hissed, "my men will chop you into shark chum."

"I know. But I don't think you will. You see, I think you need help—and my companions and I may be able to provide it. But only if you're frank with us."

"What makes you think I need any help? Least of all from the Authority," she added with a sneer, all pretense gone. "That *is* who sent you, isn't it?"

"Yes, and our mission leader is firmly convinced you're a Transhumanist, because that seems to be the only possibility. And yet, we know those men chasing you in Port Royal were time travelers . . . and we're certain that *they* were Transhumanists. Very perplexing. That's why I've been sort of assigned to try and find out more about you."

"And I thought you liked me! I'm crushed!" Her sarcasm somehow lacked a hard edge.

"Actually, I do. That's why I'm still hoping, in the teeth of all logic, that you're not really a Transhumanist. It's also why I hope I can talk you into accepting our help. Whatever you may say, or think, I believe you need it."

"Why?" she challenged. "And what kind of help can you and your party give me, even if I wanted it?"

"As to the latter...I don't know, at least not yet. But before you decide you're in no need of allies, you ought to know this: there is at least one Transhumanist in this fleet. We've spotted him aboard *Oxford*. It seems they're still after you."

Her features revealed her startlement for only a split second before closing up again like shutters. "I'll deal with them in my own way," she said stonily.

"I only hope your confidence is justified. Oh, by the way, what's your real name?"

"It really is Zenobia." She paused and seemed to reach a decision. "Zenobia, Category Thirteen Delta, Twenty-Fourth Degree."

He stared. "So you really are—"

"Yes. Sorry to disappoint you. And if you knew anything about the Transhuman Dispensation, that *Delta* would tell you that it's an unusual designation—a non-standard genetic upgrade tailored for a particular purpose. Specifically, I was...designed to be instrumental in the establishment of a cult among the slaves in Saint Domingue, which will eventually become Haiti—a variation on Voodoo which will bear fruit at a much later time, calculated by a highly advanced form of mathematical sociodynamics, like all the other sociological time-bombs with which the Movement has been filling the out-of-the-way parts of the human past. Everything about me—including the bionics you've observed—was intended to maximize my effectiveness in that role." She smiled slightly. "By ancestry, I'm not altogether African. I didn't need to be. I was darkened up, and my features slightly altered, by resequencing of my DNA. The side effects weren't too unpleasant."

Why is she telling me all this? wondered Boyer from

the depths of his shock. But the important thing was to induce her to keep on telling it. "Then why were your fellow Transhumanists pursuing you?"

"They're no longer 'my fellow Transhumanists.'" Her eyes grew very hard. "The cult I was supposed to found was one of unspeakable foulness and depravity—a cancerous growth within the body of *Vodou*. I could no longer stomach it. And besides . . . do you know what it's like for women in the Movement?"

"I can't honestly say I do, although I've always understood that they were regarded primarily as breeding stock."

"It may not be as bad as it once was. Ever since the Movement went underground, it can't afford to waste any of its resources. And there were always exceptions for special purposes. In my case, for example, they wanted a woman because women traditionally had a prominent religious role in West African societies. But the attitude was always there. Almost never anything blatantly abusive or grossly degrading, you understand. Just small things. Constant, demeaning small things." She grew silent, and seemed to forget his presence.

"So you deserted," he prompted after a moment. "But how—?"

She raised her left arm. On its underside, a few inches from the armpit, was a scar, surrounded by burn tissue as though a wound had been very crudely cauterized.

"I cut out my TRD," she stated matter-of-factly, "and threw it away. Without its built-in tracking feature, they were no longer able to follow my movements. I got out of Haiti and crossed over to Jamaica. There, I made my way into the Blue Mountains and took up with the Maroons there. I hadn't been given this century's English, but working back from our own language I was able to learn how to communicate with them."

"That must have been very difficult," offered Boyer, inadequately. He was trying to imagine the epic of escape and survival that Zenobia was skimming over in a few brief sentences.

"Not as much as you might think. You see, I still had my...special features. I was able to set myself up as a leader among them." She gave him a challenging smile. "I've found I actually *like* this century better. You'd be surprised at all the things I don't miss. Except...people I can talk to. People who can understand."

Yes, the Maroons probably have their limitations in that area, Boyer thought. He decided he could stop wondering why she was being so loquacious with him.

"Is piracy one of the things about the era that you like?" he risked asking. "It must be a terrific advantage, knowing in advance what's going to happen next."

"But I don't. I was never an historian. And I wasn't given any orientation in anything except the religions and folkways the slaves brought from Africa. I didn't need to know anything more—besides being a mere woman. No, I've had to make my own way without any real foreknowledge."

So you don't know what's going to happen to HMS Oxford *tomorrow night, do you?* Boyer filed the datum away in his mind.

"And yes," she continued, "I like some things about it. For one thing, it gives me a 'support system' in the form of the Brethren of the Coast. You saw in Port Royal how useful that can be when my former...

employers come looking for me. And I never know when they're going to be looking for me."

Boyer thought he saw a perfect opening. "Then you admit, in effect, that you *do* sometimes need help. Welcome to the human race! Maybe we can offer you some. And as you tell the story, we're natural allies."

"No!" Zenobia's vehemence rocked him back. Her eyes, artificial though they might be, were like burning black coals. "I hate the Transhumanists, but I hate the Authority—and the whole society it's a part of—just as much! My ancestors were Transhumanists back when the Movement ruled Earth. Do you know what was done to them in the late twenty-third century when the Dispensation was overthrown? Do you?"

"I think I have a general idea," said Boyer, recalling the way Earth had been washed clean of the Transhumanist aberration with a torrent of blood.

"Then you know why my loyalties are to nobody but myself and my men. And why I've chosen to strand myself in the past: it's a better neighborhood! You may think my Maroons are barely above the level of savages, but they're *clean!*" She drew a deep breath. "Tell your mission leader that. I think you'd better leave. The crew are starting to get curious."

"Very well." Boyer turned to go, then paused. "Just one thing I'm still curious about, Zenobia. Those 'demons' you described to your men, that night—"

"No. I think I've already told you enough. Maybe too much."

"All right. I'll go." As he clambered over the rail, he paused once more. "Anyway, maybe I'll see you tomorrow when you come aboard *Oxford* for the captains' council."

"Maybe." A ghost of a smile came back to life, and as she turned away he was barely able to hear her add, "I hope so."

"You *what?*" exclaimed Jason when Boyer reported to him aboard *Oxford*. Mondrago muttered something, the only intelligible word of which was "Civilians!"

"That's right, Commander," Boyer admitted unflinchingly. "I revealed that we're time travelers, and that we know she's one. It seemed the only way to induce her to open up. And it did." He proceeded to relate Zenobia's story. "And so," he concluded, "she's out for herself now. She's not inclined to join us, but she's hardly likely to tell the Transhumanists about us."

"What if she *had* still been on speaking terms with them?" Mondrago demanded. "How could you be sure she wasn't?"

"I couldn't be sure," Boyer admitted. He turned to Jason. "I'm sorry, Commander. I know I took a risk, in violation of orders. But . . . I felt a need to be honest with her."

Jason considered for a moment. "All right. What's done is done, and you did obtain some valuable information. And I gather that there are a couple of things you didn't reveal. One is that we know the 'demons' are Teloi."

"That's right. I was hoping she'd volunteer some information about them, but she didn't. Maybe she doesn't know what they really are."

"I suppose that's possible. Same goes for the spacecraft wreckage Asamoa found. You didn't tell her about that either, did you?"

"No. I felt I'd already told her enough—"

"That's one way to put it," Mondrago interjected.

"—and for that reason I also didn't tell her about the *Oxford* explosion, even though I really wanted to. Commander, we've *got* to warn her about that!"

"Why?" Mondrago sounded genuinely puzzled.

Jason shushed him. "Maybe. But for now, no more revelations without my express permission. We've got to hold on to all the cards we have left to play." Then, as an afterthought: "Oh, one other thing, Henri. Don't tell Nesbit about any of this. He might have a stroke. And," he added, addressing Mondrago before the latter could open his mouth, "*don't* say it!"

CHAPTER THIRTEEN

Morgan had a great bowl of rum punch set up on *Oxford's* quarterdeck. The captains needed to have their wits more or less about them for their council where the fleet's destination would be chosen and the articles approved The real drinking would begin afterwards.

The council would be held on deck in the afternoon sun, in full view of the crew crowding around. It was part of the overall rough-and-ready democracy of buccaneer society, unique in this century. Jason and his companions had elbowed their way into a good position, against the starboard rail in the waist just forward of the quarterdeck, for viewing the proceedings, which Grenfell would have cut off one of his own arms rather than miss. From there, they watched the procession of small boats arrive carrying the captains.

Nesbit's jitters had waxed as the day had progressed. He glanced around the deck as though expecting it to erupt in flames at any moment. "Are you *sure* the explosion isn't supposed to happen yet?" he asked Grenfell, not for the first time.

"Quite sure, Irving," Grenfell sighed. "The historical record is quite clear. It doesn't occur until late at night, well after the captains' conference has adjourned and the subsequent party has been in progress for some time. We'll have plenty of time to slip off the ship and steal a boat."

"But what if someone sees us and raises the alarm?"

"We've been over all that, Irving. No one will be in any condition to notice our departure."

Jason paid no attention to the conversation. He was watching the captains as they clambered up the gangway one by one and came aboard. The French captains looked like what they were: men whose cupidity just barely had the upper hand over their smoldering resentment. All, regardless of nationality, were about as villainous-looking a crew as Jason would have expected. Grenfell thought he could identify some of them by name: Richard Norman, captain of the *Lilly,* Joseph Bradley of the *Mayflower,* Richard Dobson of the *Fortune,* Lawrence Prince of the *Pearl,* John Morris of the *Dolphin* (a particularly close associate of Morgan's) and others. The Dutch were represented by Bernard Claesen Speirdyke, whose name his English associates perhaps understandably shortened to Captain Bart. Morgan greeted each of them effusively, generally confirming Grenfell's guesses as to their identity. For this occasion he was dressed as they had first seen him in Port Royal, in his flamboyant version of gentleman's attire as he felt befitted the Admiral of the Coast.

One of the last to come aboard took a while to get up the gangway, for he was a very big man indeed, and presumably very strong as well, judging from his almost simian arms. He was also, Jason thought, one of the ugliest human beings he had ever seen. His hair, parted in the middle of his massive head, and his drooping mustache were a yellow suggesting exceptionally greasy butter. His eyes, under beetling brow ridges and a notably low and sloping forehead, were a grey so pale as to be practically colorless; they were like empty holes in a face that was hideously scarred and screwed up into a seemingly permanent scowl, lower lip outthrust.

"So much for evolution," Jason heard Mondrago mutter.

"Roche Braziliano!" Morgan exclaimed. "I hadn't dared hope that you'd be able to make this rendezvous. Welcome! Thrice welcome! We'll drink later." The new arrival's scowl went down a couple of notches of intensity; Jason got the impression that this was his equivalent of a smile. He gave a couple of grunts; Morgan beamed in apparent agreement with whatever the grunts signified.

Grenfell looked fascinated. "Well, well! We never knew that Roche Braziliano was involved in this particular expedition. It's recorded that he raided Campeche in 1669, but that could be later in the year."

Da Cunha looked askance at the name. "If he's Brazilian, I'm Tibetan!"

"Actually," Grenfell explained, "he was born Gerrit Gerritszoon at Groningen in the Netherlands. His family moved to Brazil during the mid-1600s when the Dutch controlled it. When the Portuguese recaptured it, he made his way to Jamaica and joined the buccaneers after leading a mutiny. He rose rapidly to the status of captain—of a vessel stolen from other pirates. His greatest claim to fame is the time he was captured by the Spanish at Campeche. He escaped by tricking the local governor, by means of a forged letter, into thinking his followers were standing ready to avenge him if he was hanged."

"He must be cleverer than he looks," said Da Cunha in a damning-with-faint-praise tone.

"True. Evidently, he could even read and write. Afterwards, he got back in business by buying a new ship from L'Ollonais, who was an associate of his."

"What a surprise," commented Mondrago.

"Finally, I should mention that he is widely regarded among his fellow buccaneers as being . . . well, insane."

Mondrago stared at the throng around him. "How could anybody *tell*?"

"How did they even *notice*?" Da Cunha added.

"It might have had something to do with his practice of cutting the limbs off Spanish farmers and roasting them alive over pits if they refused to hand over their pigs to him. Also . . . if he ever offers you a drink, I advise you to accept it. He was noted for killing anyone who didn't."

Zenobia was the last to arrive. As she strode like a lioness across the deck to greet Morgan, she ostentatiously ignored both leers and surreptitious signs against evil. But she exchanged a brief eye-contact with Boyer and flashed a smile at him before the captains got down to business, surrounded by the audience crowding the deck and clinging to the shrouds and ratlines. When it came to their leaders' decision-making proceedings, buccaneers were evidently believers in "transparency."

"My friends," Morgan began after wetting his throat

with rum punch, "I propose that we first settle on the articles to govern our company for the duration of our voyage." There was a chorus of affirmative-sounding noises.

"This is a departure from the usual procedure," Grenfell whispered in Jason's ear. "Generally, pirates would settle on a target first, then hammer out the articles. I suspect that Morgan's articles are standard ones, and are so well known and so widely accepted that in this case it's mere routine, to be gotten out of the way at once, without much discussion."

And so it proved. First came the not unimportant matter of compensation. Plunder was to be allocated on a basis of one share for each common pirate, while a master's mate got two and a captain got five. As Admiral of the Coast, Morgan would get six. Ships' boys had to settle for half a share. There were additional bonuses for specialists: a carpenter got a hundred and fifty pieces of eight, a surgeon two hundred and fifty. (Boyer and Nesbit had to endure their companions' elbows in the ribs at that.) And then came the provisions for recompense for serious wounds. Anyone who lost an arm got six hundred pieces of eight if it was the right and five hundred if the left. For the right and left legs it was five hundred and four hundred respectively. And so forth, down through lost eyes and fingers.

"Disability insurance among pirates!" said Nesbit wonderingly. "I never would have thought it."

"It was a quite standard element of these articles," Grenfell assured him. "As was incentive pay," he added as bonuses for various acts of bravery in battle were enumerated. "In some ways, the Brethren of the Coast were centuries ahead of their times."

"But what if they didn't capture any booty?" Da Cunha sounded curious.

"Then nobody got anything. The basic rule was: *no prey, no pay.*"

"Which must be quite an incentive in itself," Jason reflected. It was yet another reason why the buccaneers fought better than their ill-paid Spanish adversaries.

Next the captains turned to the provisions of the articles governing shipboard conduct. These too were approved expeditiously. Most were fairly commonsensical. Fighting was prohibited, as was gambling—Jason suspected that the latter was considered likely to lead the former. Theft, cheating on the division of spoils, and failure to keep one's arms fit for action were strongly interdicted. Punishments for violations included death and marooning (which, no doubt, amounted to merely an elaborate and gratuitously cruel sentence of death), but in some cases they were left up to the discretion of the captain and company. Then came a provision that piqued Jason's interest. When it was read out, there was no dissent, and indeed a mutter of agreement arose from the spectators:

"Any man who shall, in the hold, snap his firelock, or light matches, or smoke tobacco, or carry a lighted candle uncovered by a lanthorn, shall receive Moses' Law."

"'Moses' Law'?" queried Nesbit in an undertone. "I didn't know these people were Jewish."

Grenfell smiled. "It means thirty-nine lashes on your bare back. There were very few offenses for which buccaneers were willing to agree to flogging as a punishment. This was one of them. However wild and crazy these men may seem in most respects, they're only too well aware that the ships they live aboard are floating fire bombs."

"And they're not likely to get drunk enough to forget that," Jason mused. It made what history said was going to happen to *Oxford* more difficult to understand—downright puzzling, in fact.

After the articles were finalized and signed or marked by all the captains, there followed a brief discussion on their supplies of fresh meat. This too had an air almost of routine. Their favorite was tortoise—and, indeed, the time travelers had found it delicious. It was agreed that they would supplement their supply of it with pork, obtained along the south coast of Hispaniola by nocturnal raids on Spanish hog yards, where Roche Braziliano's reputation would doubtless help predispose the proprietors to a cooperative attitude.

Finally, Morgan stood up with an air of getting down to the real business. "And now we must choose our destination." He motioned to a pair of men, who set up a large cowhide map of the Caribbean. It was crude, but it looked to be about as accurate as the current state of cartography permitted. "Everyone may have his say, of course, in accordance with the rules of the Brotherhood. But I want to hear no cautious, timorous ideas." He swaggered over to a rail and theatrically pounded *Oxford*'s heavy timbers with his fist. "This is a true fighting ship—the greatest ship any of us have ever had. Now is our chance to show the Dons that we can strike them where we will. This is a time for boldness! Let no one propose small, easy targets." Abruptly, his eyes twinkled and his tone turned mischievous. "Let no one propose Portobello either. I don't think we'd find much there."

There was general predatory laughter at Morgan's pleasantry—which, of course, was his way of reminding them of his coup of the previous year, when he had done what Francis Drake had failed to do. "Campeche?" Captain Dobson suggested hesitantly after it had died down.

"Come, I said no lesser towns," Morgan reminded him.

"Havana?" someone else offered, in a French-accented voice that suggested he himself didn't take the idea seriously.

"Bah!" spat a third captain. "That's not a city, it's a fortress. One of my men was once held prisoner in one of those three great castles that guard it. He says it would take fifteen hundred men to even attempt it. We've got less than two thirds of that."

Other names were tossed back and forth. Finally, Roche Braziliano spoke up in a basso whose Dutch accent was so thick as to be almost incomprehensible. *Hey, he can talk!* Jason thought. "You don't fool me, Henry. You already know where you want to go. Why don't you just go ahead and tell us?"

"That's right, Captain, let's hear it!" Zenobia called out. "Don't keep us waiting."

Morgan let a dramatic pause last just long enough. Then he drew his cutlass, placed its point on the map at a spot on the northern coast of what would one day be called Columbia, and spoke one word. "Cartagena!"

The stunned silence was followed by a flabbergasted hubbub.

"Hear me!" roared Morgan. "It's the greatest port in all of Spain's empire. It's where they collect all the treasure of Peru! Imagine the booty! And remember, Drake took it. If Drake could do it, so can we."

"But that was in our great-grandsires' day!" Captain Norman protested. "The Spaniards learned their lesson from it. Since then they've ringed the lagoons with castles, bristling with guns."

"L'Ollonais tried it, and failed," rumbled Roche Braziliano lugubriously.

"L'Ollonais didn't have this ship! *Oxford*'s guns can silence those batteries, and afterwards warehouses full of silver will be ours for the taking! And besides, the strength of Cartagena's defenses works to our advantage, in a way, because it's surely made the Dons overconfident." Morgan's dark eyes darted around and spotted Jason. "Isn't that so, Jason? You spent time among the Spaniards, so you know how they think."

"Aye, Captain!" Jason felt he ought to add something. He recalled a story Grenfell had related. "They say that one day the king of Spain was looking out a window of his palace toward the west. When his courtiers asked him why, he said he expected to be able to see the walls of Cartagena across the ocean, considering how much money he'd spent on them."

"There! You see? You see?" urged Morgan after the laughter had subsided. "The Dons will never dream that we'll dare to attack Cartagena, because they don't know we've got *Oxford*. Shall we pass up this chance?"

"No! No!" came the shouts.

"We'll lose a lot of men," one pessimistic soul demurred.

Morgan's eyes sparkled with Welsh devilment, and he spoke with his irresistible Welsh lilt. "Well, the fewer of us who're left afterwards to divide the spoils, the larger the shares!"

Grenfell had mentioned that Morgan had used

this appeal, at once devil-may-care and cold-blooded, before Portobello. Now it worked its magic again, with the aid of the man's sheer force of personality. The shouts of agreement drowned out any remaining voices of caution.

"Cartagena it is!" Morgan beamed, thrust his tankard into the punch bowl and, after a swallow, poured it out. "Away with this treacle! What a way to ruin perfectly good rum! Captains, you must later come to the great cabin, where a feast is being set out for us. But first, I see the rum-barrels are being hauled up from below decks. Let us all toast the new year, and the certain riches that lie before us!" To uproarious shouts, Morgan and the captains began to lead the toasts.

Jason hardly noticed. He had spotted the Transhumanist Mondrago had previously identified. He had some kind of bionics, as the sensor in the butt of the pistol tied securely to Jason's belt confirmed. And he was looking very intently in Zenobia's direction.

"Alexandre," he murmured, "keep that man under close but inconspicuous surveillance. And Henri, whenever you can get Zenobia alone, warn her of him."

"Right, Commander," said Boyer. Then, after a slight hesitation: "Do I have your permission to tell her what's going to happen to this ship tonight?"

"You do. She needs to know anyway." Jason glanced at the Transhumanist again. He wasn't looking after Zenobia anymore, but seemed to be anticipating something else. "I don't like this. I don't like it at all."

CHAPTER FOURTEEN

The tropical dusk fell on a scene of revelry.

The toasts Morgan led—including one to His Majesty the King, which he proposed with a deadpan seriousness that everyone was careful to emulate—were only the beginning. The company toasted anything they could think of, including the whores back in Port Royal, bless 'em. This led to a debate among several loyal clients as to which lady represented the gold standard of the profession.

"Salt-Beef Peg, she's the best," declared one buccaneer stoutly. His explanation of the appropriateness of her name left Nesbit looking as though he was in shock.

"Ah, you're daft!" scoffed a skeptic. "Buttock-de-Clink Jenny will wear you out!" He proceeded to illustrate his case in terms that made even Mondrago blush.

"You're both wrong," said a third with condescending certitude. "No-Conscience Nan is the one." He was only a few words into his supporting arguments when Da Cunha excused herself, telling Jason she'd observe the Transhumanist from somewhere else.

None of this intellectual disquisition led to an actual fight, for everyone was far too merry for that. Guns began to be discharged, as was permissible in circumstances such as these, as long as they were above decks and fired into the air. Likewise, candles were brought out as the black-velvet tropical night descended. The sounds of fiddles and guitars, and voices raised in song in various languages, arose. Grenfell had mentioned the fondness for music of seamen, who had to make their own entertainment.

Jason was almost hypnotized by the sea-shanties—not to mention the ongoing explication of the qualities of No-Conscience Nan—when he felt a tug on his sleeve. It was Grenfell. He pointed forward along the rail against which they stood, not far from the forecastle, where no one was paying any attention. The Transhumanist, unnoticed by the drunken revelers, was helping two drenched men over the side.

It drove all thoughts of No-Conscience Nan from Jason's mind. He activated his sensor display. Two tiny blue dots flashed. *Do they have artificial gill implants?* he wondered. *Or are they just very good swimmers? It depends on how far they've had to come.* Not that it mattered. One way or another, they were here, and now were beginning to move inconspicuously aft, sidling through the merrymakers. And Jason could think of no way to do anything about it without interrupting the party with a conspicuous commotion.

"I don't understand," Grenfell was whispering in his ear. "Zenobia may not be an historian, but they have historians working for them. They must know what history says is going to happen to this ship tonight. So why are they trying to get *on* rather than *off?*"

"They all look like they belong to the low-initiative castes that can be suicide-conditioned. But there's something else that's puzzling," Jason whispered back, more to himself than to Grenfell. The new arrivals had belaying pins—the club-shaped batons used to secure running rigging, and secondarily as cudgels when the need arose—stuck through the belt-ropes around their waists. *Now why bring those?* he wondered. There were racks of them all over *Oxford*'s main deck.

Then his attention was distracted again, this time by Mondrago. The Corsican was pointing aft, where Morgan was waving farewell to the celebrants and leading the captains toward the hatch leading down to the great cabin where their feast awaited. Zenobia was starting to follow, at the back of the procession. All at once, the three Transhumanists started working their way stealthily in that direction.

Then Jason saw that Boyer had maneuvered himself onto the quarterdeck and now was moving swiftly to intercept her.

"Zenobia!"

She halted at the sound of Boyer's low voice and looked back over her shoulder. He gestured to her to come. She hesitated a second or two, then said something to one of the other captains before turning around to join him.

"What do you want?" she hissed. "I've got to get below to the great cabin with the others or they'll think I'm—"

"Zenobia!" he cut her off. "Remember the Transhumanist I told you about? Well, he's up there toward the forecastle, watching you carefully. My mission leader thinks something is about to happen."

"I told you before: I'll deal with them in my own way, and I don't want you people's help." The look she gave him wasn't quite as harsh as her words. "But thanks for the warning. And now I have to—"

"Listen to me! There's something else. Our party includes an historian specializing in seventeenth-century piracy, and he's convinced that this ship is going to blow up sometime tonight with the loss of two or three hundred lives."

Her eyes grew round, then instantly narrowed with suspicion. "If you think that, then what are you doing here?"

"There are questions about the cause of the explosion—historical puzzles we'd hoped to solve. But we're going to be getting off the ship very soon. Come with us!"

"Ha! Your mission leader doesn't care if I live or die!"

"*I* care!"

Their eyes met for a couple of heartbeats before hers slid aside. "How do I know this isn't some trick to make me put myself in the hands of your party for interrogation?"

"Do you believe I'd lend myself to something like that? Do you truly believe it?"

He could barely hear her "No," just before . . .

"I think I have it, Commander!"

"What?" Jason turned away from the Transhumanists he had been watching intently, to meet Grenfell's excited face.

"Yes! The accounts suggest that Morgan and the other captains survived the explosion because they were sitting down to dinner in the great cabin, whose sturdy construction shielded them from the blast and allowed them to be thrown free. So if the Transhumanists want Zenobia dead—"

Realization burst on Jason. "Yes! Then they're here to make sure she *isn't* in that cabin! And," he added, looking across the main deck and abaft where Boyer had Zenobia in deep conversation, "we're helping them!"

Without pausing to formulate a plan, and ignoring the odd looks they were starting to get from those nearby, he turned to Mondrago, Grenfell and Nesbit. "Let's move!"

They stared at him. Nesbit spoke up. "Commander, I must protest! We'll give ourselves away, and create an unhistorical—"

"Irving," said Jason with a chilling grin, "I don't think any witnesses are going to be alive for long." He turned and shouted athwartships to Pauline Da Cunha, where she stood against the port rail on the far side of a hatch, open to allow air below decks. He shouted in Standard International English. "Let's grab Zenobia and then get off this ship!" Then, ignoring the stares of the startled pirates around him, he went into action without waiting to see if he was being followed.

The nearest Transhumanist swung toward him, and in another fraction of a second Jason understood why they had brought their own belaying pins.

Boyer spun around at the sound of Jason's shout, just in time to see Jason grasp a Transhumanist by his right arm, the hand of which held a belaying pin, and twist the arm upward. As he did, a spear of light, crackling with ionized air, shot out the end of the belaying pin and struck a yardarm, which burst into flame.

Disguised laser pistol flashed though his mind, as pandemonium broke loose among the suddenly sober pirates, face to face with the manifestly supernatural.

He glimpsed another Trasnhumanist level a belaying pin in their direction, seeking a field of fire through the chaos of panic-stricken pirates. He threw himself against Zenobia, knocking her off-balance, just as the laser beam flashed past, burning a hole in a bulwark. He saw the Transhumanist prepare for a second shot. . . .

It was no time for sublety. Jason wrenched the arm sideways, almost dislocating the shoulder, and pushed the Tranhumanist forward, delivering a punch to the kidney with his free hand while bringing a knee up, hard, into the face. But the man, with gene-enhanced tenacity, continued to struggle while maintaining his grip on the belaying pin.

Jason managed to spare an instant for a glance around. Nearby and slightly forward, Mondrago was struggling with another Transhumanist, and that one's *faux* belaying pin was spinning across the deck to a scupper, where it fell into the sea. Across the deck, on the far side of the open hatch, Da Cunha tackled the third Transhumanist, who was drawing a bead on Zenobia and Boyer, and sent the shot wild.

"Henri!" Jason yelled, as loudly as possible in the midst of his straining efforts to keep the Transhumanist immobilized. "Tell her to come with you or else get down into the captain's cabin right now, if she wants to live! And everybody, over the side!"

But Boyer couldn't hear him over the general uproar.

He grabbed Zenobia by an arm and tried to pull her over to the quarterdeck's starboard rail.

Mondrago placed a knee in the small of his face-down opponent's back, wrapped an arm around the man's neck, and jerked viciously back and upward, breaking the spine. Then he jumped up and scrambled to obey Jason's orders, going to the rail. Grenfell did the same. Nesbit was still stunned into immobility.

Boyer was clearly having trouble getting Zenobia to starboard—she still seemed confused and uncertain. But then Da Cunha finished off the Transhumanist she had tackled with a precise and economical punch to the temple, then sprang to her feet and rushed diagonally across the quarterdeck through the milling crowd. She grabbed Zenobia's other arm and, together with Boyer, hustled her forward.

All of this Jason took in within the space of a moment. Then the Transhumanist, with a sudden surge of strength, reared up and almost got his right hand free. His exertions sent another laser bolt skyward. Jason slammed him back down and they rolled across the deck toward the open hatch. Jason managed to bring them to a halt inches before they fell in, with himself on top. He managed to get his left knee atop the Transhumanist's left wrist, immobilizing it. Then, grabbing the right wrist with both hands, he slammed it down hard on the edge of the hatch, seeking to dislodge the belaying pin.

He succeeded. But just before the belaying pin fell down into the gun deck, the Transhumanist's right hand convulsed once more, and another laser bolt flashed . . . this time downward, through the hatch.

Jason heard a crackling sound from below decks,

and his nose caught the rotten-eggs smell of burning black powder. Looking over the edge of the hatch, he saw flame running along the line of what must be a carelessly spilled trail of powder, leading to the forward magazine.

All around him, the panic rose to crescendo, for the pirates now knew themselves for dead men.

Jason raised his right hand, stiffened it into a blade, and brought it down on the Transhumanist's upturned throat, crushing his larynx, then leaped to his feet before the man had finished spasming in death. *"Over the side—NOW!"* he yelled as he sprinted back to the starboard rail.

Mondrago and Grenfell began to scramble over the rail. Nesbit still stood paralyzed. Da Cunha rushed to obey, leaving Zenobia still standing confused with Boyer urging her on.

Jason grabbed Nesbit's arm and practically flung him over the rail, his arms and legs flailing. Then he jumped himself, a fractional second after Mondrago, Grenfell and Da Cunha. As he went over the side, he shot a glance toward the quarterdeck, barely in time to see that Boyer was in a position to jump but that Zenobia still hesitated.

He saw Boyer turn back and push Zenobia overboard, just before the world turned to fire and noise.

If they had still been on deck, the concussion would have killed them. As it was, they were all in midair and the shock wave propelled them further out, ahead of the blast that engulfed Boyer as it broke *Oxford* apart. The sound that accompanied it was more than a sound; it was like a physical thing that stunned and shattered them. But then they hit the surface and were frantically treading water and praying that none of the flaming debris that rained from the sky would fall on them.

They could all swim—it was one of the abilities the Authority required of would-be time travelers—so Jason was confident that they would all survive. *Except, of course, Henri,* a ghastly inner voice reminded him. He couldn't let himself think about that. Not yet. He swam in the darkness until he found a floating yardarm to cling to. Presently, two others joined him. One was Grenfell, bleeding from a wound to the side of his head and seemingly half-stunned. The other was Nesbit, who had grasped the historian and was swimming for both of them.

In any other circumstances, Jason would have been immobilized by shock at the sight of Nesbit doing something useful. But at the moment he had other things on his mind. "Did either of you see Alexandre or Pauline?" They both shook their heads. "Well, I saw them both get off. If they landed in the water conscious, they ought to be all right. And," he added, bringing up his map display, "the current will take us northeast, past Cow Island to the shore of Hispaniola's southern peninsula."

"Henri didn't get off, did he?" asked Grenfell.

"No," answered another voice before Jason could respond.

Zenobia emerged from the darkness, clinging to a piece of flotsam. In the light of *Oxford*'s burning wreckage, her face looked calm . . . almost dangerously so. She hooked an arm over the yardarm and caught her breath. She drifted closer to Jason. Her eyes held an odd emptiness.

"As I went over the side, I saw the stern gallery get blown out. I could have sworn I saw human figures being thrown free. Those were the captains, in the great cabin, weren't they?"

"Yes," Grenfell told her. "History says they, including Morgan, survive."

"I was supposed to have been there. Those Transhumanists were there to keep me outside so I'd be sure to die, weren't they?"

"That's right," said Jason.

"Henri saved my life—again. He stayed aboard just long enough to push me off. He's dead because of them...and me." She spoke in level tones. But the light of the flames reflected something in her eyes that caused Jason to shiver in a way that could not be accounted for by the warm tropical water in which he floated. "You're the mission leader, aren't you?"

"Yes. Commander Jason Thanou, at your service."

"Thanou!" A smile almost twitched into life. "We've heard of you. In fact, you have quite a reputation in the underground. The word is, you'd kill Transhumanists as soon as look at them."

"Maybe not all Transhumanists."

"Then possibly we can work something out. I think we both have someone to avenge."

"I think we just might."

They watched the burning, broken *Oxford* founder and go down in a cloud of steam, taking the last light with it.

CHAPTER FIFTEEN

It was still dark when they finally washed ashore on the strip of sand, too narrow to be called a beach, just east of what would one day be called Baie D'Aquin, although Jason doubted it was called anything now.

In a way, Jason decided, it was worse to have ground under his feet. It left his mind freer to contemplate the fact that, for the third time, a civilian member of a party he led had been killed. *After Sidney Nagel,* he thought dismally, *I told myself that surely it must only feel this way the first time. After Bryan Landry, I wasn't so sure that's true. Now I know it isn't.*

He busied himself with helping Nesbit get the still unsteady Grenfell onto the sand and doing what little examination was possible by the light of a half moon that intermittently appeared between drifting clouds. The historian insisted he was all right, but Jason ripped off a strip from the hem of his shirt, and Nesbit, who actually seemed to want to be useful, bound his head with it. Then Jason took stock.

They had nothing but the drenched clothes on

their backs, save that his pistol with its hidden sensor was still tied to his rope-belt. Naturally, he had no powder and shot for it. All their other possessions, including, of course, their muskets, now lay on the sea-bottom with *Oxford*. Zenobia had a dagger, and Jason decided it was just as well that she and they now seemed to be allies.

He activated his map display and called up the locations of the team's TRDs. Besides Nesbit's and Grenfell's, bunched together with his, two others that must denote Mondrago and Da Cunha were on the shore a short distance west. Although, he glumly reminded himself, that didn't necessarily mean they were alive, any more than was Boyer, whose nearly indestructible TRD showed, mockingly, at the location of the sunken *Oxford*. By retrieval time, after a few months at the bottom of the sea, he doubted that there would be much left in the way of remains. He hoped the sea-creatures would leave nothing at all, for if anything did appear on the displacer stage, it probably wouldn't be very edifying.

Presently the other two Service members' TRDs began to move on the display, almost causing Jason to go weak with relief. By sheer good fortune, they were moving eastward. He decided against calling out to them, not knowing who or what was in the thick jungle that fringed the shore. So he simply waited, and soon they appeared, splashing along in the shallows that lapped a strand almost too narrow to be walked on. Jason introduced them to Zenobia, whose presence they seemed to take in stride.

"What now, sir?" asked Da Cunha.

"With Henri gone, Zenobia has more knowledge of

Hispaniola than any of the rest of us." Jason turned to the renegade Transhumanist. "How about it? Is there anyone we should try and seek out on this island once it's daylight? What about the cult you were supposed to found before you deserted? Are there any of its members you think you can still trust?"

"No. Absolutely not. They're hopelessly corrupted, and under the control of the Transhumanists and . . . Yes. We've got to avoid them at all costs."

Jason noted, without comment, that she used *Transhumanists* in the third person. Presumably any lingering loyalties she might have felt had gone down with the *Oxford*. He also noted the way she had cut herself off, without elaboration, after mentioning them.

"Them and those 'demons' you warn your Maroon followers about?" Jason asked in a carefully offhand tone.

Her head jerked up in the moonlight. "What are you talking about?"

"Oh . . . Henri mentioned something about it. He said you described them physically."

"I don't know what you mean."

Jason dropped the subject. Zenobia clearly didn't want to be drawn out on the subject of the Teloi, and his alliance with her was still too young and fragile for any pushing or prodding. "Well, then, what about your Maroons? Will they come ashore looking for you?"

"I doubt it. When I don't turn up among the captains who survived the explosion, they'll assume I'm dead. They'll elect a new captain and either go home to Jamaica or continue to follow Morgan."

Grenfell spoke up. "Speaking of Morgan . . . remember how it was agreed that the fleet was going to do some raiding along the south coast of Hispaniola to augment the meat supplies before heading for South America? Well, history says Morgan did precisely that, starting about a week after the *Oxford* disaster, before holding a second rendezvous a month later at Saona Island, which is off the southeastern end of Hispaniola. That means he's going to be working his way eastward along this shore."

"So," Jason said thoughtfully, "we need to get moving ourselves, so we can be at one of the places he's going to raid at the time he raids it, and get picked up."

"But, Commander," said Nesbit, "are we sure we *want* to be picked up by Morgan? Whatever he plans to do now, I somehow doubt if it's going to be either pleasant or safe. Why not stay here in Hispaniola and lay low, as people say?"

"Because of the Observer Effect, Irving," Jason explained. "Morgan's career is historically documented. As long as we're with him, the Transhumanists are limited in the action they can take against us. If they tried to swoop down and wipe out his fleet, *something* would prevent it. Otherwise, it would already be part of recorded history, like the *Oxford* explosion. They know this; they were aboard *Oxford* simply to make sure Zenobia was in a position to get killed. They had no idea they were going to *cause* the explosion." *With a little help from me,* he thought with a pang of guilt. "On the other hand, practically anything can happen in the historyless wilds of Hispaniola. Here, they don't have to be careful."

"And besides," said Mondrago, "if we sit here on our dead asses for the next four and a half months, even if we survive, we won't be accomplishing our mission." He gave Zenobia a quick sideways glance, then met Jason's eyes. Expressions were hard to make out in the moonlight, but they understood each other. The Corsican was silently reminding him that they still had learned nothing about the origin of the spacecraft wreck, and that what little they knew about the Teloi involvement in this time and place simply raised new questions. He was doing it silently because he knew that it was too soon to be mentioning these matters aloud in Zenobia's hearing.

Jason only hoped that Nesbit and Grenfell wouldn't blurt anything out. They didn't. *Maybe sheer exhaustion is catching up with them*, he thought. *It certainly is with me.*

"All right, then," he said. "We'll follow the coast east when it's light. My map display will help. For now, let's try and get as much rest as we can. It's not long before daybreak."

Dawn revealed the Massif de la Selle (where Sam Asamoa would find the century-and-a-quarter-old wreckage of a twenty-fourth-century spacecraft lying in the 1790s) to the northeast, and the Massif de la Hotte to the northwest, both rising beyond a jungle that came almost to the water. In fact, there was a kind of very low tree whose branches touched the water. It bore a kind of fruit that they all gazed at hungrily. Nesbit reached out to pluck one.

"Don't!" Zenobia snapped. "This is the *mançanilla*, or dwarf-apple tree. The apples are poisonous; eat them and you'll go mad with thirst and die. In fact, you're going to get a rash on your hand if it brushed the leaves."

"Thank God we've got you with us," said Jason. "You

can tell us what is and isn't safe to eat. Now, Roderick, what can you tell me about Morgan's schedule? You said he's going to start out after about a week."

"So says Esquemeling's account. I'll try to remember the details. Morgan takes a few days to get to the southernmost point of Hispaniola, where he has a lot of trouble rounding the cape—in fact, he beats against contrary winds for three weeks. Once he gets past that, it's not far to Ocoa, which he raids."

"So it sounds like he's going to be at Ocoa roughly five weeks from now." Jason summoned up his map display. His heart sank at the trek that lay before them. The straight-line distance to Ocoa was just over a hundred and fifty miles, but trying to follow the direct route would take them over mountains. No, they would have to follow the coast, which he guesstimated would add another fifty to seventy miles. And if this stretch of coast was a fair sample . . .

He had fairly little doubt that he himself, Mondrago and Da Cunha could do it. He had even less doubt in Zenobia's case. He was reasonably confident that Grenfell was up to it. And he allowed himself to hope that Nesbit's official qualifications were genuine.

"All right, people," he said as briskly as he could manage, "let's go for a walk on the beach."

It was even worse than Jason had anticipated. The jungle vegetation frequently made the shoreline impassible, forcing them to either wade through the shallows or work their way around it by going inland. This often meant splashing through marshes and entering forests full of what Zenobia said were called prickle-palms, a name they all came to agree was only too apt.

Numerous streams provided drinking water, and thanks to Zenobia's knowledge of the vegetation they didn't starve. In fact, edible fruit was fairly abundant. But fruit is not very filling, and they were often hungry despite the occasional land tortoises they were able to catch and cook over fires Jason started with his flintlock. Lack of adequate food conspired with their constant exertions to render them chronically weary.

And always there were the tormenting insects: large blood-sucking flies as well as tiny stinging and biting gnats. Having no animal grease to smear on themselves (they sometimes sighted the wild pigs and cattle with which Hispaniola abounded, but rather few, and they had no practicable means of catching them), they took to carrying palm-branches to use as whisks. And at night, the din of a billion crickets made sleep difficult despite their fatigue.

The saving grace was that, as Zenobia assured them (confirmed by Esquemeling, according to Grenfell), none of the local scorpions or serpents were poisonous. Nor did their route bring them to the major rivers favored by the crocodiles, which were renowned for their monstrous size and omnivoracious appetites. The relative paucity of wild pigs and cattle in this part of Hispaniola was also fortuitous, according to Zenobia, because that was why they never encountered the wild dogs that preyed on those animals.

Something else they never encountered was people. Zenobia agreed with Grenfell that the French colony of Saint Domingue was centered to the northeast, and had not yet expanded into these southern wilds. Jason recalled the Spanish policy of concentrating their populations around the defensible towns, which had left the coasts to bands of *boucan* hunters. He had half expected to run into some of the latter. But Grenfell assured him that by this date most of them had gone into piracy. Occasionally they spotted Indians in the distance, but only fleetingly as they melted into the forest, having learned that pirates were best avoided.

As the weeks passed, their pace actually picked up somewhat, as they adjusted to the conditions of their trek. Nesbit in particular proved to be surprisingly little of a burden. Except in the earliest stages of the journey, there was hardly any of the whining Jason had dreaded. It was as though hardship brought something out in him . . . or, perhaps, burned something away. To an even greater extent than the other men, he grew almost unrecognizable under his sun-blackened skin and shaggy hair and beard.

After a time the shoreline turned southeastward. They passed what would, in later centuries, be the borderline between Haiti and the Dominican Republic, which Jason celebrated as a benchmark of progress. They continued on down to Hispaniola's southernmost point of land, with the island of Isla Beata visible beyond a channel.

"Is there any chance we'll sight Morgan's ships here?" Nesbit asked Grenfell hopefully.

"I doubt it. They're probably too far out to sea, trying to round the cape. And even if we did, what good would it do us?"

"Er . . . perhaps we could build a signal fire."

"Morgan would hardly be likely to respond to it; he has no reason to suppose any of his people are ashore on Hispaniola. And in the contrary winds he's fighting, he wouldn't be able to put boats ashore on this point of land even if he wanted to."

It proved to be academic in any case; they sighted no sails. So they wearily turned northeastward, passing between the coast and Laguna de Oviedo on their left. This was flat country, but it also had some significant streams. There were fords...but that was where the crocodiles liked to congregate. They had to be very careful. Beyond that, the mountains of the eastern end of the Massif de la Selle came down almost to the water, and the going got very rugged indeed. Sometimes they had to detour inland to avoid a rocky headland.

One day they had to take an unusually long such detour. They were in a glade, with the top of the coastal jungle below and the late-morning sun gleaming on the blue Carribean beyond to the east, when Jason thought he heard a sound that had no place here and now.

No, he thought, shaking his head. *Just my imagination. Too much tropical sun.*

But then Mondrago met his eyes, and he knew the Corsican had heard the same thing. And then the humming sound grew too loud to deny. And a certain tiny blue light began to flash for attention at the edge of his field of vision—the light of his brain implant's feature (little used in past eras, but helpful to the Hesperian Colonial Rangers) which detected nearby use of the grav repulsion technology whose characteristic hum he had heard.

A few yards over the glade, an area of sky—a shockingly large area, thought Jason—began to shimmer and waver, as was characteristic when a refraction field or "invisibility field" was powering down, ceasing to disrupt visible frequencies of light and causing them to bend—or, more properly, "slip"—a hundred and eighty degrees around the object the field enclosed.

Then, abruptly, the field was switched off and that object stood revealed in all its howlingly anachronistic solidity: a small spacecraft, floating above the glade.

"Don't anybody move," Jason said in a flat, cold voice as he saw the dorsal weapon turret swivel to target the small, tattered group.

CHAPTER SIXTEEN

The spacecraft was about as small as vessels equipped with the negative-mass drive came: somewhat over eighty feet long, shaped rather like a rather thick blunt-nosed arrowhead with the housings of the drive's twin nacelles causing the sides to bulge. It was typical of craft of its class in all respects, and clearly its owners were from approximately Jason's own time. Such vessels were used for a variety of specialized roles, for which modular options were available . . . including the option of a turret for a weapon-grade laser like the one into whose orifice they now gazed. Looking more closely, Jason thought to identify the model as . . .

"A Kestrel," said Mondrago in a low voice, confirming his supposition. "Escobar-Ramakrishnan Spacecraft makes it in a gunship model—in fact, this is pretty much it. Notice the weapon pods attached to the hardpoints. Those are Firebird missile launchers. I don't know why they think they need stuff like that in this era. They probably just left them on because they're a standard feature of this model."

"Sounds like you're familiar with it."

"We sometimes used them in Shahinian's Irregulars," Mondrago nodded, referring to his former life as a merc. "Flying them wasn't my job, but I checked out as a relief pilot."

"I see." Jason filed the last datum away for future reference. He himself was a qualified pilot, but the Kestrel was new to him, and in any event he was rusty.

The Kestrel extended its landing legs and settled down onto them with a wheeze. Its ventral hatch hummed open and lowered the access ramp to the ground. In any other circumstances, Jason would have been bemused to see two men dressed and tattooed as pirates descend that ramp, armed with laser carbines. They were to all appearances African, which might or might not mean anything in the case of Transhumanists. Their ethnicity did nothing to disguise their membership in the enforcer castes, if one knew the signs.

"Hands in the air!" one of them snapped. He then ran a sensor over the group. He smiled when it flashed at Jason's pistol. He took it and smashed the butt against a rock. Zenobia's dagger was also confiscated. Then they were motioned inside the Kestrel.

Passing through the open airlock, they entered at the rear of the main cabin. The Kestrel was not a vessel designed for long-term occupancy. At the forward end of the cabin was a small, raised control bridge with seats for a pilot and a copilot/communications officer; otherwise, the cabin held seating for a weapons operator at a small console and for five passengers. Aft of the cabin was a cargo hold, and then the engineering section, including the photon drive used for maneuvering in a significant gravity field once the ship rose above the altitudes where grav repulsion's efficiency dropped off.

Under the prodding of the laser carbines, they moved forward toward the bridge, where a man sat on the pilot's seat to the left, which he had swiveled around, and draped a leg negligently over an armrest. The goon carrying Jason's pistol handed it to him with a mutter of explanation. He stood up as they approached and smiled down at them.

Jason recalled Franco, Category Five, Seventy-Sixth Degree, whose acquaintance he had made in fifth-century-B.C. Athens: a leader-caste Transhumanist genetically tailored to fit the Classical Greek ideal of god-like appearance. Now he saw the West African version. If Zenobia had been male, this would have been her.

Not that affinity of origin implied friendship. The air between their eyes seemed to sizzle with the look they gave each other.

"You!" she spat.

"Yes," the man said lazily. "Romain, Category Three, Eighty-Ninth Degree," he added in an aside in Jason's direction. "I considered this important enough to warrant my personal attention. And not just because of the chance to recapture you, Zenobia." He turned his magnetic dark eyes on Jason. "After your encounter with my men in Port Royal, I had the imagery from their leader's recorder implant run through this ship's database, and we were able to identify you. I could hardly believe my good fortune at such a bonus: Jason Thanou himself! We have accounts to settle with you. Oh, yes, a number of them." His expression was that which a shark would form if it could smile.

"I suppose I should be flattered," said Jason. "Just out of curiosity, how did you locate us?"

"It wasn't easy, given the amount of ground we had to cover. That's why you've made it this far. But this ship has a long-range version of the kind of sensor you have, or had, in this." Romain held up Jason's pistol, with its damaged butt. "So you, as well as Zenobia, unintentionally enabled us to find you, with your brain implant." He gave a sarcastic *tsk-tsk*. "Whatever became of your precious Human Integrity Act?"

With a sick feeling, Jason realized it made sense. His miniaturized version had only been able to detect active bionics at a range of a few yards; the Kestrel could doubtless carry a full-sized model. "Still," he said, ignoring the last jab, "you went to a lot of trouble. Once again, I feel flattered."

"Don't. We would have done it anyway, just to get this traitor. And now she's going to have the opportunity to expiate her treason." Romain's eyes took on a new avidity as they rested on Zenobia, though he continued to address Jason. "We are in this part of Hispaniola because we are expanding our cult into the Spanish-held eastern part. We are working our way east, just as you were, putting on . . . shows for our new converts. We plan to hold a climactic one near Ocoa, and she will be very useful in it. Yes . . . very useful."

Zenobia refused to be baited, or to react in any way; she might as well have been an ebony statue. Romain turned away from her and ran his eyes ever Jason and his followers. "There will be another event before that, and one of you will be able to be of assistance. So you see: even Pugs can lend purpose to their otherwise pointless existence by being useful to us, their supplanters."

Jason did his best to emulate Zenobia's cold impassivity. Behind his expressionlessness, he was reflecting that they were being taken precisely where they had wanted to go. It puzzled him until he remembered that the Transhumanists, aside from a few specialists, weren't interested in human history—indeed, they prided themselves on their indifference to such irrelevancies. So perhaps Romain, unlike Grenfell, didn't know in detail the itinerary of Henry Morgan's movements after the *Oxford* disaster. If not, Jason devoutly hoped that none of his people would blurt out anything to enlighten him. His ignorance was one of the very few cards they had to play.

"The fact remains," he said, taking up where he had left off and pointedly ignoring everything Romain had said, "you've gone to a lot of trouble—starting with temporally displacing this ship over seven hundred years. That must have represented a staggering effort even for you." Romain, as though recognizing a pathetic effort to draw him out, merely grinned lazily. "I can't help wondering," Jason continued in tones of casual curiosity, "if it might somehow be connected with the presence of the Teloi in the here-and-now."

It was deeply satisfying to see Romain's grin freeze into startled immobility. Zenobia stared at him wide-eyed. "Then you—"

"Yes, we know," Jason sighed. "You see, the Teloi and I go back a long way. I recognized them in your description of a 'demon,' as repeated by Henri Boyer. I haven't told you that because I haven't wanted to pressure you, hoping that you'd voluntarily come forward with what you know. But you never did. And there's no point in being coy any longer, is there?" He met her eyes, and for an instant Romain was almost forgotten. "I'm genuinely curious. You've been unwilling to say anything about them, even to Henri. In fact, you've pretended not to know what I was talking about. Why?"

"Why do you think? It's called *shame*. Shame that I ever took part in Romain's foul cult that has tried to set them up as gods."

"Gods?" Jason glanced at Romain, who had rediscovered his equanimity and was looking on with smiling complacency as Zenobia continued.

"Yes. It was one of the things I could no longer stomach—one of the things that caused me to run off and start a counter-cult of my own, to try and undo some of the harm I had done. I hoped to establish a tradition that identified them as agents of evil."

"Yes," Romain interjected, "we've learned of your activities among the Jamaican Maroons." His expression turned ugly, and his eyes held the fire that burns behind the eyes of the zealot, whether the zealotry is of religion or of its substitute, ideology. "You, like all of us, were designed to fulfill a specific function in the restoration of the Transhuman Dispensation. You were given your particular abilities and characteristics to enable you to serve a purpose in our great work of transcending the primordial chaos of random evolutionary processes. So in addition to betraying us, you betrayed yourself. You're lower than a Pug!"

"Yes, I am," she flung in his face, "but I'm gradually working up to their level from yours!"

With a movement of almost invisible swiftness, Romain struck her an open-handed blow across the face, with a force Jason thought must surely break her neck. It rocked her head back, but that was all. She turned back around and looked Romain in the eye with silent defiance. Jaw working, he smashed her across the face again, from the opposite side, even harder, with an even more obscenely loud *smack*. This time she almost lost her balance, and when she turned to him there was a trickle of blood from a split lip. But she still made no sound, and she held herself straight, and her eyes again met his with cool contempt.

Jason had previously thought Zenobia was magnificent-looking. He'd had no idea.

Romain brought his breathing under control. "Secure them in the passenger seats," he muttered to the goons. "We depart."

Jason was strapped into a seat just across from Zenobia. So by turning his head to the left he was able to see as Romain leaned over her and spoke quietly. "In the end, you will be of service to the Movement after all . . . and you know what kind of service. Oh, yes, you know. And your treason will make you even more useful, for when we use you in the rite it will clearly show the power of our cult over yours. Think about that as you await it." He stood up and paused. "But for the rite we plan first, we will need another. Women or children always seem to make a greater impact, and unfortunately we have no children available." His eye went to Pauline Da Cunha. "Yes. Her, I think." Then he turned and went to the pilot seat.

In the course of the short flight, Jason had no chance to ask Zenobia just exactly what Romain meant. And she sat with a face frozen in horror.

Their flight was a short one, to another upland glade, this one in the low hills only a few miles north of the Bahia de Neiba. Here they waited for a few days while various escaped slaves trickled in.

Jason, Mondrago and Da Cunha knew all too well the Transhumanists' utter ruthlessness in dealing with prisoners—knowledge they chose not to share with Nesbit and Grenfell. They engaged in a few whispered discussions on the topic of attempting escape, only to reject it as futile. They were too closely guarded.

Zenobia remained largely uncommunicative, but Jason was able to sound her out about a few things in their rare moments of relative privacy. In particular, he wanted all the information she could give him about the Transhumanists' cult and its West African origins.

"The innumerable deities, or *loa,* are divided into two classes, or families," she explained. "The Rada and the Petro. The Rada are the 'good' ones, but they're kind of slow and lazy; they can't do much for you. The Petro are powerful and fast-acting. They're also basically wicked, but with the proper rites—including a lot of animal sacrifice—they can be made to do good things for you in exchange for a promise of service." It seemed to Jason that she hesitated a fraction of a second before the word *animal.* "The Transhumanists are spreading the notion of a new kind of Petro which is particularly powerful and which, unlike the others, actually appears incarnate to the worshipers."

"The Teloi," Jason nodded. "Why are they willing to play this role? And how can they still be alive? And what are they doing in this part of the planet, anyway?"

"I don't know any of that. I was told very little beyond what I needed to know." And Jason could get no more out of her.

Finally, one night, the preparations were complete. Several small, thatched houselike structures were set up around an open space containing a large silk-cotton tree, in front of which was a closed wooden coffin. Into this torchlit space the prisoners were herded, naked and bound. All around were the local escaped slaves, staring from the shadows. The adepts—the Transhumanist goons and a few cult members from Saint Domingue to the west—wore red robes and head coverings resembling various animals, and they began to dance to the beat of drums. Then Romain stepped forward and raised his deep, compelling voice—bionically enhanced in the subsonic range like Zenobia's—in a chant that everyone joined. Jason could not understand the words.

Gradually the chanting rose in pitch and tempo until it seemed about to climax. Suddenly, Romain raised his arms and all sound stopped. Above the clearing, the stars were occluded by the Kestrel, its invisibility field now deactivated, and a searchlight flooded the clearing. The worshipers moaned ecstatically. By the time they had blinked away the dazzlement of that light and could see again, a robed figure that had not been there before had stepped from the jungle and stood in the clearing.

The moaning intensified as the throng fell to their faces.

Jason stared at the seven-and-a-half-foot humanoid, with its crown of shimmering hair that seemed to be spun from silver and gold. Even in the torchlight, there could be no possible doubt that this was a Teloi. The long, sharp-featured face with its uptilted cheekbones and brow ridges and its enormous oblique eyes was unmistakable. But for some reason he couldn't put his finger on, this one was subtly different from the

Teloi he had known in the Bronze Age and in Classical Greece. The species was undoubtedly the same, but the aspect of languid, almost studied decadence that Jason remembered was missing, replaced by a kind of dynamic harshness.

A dog was brought forth. All four of its paws were chopped off, and it was buried alive, putting an end to its howls and whimpers.

There was a series of responsive chants which seemed to be signifying that the dog was insufficient. Then Romain and the two goons walked toward the group of bound prisoners. They carried thin cords. They untied Pauline Da Cunha.

"Zenobia, what's happening?" she demanded as the goons tied her again, this time with the cords they carried. Zenobia made no reply. She seemed unable to speak.

Romain stepped in front of Jason and spoke softly in Standard International English. "The cords are thin, but they have the tensile strength of cello strings. They are, you see, made from the well-cured intestines of the previous sacrificial victims, who therefore in a sense bind their successors. Rather poetic." He smiled and then turned and walked away.

All at once, Jason understood. He watched as they used the cords to drag the still bewildered Da Cunha to the coffin . . . which served as a low table, onto which they tied her.

Jason turned a searing look on Zenobia. "Why didn't you tell me?" he rasped.

"I couldn't," she whispered, not meeting his eyes. Then she looked up and spoke defiantly. "What good would it have done you—or her—to know in advance?"

Jason had no answer. He turned toward the coffin as the knife descended on the naked figure stretched out on it, and the blood and the screams began.

Afterwards, Jason's recollections of what happened were never entirely clear. But he forced himself to remember as much as possible. He needed to remember it.

He and Zenobia were the only ones who watched it all. Mondrago shouted Corsican curses until one of the goons came over and knocked him unconscious. Nesbit soon fainted. Grenfell withdrew into a state of shock and simply hung against his bonds, saliva drooling from a corner of his mouth.

Jason wanted with all his soul to join them in oblivion. But he made himself watch. He vomited when the quartering commenced, but he still watched. He watched the cooking, and smelled it.

The new converts were not allowed to share in the meat—that was only for the adepts, and even they consumed only a small amount. This was a sacrifice to the Teloi "god," and he did most of the eating.

Finally it was over. Words were spoken and chanted which seemed to indicate that the Teloi found the sacrifice adequate. The hovering Kestrel speared the clearing with another blinding beam of light, under cover of which the Teloi turned and walked back into the jungle.

Romain walked over to stand before Jason and Zenobia. His face wore a look of dreamy satiety. His mouth gleamed with grease. With his right hand he held a wet mass of guts in front of Zenobia's face.

"They'll be dried and cured, and used to bind

you—the prize victim—at the climactic ceremony. As I said, one leads the next." He turned to Jason and smiled, licking the grease from his lips. "See, I told you. Even Pugs can have their uses."

Jason said nothing. His expression did not change. He held Romain's eyes as long as possible, while imprinting on his memory every smallest detail of that face.

CHAPTER SEVENTEEN

The remains of the sacrifice were burned. As it happened, Pauline Da Cunha's TRD, in addition to her deactivated brain implant, was still among those remains, and therefore fell down into the heap of greasy ash where the closed coffin had been. The little light on Jason's map display would remain there, as a reminder he didn't need.

They remained there for a few days. The climactic ceremony of which Romain had spoken was to be held in another upland clearing, this time northeast of the Bahia de Ocoa, only about thirty-five miles as the crow or the Kestrel flew. But Romain wanted to give his adepts time to fan out ahead as "advance men," spreading the word and gathering the believers. In the meantime, the prisoners were kept outside rather than aboard the Kestrel, bound even when eating tasteless rations twice a day under watchful guard, prey to the insects at all times.

Grenfell barely seemed to notice the endless, hellish discomfort. He had returned to awareness, but his personality had yet to reassert itself. Most of him was still sheltering in a place where what he had witnessed had never happened.

Nesbit was different. After regaining consciousness, he had gone through a brief spell of trembling reaction. But since then, the transformation Jason had noticed in the course of their trek seemed to pass to its next stage, as though horror had completed the work that mere hardship had begun. He would, Jason was increasingly certain, hold.

The other two were simply stoical in their own individual ways. Anyone who hadn't known Mondrago as Jason did would never have guessed at what was being stored up behind the expressionless façade of a man in whose very genes slumbered the tradition of vendetta. As for Zenobia, she waited in silent inscrutability.

It was after dark of the second night when the tall figure of the Teloi entered the circle of firelight and approached them. This time, instead of a robe he was wearing a kind of form-fitting jumpsuit that looked utilitarian to an un-Teloi-like degree. His expression held in full the Teloi arrogance, but it was a kind of austere arrogance which somehow wasn't true to type as Jason knew it. His huge, strange eyes ran over the entire huddled group of seated, bound figures before looking Jason full in the face.

"I am told that you speak our language," he said in that tongue. His voice had the disturbing quality Jason remembered, but it formed words in a more clipped fashion than he recalled.

"Badly. You imposed it on the speech centers of my brain without proper preparation, in a brute-force way." Privately, Jason noted that the Teloi had referred only to him, apparently unaware that Mondrago shared his imperfect knowledge of the language, having acquired it by direct neural induction on preparation for their expedition to the Athens of Themistocles. He had no intention of revealing the fact, and he knew he could count on Mondrago's tight-lipped silence.

"'We' imposed it?" the Teloi queried. Then his thin lips curled with disdain. "Oh, yes. You mean the *Oratioi'Zhonglu*."

"Er . . . the . . . ?"

"They were a *zhonglu*—that is, a . . ." The Teloi looked annoyed and seemed to decide that trying to explain the term was more trouble than it was worth— or perhaps its meaning was so obvious to him that it could hardly be put into words. "A group of individuals of my race who, a long time ago, arranged to isolate themselves on this planet so they could play at being gods among a slave-race of their own creation."

"A very long time ago," said Jason, nodding slowly. "About a hundred thousand local years. So you're not one of them?"

The Teloi seemed to find the question insulting. "Do not confuse me and my comrades with those contemptible, degenerate fools! They're all dead by now. And they were typical of our race in those days. Our ancestors had sought to turn their posterity into gods by genetic engineering. Instead, they produced useless parasites who could find no better use for their near-immortal lives than to find ever-new frivolities and depravities to hold at bay the meaninglessness of those lives. It was because of the decadence of those like the *Oratioi'Zhonglu* that we lost the war with the Nagommo."

"Ah, yes, the Nagommo." Jason reviewed in is mind what he knew of that amphibious race and its long war of mutual genocide against the Teloi. In 1628 B.C. he had watched the death of what he was coldly certain was the last Nagom in the universe: Oannes, a survivor of a Nagommo battlecruiser that had crash-landed in the Persian Gulf in the fourth millennium B.C. Its crew had taught the rudiments of civilization to the rebellious human slaves of the Teloi in that region. In the meantime, their race had gone on to win the war, but at too great a cost, for they had laid the groundwork for their own eventual extinction. Jason, who had looked on their graveyard homeworld, decided not to mention that, for this Teloi might not be aware of it, and Jason had no desire to give him satisfaction. "We were under the impression that they had destroyed your race."

"Ah, no!" The Teloi knelt down and brought his face close to Jason's. His eyes, with the deep blue irises and pale-blue "whites," were incandescent with fanatical hate. "The war against the Nagommo was our salvation, for it gave to our hollow lives a purpose: the extermination of those nauseating, slimy vermin. Admittedly, most of our race were too far gone in degeneracy to dedicate themselves to that purpose. But some of us did. We formed the *Tuova'Zhonglu*, a ..." Once again he seemed stymied at trying to explain what *zhonglu* meant. "A new military organization ... no, society, with its own culture of duty and sacrifice, rejecting all the idle pleasure-seeking and aesthetic dilettantism of our fellows.

"But we were not enough—never enough. The useless, effete majority never gave us the support we needed. That was why we lost the war. No, we

never really *lost* it—we were betrayed! If our race
had united behind us and accepted our leadership,
we would have obliterated the Nagommo!

"In the end, those who had failed us perished as
they deserved, for they had proven themselves unworthy
of us. But our race was not destroyed—it was purified!
Its worthwhile members—the hard, incorruptible core
of the military—escaped from the final cataclysm into
space. Even now we cruise the star-trails, spending long
periods in suspended animation to prolong our lives,
gradually and inconspicuously gathering our strength
for the inevitable day when the universe will know
its natural masters!"

My God, Jason thought. *We're not just dealing with
Teloi. We're dealing with the Teloi version of fascists!*

I'm beginning to appreciate Zeus.

"One question," he ventured. "Since you had nothing
to do with the, uh, *Oratioi'Zhonglu* here on Earth, how
did you know that I can understand your language?"

"I told him," said a voice from the shadows, loath-
somely familiar even when speaking Teloi.

Romain stepped into the light, smiling his trade-
mark lazy smile. Jason carefully kept his face and
voice expressionless.

"And how did *you* know?"

Before replying to Jason, Romain turned to the
Teloi. "I can communicate with him more readily in
our own language," he explained. The Teloi gave an
imperious gesture of acquiescence, and turned to go.

"One moment," said Jason. "What name should I
call you by?"

The Teloi paused to consider. "I understand the
Oratioi'Zhonglu adopted names remembered in your

various cultures as those of gods. Appropriate, inasmuch as they created you." For the first time, a hint of a smile flickered across that cold face. "You may call me...Ahriman." He turned on his heel and was gone.

"These lunatics," said Romain in Standard International English, "are too arrogant to have any interest in learning our language. A good thing for us, from the standpoint of security. And now, to answer your question, I know because it was one of the things we learned via a message-drop—we use the same system you do, you see—from our mission leader in fifth-century-B.C. Greece."

"Franco, Category Five, Seventy-Sixth Degree," Jason nodded. "I remember him well. In fact, I killed him."

"So we surmised from the fragmentary report of the one member of that expedition who got back alive, and from the fact that Franco's body, when it appeared at our displacer, had a laser burn in addition to its other injuries."

"You don't sound as resentful as I would have expected."

"Franco was a boasting fool, and deserved what he got. But for all his incompetence, he did provide us with some extremely valuable information. You see, whatever my associate Ahriman says about his contempt for the *Oratioi'Zhonglu*—which I gather they reciprocated in a supercilious sort of way—the two factions did communicate with each other from time to time. Thus the 'gods' here on Earth knew a little something of the movement schedules of the surviving Teloi military—very long-term schedules, as you might expect of beings whose lifespan is measured in tens of thousands of years. So Franco was able to learn from

Zeus that a Teloi battlestation is due to pass through this system in the spring of 1669."

Jason sat up, as far as his bonds would permit. "So this is why you went to the colossal effort of temporally displacing a spacecraft!"

"Precisely." Romain's smile went up a notch of smugness. "As soon as we got Franco's message drop, we knew we had a golden opportunity. We were going to send an expedition to this general period anyway, to establish our cult among the slave population of these islands—a seed to germinate for centuries inside the larger body of Voodoo. So we sent the Kestrel here, and used it to establish contact with them."

"But you said the battlestation isn't due until spring."

"A small advance party was already here, led by Ahriman. We already knew their language, of course, having made contact with the 'gods' some time earlier than the fifth century B.C."

"So Franco told me." *Franco told me a lot of things,* Jason did not add. *Just as you are doing now. You may sneer at him as a braggart, but you're a lot like him. I imagine all you leader-caste types are. It must be hell, having nobody except your gene-tailored yes-men to talk to. Having a new ear to vent to must be a hard temptation to resist.*

And I've got to keep the flow of revelations coming, even if it means conversing with a creature like you, close enough to smell your breath.

"It turned out we were natural allies. Ahriman agreed to pose as a *loa* of the Petro family, appearing in the actual flesh. It makes quite an impression, as you've seen." Romain leaned forward, and his affectation of catlike complacency slid away to reveal sheer, undignified gloating. "Furthermore, when the battlestation makes its pass of Earth, they're going to share with us their military technology. It's more advanced than that of our era in a number of areas. Once our underground organization has that data... well, who knows? Maybe it won't *need* to be underground anymore."

Jason did not allow himself to consider the alarming implications of what Romain was saying, lest the Transhumanist have the satisfaction of seeing his reaction. "I don't quite understand the deal," he said evenly. "Why should they agree to do all this for you? What can you do for them in return?"

"Well, for one thing, we allow them the use of our vessel from time to time. In fact, we've promised to make them a present of it. It's not too comfortable for them, being designed for humans, but invisibility makes up for a lot of discomfort."

Jason nodded, recalling having noted while in ancient Greece that the refraction field was an odd lacuna in Teloi technology. "Still, that doesn't seem like enough. There must be more."

"Oh, indeed there is!" Romain's mocking smile was back. "We've told them that, a little less than five centuries from now, humans are going to begin planting extrasolar colonies. We've agreed to tell them the locations of those colonies, and their dates of foundation, so that Teloi warships can be on hand to destroy them in their infancy. After which we've assured them that the Transhuman Dispensation, having reestablished its rule over Earth, will restrict itself to the solar system and leave the galaxy to them."

Jason could only stare, speechless.

"But the Teloi *can't* prevent the colonies from being founded!" blurted Nesbit, speaking up for the first time. "The Observer Effect—"

"Of course they can't. But *they* don't know that." Romain's smile widened. "We haven't been entirely candid with them about the nature of time travel."

"Your friend Franco also tried to play the Teloi for suckers with false promises involving time travel," Mondrago pointed out. "When they found out the truth, they were a little upset. In fact, they and Franco's men mostly wiped each other out."

"Franco, as you have already heard me indicate, was a fool. He made promises whose falsity quickly became apparent. I don't. By the time these Teloi simpletons learn that they have been duped, it will be centuries too late."

"Aren't you worried that *I'll* tell Ahriman?" asked Jason. "Remember, I speak his language."

"Not particularly. In the first place, I don't plan to allow you an opportunity to do so. In the second place, he wouldn't believe you. As you've doubtless observed, these *Tuova'Zhonglu* Teloi are mad. They live in a universe of what they want to believe. And in the third place . . . I would be displeased if you did. You would be well advised to avoid displeasing me."

"Why? What have I got to lose? I'm as good as dead anyway. You wouldn't be telling me all this otherwise."

"Quite true. But the *way* you die is something else." Romain indicated Zenobia, who had continued to sit like a statue. "She, as I have said, will be the sacrifice at the great ceremony shortly, thus demonstrating the power of our pet *loa* over her. She will die as did your friend . . . your *tasty* friend. But we will have use for the rest of you later. You can go the same way—or it can be worse. Much worse. It can be made to last a very long time, by taking nonessential parts one by one and consuming them while you are still alive to watch. Considering who you are, I am leaning in that direction anyway. So don't provoke me."

Jason met his eyes. It had to be said. "There are some things that I never knew even Transhumanists did."

"Ordinarily, you would be correct. And I will own to a degree of squeamishness at first. But since then, I've found that what began simply as a matter of showmanship has become more and more strangely . . . habit-forming. And, of course, scruples do not apply when dealing with Pugs." Romain gave Jason one more look, licked his lips, and was gone, leaving them sitting silently in the shadows.

CHAPTER EIGHTEEN

The day finally came when they were herded aboard the Kestrel, with Grenfell moving listlessly, still detached from the proceedings. Two goons strapped them into the four rear passenger seats. Ahriman seated himself awkwardly into the forward one, next to the weapons station. Recalling Romain's words, Jason decided against any attempt to communicate with him.

For a trip this short, the photon drive would have been superfluous. The grav repulsors, whose primary use was to provide the lift that enabled the photon drive to easily attain orbital space, had some lateral movement capability and could be used as a secondary form of propulsion for atmospheric maneuvering at low altitudes. So the Kestrel drifted, invisible and almost silent, on an east-by-northeast course that took it over the northern shore of the Bahia de Ocoa.

Hispaniola's principal town of Santo Domingo was only a little further east, and this was one of the areas where the authorities had forced the population to concentrate itself, making it more defensible, but, as Grenfell had once explained, effectively leaving most of the coastline to the buccaneers. Their flight took them over areas where the Spanish presence was visible, at least in the lowlands. But their destination was up in the hills to the north of the tiny port of Ocoa, an area where runaway slaves lurked.

Not that Jason was able to observe the scenery below from where he sat, bound to his seat. Nor would he have paid any attention if he had been. His thoughts were focused exclusively on one problem: escape.

Unfortunately, there seemed no solution to that problem.

The one advantage he had was his brain implant's map display. If they could somehow slip their bonds and elude the extremely thorough watchfulness of Romain and his goons, they would be able to find their way to wherever they decided to go. But his very use of that brain implant would expose them to detection by the Kestrel's sensor that had found them in the first place.

"I can only think of one possibility," he whispered to Mondrago as they sat, bound as usual, in the torchlit clearing the night after their arrival, watching preparations that included the construction of a closed coffin by cult adepts high-ranking enough to be trusted with knowledge of the Kestrel. "If Zenobia and I go in one direction—or, better still, two different directions—and the other three of you go another, they wouldn't be able to track your group because none of you have any bionics. You could maybe lead Nesbit and Grenfell to safety."

"Do you really think I'd leave you and Zenobia to . . . what Romain has planned for you?"

"You'll damned well do it if I put it in the form of a direct order! *Somebody* has got to get back with the information we now possess."

Mondrago didn't meet Jason's eyes. "Well, it's all academic anyway, isn't it? Before we can even think about eluding pursuit, we have to get away in the first place. And they don't show any signs of letting us do that."

Jason knew what he meant. If anything, they were under more thorough watch than ever, because more of Romain's goons had been waiting here, under the command of the middle-level type Jason recognized from Port Royal by the bandage that circled his head and covered the hole where his right ear had been. The look he had given Zenobia had not been pleasant, and Jason had overheard Romain sternly explaining to him that she must be preserved intact for the sacrifice.

"One good thing," he told Mondrago and Zenobia. "So far, we've made no attempt to escape, so the guards have gotten slack. Their procedures have become a matter of routine, and their vigilance is relaxed."

"Something else," said Zenobia. "My eyes are bionic—"

"Yes, Henri told us."

"But they have an additional feature I never mentioned to him: night vision."

"All right; that's two things in our favor."

"Actually," said Mondrago—hesitantly, it seemed to Jason—"there's a third." Looking around to make sure none of the goons were watching, he put his bound hands inside his breeches and drew out a small general-purpose knife. Jason couldn't imagine how he had been concealing it in there without cutting

himself. Mondrago quickly pushed it back down out
of sight. "One of the cult adepts dropped it the night
of the . . . sacrifice. I scooped it up afterwards when I
came to and he was still in the kind of dreamy state
you've seen them in after . . ." He couldn't continue.

"You didn't tell me. Why?"

"I had a pretty good idea that, if there seemed
to be a chance of escape, you'd give me the kind of
orders you've just given me."

"Well," Jason sighed, "it's still not a very good
chance. And even if it was, we'd just be back face
to face with the *other* problem: their ability to locate
me and Zenobia." Unbidden, there came into his mind
the ancient joke about the First Principle of Military
Leadership: *Never give an order you know won't be
obeyed.* Despite what he had said earlier, he was by
no means confident that Mondrago would obey an
order to leave him and Zenobia to their fate. And he
was honest enough to admit to himself that he didn't
relish the role of decoy. "For now, let's wait and see."

But he knew they didn't have much time left. The
coffin was almost finished.

Early the following morning, there was a commotion. Romain and Ahriman engaged in what seemed
to be a hurried colloquy, after which the Teloi and
two goons boarded the Kestrel. Romain spoke briefly
to One-Ear—Jason got the impression that the latter
was being left temporarily in charge—and then followed Ahriman aboard. The cult adepts moaned softly
and made signs as the Kestrel rose into the sky and
vanished within its refraction field.

"What's going on?" Nesbit whispered.

"I don't know," Jason replied. "Evidently something has come up that requires Romain's and Ahriman's presence elsewhere."

"Maybe even somewhere off-planet," Zenobia speculated.

"Wherever they've gone," said Mondrago, "they've taken the Kestrel's sensors with them." His eyes met Jason's. "It's now or never, sir."

"You're right. After we've been fed breakfast, start working on your bonds whenever no guards are watching." Jason worked his way around and whispered to the others. "All right, here's what we're going to do..."

One-Ear must have gotten renewed warnings about Zenobia from Romain, for he largely stayed away from the prisoners. That, and the fact that he was now somewhat shorthanded, gave Mondrago frequent opportunities to inconspicuously saw at his bonds, awkwardly grasping the knife behind the small of his back and maintaining a stoic silence whenever he inadvertently cut his wrists. After his hands were free, he kept them together, underneath him, whenever a guard came by. When no guard was about, he worked his way up against Jason and freed his hands.

That was as far as they had gotten when darkness fell and one of the guards approached with their nighttime rations. This had become so routine that the guard was unarmed, save with a knife thrust through his belt-rope, and had no backup. One-Ear and the rest of his men were in the distance, around a flickering fire. As always, the guard carried a tray with five bowls of glop about the consistency of thin gravy, which they were to grasp with their bound hands and slurp down. When he came to Mondrago and bent down, the Corsican raised his hands as usual. As far as could be seen in the night, they were still bound. And they concealed the knife held under Mondrago's right wrist.

With a movement of almost invisible swiftness, Mondrago flipped the knife up. His left hand went up and behind the goon's head and pulled it down and forward, while simultaneously he thrust the knife under the chin and up through the tongue and into the brain.

It probably wouldn't have worked, given the goon's genetically upgraded reflexes, had it been anyone but Mondrago. As it was, the goon never made a sound. There was the merest trickle of blood, as usual in cases of instantaneous death.

Mondrago lowered the goon to his knees and, using a nearby stick, propped the body into a kneeling position. Swiftly, before anyone could notice anything amiss, he handed the goon's knife to Jason. The two of them swiftly cut the ropes binding their ankles, then freed the others, cautioning them to silence. The last was hardly necessary in Grenfell's case, although awareness seemed to be awakening in his eyes.

"All right," Jason whispered. "Before anybody over there at the fire notices that this goon hasn't moved in a long time, let's crawl—very slowly and quietly—over to the edge of the clearing." He activated his map display. "Once we're in the jungle, we'll head in that direction, which is south. Zenobia, lead the way. Irving, can I depend on you to make sure Roderick keeps moving?"

"Yes, you can," said Nesbit steadily.

"Good. Alexandre and I will bring up the rear."

They were beyond the clearing, and up and running on their stiffened legs, before they heard the sound of shouting from behind.

Following Zenobia, they were able to outdistance their pursuers, who were blundering through the darkened jungle with the aid of torches. But Jason was only too well aware that in daylight they would lose that advantage, and that One-Ear's cult adepts, escaped slaves all, were more jungle-wise than any of them except possibly Zenobia. He also knew that One-Ear would never give up the pursuit and face Romain's wrath for losing the prisoners. So he urged his people ever onward through the night, gaining as much of a lead as they could. Nesbit was as good as his word, keeping Grenfell running whenever the historian seemed about to sink into vagueness.

Still, Jason couldn't free himself of the feeling that, given the Transhumanists' lack of scruples about bringing high-tech equipment into the past, One-Ear might very well have a means of communicating with the Kestrel. He could only hope that One-Ear, in the immemorial way of underlings everywhere, would try to recapture the escapees on his own rather than immediately summoning the spacecraft, lest Romain conclude that he couldn't handle his own problems.

Instead of brooding about it, he concentrated on their route. The tiny port of Ocoa lay about fifteen miles south-southwest. He had no intention of actually going there, given how the Spaniards felt about pirates. But Grenfell had said that Morgan was due to land raiders in its vicinity to supplement his water and meat supplies, although he had been unable to be precise about locations or dates. So Jason led them down the slopes into the coastal lowlands along the eastern shore of the Bahia de Ocoa, where there were ranches the pirates might raid.

"Of course," said Zenobia as they made one of their occasional stops for water along the Rio Ocoa, which they dare not follow consistently for fear of discovery, "they might raid on the *other* side of Ocoa, further southeast."

"But that would put them closer to the Spanish stronghold of Santo Domingo," Jason argued. "No, my hunch is that they'll land north of Ocoa."

"Unless they've already come and gone."

"I prefer not to assume that." Jason stood up. "All right. Let's go. Irving, is Roderick in shape to get moving?"

"Yes, I think so." Nesbit murmured something in Grenfell's ear. The historian nodded slowly and got to his feet.

They resumed their trek, leaving the Rio Ocoa behind and following a smaller stream southwestward, occasionally glimpsing the Bahia ahead whenever the vegetation grew thin enough. Finally they entered the fringes of the coastal plain, and Jason turned out to be right that there were ranches here.

Unfortunately, those ranches showed signs of having already been raided. There were burned-out sheds, and fly-swarming carcasses of cattle and horses lying about.

Jason had difficulty meeting his companions' eyes, especially Zenobia's. "This all looks very recent," he said. "Maybe—"

All at once, a sound of shouting and musketry was heard. They ran behind a ruined building as a ragged line of men, apparently Spaniards, broke into the cleared area, plainly beating a retreat. Their retreat turned into a rout as another line of men—clearly pirates this time—appeared behind them, pausing to fire their expensive muskets with their famous marksmanship, bringing several Spaniards down and then breaking into a charge.

Jason stepped around a corner of the ruin and started to wave his arms in the direction of the pirates. "Over here!" he shouted . . . then doubled over, breath whooshing out, as the butt of a laser carbine smashed into his stomach.

Before he could straighten up, he was shoved back behind the wall among his companions. A goon stepped quickly around the corner, covering them all with the laser carbine. "No one move or make a sound," he commanded.

Jason sensed rather than saw Zenobia bunching her muscles to spring. The goon smiled lazily and pointed the laser carbine at her midriff. "Don't be a silly bitch. Nobody's *that* fast." He sounded almost bored. One muscle at a time, Zenobia uncoiled. The goon smiled again, then moved his lower jaw in a way that Jason recognized: he was activating an implanted short-range communicator. "I have them. I'm at—"

With a roar, a large figure burst around the corner of the ruined wall, waving a cutlass overhead. The goon swung around. Before he could bring the laser carbine into line, the cutlass came down, smashing the weapon out of the goon's hands. At the same moment, Zenobia leaped forward. She grasped the Transhumanist's left wrist and wrenched the arm back up behind him, while clamping her right arm around his throat.

With a bellow of triumph, the new arrival thrust his cutlass into the goon's midriff, gave it a vicious twist, and yanked it out, trailing a rope of guts.

As Zenobia let the body fall, their rescuer wiped his sweat-soaked dirty-blond hair back, revealing the Neanderthaloid countenance of Roche Braziliano.

I never thought I'd be grateful to see a face like that, Jason thought.

"Zenobia!" rumbled the pirate in his almost impenetrable Dutch accent. His scowl almost entirely smoothed itself out, which Jason suspected constituted his version of a toothy grin. "It's you! And you—Jason, *ja?*—I remember from the *Oxford.* How come you to be here?"

"It's a long story. We were blown free of the *Oxford* and got ashore. Some renegades who still have a grudge against Zenobia from her time here in Hispaniola have been chasing us. This was one of them. We're in your debt."

"Well, Captain Morgan will be glad to see you. Come along, we'll be heading back to the beach as soon as we've finished whipping these dogs of Spaniards back to their kennels." As he turned to go, he noticed—seemingly for the first time—the wrecked laser carbine on the ground. His scowl returned, and his pale-gray eyes blinked repeatedly as he gazed at something that had no business existing in his world. He gave a puzzled grunt. "Ah ... what is ...?"

"Never mind," said Zenobia, and Jason realized she had activated her vocal implant. "It's nothing. Let's go. Captain Morgan will want to see us."

"Uh ... *ja,*" grunted Roche Braziliano as the subsonic wave did its work. "You're right. Let's go."

⊹   ⊹   ⊹

"We landed a party near here a few days ago," explained Henry Morgan, leaning on the side of a beached boat as the returning pirates filed past. Zenobia had already returned to *Rolling-Calf* and a rapturous reception by her Maroons. "They gathered in a lot of good meat. The Dons took exception. They brought in three or four hundred men from Santo Domingo and gathered in all the animals from the farms we hadn't raided, so when we landed again this morning we found nothing. So we sent fifty men further inland. The Dons thought they'd be clever. They left a great herd of cattle where it would be sure to be found, lying in wait nearby. After our men had killed a large number of the beasts and were starting to haul the meat away, they attacked from ambush. They probably thought we'd flee in disorder like they would. But our men know how to retreat in good order, pausing at every opportunity to take toll with their muskets. Eventually the Spaniards, being Spaniards, lost heart and started to retreat themselves. We pursued them and wiped out most of them, although we'd had to abandon all the meat. It was in the course of that pursuit that Roche ran into you." He grinned. "What excellent fortune! Of course, it's too bad about Henri; he was a good man, and it's always a shame to lose a ship's carpenter. And I gather Roderick isn't quite himself—that sometimes happens to men who go through great hardship, but they often get over it. And it's a pity about your mistress drowning, Jason. A good-looking piece, in a Portuguese sort of way."

"Yes," said Jason noncommittally. They hadn't been forthcoming about Pauline Da Cunha's death, merely saying that she as well as Boyer had gone down with the *Oxford*.

"Still," Morgan continued, "the rest of you had the luck of the Devil, being blown clear and then washing ashore and finding each other on the beach. And then you walked all the way here! That story ought to be good for free drinks for the rest of your lives! You must have made very good time." Morgan's dark eyes narrowed, and Jason reminded himself that, whatever else he was, this man was very shrewd. "You know, there's one thing I still don't quite understand. You headed east at best speed, toward the Spanish-settled region around here... like walking into the lion's den, you might say." Morgan's eyes narrowed still further. "If one didn't know better, it's almost as though you knew I was going to be here."

Very, very shrewd. "It was just a lucky guess, Captain. I figured you'd need to raid the southern coast of Hispaniola to replenish your supplies, so I thought this offered the best chance of encountering you somewhere."

"Hmm. It was still what people call a long chance. It's almost enough to make you believe what fools say about Zenobia!" Morgan laughed, just a trifle uneasily, then abruptly dismissed the subject. "Anyway, as old Will Shakespeare said, all's well that ends well. Tomorrow, I'm going to lead a couple of hundred men back here to finish off those Spaniards from Santo Domingo. Then we'll start working our way east— damn these contrary winds!—toward Saona Island, off the southeast tip of Hispaniola, where I've called a second rendezvous."

Nesbit's curiosity seemed to overcome his hesitancy. "Er, Captain, didn't the destruction of *Oxford* cause any of the Brotherhood any, well, misgivings about following you, for fear of bad luck?"

Morgan looked at him as though he considered the question an odd one. "Of course not. The fact that I survived it was a sign of excellent luck! Any pirate worth his salt would want to follow a captain who got out of *that* alive along with only ten others, when over two hundred went down!"

"But all those dead men!"

"Well, it helped that a lot of them were still floating the next day."

"Ah," Nesbit nodded. "You mean you were able to give them Christian burial."

"No! We were able to get their rings and other jewelry off." Morgan roared with laughter. "Oh, yes, a few of the Frogs crawled away, but only the ones who'd been looking for an excuse to do so anyway. As far as the others are concerned, I lead a charmed life!"

Jason nodded to himself, recalling that Grenfell had said much the same thing about the seemingly paradoxical effect of the *Oxford* disaster on Morgan's reputation. Now the historian was only fitfully able to supply such insights. Their reunion with Morgan's company had seemed to rekindle his awareness of—and interest in—his surroundings, which gave Jason cause for cautious hope. But for now, at least, they were going to have to get along without the foreknowledge of events that he had provided.

"But," continued Morgan, his mood visibly darkening, "there's no denying that the loss of *Oxford* is a heavy blow. Without her, I suppose we'll have to pick a destination less tough than Cartagena." He shook his head sadly, then stood up straight. "Well, we'll deal with that at Saona Island. For now, let's get back to Dick Norman's *Lilly*, my new flagship, where a man can get a drink!"

CHAPTER NINETEEN

The next day, Morgan's landing party found no Spanish troops and had to content itself with some random vandalism in the region. It proved a harbinger of frustrations to come.

Behind schedule and seething with impatience, Morgan set his course for Saona Island. It took weeks, tacking and beating against particularly foul contrary trade winds. It was hellish aboard the small ships, rolling and pitching and exposed to the whipping spray. Jason could only give thanks that all members of his party were, like himself, not susceptible to motion sickness. He had insisted on it as a special qualification for this particular mission, hoping (unsuccessfully, as it turned out) to exclude Nesbit.

Finally arriving at Saona Island, they found that none of the other ships Morgan had summoned from Port Royal and the other buccaneer centers had arrived yet. Those had also had to sail to windward, and they had further to come. As they began to straggle in, word came that some had simply given up.

So Morgan, lest his fleet run low on supplies again, had sent an expedition of a hundred and fifty men back to Hispaniola, to pillage the rich environs of Santo Domingo itself. But the Spaniards were forewarned as they so often were—it was a chronic problem, with coastal settlers and fishermen and Indians eager to report sightings of pirate ships in hope of reward. And by now Morgan's diabolical reputation as the nemesis of the Spanish empire was such as to make him a particular target. So the party found well-prepared troops in a strong defensive position, and returned empty-handed.

At last, all the ships that were going to come were assembled at Saona Island. Morgan received reports that three of them had turned back, unable to make further headway against the trade winds because of stress to their hulls or exhaustion of their crews. He also learned that the Spaniards of Cartagena had rejoiced at the news of the *Oxford* disaster.

"The silly papist fools claim their city's patron saint, Nuestra Señora de Popa, set off the explosion," one of the captains told the council Morgan had called aboard *Lilly*. "They even say she was seen emerging from the water, her clothes all wet, after swimming back from Cow Island!" Jason, who knew the real cause, dutifully joined in the chuckles.

Morgan was not amused. He looked out over the rail at the other ships. "Well, it's clear we can't expect any more ships to come. So we're only nine ships and less than six hundred men. And this one, with only fourteen light guns, is the most heavily armed ship we've got. We all know we can't attempt Cartagena without *Oxford*. I say, let's set our course for Caracas and the towns along the coast of the Spanish Main to the east of it."

"But," someone objected, "that's to the southeast of here. It would be a long haul to windward. And after the beating our ships have already taken...!" A murmur of weary agreement arose. The accented voice of one of the French buccaneers who had stuck with Morgan interrupted it.

"There's another possibility, *mes amis*. I was with L'Ollonais when he sacked Maracaibo. True, the approaches are treacherous, but I know them well. And small, shallow-draft ships like ours will be ideal for them."

"But L'Ollonais picked it clean!" Zenobia objected.

"Ah, but that was more than two years ago, *non*?"

"That's right!" said Morgan, suddenly charged with the predatory eagerness he knew so well how to instill in others. "You know how it is with Spanish cities. Even after we pillage them, the ruling groups are still stuck there—they need the king's permission to relocate somewhere else. So they build their wealth back up, which doesn't take long. There's always a new mule train coming in with more silver. Maracaibo will be a fat prize again." Jason, from his experiences in the twentieth century, recalled that burglars who had robbed an affluent house would often hit the same house again after giving the insurance company time to restock it.

"They also send messages to Madrid asking for money and engineers to build new fortifications," said Roche Braziliano in the lugubrious tone for which his face was so well suited.

"But that takes time! What could they have done

in two years?" Morgan's eyes twinkled with his infectious pleasure at his own cleverness. "And besides . . . getting there will mean dropping due south, with the trade winds to port. An easy voyage."

Summoning up his map display and enlarging its scale to include the entire Caribbean, Jason saw that Morgan was right. The proposed target lay across the Caribbean on the northern coast of South America. There, the great Gulf of Venezuela was connected by a narrow channel to the almost equally large Laguna de Maracaibo, a lake—actually a fresh-water lagoon—measuring eighty-six miles from north to south and sixty miles east to west. He zoomed the map in on the lake and saw that the town of Maracaibo was situated near the southern end of the channel. On the southeastern shore of the lake was another substantial town, called Gibraltar. The surrounding country was a fertile lowland plain, encircled by mountains.

The lake, he thought, bore a striking resemblance to a bottle. *What happens*, he wondered, *if somebody plugs it while we're inside?*

But he could see that Morgan's last point had swayed the doubters. There was little further discussion.

The southward voyage was almost as uneventful as Morgan had promised. They stopped at the island of Ruba, the future Aruba—a Spanish possession whose Indian inhabitants nevertheless habitually did business with passing buccaneers. They did so now, and after buying supplies from them Morgan continued on to the Gulf of Venezuela, sailing at night, keeping to the middle of the entrance to stay out of sight of Spanish watchtowers. The French pirate guided them through the shallow, sandbar-laced waters of the gulf, and on the night of March 8 they anchored outside the narrow twelve-foot-deep channel that gave entry to the lake.

At first light, they began to cautiously negotiate the entrance to the channel, working their way between the two small islands of San Carlos and Zapara. It was tricky navigation. But the morning light revealed that that was the least of their problems.

"Well-positioned fortress," Mondrago commented dispassionately, studying the battlements on the eastern shore of San Carlos, looming over a sandy beach, barely three hundred yards from the channel.

"And one which the Spaniards have evidently built since L'Ollonais was here," said Jason, glancing at *Lilly*'s quarterdeck where the Frenchman was making embarrassed excuses to Morgan.

"Here's where we could have used *Oxford*'s thirty-four guns," he heard Morgan rumble. "As it is, there's only one way. We'll have to land on that beach and take it by storm."

Jason didn't listen to whatever else Morgan said, for at that moment his attention was distracted by a blue dot at the edge of his field of vision. He activated his map display to confirm something he decided to keep to himself for the present.

Half of the company went ashore that afternoon, in a stiff breeze which gradually developed into something resembling a squall. The boat carrying Jason and Mondrago capsized, and they splashed through the surf with viciously blowing sand stinging their eyes and Spanish cannonballs, fired from above, kicking up sprays of sand and water around them.

But not many balls. Mondrago had counted eleven cannon muzzles protruding from the crenels above, but they were being fired slowly, one at a time. That, and supporting fire from the ships, enabled the buccaneers to fight their way to the ridge of sand that provided the only cover available.

"What's wrong with them?" Mondrago wondered aloud as they hugged the sand. "They could murder us, given a decent rate of fire. Not that I'm complaining, mind you."

"I suspect that fort is seriously undermanned—a typical result of the Spanish crown's peso-pinching, as Roderick once mentioned. They haven't got enough men to serve all the guns. And the ones they have got probably aren't all that well-trained."

Morgan, who believed in leading from the front, had come ashore. "All right," he called out. "We wait here until dusk. Then we'll rush for the walls. We won't be able to run very fast, uphill in the sand, but under cover of dark we ought to be able to cross the open space. Make sure of your weapons."

Jason and Mondrago complied. Their wonderful muskets, of course, lay at the bottom of the sea off Cow Island with HMS *Oxford*—Mondrago had never entirely gotten over that—but Morgan had given them flintlock pistols from a common store of surplus equipment. Not that they could have used the muskets at the moment, for the battlements were beyond effective range. Everyone had to lie low and take it. So when the abrupt tropical darkness fell, just after a final volley from the fort's guns, it was a very frustrated line of buccaneers that rose from behind the sand ridge on Morgan's command and surged forward.

Strangely, there was no fire from the fort. They

reached the base of the rough stone wall and hugged it, staring at each other in the moonlight, bewildered.

"Where the devil's a gate?" demanded Morgan.

They soon found one. "We need a ram," someone said.

"Faugh!" Morgan reared back and, with all the force of his large body, kicked the gate with his sea-booted foot. It swung open. After an instant of stunned immobility, the buccaneers swarmed in with a roar.

The fort was deserted. They all burst out laughing.

"The buggers must have slipped away just before dark, after firing that last volley!" someone crowed, slapping Jason on the back.

"After the visit by L'Ollonais, they were probably pissing in their pants with fear," opined the Frenchman. "Now the way to Maracaibo is open!"

"Wait!" thundered Morgan. "Wait, you swabs! I don't like this—it's too easy. I want every inch of this fort searched."

The buccaneers began to fan out across the courtyard into the buildings, where they struck flints to light torches. Jason and Mondrago attached themselves to a group that Morgan led into the largest structure, which they began to search room by room.

It was then that Jason smelled an acrid aroma.

Mondrago must have detected it at the same instant. "Isn't that—?" he began.

But Jason had already locked eyes with Morgan . . . and Morgan had broken into a run. They followed him down a short stony corridor into the chamber at the far end, where they stopped, paralyzed.

It was the fort's powder magazine. A long, slow-burning fuse led straight to a mountain of piled gunpowder barrels. The flame was just short of them.

For an eternal instant, Jason knew himself to be a dead man. It was the same knowledge that held them all immobilized.

All but one. Henry Morgan didn't really look like he was built for speed, but he sprang forward without a second's hesitation, straight for the powder barrels, and stamped a foot down on the fuse. The flame went out.

In dead silence, the rest of them shuffled forward. Another smell was now added to that of smoke. Someone had had a little accident.

They all looked down. There was no more than an inch of fuse left. With a collective *whoosh*, everyone breathed again.

"Huzza for Captain Morgan!" somebody shouted in an unsteady voice. The rest of the buccaneers whose lives had just been saved came running to see what the cheering was about.

In addition to the huge store of powder that was to have been their death, the abandoned fort proved to contain a wealth of weapons. Jason and Mondrago got new muskets—not as good as the ones they'd lost, of course, and they would have to get along without laser target designators.

The next morning Morgan ordered the cannons spiked and, for good measure, buried in the sand. He had no intention of leaving any of his small force behind to garrison the fort, and he didn't want any Spanish reoccupiers to be able to contest his fleet's departure when they came back through this channel. The supplies of arms and ammunition were then loaded aboard the ships and they set sail. But then they came up against what was known as the Maracaibo

Bar: a shallow bank of quicksand around which the ships couldn't find a way without spending more time than Morgan wanted to waste.

So they fell back on a Morgan hallmark: the forty-foot, single-sail canoes that his ships always towed or carried. They were able to inconspicuously go places the seagoing ships couldn't. In Morgan's epic two-year ravaging of Central America, and in his taking of Portobello the year before, they had been his secret weapons. And so they proved now, as the men crowded aboard, sat at their benches and manned the paddles. Despite the handicap of paddling into the wind, they soon reached the shore at the foot of Maracaibo's Fort de la Barra. It turned out to be another empty fort, but this time without any traps.

"I've got to give that crazy bastard L'Ollonais credit," Morgan admitted as they walked down the deserted main street of Maracaibo. "Thanks to him, most Spaniards are so terrified of us they don't even try to resist. The more we have a reputation for doing the kind of things he did, the less we have to actually do them." He laughed. "They even make up stories about us, and come to believe the stories. I've heard that some of them even expect us to *eat* them!"

Jason and Mondrago exchanged an uneasy glance.

"According to one of our few prisoners," Morgan went on, "the captain of the garrison here called a muster of all able-bodied men. He had drums beaten, flags flown and bells rung. The poor sod found himself standing all alone in the square, looking stupid."

As they walked on, buccaneers were searching the houses on either side, alert for ambushes. But the houses were empty, their doors ajar. Just off the town square they passed a Catholic church where the buccaneers were amusing themselves by smashing crucifixes, desecrating icons and urinating into fonts like the good Protestants they were. A musket-shot rang out and the head of a saint's statue exploded. "Belay that!" Morgan shouted. "You might hit somebody."

Nesbit spoke up timidly. "Ah, Captain, how will you obtain any, well, loot now that the inhabitants have fled and hidden their valuables?"

"Oh, they always do that," said Morgan, serenely unconcerned. "Starting tomorrow, we'll start going out into the countryside to round people up. They'll ransom themselves, after questioning with the usual ceremonies." Nesbit, who now knew what that meant, blanched. "It ought to take us two or three weeks to clean out the region here around Maracaibo. Then we'll sail south to Gibraltar, at the other end of the lake."

As soon as Morgan had moved on, Nesbit turned to Jason anxiously. He had surprised Jason with his capacity to endure privations and hardships, but this was something else. "Commander, surely *we* are not going to be expected to . . . that is, actually participate in . . ."

"I'm going to do my best to arrange things so that we aren't directly involved," said Jason. It was an issue he had always hoped would not arise. He now saw that hope had been unrealistic. "But I'm afraid you may *see* some things that . . . well, we just have to stay in character."

All at once, Grenfell spoke up. He had been walking as usual with Nesbit, who since their escape in Hispaniola had more and more become his caregiver. "Anyone who shies away, or questions the methods, is suspect." His voice was hollow but alive.

"That's right, Roderick," Jason said immediately and enthusiastically, for he always tried to encourage the historian's increasingly frequent awakenings into full awareness.

"Well," Nesbit said, somewhat reassured, "however unpleasant our proximity to Morgan's historically attested exploits may be, at least your theory about the Observer Effect seems to stand confirmed."

"So it does," Mondrago nodded. "Ever since we rejoined Morgan, the Transhumanists haven't tried any funny business with us."

"Yet." Jason saw the dampening effect that one word had on his companions, but he had to be honest with them. "I didn't tell you before. But as we were entering the channel, just before our landing at the fort at San Carlos, the gravitic sensor feature of my brain implant picked up something just north of us,"

"So Romain is shadowing us," Mondrago stated rather than asked. "Have you picked it up since then?"

"No. They must have inadvertently strayed into the very short range of my sensor for that instant. So they're biding their time, hovering over the Gulf of Venezuela in the Kestrel's refraction field, totally undetectable in this era, awaiting an opportunity. We have to be on the alert for anything."

It was a very subdued group that returned to the waterfront.

CHAPTER TWENTY

Don Alonzo de Campos y Espinosa was, for the first time in years, a happy man.

He was, after all, vice admiral in command of the Armada de Barlovento—the "Windward Fleet" which was permanently stationed at Havana for the protection of Spain's colonies and the suppression of the heretic pirates. But for literally decades it had only been stationed there on paper, as was so often the case with things in the Spanish empire. The navy and the Council of the Indies had bickered endlessly while influential royal favorites had siphoned off one ship after another for their own use. Finally the depredations of the pirates—and especially that demon in human form, Henry Morgan—had grown to such proportions that the queen-regent Mariana and her regency council who governed for the mentally incompetent Carlos II had been forced to order the armada to actually set sail from Spain. But by then only five of its original dozen ships remained. That had been a year ago. Its arrival should have instantly tilted the balance of power in the Indies, for its powerfully armed ships could have obliterated the pirates' small, lightly-armed vessels without breaking a sweat. But at once the deadening tentacles of the overcentralized Spanish bureaucracy had begun to close over him, limiting his freedom of action. As always, the protection of the treasure fleets had come first, for they carried the stream of silver that prevented—or at least postponed—yet another bankruptcy of the Spanish monarchy. He had been shackled to that task, gnashing his teeth with frustration, while that never-to-be-sufficiently-damned Morgan had plundered Portobello and gotten away with his swag.

After six months of this, lack of results—although no fault of his—had caused the queen-regent to order two of his ships back to Spain. So his "fleet" was now down to three ships. Unable to effectively patrol the vast area for which he was responsible, he had come to depend more and more on a network of informers. They had reported tavern gossip of Morgan's plans to descend on the Main. Reasoning that the pirates would head east in order to take advantage of the trade winds, he had set sail for Puerto Rico and then back to Hispaniola. There, in late March, he had learned of the repulse of Morgan's men from Santo Domingo after their various cattle hunts. He had also been able to question a Dutch trader who had sold meat to pirates who had blabbed the word "Maracaibo.".

Afire with eagerness, he had immediately sent his ships racing south. And now he lay at anchor in the Gulf of Venezuela, and savored the knowledge that, at long last, Morgan lay inescapably in his grasp.

He stood on the quarterdeck of his flagship, the mighty forty-eight-gun galleon *Magdalena*. Looking out over the water, he surveyed his other two ships: *San Luis* and *Nuestra Señora de la Soledad*, with thirty-eight guns and twenty-four guns respectively. Even Morgan's flagship was a mere fourteen-gun sloop. The rest of the pirate ships were little more than glorified ketches, not a real warship in the lot. In a sea-fight, Morgan would stand no chance at all.

And it now appeared that the only way Morgan would be able to avoid such a fight—and under the most unfavorable circumstances, at that—would be by surrendering. After which he would die.

Don Alonzo turned back to the mestizo, a corporal in the local militia, who had just finished relating to him the tale of Morgan's capture of Maracaibo. "And so you say that the people here ran away and made no resistance?"

"That is true, *Almirante*," the mestizo stammered, fidgeting and wringing his hat in his hands as he addressed a man so many strata above himself in the social hierarchy of the Spanish empire as to seem almost an angelic being. "The pirates are more like ferocious beasts than men! They can appear from nowhere by sorcery! They would have devoured us all! They—"

Don Alonzo waved the wretch to silence, disgusted. His position required him to be diplomatic, whether dealing with colonial governors or cultivating informers, but privately he despised everyone in the New World. Corruption and rot were everywhere. The administrators sent out from Spain were bad enough: they bought their positions and then recouped their investment by graft and bribe-taking. Still worse were the Creoles, Spanish-descended but born in the colonies and unworthy of the blood in their veins. They had sunk into a sensual tropical torpor, devoid of ideals or honor and utterly lost to the stern crusading spirit that had swept the Moors back into Africa and conquered whole heathen empires in Mexico and Peru. Instead of laying down their lives for their king and their faith, they preferred to grovel in the mud and let the pirates walk over them in the hope (usually vain) of preserving their material possessions. Yes, they were beneath contempt. And mestizos like this one were simply beneath notice. Not to mention Indian *peons* and black slaves and the *zambos* that resulted from mixing the two.

"And afterwards," he resumed, "Morgan sailed on down the lake to Gibraltar, and is there now?"

"Yes, *Almirante*. He has been there for weeks, torturing and pillaging."

"Ah." Don Alonzo turned away, for it would not do to let this lowborn lout see eagerness trembling on the chiseled features of an *hidalgo* of Spain. Behind him, he heard *Magdalena's* captain hustle the corporal off the quarterdeck.

"Have the local pilots been brought aboard?" he demanded after a few moments.

"They have, *Almirante*," reported the flag captain. "They assure me that they can guide our ships through the hazards of the Gulf. But," he cautioned, "they tell me our ships are so deep-drafted that they cannot promise to bring us safely past the Bar of Maracaibo into the channel."

"Nor will they need to do so." Don Alonzo swung around, and now he could let his avidity show. "Don't you see? We don't need to proceed on down into the Laguna de Maracaibo and seek Morgan out. *He* must come to *us!* There's no way out of the lake except through the one eight-hundred-yard-wide channel. All we have to do is wait for him there. Any one of our three ships could blow his entire fleet out of the water."

The captain's eyes lit up. "So Morgan is trapped! He's in a bottle and we'll be the cork."

"Yes. This time we have him—he can't possibly get away." The thought energized Don Alonzo and he began rapping out orders. "We'll leave nothing to chance—remember, this is Morgan we're dealing with. Put couriers ashore with letters for the governors of Mérida and other towns requesting whatever ships and men they can send. And as soon as we arrive at the channel-mouth, we'll reoccupy the fort on San Carlos—it will be like an unsinkable fourth ship for us."

"Yes, *Almirante*." The flag captain hastened to obey.

Don Alonzo looked out over the water and sighed with contentment. The hour of divine justice had arrived for the diabolical Henry Morgan, and he himself was going to have the honor of being God's instrument.

He set himself a penance for reflecting that it also wouldn't do his career a bit of harm.

It was now mid-April. After raking over Maracaibo and the area thirty miles around it, Morgan's fleet had set sail down the lake. Following a token cannonade from Gibraltar's fort, the people of that town had fled like those of Maracaibo. Here again, the buccaneers had spent weeks scouring the surrounding countryside for prisoners. Now the fleet—grown to fourteen vessels as a result of captures, including a merchantman from Cuba that was larger than anything else Morgan had—was preparing to depart, groaning with loot.

That loot included more than the expected gold, silver and other valuables. The holds also contained slaves stolen from the local planters, who could be sold in Jamaica to feed the voracious demands of the burgeoning sugar plantations. Jason had noted that Zenobia's crew had no more trouble with this than any of the other pirates. No one in this century had any moral objection to slavery as an institution, as opposed to objecting to *being* a slave. But it was something with which Jason and his companions were less than comfortable.

Nor was that all. There had been worse. Much worse.

They sat at a rough table outside a dockside tavern, drinking plundered Spanish wine, as some last remaining cargo was loaded aboard. No one was much more talkative than Grenfell. Even Mondrago, who was hardened to battlefield behavior in many eras, stared into his wine-cup moodily. "Now I understand why pirates get drunk so much."

Nesbit, who was not so hardened, wore a haunted look. "One time," he said to no one in particular, "I saw burning matches tied between a prisoner's fingers. I saw men racked until their joints popped out. I saw a man's wrists tied together behind his back and his arms lifted straight up over his head so they broke behind the shoulders. I saw another man's face scorched with burning palm leaves until skin was hanging off in strips. I saw—"

"We all saw this stuff, Irving," said Jason. "I witnessed a woolding." It had taken all his gift of gab to avoid having to actually participate without incurring suspicion. He turned to Zenobia, who looked less affected than any of them...but then, she was accustomed to it. "At least your Maroons weren't as bad as some."

"Even though, as escaped slaves, they have reason to have a lot of resentment stored up," Mondrago added.

"I do my best," she said shortly and tossed off some wine. When she next spoke, it was with a note of defensiveness. "You can't view all this in isolation. Do you have any conception of the things the Spaniards do to prisoners? When they take a crew of 'heretics' in what they consider their waters, they cut off their hands, feet, noses and ears, and then smear them with honey, tie them to trees and leave them for the insects. Have you heard the story of what happened after the Spanish reconquest of Providence Island from the buccaneers in 1666? Under the terms of surrender, the prisoners were supposed to be returned to Jamaica. In fact they were taken to Portobello and worked to death in an enclosure knee-deep in water and exposed to the sun, packed together and chained to the floor, subjected to constant beatings. When Morgan took Portobello, he and his men liberated the few survivors...or what was left of them. They weren't likely to forget those men's stories." She took another swig of wine. "You just can't apply your standards here."

All at once, Roderick Grenfell spoke, so crisply that at first they didn't even recognize his voice. "At the same time, the more lurid stories—crucifixions, and sexual mutilation of female prisoners, and deliberate starvation of women and children—have proven to be exaggerations by Esquemeling, as has long been suspected. Doubtless his publishers wanted such sensational embellishments." Then, just as abruptly, he fell silent.

They all stared at him. It was the longest and most articulate statement they had heard out of him since that night in the hills north of the Bahia de Neiba. Eagerly, but keeping his voice calm, Jason spoke.

"That's very interesting, Roderick. Can you tell us more? Can you tell us what's going to happen to Morgan and his fleet next, after they leave Gibraltar?"

"What?" Grenfell blinked several times and met Jason's eyes ... but only briefly. His eyes slid away and he fell silent as the shadows settled over his mind again.

Jason let out his breath. The historian was improving, and Jason had no doubt that twenty-fourth-century therapists would be able to bring him around after their retrieval. But he was nowhere near fully functional now, so the group was going to have to continue to get along without detailed foreknowledge of events.

They saw Morgan advancing along the quay, ordering the last men aboard. "So, Captain," Zenobia called out, "we're off to Maracaibo and the open sea?"

"Yes, and not a minute too soon," Morgan replied, looking preoccupied. "We don't know what's going on up there ... surely the Spaniards sent messengers to Cartagena or even Panama. We need to *move.* I've released all the prisoners who've already paid their ransoms, keeping only four as security for the money still owed us." He scowled. "The freed prisoners wanted me to turn that slave over to them—the one who gave us so much valuable information on them."

If it had been possible, Zenobia would have paled. "They'd burn him alive!"

Jason knew what she meant. The buccaneers had forced the slave to kill some of the Spanish captives—a kind of initiation. He had cooperated with no noticeable hesitancy. *I wonder why?* Jason thought ironically.

"I know," said Morgan grimly. "Well, to hell with them. He was a help to us. He comes with us, and goes free. I pay my debts." Morgan moved on.

"Well," said Mondrago, quaffing the last of his wine, "we'll find out soon enough what comes next, with or without Roderick's help."

Don Alonzo de Campos y Espinosa nodded in satisfaction as the flag captain concluded his report.

"So, *Almirante*, those seventy local militiamen are now at the fort on San Carlos, to reinforce the forty of our own troops already there. And they are fully provisioned."

"Good. This time Morgan won't encounter a token garrison, as he did when he first arrived. Nine men, to serve eleven cannon!" Don Alonzo muttered with disgust.

Finding the fort deserted had been an unanticipated stroke of luck, for he had expected to have to overcome a pirate garrison. But Morgan must have gotten too greedy, wanting every available man for ransacking the coastal towns. He would live to regret his greed . . . but not for long. The Spaniards had unburied the fort's cannons and gotten six of them back in working order, and provided others from the ships.

"Send another twenty-four of our musketeers to reinforce the fort," he ordered. "We have more than enough aboard our ships."

"Yes, *Almirante*." The flag captain hurried off.

Don Alonzo walked to the quarterdeck rail and surveyed the other two ships of his command. It had not been easy, getting them all on station and holding that station, for gales from the north had threatened to blow them onto the reefs. He had ordered ballast thrown overboard to lighten ship, and the crisis had passed. *Not surprisingly,* he thought with a touch of pride in the Armada Barlovento. These were not the fat galleons of the treasure fleets, stuffed with cargo and passengers and meddling royal notaries, and captained by time-servers who had bought their lucrative commissions. No, these were fighting ships manned by trained soldiers. And now they were in position across the narrow channel that was Morgan's only escape route. The bottle was corked.

As he turned to go below to his cabin, he happened to glance northward, at the sky over the Gulf of Venezuela. *There!* He blinked and it was gone.

It wasn't the first time he had thought he glimpsed it: a little area of sky that somehow rippled or wavered, as though something was there and yet not there, hovering above the waters.

Ridiculous! he chided himself. Everyone knew that the eyes could play tricks in the dazzling sunlight of the tropics. He shook his head as though to clear it of nonsense and descended the ladder to his cabin.

CHAPTER TWENTY-ONE

"All right, everyone," said a grim Henry Morgan to the assembled captains and the *Lilly*'s crewmen who crowded around the quarterdeck. "The boat has returned. And what the old Spaniard told us is true."

There was a dead silence, broken only by a more than usually eloquent grunt from Roche Braziliano.

They had arrived at Maracaibo the day before, after a four-day voyage up the lake from Gibraltar. They had found the town deserted save for one sick old man who—perhaps resentful at his fellows for leaving him behind—had told them that three Spanish ships lay in wait at the narrowest point of the channel, where the fort was now fully manned and armed, and could have commanded the passage by itself. Morgan had immediately sent his fastest boat to investigate. It had returned today with confirmation.

"And it's even worse than we thought," Morgan continued inexorably. "These aren't just any Spanish ships. They're war galleons, with forty-eight, thirty-eight and twenty-four guns. There's no question—it's got to be the Armada de Barlovento. And they have us trapped."

"How did they know we were here?" Roche Braziliano wondered, furrowing his brow so intensely it practically disappeared.

"How else?" said Zenobia scornfully. "Loose talk by some of our men back in Hispaniola."

"Naturally," said Mondrago in a sneering undertone, and even at this moment Jason had to smile. The Corsican was what might be called a security snob. He was firmly convinced—not altogether without reason—that no one in past eras had had any inkling of counterintelligence.

Everyone else broke into a babble of nervous muttering, knowing that the least of those three Spanish ships was more than a match for their entire fleet. Morgan was uncharacteristically silent, seemingly lost in thought, which added to the general nervousness. If *he* was discouraged...

Suddenly, Morgan stood up and the hubbub stilled. All eyes were riveted on him. The brooding silence stretched.

"Well, there's only one thing to do," he said slowly. "I'll send a letter to the Spanish admiral—"

What's this? He's going to surrender? thought Jason incredulously. *That can't be... can it?*

"—demanding that he pay us a hefty ransom, and telling him that otherwise we'll burn Maracaibo to a cinder."

For a couple of heartbeats, everyone goggled in absolute silence. Then an explosion of laughter and cheering burst forth, with an unmistakable undertone of relief. This was still Henry Morgan.

Jason was certain that his lower jaw must be touching the deck.

Morgan must have noticed his expression, for he turned to him with a smile and spoke as though explaining something that ought to be self-evident. "Remember, Jason: always behave as though you have the upper hand."

"Even when you don't?"

Morgan's smile widened. "*Especially* when you don't!"

The captain of *Magdalena* looked like he was in danger of having a stroke.

"Morgan's insolence is beyond belief! Is there no limit to the effrontery of this scoundrel? Surely he must be possessed by the Devil. With your permission, *Almirante*, I will immediately order the hanging of the pirate scum who brought us this insultingly preposterous demand."

Don Alonzo gestured his flag captain to silence. He turned back to the heavy oaken table in his cabin and ran his eyes over Morgan's letter one more time. He shook his head.

"No. For one thing, I must reluctantly admire this messenger's boldness. And besides, I intend to use him to convey my reply to Morgan."

"*What?* But . . . but surely, *Almirante*, you do not mean to dignify this letter with a response!"

"But I do. I will make Morgan a counterproposal. If he will off-load his captives and all his loot and slaves, and return to Jamaica peaceably, I will offer to allow him to pass unmolested."

The flag captain tried several times to speak. When he finally succeeded, it was in a voice choked by the conflict between his indignation and his fear of straying over the line into insubordination. "*Almirante*, you would demean yourself by negotiating with this Lutheran pig! And your orders are to exterminate piracy in these waters. Surely you cannot intend to disregard those orders by letting him go!"

Don Alonzo shot him an irritated look. "Don't be absurd. As you yourself have repeatedly pointed out, Morgan is both a heretic and a pirate."

"Ah!" The flag captain's features smoothed themselves out into a smile as understanding dawned. "And either would suffice to release you from any promises to him."

"You've grasped it. Now please summon my secretary so I can dictate a letter."

"Well," said Morgan two days later, "I'll say this for Don Alonzo. At least the tone of his letter is appropriately courteous, as one gentleman to another. Not like Don Agustín de Bracamonte, the governor of Panama." Blood rushed to his face and he scowled at the recollection. "After I captured Portobello last year I sent him a letter demanding ransom for the city. Do you know what he wrote in reply? He called me a *pirate!* Me! A pirate! Can you imagine? When I had a perfectly legal commission from Governor Modyford, with everything in order. A *pirate!* Ha!" Morgan got himself under control with an effort, and soothed his injured feelings with a slug of rum. After a year, he was obviously still seething about it.

They sat in the desecrated church near the square, which Morgan had been using for his headquarters. Several of the captains were there, as were some members of *Lilly*'s crew, including Jason. Zenobia spoke up as soon as Morgan had regained his composure.

"Courteous or not, do you really believe his offer of free passage?"

"No. I believe he wants to lure us into the channel and sink us without the treasure going to the bottom in deep water. But I owe it to the men to put this before them fairly." Morgan finished his rum and stood up. "Come on. They all ought to be gathered in the square by now."

They walked the short distance to the marketplace, which was packed with almost the entire personnel of the fleet, waiting in uncharacteristic silence. Morgan hitched himself up on a cart and waved Don Alonzo's letter.

"We have the Spanish admiral's reply," he began, then proceeded to read them the letter. Afterwards he handed it to a French buccaneer to translate for the benefit of his countrymen in the crowd. Then he stepped forward and addressed the still-silent assembly.

"You've heard Don Alonzo's offer: we can go back to Jamaica in safety if we go empty-handed. You've also heard his warning that he'll put every one of us to the sword if we refuse. So what is our choice to be?"

An indignant roar arose.

"Trust a Spaniard?" someone jeered over the din.

"Those men on Providence Island did," shouted someone else. "And we saw what happened to them, in the dungeons at Portobello!"

The roar grew ugly.

"But," came a hesitant demurer, "this Don *might* be a man of his word. And—" Whatever else the speaker was going to say was drowned in catcalls. One bellowing voice rose over them.

"I don't give a tinker's damn if he *is* being honest!

Are we to meekly give up all we've fought for and slink back to Port Royal as beggars, to starve or maybe sell ourselves into indenture so we can at least eat slops?"

Now the roar rose to a unanimous thunder of *No! No!*

Morgan stepped forward and raised his arms. The noise instantly subsided.

"All right. We're agreed. We'll fight rather than accept the Spaniard's offer. So we're back to the question of *how* to fight when we stand no chance at all."

This brought them back down to Earth. A gloomy silence settled over the square. Morgan, with his usual uncanny sense of timing, let it last just long enough.

"No, we stand no chance in the kind of fight they expect—that is, if we do it their way, which is the only way they know. But there's another way." Again, Morgan paused for a precisely calibrated moment. "I'm thinking of that big Cuban merchant ship we captured at Gibraltar. Here's my idea." He outlined it in a few swift sentences, and as he spoke the buccaneers' silence turned to one of excited eagerness.

Out of the corner of his eye, Jason noticed Grenfell stirring. The historian blinked several times, and his eyes seemed to clear. "*Yes!* I remember now. How could I have forgotten?" Nesbit clasped his shoulder, then turned and met Jason's eyes. They exchanged a nod.

"Now," Morgan concluded, "that's just a rough idea. To make it work, I need everyone's ideas. The first question is: *can* it work?"

"Aye, Captain!" someone called out. "I've worked with such things before. We have all the materials we need."

"Good! You'll show everyone what to do. Can anybody think of any problems?"

"That Cuban tub doesn't have many gunports," Captain Lawrence Prince pointed out.

"So we'll cut new ones," said the first speaker.

Not for the first time, Jason couldn't help being struck by the rude, crude but democratic way the buccaneers reached decisions and then brainstormed the best way of implementing them—so different from the rigidly top-down management style of the Spaniards and, indeed, of everyone in this century. Cruel, greedy and debauched the Brethren of the Coast might be, but they were a straw in the wind of the future—a wind that was going to blow away the last lingering cobwebs of feudalism.

"The people who fled from this town are still hiding in the surrounding hills," observed Captain John Morris, always a voice of caution. "They'll be able to spy on us, and get word to the Spanish admiral of what we're up to."

To Jason's surprise Mondrago piped up. "I might be able to help with that, Captain. I know something about, well, keeping things you're doing secret and maybe making the enemy think you're doing something else." The current language held no such word as *disinformation*.

"Splendid! What do you suggest?"

"Well," said the Corscian, ignoring Nesbit's obvious disapproval of his potential impropriety, "first of all, the prisoners and the slaves must be kept shut away in isolation, so they can see nothing of what's going on, and carefully guarded so they can't escape."

"Excellent idea." Morgan beamed. "All right, everyone, let's get busy. Meanwhile, I'll send the Spanish admiral another letter to gain us a little time."

⚜   ⚜   ⚜

"All well and good," Nesbit had persisted. "But what about you, personally? Our escape from the Transhumanists has left us in possession of absolutely priceless information about them and their Teloi allies. It is essential that we remain alive until our retrieval date—especially you, with the imagery on your recorder implant. It would be irresponsible to risk your life in the pursuit of mere adventure!"

"Why, Irving!" Jason had grinned. "I thought you were the one lusting for adventure."

Nesbit had had the grace to look abashed. "I've come to understand the classic literary definition of 'adventure': someone *else* having a horrible time hundreds of years ago and thousands of miles away."

"With you sitting in an easy chair, reading about it and sipping a tall cool one," Jason had finished for him. "But more to the point, Roderick has been able to assure us that the crew of *Satisfaction* got away alive. So for once, adventure should be risk-free."

Nesbit had had no answer for that. So now Jason and the other eleven volunteers who crewed *Satisfaction* gazed ahead in the dawn as a strong wind out of the lagoon filled their sails and swept their ship and two others alongside it—including *Lilly*, with Morgan aboard—toward the waiting galleons. The smaller vessels, *Rolling-Calf* among them, followed slightly behind.

As they came into range, fiery broadsides belched from the Spanish ships, followed a second later by the crashing report of the guns. Cannonballs whistled overhead, punching through the canvass of the sails. Morgan's ships returned fire, but the sound of their guns seemed weak and futile against the thunder of the Spanish broadsides. Nevertheless, they continued on down the wind, drawing closer and closer, even though deadly splinters were starting to fly as the Spanish scored hits.

As they approached, Jason allowed himself to feel relief. Despite all their precautions, a black captive who may have had knowledge of what they were about had escaped. (Mondrago was still fulminating about it, declaring that these people were unteachable.) But evidently the escapee hadn't made it to the Spanish fleet, or if he had his warning had gone unheeded.

"It's time!" Jason called out to the others as the Spanish flagship loomed ahead. No further steering was needed now; the wind could do it all. "Abandon ship!"

He scurried across the deck, amid the smell of tar, pitch and brimstone smeared over palm leaves. Men ran about, lighting the fuses of the "cannons"— logs filled with gunpowder—that jutted from the new gunports. Other men emerged from the hold, where the shipwrights had removed all superfluous partitions. They waited just long enough to hurl grappling hooks at the galleon *Satisfaction* was now almost touching, catching its rigging. Then, one by one, everyone jumped over the stern, out of sight of the Spaniards. Jason paused a second, smiling, and wished godspeed to the "crewmen" who were remaining aboard—the ones made out of combustible materials on wooden frames, with soft *montera* hats atop their heads and cutlasses propped at their sides. Then he went over the side into the water and swam to one of the canoes that *Satisfaction* had been towing at a distance.

Behind him, the two ships collided.

✠   ✠   ✠

Don Alonzo watched through his spyglass with growing amazement as the pirate ships continued to bear down on *Magdalena*, making no attempt to draw away. His gunners had repeatedly lowered the muzzles of their guns as the range closed, and now they were firing point-blank. He could see the cutlass-wielding figures aboard Morgan's new flagship, and even though they were heretics he had to admire their unmoving steadiness under fire. Yes, he had been right; they were going for a boarding action.

On and on the ship came, propelled by the stiff morning wind, heedless of the cannonade, until with a grinding crash it rammed into *Magdalena*, entangling the two ships' rigging with the help of grappling hooks. The Spanish infantry, drilled to a high pitch of anticipation, didn't wait for the pirates to board but swarmed forward with a shout, scrambling over the side onto the pirate ship's deck...where they stood, bewildered.

Something is wrong, thought Don Alonzo, watching from the poop. *Why aren't they fighting?* He saw one of his men step up to a motionless pirate and tap his cutlass, which fell to the deck.

At that moment, the wind blew the smell of tar over palm leaves into his nostrils.

The day before, one of the informants from shore—a black who had escaped from captivity—had claimed that Morgan wasn't really turning the Cuban merchantman into his new flagship. But when he had told Don Alonzo what the pirates *were* doing to it, the admiral had scoffed, for what he had described involved a specialized branch of naval expertise, surely beyond the capabilities of this scruffy rabble of pirates.

Now he remembered what that black man had told him. And with the recollection came the most dreaded word anyone could hear in the naval warfare of the Age of Sail: *Fireship!*

Just as the word flashed through his brain, Hell erupted.

CHAPTER TWENTY-TWO

The Spanish boarders were literally blown aloft as *Satisfaction* went up in a veritable fireball, and a shower of flaming debris rained down into *Magdalena's* flammable sails and rigging. The canvas sails and fat-covered ropes caught fire immediately, and the strong south wind swept the conflagration over the decks and up the masts. Fleeing, screaming men were wrapped in flame before they could jump overboard.

"Fight the fires!" roared Don Alonzo, who had ordered barrels of water placed on the decks for this very purpose. "Cut the grappling lines and push off! Throw planks overboard for the men in the water!"

But his orders could not be carried out in the roaring inferno that *Magdalena* was swiftly becoming. As the fire began to engulf the stern, the flag captain turned to him. "*Almirante*, you must abandon ship before you are trapped by the flames! I will have a rope ladder lowered for you."

Heartsick, Don Alonzo nodded.

✠   ✠   ✠

From their canoe, Jason and the men with him watched the incredible Spanish debacle unfold as the sun rose higher in the smoky sky.

They saw the burning *Magdalena* go down bow-first in a hiss of steam, and as she did, chaos and confusion infected the rest of the Spanish squadron. *Soledad*, the smallest Spanish ship, tried desperately to break off from the vicinity of the fire, but her rigging grew so tangled that she soon ceased to be navigable. Unable to maneuver, she was soon swarmed by buccaneer craft led by *Lilly* and a wave of boarders led by Morgan himself poured up her sides as her panic-stricken crew jumped overboard. The third galleon, *San Luis*, headed for the protection of the fort's guns, but ran aground. Her crew began to frantically offload as much of her provisions and munitions as possible.

And, in the same direction, they saw a longboat making for San Carlos, carrying a passenger wearing a splendid, if bedraggled and soot-stained cloak.

"It must be the Spanish admiral!" someone in another canoe shouted. "After him!"

Jason and the others grasped their paddles and started in pursuit. But the longboat had too great a head start, and the canoes had to pull away as Don Alonzo stumbled ashore on the beach under the fortress walls. Shortly afterwards, smoke began to rise from *San Luis*.

"Yes, *Almirante*," reported the captain of *San Luis*, "I scuttled my ship and burned her down to the waterline."

"Good," said Don Alonzo, looking out from the fort's battlements. "That's one ship Morgan won't have."

He could barely force the words out through a throat choked with fury as he saw Morgan's flag flying from *Soledad*. He also saw pirate boats clustered where *Magdalena* had sunk, and divers plunging down into the waters to retrieve loot from the wreck.

By a supreme effort of will, he forced both rage and depression from his mind, clearing it for what must now be done. He turned and looked down into a courtyard crowded with the crew of *San Luis* and whatever survivors of the other two ships as had made it ashore, as well as with the garrison. All were milling about, stunned.

"We must get these men in order immediately," he told the fort's castellan, "and prepare for an attack. Morgan will undoubtedly mount one as soon as he is able, for he knows he must take this fort." He drew himself up and gazed sternly at the semicircle of dejected officers before him. When he spoke, it was as though they heard the ringing voice of the old Spain, the Spain of the *Reconquista*. "Remember: *we still have Morgan trapped!* He still must pass through this channel, which our guns command. The messengers we sent out a week ago must have reached Mérida and Caracas and their other destinations, which means that ships and men are on their way. All we have to do is keep Morgan bottled up until they arrive. Time is on our side, gentlemen!"

"Time is on their side," Henry Morgan admitted that night as he and his captains met under the stars on the quarterdeck of *Soledad*. ("I've had a lot of flagships lately," he had quipped.) Elsewhere, the buccaneers were celebrating the miraculous annihilation of the Armada de Barlovento. But here the mood was, if not precisely sober—there was too much rum flowing for that—certainly somewhat subdued.

"We've seen that storming the fort from the beach isn't going to work," he continued. "Isn't that right, Jason?"

"Aye, captain." Jason had been part of a landing force Morgan had put ashore late that very afternoon, hoping to ride the momentum of his incredible victory at sea and take the fort while its defenders were still demoralized. "The Spanish admiral must have put heart into that garrison. We tried to rush the walls at dusk. But we could do nothing, with only muskets and fire-balls." The latter, the primitive grenades of the period, were favorite pirate weapons. But they had proven ineffectual against the blistering fire from walls that this time were fully manned and resupplied with artillery. "We lost thirty men dead and a lot more wounded before returning to the ships."

"Well," said Zenobia, "we'll have to do something about that fort. You know damned well that the Spanish admiral sent for reinforcements as soon as he got here. We've got to leave before they arrive, and those guns would play havoc with us as we tried to run the channel."

"True," Morgan nodded, with a thoughtful swallow of rum. "But on the other hand, we have allies."

"We do?" Roche Braziliano's scowl deepened with perplexity. "Who?"

"Why, the good citizens of Maracaibo!" Morgan grinned. "They want us gone as soon as possible, with their city unburned. That means their interests are closer to ours than to Don Alonzo's. I'll send him a letter offering to leave the town standing in exchange for free passage out."

"He won't accept it," one of the captains predicted. "He'd see a dozen Maracaibos burned rather than let us escape."

"Of course he won't. But at the same time I'll tell the locals we'll release the prisoners, spare the city and leave in exchange for a ransom. They'll pay it—especially after I let them bargain me down a bit. But after they do, I'll tell them that we *can't* leave with the fortress guns commanding the channel, and that they have to send representatives to Don Alonzo and persuade him to let us go. To encourage them to do their utmost, I'll keep their fellow townspeople as hostages."

Zenobia's teeth flashed white against her dark face in the light of the ship's lanterns. "Very clever, Captain. Do you think it will work?"

"It's worth a try." Morgan finished his rum. "And now I have a guest awaiting me in the cabin: the pilot of *Magdalena*. We fished him out of the water."

"Throw him back in," grunted Roche Braziliano. "With his big toes tied together."

"That would hardly be the act of a gentleman," declared Morgan with a loftiness Jason thought he carried off surprisingly well. "I am treating him as an honored prisoner of war. And besides," he continued, with a slowly spreading smile, "he's so grateful for— and probably surprised by—his generous treatment that he's proving a useful source of information on various things I need to know . . . such as how Don Alonzo de Campos y Espinosa's mind works."

The delegation of Maracaibo's leading citizens cringed before Don Alonzo's wrath.

"You contemptible, pusillanimous cowards!" the admiral roared, standing up behind his desk in the castellan's office and leaning forward as though to intensify his glare. "You make me ashamed to call myself a Spaniard! Instead of standing and fighting when these pirates first arrived, you fled for your miserable lives. And now you've groveled at Morgan's feet, paying the ransom he demands for sparing your wretched town."

"Oh, no, *Almirante*," one merchant denied timidly. "Rest assured, we didn't pay the ransom he wanted. We got him down from thirty thousand pieces of eight to only twenty thousand. Alas, he wouldn't budge on the five hundred beeves, but—"

"Silence, clown! I don't want to hear about the haggling of greasy hucksters. In the end, you paid. And now you come crawling to me, begging me to forget my duty and let Morgan sail away with his loot. Your degradation is so complete that you're willing to act as this heretic pirate's spokesmen!"

"No, *Almirante*," protested one man, bolder than the rest. "We speak not for Morgan but for our families and friends he is holding as hostages. They will be at Morgan's mercy if you do not let his fleet go unmolested."

"He can hang the lot for all I care! You have no one but your own craven selves to blame. Creep back to Morgan and tell him that I know my duty to my king, and that no threats to unworthy subjects like you will prevent me for carrying it out. Now get out of my sight! You disgust me."

As the soldiers hustled the delegation out, Don Alonzo got his breathing under control and turned to the castellan. "Are my orders concerning the landward approaches to the fort being carried out?"

"Yes, *Almirante*. New trenches and earthworks have been prepared in those positions, and procedures for moving our artillery there on short notice have been put in place and practiced."

"Good. We've repulsed Morgan when he attacked from the sea; he won't try that again. And remember what happened at Portobello. He put his men ashore with those canoes of his and took the great fortresses guarding that city by assault from the land side, where they were most vulnerable. It's a weakness of all our works, including this one—they're designed to control sea approaches. But I don't intend for that to happen here."

"It won't, *Almirante*," the castellan stated emphatically. "You have my word: this fort will not be taken by a land assault."

He turned out to be right.

"Well," said Henry Morgan philosophically to the group on *Soledad*'s quarterdeck, "it was worth a try. And the time hasn't been wasted. We've finished getting all we can out of *Magdalena*." His eyes held an avaricious gleam. "Fifteen or twenty thousand pieces of eight—it's hard to say exactly, since some of it was melted into globs of silver by the fire." The gleam died, and he gave a disappointed headshake. "According to my friend the pilot, there was a total of *forty* thousand aboard. But that's all the divers can reach."

Mondrago leaned over and whispered in Jason's ear. "He's being awfully nonchalant for somebody who's still bottled up here."

"And who knows that time is against him," Jason whispered back. "He must have something up his sleeve."

Grenfell spoke hesitantly. "I think I'm beginning to remember..." But his voice trailed vaguely off.

"So what does that bring our total up to?" Zenobia wanted to know.

"Ah, yes!" Morgan's eyes lit up again. "Counting that and also the ransom from the townspeople, it comes to at least 250,000 pieces of eight." There was a collective gasp. "And that's just the money and jewels; it doesn't count the merchandise—of which there's quite a lot—and the slaves."

"That's more than we got at Portobello," someone breathed in a tone of what could only be called reverence.

"And more than L'Ollonais got when he came here," rumbled Roche Braziliano, almost forgetting to scowl. Everyone else was speechless. This was a haul of legendary proportions.

"We'll make the division now," Morgan continued. "Each ship will carry its own crew's share. Putting it all aboard one ship would be risky." He didn't elaborate on whether the risk was of storms at sea or of the one ship's captain getting funny ideas.

Jason could keep silent no longer. "Ah, Captain... I hate to mention it, but this treasure won't do us much good unless we can get home with it." There was a general muttering as everyone came down from the clouds of cupidity with a bump.

"Oh, that," said Morgan, as though voicing an afterthought with a Welsh lilt. "Well, I think I might have an idea. You see, I've been talking to the Spanish pilot about Don Alonzo. He's told me quite a lot. For example, he's confirmed that Don Alonzo never had any intention of honoring his promise of free passage."

He shook his head sadly, as though disillusioned to the core of his sensitive soul by the depths of human perfidy. "Anyway, between things he's told me, and what our scouting boats have reported about the work the Spaniards have been doing on the landward side of the fort, it's clear to me that they expect us to attack from that direction, the way we did at Portobello."

"Makes sense," nodded Zenobia. "Too bad their artillery would blow us to bloody rags."

"Still," Morgan mused, "it seems a shame to disappoint them. Here's my plan..."

As he spoke, Grenfell's eyes cleared and he began nodding excitedly.

Don Alonzo stood on the battlements in the afternoon sun and watched the parade of canoes through his spyglass.

The pirate fleet lay beyond gunshot, and there its ships loaded men into canoes—about twenty men per canoe. Then the canoes were rowed ashore to a spot toward the island's far end, beyond a line of mangroves. Then they would return to the ships—slowly, for on the return trip they carried only a couple of oarsmen—to pick up another load of men. It had been going on for hours. Now it appeared that the last of the canoes were headed back to the ships.

"Have you kept a tally of canoes and men as I instructed?" Don Alonzo demanded of the castellan.

"I have, *Almirante*. The total number of men who have gone ashore and remained there comes to more than half of Morgan's entire force."

"And now they wait concealed behind those mangroves, from which they will undoubtedly emerge and attack us tonight," said Don Alonzo with a satisfied nod, pleased at the confirmation of his prediction. "But we are ready for them."

"Indeed, *Almirante*." The two men looked down over the parapet, where the last of the great cannon, on its cumbersome four-wheeled garrison carriage, was being laboriously trundled along the ramp prepared for the purpose, and emplaced in its new position on the landward earthworks, to join all its fellows. It had been an exhausting task, and the men now rested beside their guns. Behind them were neat stacks of ammunition—not the ship-smashing round shot, but case shot whose spreading pattern of musket balls and scrap metal could shred whole squads of advancing infantry at short range. Companies of musketeers also rested at their stations along the line of fortifications. All that firepower was perfectly positioned to cover the cleared area that the attackers must cross.

"We will slaughter them when they advance beyond the mangroves into the open," the castellan stated confidently. "The darkness won't shield them—there'll be enough of a moon, and as you can see we have an ample supply of torches prepared." Then, with the barest hesitation: "Er, *Almirante*, it is of course unnecessary to point out that we now have no guns pointing seaward."

"Nor do we need them. This is the one time when we can be absolutely certain that Morgan is *not* going to try to run the channel." Don Alonzo waved in the direction of the mangroves. "Not even a godless pirate would sail away and leave the majority of his own men stranded."

"Ah." The castellan nodded. "I understand."

⚜   ⚜   ⚜

Jason couldn't decide which was more unpleasant: the brackish bilge-water in which he lay flat on his back, or the highly aromatic buccaneers pressed tightly against him, sardinelike, in the bottom of the canoe.

None too soon, the seemingly empty canoe scraped against the side of *Soledad*—the side hidden from the view of the fort, naturally. The concealed men in the canoe got stiffly up and climbed aboard using ropes hanging from the rail. They hastened below, out of sight.

The gun deck was crowded with other wet, tired but grinning men who had gone ashore sitting up in the canoes, fully armed and conspicuous, and then, concealed by the mangroves, laid down behind the gunwales and returned to the ships, supine and invisible. One of them was Mondrago.

"Well," he greeted Jason, "yours was one of the last canoes. I heard Morgan say we mustn't overdo it; the Spaniards will never believe that we've landed any more men than those that have already shuttled back and forth between ships and shore." He gave his head an incredulous shake. He had still not gotten over his awe at Morgan's preposterously simple but brilliant ploy.

Morgan came down the ladder, greeting men by name and cracking jokes. "When do you plan to set sail, Captain?" asked Jason.

"Oh, I don't think I'll set sail at all, at least at first. It would make us more conspicuous. No, I believe that after nightfall I'll simply weigh anchor and let the ebbing tide carry us out of the channel. With all the sails furled, we'll be almost invisible at night. When we draw level with the fort, *then* we'll pile on all the canvas we've got."

⚜   ⚜   ⚜

"Hasn't the patrol been heard from yet?" demanded Don Alonzo irritably, staring into the darkness beyond the landward fortifications.

The sun had set and no attack had come. Finally, in a fit of impatience, he had ordered a patrol to be sent out to probe beyond the mangrove barrier and, perhaps, prick the pirates into some reaction—or at least find out what they were up to, and why the expected attack hadn't materialized.

"No, *Almirante*," the castellan reported. "They should have made some kind of contact with the pirates by now. But—"

"*Ships in the channel!*" screamed a lookout from the seaward battlements.

Don Alonzo and the castellan stared at each other wide-eyed. Then they ran along the ramparts to the seaward side, where they could gaze out over the channel. Even in the moonlight, Don Alonzo could see it was thick with pirate vessels. As he watched, their sails began to blossom out and catch the night breeze, and they swept ahead faster.

"Get the guns back up here!" he bellowed.

"Impossible, *Almirante*," protested the castellan. And Don Alonzo knew he was right. Manhandling those guns to the landward side had been an afternoon's work.

"*Almirante*," someone else cried out, "the patrol is back."

The young *teniente* in command of the patrol ran up and dropped to one knee, gasping for breath. "Your pardon, *Almirante*, but we advanced cautiously to the mangroves and beyond, and encountered no one. So we continued on, which is why I am so late in reporting." He took another deep breath. "We found nothing, anywhere."

"*What?*" Don Alonzo loomed over the young man, seething with fury. "Idiot! You must have missed them!"

"As God is my witness, *Almirante*, there is not a single pirate on this island!"

And as the pirate ships vanished into the dark of the Gulf of Venezuela, seven guns crashed out in a mocking farewell salute.

CHAPTER TWENTY-THREE

When it came to weather, Henry Morgan's luck had always been as legendary as it was with most other things. In all his expeditions he had never encountered a really dangerous storm at sea.

But in the Caribbean, no one's weather-luck can last forever. Morgan's chose to run out the day after their departure from the Laguna de Maracaibo, when they still had to worry about being driven back onto the shore.

"Is this technically a hurricane?" shouted Mondrago over the howling of the wind, the crashing of the thunder and the creaking and groaning of the ship's frame as he and Jason clung to the shrouds and ratlines for dear life, lashed by rain and spray.

Jason was opening his mouth to reply when *Soledad*—Morgan hadn't gotten around to renaming her—plunged down yet another mountainous wave into the trough below. A sheet of water roared the length of the ship, battering the wind from their lungs and almost knocking them off their feet. The ship struggled aright, wallowing, as water poured off the deck into the scuppers through the waterways along the bulwarks. Jason lost his grip but managed to grab a mainmast backstay before he could be swept overboard. He coughed out the salt water that had forced itself in before he had managed to close his mouth, and gasped for breath.

"This isn't quite hurricane season," he finally wheezed. "It generally begins in June. And the normal hurricane area is further north. But this is a damned serious tropical storm." He'd barely finished the sentence before he had to duck to avoid being brained by a flying piece of broken tackle. The ropes of loose rigging were like whips in the wind.

Morgan, fearful of finding himself back ashore and at the highly problematical mercy of the Spaniards, had tried anchoring in five- or six-fathom water—about thirty to thirty-six feet deep—and riding out the storm. But the tempest had intensified, and he'd had no choice but to weigh anchor and face into the waves. Jason and Mondrago were part of the shift now laboring topside to keep the ship afloat. Nesbit and Grenfell were both below, manning the pumps. Jason tried to imagine what it must be like aboard the undecked boats.

"I tell you," an older than-average buccaneer cried out a few feet from them, "this fleet is cursed! It's *her!*" He pointed theatrically across the water. Even in the gloom, *Rolling-Calf* was close enough to be seen. "Everybody knows a woman at sea is bad luck. She's bought it on all our ships."

A brief lull in the wind allowed another man to make himself heard. "She's not just a woman—she's a witch! They can stir up hurricanes by tossing a pinch of sea sand into the air, or by stirring the water in a pot with their bare feet."

"And who knows what a *black* witch can do?" jittered the first man. "That must be it. She wants to sink us all!"

"But," Jason pointed out, "she's caught in this storm with the rest of us."

"Ah, have you no wit, mate? The Devil takes care of his own—he'll pluck her out while the rest of us drown. I once knew a man who said he saw—"

"Belay that talk!" bellowed Henry Morgan, making his unsteady way toward them along the rolling, lurching deck. "What are you, seamen or frightened children? We're all in this together—everyone in the fleet. Now put your backs into—"

Whatever else he was going to say vanished tracelessly in a shrieking roar of renewed wind, and *Soledad* breasted a wave even more titanic than the last one. This time the helmsman was unable to keep her bow-on, and as she came down she slewed to starboard. So the brutal onrush of foaming seawater went athwartships, causing her to heel over.

Jason, alongside the starboard rail, clung desperately to the backstay. But it snapped free, and he went over the side. Mondrago tried to grasp him by the arm, but failed. At that moment Morgan, who hadn't been grasping anything secure, slid to starboard and his heavy body crashed into Mondrago's.

The three of them hit the water almost together.

Jason, his lungs almost rupturing with the agony of suffocation, struggled up to the surface. Frantically treading water while sucking in wheezing gasps of breath, he saw that the sudden gust had subsided and they were again between waves. He also saw the bobbing heads of Morgan and Mondrago not far away. And he saw *Soledad*'s receding stern.

He knew that crying after her for help would be futile, even had his lungs been up to outshouting the wind. A hopelessness too leaden for panic suffused him.

Then a female voice came thinly through the wind, crying "Grab the lines!" He looked around and saw *Rolling-Calf* coming alongside in the relatively calm water. Crewmen were flinging out ropes, one of which splashed into the water nearby. With more strength than he'd thought he had left in him, he swam for it and clutched it, winding it around his midriff. A pair of Maroons hauled him aboard. As he collapsed on the deck and lay there drawing heaving, shuddering breaths, he watched Mondrago being likewise lifted of the gunwale, as was Morgan—with somewhat more difficulty—after another moment.

"Captain Morgan!" said Zenobia, descending from the poop. "Thank God! And—" She turned to the other two rescued men, and halted as her eyes met Jason's.

"Thank you," he said, inadequately.

"Well, well!" Her mocking smile was back. "Who would ever have thought I'd save . . ." Her voice trailed off as she remembered Morgan was in earshot. He got laboriously to his feet.

"Aye, lass, thank you indeed!" Morgan looked at the sky. "What do you think? Is the worst past?"

"I fear not, Captain. This is just a lull. There's more yet to come." Zenobia stepped back up to the poop, and the three men joined her. She pointed over the taffrail. "Look back there. You see—"

A scream split the air. They whirled and saw one of the Maroons, standing amidships, pointing aloft. He fell to his knees, moaning. His crewmates followed suit.

Jason and the others looked up. Overhead, an

arrowhead-shaped segment of the leaden sky was rippling and wavering in a way that was clearly unnatural. Still more unnatural was the sudden appearance, about midway along that region's length, of a sharply defined rectangle of dim light seemingly suspended in midair.

Jason barely had time to recognize what he was seeing when his body was seized in an invisible, rubbery, unbreakable grip. He and the others on the poop began to float upward, toward the rectangle of light.

A roar of enraged incomprehension burst from Morgan's lips as his feet lost contact with the deck. It subsided into inarticulate grunts as he struggled and thrashed in midair against the immaterial force holding him. The other three did nothing. They knew too well what was happening to them, and the uselessness of resistance.

They ascended more and more swiftly, borne aloft by that irresistible force, and the open rectangle—the Kestrel's cargo hatch—engulfed them. A refraction field was carried by a grid in a vehicle's surface, and formed mere millimeters from that surface, so that when the hatch slid aside it left a gap in the field. Once inside the partly empty space that was the cargo hold, they hung suspended just under the hemispherical device set in the overhead which projected the remotely focused gravitic effect known as a tractor beam. Then the hatch slid shut below them with a clang, forming a deck onto which they were unceremoniously dumped as the tractor beam was switched off. Through the bulkheads came the hum that told Jason that they were bound somewhere else on the wings of grav repulsion, leaving Morgan's storm-tossed fleet behind.

For a moment, they simply lay there in silence.

In that moment, Jason had time to stare at Morgan and think, *This can't be right! What happened to the Observer Effect? We've been counting on it. Nothing is supposed to happen to Morgan at this point. Something should have prevented them from grabbing him! History says he got back from Maracaibo, pillaged Panama the following year, got knighted and made Lieutenant Governor of Jamaica, and so forth.*

He felt a sickening sensation of mental free fall as his accustomed structure of assumptions seemed to crumble away from beneath his feet, leaving him plunging into a chaos that did not bear contemplating.

So perhaps I know how Morgan feels right now.

But Morgan recovered before he did. The buccaneer admiral stood slowly up. He instinctively started to draw the cutlass at his side, but then dropped his hand as though recognizing the gesture's futility. He looked around slowly in the dim electric light. He seemed to take in the background hum, a type of sound that had never been heard on Earth in 1669. His eyes—quite black in that illumination—were wide as they stared at surroundings that held not a single familiar or even comprehensible reference point. Those eyes took in the composite plasteel of the decks and bulkheads, which his world could never have cast in metal. They blinked at the lights that shone without fire. Then they finally came to rest on his three companions . . . and particularly on Zenobia.

I was wrong, Jason decided. *I can't know what he's feeling. He's a highly intelligent man—a bleeding genius in a low kind of way—but he's still a product of a society that hasn't entirely left the Middle Ages behind. His eyes—the eyes of a man who fears very little—hold a kind of fear I can never feel, because I grew up in a society that accepts rationalism as unquestioningly as the Middle Ages accepted the supernatural.*

Sooner than Jason would have thought possible, Morgan found his voice. "So," he said slowly to Zenobia, "you really *are* a—"

Zenobia shook her head. "No, Captain Morgan. It's not what you think. This has nothing to do with the powers of darkness. We're in a vessel that can fly through the air—but not by sorcery. The people who command it are very evil, but they're not witches or warlocks. Their evil is of the ordinary human sort— and we all know the kinds of things we're capable of doing to each other without any help from Satan."

"And these people who've captured us are our enemies," Jason put in. "Actually, some of them *aren't* human. But even those are not demons, even though Zenobia's Maroon followers believe they are."

"And the Maroons really aren't all that far wrong," Mondrago muttered. Jason reflected that it was just as well that Irving Nesbit was still aboard *Soledad*. He probably would have been going into cardiac arrest at this point, listening to the frankness with which they were speaking to Morgan, who had no right to be here at all.

Once again, Morgan stared at the three of them in turn. An average human of this century would, Jason thought, have been gibbering by now, or else too deeply in shock even to gibber. But if there was one adjective which did *not* describe Henry Morgan, it was "average." He drew himself up into an unconscious stance of command, and his features hardened into a mask of iron.

"Who are you three?" he demanded. "*What* are you?"

For a moment, Jason considered telling him they were from the Moon. That was something the seventeenth-century mind could at least fantasize about—Cyrano de Bergerac was currently fourteen years in his grave—whereas time travel didn't yet exist even as a fictional device. But he considered it only to reject it. The time for game-playing was past. He met Zenobia's eyes; she nodded, and he proceeded.

"We're from the future, Captain. A little over seven hundred years in the future, to be exact. I don't ask you to understand it. Just take my word that we can, within limits, voyage on the stream of time—as can the evil men who now have us imprisoned in their flying ship."

"'Flying ship'? Yes, so Zenobia said. But...but I saw no 'ship.' Only a square hole in the sky, in a part of the sky that seemed to flicker, or..." Morgan trailed to a bewildered halt.

"This ship can make itself invisible. And," Jason continued hastily as Morgan's jaw dropped, "this also has nothing to do with any black arts. Zenobia has told you the truth: these enemies of ours are very powerful, but their power is only that of mechanical and warlike skills that your world doesn't yet possess, just as..." Jason sought for an example Morgan would understand, for the concept of technological advancement did not come naturally in a world where the way things were done never changed noticeably over the course of any one individual's lifetime. "Just as your own ancestors in the days of Richard the Lionhearted didn't have guns, or astrolabe and sextant for navigating their ships."

They didn't? said Morgan's expression. With what

seemed almost a physical effort, he sought to come to terms with all of this. "If you haven't been born yet, and won't be born for seven centuries, then how can you be here now? By God, time isn't a sea to be voyaged on! It just . . . *is*. Once a moment has passed, it's over and done with. This is madness! It would make a chaos of all creation!"

"Believe me, you're not the only one to have thought that," said Jason with a smile. "But you know I must be speaking the truth, for you know that no one of your time could build this flying ship."

"Flying . . . But this deck is steady under my feet."

How do you explain inertial compensators? thought Jason with an inner groan. *Or grav repulsion? When Isaac Newton is twenty-seven and only just becoming a professor at Cambridge!* "The lack of a sensation of motion has to do with the same force that allows the ship to fly, and which brought us up through the air," was the best he could manage. "And remember, it's not magic. Nor is . . . that which allows us to leave our own time and visit other times."

"Hmm . . ." With a swiftness Jason knew he shouldn't find surprising, Morgan accepted the situation and began to think out its implications. "If you came from your own time, then surely you can return to it." The dark eyes gleamed with sudden avidity. "And perhaps take me with you? By God, I think I might like to see a world that builds invisible flying ships! I can imagine many possible uses for them."

I'll just bet you can. "I'm sorry, Captain. It doesn't work that way. We are all . . . anchored to the times we are born into. You are of this time, and must remain in it. We are in it for a set period, and must remain until a prearranged date only a couple of weeks from now."

"Unless our mission leader has one of the Special Ops gizmos implanted in his brain," was Mondrago's muttered qualifier in Standard International English. "Too bad we can't use that to get out of this right now."

"And it is impossible for me to return at all," interjected Zenobia. "I did what was necessary to make it impossible."

"So you marooned yourself in time," said Morgan wonderingly. "Why?"

"Because I was once one of the evil ones who now hold us captive," she stated boldly. "I could no longer stomach being used by them, for they seek to found a demon-worshiping cult of unspeakable foulness, for their own twisted purposes."

"And what are those purposes? Do they wish to plunder the past? Is that possible?"

"No, that's not their aim. They seek to prepare the way for their own planned conquest of all the Earth. And even that is only a means to their real goal, which is to distort the very nature of Man as God created him, making themselves into gods ruling over monsters. They would even blur the line God ordained between that which lives and that which does not."

There was nothing in Morgan's biography, nor in anything they themselves had seen of him, to suggest that he was noticeably religious. But his swarthy face paled. "This isn't simple, honest plundering. It's blasphemy. No, it is beyond the boundaries of blasphemy, or of madness. These men must be stopped!"

"That's why we've been sent into our past," Jason told him. "Stopping them is our duty."

"A war fought across time, in defiance of the proper order of events . . ." Morgan looked at him thoughtfully. "It's in my mind that you people, and not just your enemies, are arrogating to yourselves the powers of gods."

"Maybe. But what other choice have we, if we don't wish to simply lie down and accept defeat—a defeat that would mean the end of humanity as God intended?"

"None. And if what you say is true, I'm with you." Abruptly, Morgan turned to practicalities. "But they don't know that. Why did they seize me?"

"I don't believe they meant to. You just happened to be standing close to Zenobia and me, whose presence they can detect at a distance, by means you wouldn't understand. And *I* don't understand how it could have happened. It's not supposed to. Our histories—and yes, you're remembered in them—tell us it shouldn't."

"Well, be that as it may, they've got us all now. Where are they taking us in their flying ship?"

"I don't know for certain, but I imagine Hispaniola. If so, we ought to be arriving there any time now."

Morgan's eyes widened at the thought of the speed Jason's statement implied. "Why haven't they come to put us to the question, instead of leaving us locked in this hold?"

"They probably think they can break our spirit by leaving us alone to stew in our own fears and despair."

"Well, then, they don't know Henry Morgan! And . . . I don't think they know the three of you either."

All at once, the humming died down to silence and there was a slight bump as the Kestrel landed. The doors in the forward bulkhead slid aside, momentarily dazzling their eyes with the brighter illumination beyond. Two goon-caste guards entered the hold warily, holding laser carbines at which Morgan stared.

"They're a kind of guns," Jason murmured to him. "Very deadly ones." Morgan nodded shortly, and made no resistance when one of the goons took his cutlass and the other three's knives.

The goons deployed to the sides of the door and two other figures came forward. The first was Romain, wearing a self-satisfied smile—which vanished from his face when he saw Morgan.

"Surprise," said Jason with a slight smile of his own.

But then the second figure entered ... and Morgan's eyes bulged. Never mind what Jason and Zenobia had told him; he knew the supernatural when he saw it.

Ahriman disregarded him and turned to Romain, whose discomfiture was obvious. "What is the matter?" he demanded. "Yes, we have one unplanned captive, but what difference does one primitive local human make?"

Romain opened his mouth as though to reply, then closed it again.

Jason hoped his smile was infuriating. "You can't very well explain it to him, can you?"

CHAPTER TWENTY-FOUR

For a moment a kind of impasse held, as Romain stood gripped by indecision.

"Yes," Jason continued in the Teloi language, pressing his advantage, "as soon as your sensors told you I'd been washed over the side in the chaos of the storm and hauled aboard Zenobia's ship, you thought you had your perfect chance to grab the two of us despite the Observer Effect. And as soon as you detected my bionics and hers within a few feet of each other on *Rolling-Calf*'s poop, you *knew* you had that chance. So you seized it. But you forgot that even the most tightly focused tractor beam has a significant spread. So now you've got Henry Morgan—and no, I don't understand how that can be possible any more than you do. But it's not as much of an immediate problem for me as it is for you, because you've led Ahriman to believe that observed history, including the history of human extrasolar colonization, can be changed, and—"

"*Quiet!*" Romain came out of his paralysis, strode forward, and slapped Jason across the mouth with a force that brought the taste of blood from a cut lip. But Jason saw Ahriman's puzzled look.

"What is he talking about?" the Teloi demanded. "What is this 'Observer Effect'?"

"Nothing," Romain hastily assured him. "It's just the babbling of a mere unmodified human. And," he continued to Jason, shifting to the Standard International English Ahriman could not understand, "do you recall what I told you before about the consequences of displeasing me? You've already displeased me by escaping, so I might devise something even worse, when we resume our long-postponed schedule of ceremonies here."

Jason remembered those ceremonies only too well, as he stared into the face he had once seen shining with grease and wearing a look of dreamy satiety. But he forced himself to speak levelly, seeking to extract any and all information he could. *Keep him talking!* "So we're back in Hispaniola?"

"Yes—and while I'm gone there'll be no slackness like that of the idiot I left in charge last time. He has been . . . disciplined."

Jason wasn't about to shed any tears for One-Ear, but he was glumly certain that that worthy's successor had taken his predecessor's "discipline" to heart. There would be no escape this time. But then the words *while I'm gone* registered. "So you're depriving us of your company?"

"Only for a short time. You may be interested to learn that the Teloi battlestation is even now approaching Earth. Indeed, it has passed within the Primary Limit and has gone into free fall."

Jason unconsciously nodded. The battlestation was

presumably a pure deep-space construct, and as such lacked a photon drive for maneuvering in a planetary gravity well where its negative-mass drive could not function. It had simply killed the pseudo-velocity it had accumulated, resumed its intrinsic velocity, and was now passing through Earth's Primary Limit on a hyperbolic solar orbit. But of course none of that was his primary concern just now.

"So," Romain continued, "you and this traitor will have a little time to contemplate what is going to happen to you. Perhaps unfortunately, it won't be a very long time. Ahriman and I must leave immediately to rendezvous with the station. It was good fortune that I was able to tidy up matters by recapturing you just before our departure."

"You haven't entirely tidied things up," Jason reminded him. "There are, as you may recall, two other members of my team, who know everything I know about what you and Ahriman are up to. You don't know where they are—and they have no bionics for you to detect. Remember, you don't know how soon our party is due for retrieval."

"As to their location, they are, of course, with Morgan's fleet. And while locating them admittedly won't be as simple as it was in your case, it shouldn't take long to track them down and kill them. I saw enough of them to conclude that they'll be fairly helpless without you." Romain's façade of suave self-satisfaction slid off with its usual abruptness, revealing that which lay beneath. "Enough of this. Come."

Through all of this, Jason had been observing Morgan out of the corner of his eye. After his initial stupefaction at the sight of Ahriman the buccaneer had, with his usual adaptability, settled into watchfulness, listening carefully to the byplay. The Teloi language was, of course, purest gibberish to him. But Standard International English undoubtedly held a certain haunting familiarity—there must even be tantalizing stretches of recognizable vocabulary. It was, Jason imagined, probably not too much more difficult than Jamaican Creole would have been for a speaker of twentieth- or twenty-first-century American English. Once Morgan fell into the rhythm of it, he would be able to catch a great deal of the sense of what was being said.

Romain and Ahriman turned and left the hold. The goons motioned with their laser carbines for the prisoners to follow them...a little awkwardly in the case of the one to the left, who was burdened with a cutlass and three knives. They passed directly into the Kestrel's cabin—unoccupied save for a man sitting in the pilot's seat on the raised bridge—and proceeded forward along the central aisle with the air lock to the right and a row of passenger seats to the left. As they approached the bridge, Morgan's eyes grew round again, for he was entering a realm of technology so far advanced beyond his own as to be meaningless—the famous adage of the twentieth-century sage Clarke crossed Jason's mind. But once again his features closed up quickly into a mask of alertness. Perhaps, Jason thought, it helped that here he had at least one comforting glimpse of familiarity, for the bridge's viewscreen showed a clearing in Hispaniola's jungle-clothed uplands, with mountains looming in the background. And, as Jason watched, he began to very inconspicuously sidle a little closer to the goon who was holding his laser carbine in one hand as he cradled the confiscated cutlery in his other arm.

Romain stepped up onto the bridge. "Key in the figures for our rendezvous with the battlestation," he ordered the pilot. "We must depart as soon as the prisoners have been offloaded." The pilot obeyed, and the course instructions went into the Kestrel's computer. Romain turned around and addressed the goons. "Remove them."

The goons gestured them toward the airlock, and the one to the right began to reach for the switch that would open it. As the other one turned, he muttered with annoyance and paused to readjust the blades under his arm.

At that moment, Henry Morgan roared out an inarticulate bellow and swept one arm around, knocking the barrel of the goon's laser carbine downward. The goon got off a shot, which singed the deck between Morgan's feet, as the blades went clattering and scattered.

A twenty-fourth-century man would almost certainly not have done it, Jason reflected—later, when he had leisure for reflection—because such a man *knew* how viciously lethal weapon-grade lasers were, and that knowledge tended to immobilize him in the presence of one of those whiplashes of instantaneous death. But Morgan was conditioned to think in terms of the clumsy firearms of his own era. Now he shoved the goon back, to topple over against a passenger seat, and simultaneously scooped up his cutlass. With another roar, he raised the cutlass and brought it down in a diagonal slash through the goon's shoulder and chest, cutting open his heart. A gout of blood spurted across the cabin, splattering onto the deck.

For some very small fraction of a second, surprise held everyone else motionless. Then the second goon raised his laser carbine. Mondrago grasped it by its barrel with his right hand and shoved it upward, exposing the goon's solar plexus, to which he delivered a paralyzing punch with his left. Zenobia, in what amounted to a single movement of superhuman speed and fluidity, dropped to one knee on the deck, snatched a knife, brought it up, and hurled it. There was a faint *thunk!*, and Ahriman was standing with a surprised expression on his face and the knife's hilt protruding from the center of his forehead . . . but standing only for an instant, before his lifeless legs collapsed under him.

By then Romain, his features contorted with rage, was springing forward. But in his fury he forgot that he was on a raised bridge, and lost his balance as he stepped over the ledge. As he tried to right himself, he presented a perfect target for Jason's swift, powerful kick to his crotch. With a strangled, gasping scream, he crashed to the deck. Behind him, the pilot was only just standing up. He toppled back into his seat with a puff of superheated steam as Mondrago speared him with a crackling bolt from the laser carbine he had appropriated.

It was all over in a couple of seconds. The silent air of the cabin was heavy with the odors of death, including the subtly different Teloi ones.

Jason knelt over Romain, who was groaning in fetal position. He placed one knee in the small of the Transhumanist's back and locked his right arm around his throat, not quite tightly enough to choke him. With his left he twisted Romain's head around just enough so that their eyes could meet—and so that Romain would know that an additional, sharper twist would suffice to break his neck. The Transhumanist froze into immobility and licked his lips . . . much as Jason had once seen him lick grease from them.

"Now," said Jason said in a conversational tone of voice, "the hardest thing I've ever done in my life is to *not* kill you . . . or, better still, let Mondrago do it. You don't know about Corsicans and vendetta, do you? I'd love to let you find out. But I think I can—with great difficulty—continue to restrain myself if you do exactly as you're told. First of all, order your men outside to back off and take no action with respect to this vessel. Blink your eyes twice if you understand."

Romain blinked. Jason released his head, hauled him to his feet by an arm twisted behind his back, and shoved him up onto the bridge, to the copilot/ communications console. Romain activated the outside speaker and spoke as well as he was able. "Stand down! Withdraw to the edge of the clearing and await further orders." In the viewscreen, several armed and bewildered-looking goons backed away.

Morgan, holding his bloody cutlass in one hand and a laser carbine in the other, joined them on the bridge. With a coarse, jeering laugh, he waved the cutlass at the figures in the viewscreen, which he assumed to be a window even though the invention of plate glass lay two decades in the future. Then, as the fire and fury of combat ebbed from his brain, he turned to Zenobia, who was tearing strips of cloth from Ahriman's clothing to bind Romain's wrists together behind him. "Well, lass, you were right. He was no demon. I've never heard that demons can be killed as easily as men."

"What now, sir?" Mondrago asked Jason.

"I haven't had time to think that through," Jason admitted. Out of the habit of months, he and Mondrago spoke in seventeenth-century English. "I recall that you can fly Kestrels, but as to where we're going to take it—"

"Where were *they* going to take it, Jason?" Morgan suddenly asked. "I was able to make out some snatches of what you and this whoreson Romain were saying to each other, but I couldn't understand much beyond the fact that they were about to leave to meet someone, somewhere. In fact, I can't fully understand much of *anything*." He looked around, bewildered, at the incomprehensible control panels.

Partly to organize things in his own mind, Jason did his best to explain. "They were going to meet a... well, a great ship of their unhuman allies—the Teloi, as they're called—out beyond the air."

"Beyond the... ?"

"You see, this ship flies in the way you've observed as long as it's not too far above the Earth. As it rises higher, the... propulsive principle weakens." Jason didn't even try to explain the grav surface effect. "So above great heights it uses a—" He bumped up against the impossibility of rendering *reaction drive*. "Well, other engines, rather like... You've seen fireworks. It's more or less the same thing that makes skyrockets fly." It was as close as he could come to describing the photon drive.

Morgan looked a trifle uneasy at the thought of riding a giant skyrocket. "Then they were going to use these engines to go up and meet the great ship of the Teloi?"

"Yes, it's due to coast past the Earth very soon."

"'Coast past'?"

Jason decided against making any attempt to explain the negative-mass drive. "There is another means of propelling flying ships, which is very, very fast indeed—as it must be to travel the vast distances between the worlds. But it won't work at all except at a great distance from Earth or any other world—almost twenty thousand miles, in fact." Morgan's eyes, which had widened at the words *between the worlds*, now grew even wider. "The Teloi ship was built purely to travel the deeps of space, without ever coming very near a world, and therefore it needs *only* this kind of engine. So now, approaching Earth closely, it has had to turn that engine off and is now . . . sailing past on a fixed course, until it passes into the outer reaches again. This vessel was to rendezvous with it. In fact, the, er, instructions for that rendezvous have already been . . . Well, take my word that the ship can navigate itself to the rendezvous, if instructed to do so."

This last clearly meant nothing whatsoever to Morgan, but he seemed to simply accept it and, for a few seconds, think hard. "Jason," he finally inquired, "is this ship armed? I've seen no great guns."

"Those wouldn't work in aerial battle—never mind why. But yes, we have weapons," said Jason, recalling the Firebird missile launchers attached to the hardpoints. "Remember what I said before about skyrockets? These are even more like that." The focused-plasma drives of the little missiles, designed to burn themselves out in sprint mode, would at least produce a satisfying flare. "And they carry explosive charges of a kind of . . . well, powder that you've never seen, but which bursts with a very, *very* great force."

"Well, then, since the course is already set, I say let's keep the rendezvous." All at once, the Devil danced in Morgan's eyes. "We'll sail up beyond the clouds and scupper this damned Teloi ship!"

Romain gave a scornful snort of laughter. The others felt something akin to pity.

"Captain," said Jason slowly, keeping it simple in deference to the limitations of a seventeenth-century mind, "this is a very small ship, as such vessels go, and lightly armed. And its invisibility device would be no help, as the Teloi ship has ... means other than sight for detecting it. And besides, what I've been calling the Teloi ship is really more like a flying fortress, armed with weapons more destructive than anything you can imagine."

"Ah, but its crew are expecting this ship to meet them, and have no reason to expect an attack. We'd catch them with their breeks down around their ankles!"

"Well, er, yes. I suppose that might be true. But—"

"And besides ... Jason, I don't pretend to understand all the whys and wherefores of what you've told me about aerial seamanship. But from what I *do* understand, this fat-arsed Teloi hulk is simply drifting, or gliding, at the mercy of some kind of celestial currents. It won't be able to maneuver. *Our* ship will!"

Jason opened his mouth to reply—but nothing came. Without closing it, he turned to Mondrago and Zenobia, whose mouths were also open.

Romain wasn't laughing anymore.

"You know, come to think of it, while they're in free fall within the Primary Limit ..." Jason finally managed, before trailing off.

"I never thought of . . ." Mondrago began before likewise falling into silence.

The two of them turned slowly and stared at Morgan. Then they looked at each other again.

"What would Nesbit think?" asked Jason.

"What would Rutherford think?" countered Mondrago. There was another silence.

"*Let's do it!*" they both blurted simultaneously.

"Then it's settled! You two are buccaneers at heart after all!" Morgan beamed, then looked around and scowled. "Isn't there any rum aboard this ship?"

CHAPTER TWENTY-FIVE

The lack of perceptible motion didn't prevent Morgan from uttering a startled exclamation and reaching for something to grab hold of when Mondrago took the Kestrel aloft and the ground seemed to drop rapidly away beneath them. The goons burst from the outskirts of the clearing, firing their laser carbines at the swiftly rising gunship without effect. Jason, seated at the weapons console which brief instructions from Mondrago and his own experience with similar models had enabled him to operate, sent them scattering with a few staccato bolts from the Kestrel's laser turret. They paused to open the cargo hold's doors and dump the bodies that had been unceremoniously heaped in it. Then Mondrago gave her full power.

The grav repulsors' lateral propulsion capability fell off with altitude, but by providing enough lift to effectively cancel the Kestrel's weight they enabled it to reach orbit—or, for that matter, escape velocity—under photon drive easily and quickly. Morgan muttered horrid oaths as the landscape of Hispaniola receded and the outline of the island began to appear. Then he fell silent and simply gawked as the sky darkened to ultramarine and violet and finally velvet black, spangled with even more stars than could be seen on a clear and moonless night at sea—the unwinking stars of airless space—even though the Sun glowed in the sky. The Earth became a cloud-swirling blue curve, then a sphere as they passed that subjective boundary of human perception beyond which a planet ceases to be the world below and becomes an astronomical object hanging in the void.

"I never dreamed such wonders could be," breathed Morgan, in a tone Jason had never heard on his lips. "No one will ever believe me!"

They'd better not! The press of events had held Jason's long-term concerns at bay for a while. But now he had, for the moment, not much to do, and he could no longer push to the back of his mind the outrage that had been inflicted on all his comfortable assumptions about the immutability of recorded history. Henry Morgan, a fairly well-documented historical figure of some importance, quite simply had no business aboard this ship, going into space.

I can't let myself dwell on it, he thought sternly. *I've got to keep repeating to myself two stock phrases I always use with neophyte time travelers: "There are no paradoxes," and "Reality protects itself." They must be true. They must. I can't let myself consider the alternative, because to do so is to unlock a door beyond which lies madness, and for now I have to be able to function.*

So he concentrated on the viewscreen as Mondrago activated the superimposed "tactical" display, eliciting a new string of blasphemies from Morgan. From his position at the weapons station, Jason could see it over the shoulder of Romain, who sat bound and stonily silent in the copilot/communicator's seat. Zenobia stood behind the Transhumanist, holding a knife which she occasionally allowed to lightly touch the back of his neck, causing him to flinch. Morgan stood to her left, behind Mondrago, staring at the colored lights and data readouts that seemed to crawl across the stars in the screen. "How—?" he began, then shook his head and subsided, apparently deciding against even trying to understand, and satisfied himself with, "Is this how you'll sight the Teloi flying fort?"

"Yes," Mondrago nodded, hesitating only slightly at the word *sight*. "It won't be long now."

"Because of the course that was somehow set into the ship itself?"

"Right. You see, that course is linked to the track the target is following. So this ship knows where it's going to be at any given time—"

"'This ship knows,'" Morgan echoed hollowly, shaking his head.

"—and adjusts its course accordingly. After we... well, sight the target, I'll take over for the actual rendezvous." Actually, Jason thought, Mondrago could have done it himself—a doubly tangent trajectory— given the known orbit elements of the battlestation.

Morgan shook his head again. "So in your future time, you even have machines that *think* for you! I hope you haven't forgotten how to do it for yourselves."

"So do I," said Jason. *Although,* he added mentally, recalling some of the members of the Authority's governing council, *I sometimes wonder.*

Then, interrupting his thoughts, a light began to flash on the viewscreen.

"That's it," said Mondrago tensely. His hands flew over the board and he assumed manual control.

"But I see no ship," Morgan objected.

"It's not close enough yet. Although . . ." He turned and looked over his shoulder at Jason and spoke in twenty-fourth-century language. "Judging from the mass reading I'm getting, it won't be long now before we can see it. That thing is *big*."

Jason studied the readouts. "It's also not moving very fast. It must not have built up much in the way of intrinsic velocity before going into negative-mass drive pseudovelocity."

"Especially relative to Earth's almost-nineteen-miles-per-second orbital velocity," Mondrago nodded. "It must have some sort of thrusters, or else it would still have the intrinsic vector of the orbit in which it was originally built, whenever that was, in some far-off system. But those thrusters must be unsuitable for any kind of maneuvering, and be very weak relative to that enormous mass. Just enough to slow down and speed up a little, as they evidently did in the last system they visited."

And, Jason wondered, *what did they slow down to do? What were these deluded fanatics up to in that system, and in God knows how many others before that? I don't think I want to know.*

Before he had completed the thought, the battlestation appeared on visual, and began to grow.

Mondrago deactivated the tactical display and adjusted the visual for magnification. Morgan started as the battlestation abruptly appeared closer, but

recovered quickly—he was familiar with spyglasses—
and simply stared. So did Jason.

The battlestation was very roughly spheroidal,
but with the addition on its underside of two squat
cylinders—the drive nacelles—and some associated
superstructure that gave it a more or less recognizable fore-and-aft configuration. But it had none of
the esthetic satisfaction of normal interstellar ships,
designed with hull configurations that optimized
their drive-field geometry while affording a degree of
aerodynamic streamlining. Its maximum pseudovelocity
must surely be low, Jason thought, as he studied its
ugly, brutal massiveness, accentuated by the intricacy
of its external components. It held none of the over-
decorated, almost *art nouveau*-reminiscent look of the
Teloi technology he recalled from the Bronze Age.
But that, he reminded himself, had belonged to an
altogether different Teloi subculture.

"She's a whopper!" breathed Morgan. A calculat-
ing light awoke in his eyes. "She must hold a lot of
plunder! You know, it's too bad we have to sink her,
or whatever it is you do out here. If we could only
take her as a prize...!"

Jason goggled at him. "You're actually serious,
aren't you?"

"Well..." Morgan saw the expressions with which
everyone was regarding him, and sighed regretfully.
"Yes, I know. It was just a passing fancy. We don't
have the men—no offense, Zenobia—to board her."

The battlestation continued to wax in the screen.
On its side was a horizontal rectangular opening,
glowing with interior lighting from behind the atmosphere curtain.

Romain spoke up in a tone of vicious gloating. "That is a hangar bay. It can easily admit a vessel twice as large as this one." Morgan, who still hadn't entirely grasped the size of the battlestation, stared at him. Sensing an advantage, Romain altered his tone to one of wheedling. "Surely you can see the hopelessness of this quixotic venture. If you surrender now and turn control of this ship over to me, I'll intercede for you with the Teloi. I promise I'll persuade them to spare your—*uh!*"

"Shut up, you lying piece of pig shit," said Zenobia, who had cuffed him across the back of the head. "Just do as you've been told."

The Kestrel swung around as Mondrago began to match vectors with the battlestation. The grav repulsors' efficiency was minimal at this distance from Earth's surface, but it was still measurable, and nudges with it, in conjunction with the photon drive, afforded a degree of maneuverability beyond the dreams of the pioneering astronauts of the early space age with their chemical-fuel rockets. They began to jockey into position for rendezvous.

The communicator in front of Romain beeped and flashed for attention. Zenobia cut Romain's bonds and stood back out of the video pickup, knife held ready. "All right," said Jason. "Answer it as you've been instructed. And you'd better be convincing. Remember, I understand the Teloi language. If you betray us, you'll die before we do—and *our* deaths will be quick and clean."

Romain shot him a look of unspeakable hate, but activated the communicator. Morgan, who had been warned to expect voices and images from across a distance, didn't look too startled when a Teloi appeared on the video screen, wearing a jumpsuit like Ahriman's with decorative touches that gave it, even across the gulf of races and cultures, the unmistakable look of a military uniform. In the background was a vast, theaterlike control center, teeming with other Teloi.

"This is Romain, Category Three, Eighty-Ninth Degree. I wish to come aboard in accordance with our agreement."

The Teloi did not deign to directly acknowledge. "Where is he whom you know as 'Ahriman'?"

"Ah . . . I regret to say that he suffered a fatal accident on the planet's surface."

The Teloi's features barely twitched. "That is unfortunate."

"Most unfortunate. But . . . well, conditions down there are dangerous and primitive."

"How could conditions be otherwise, among humans?" the Teloi remarked with a sneer—or, more accurately, with an intensification of his permanent sneer. "I will require a full report on the circumstances of his death later. For now, your vessel's transponder confirms your identity. You may come ahead and dock in the hangar bay." Without another word, the Teloi cut the connection.

"Arrogant bastard," commented Morgan, who of course hadn't understood a word. He held his cutlass leveled on Romain while Zenobia tied him up again.

Mondrago brought the Kestrel in. The battlestation swelled in the viewscreen, and swelled, and swelled, until it filled the entire screen: a nightmare vision of raw, dystopian technology, a titanic death machine that had for centuries roamed the stars at the service of a demented dream.

Even Morgan seemed taken aback. "Jason, these, er, skyrockets of yours...You say they hold an explosive charge of a kind of gunpowder I've never heard of?"

"Yes, you might say that. It's called *deuterium*." The earliest fission-fusion nuclear explosives had, of necessity, been cataclysmic in their effects. Now, with laser-triggered deuterium fusion, it was possible to produce finely calibrated "dial-a-yield" warheads. There were even such things as nuclear *grenades*, although in practice they hardly ever got issued.

The Firebird missile's warhead could be set as low as 0.0001 kiloton (using the traditional measure of thousands of tons of a twentieth-century chemical explosive called TNT). It could also be set as high as 0.01 kiloton, destroying any target but a very hardened one at a radius of one hundred yards and inflicting significant damage, especially to electronics and unprotected personnel, at twice that radius.

Mondrago had programmed these for the maximum.

"Deuterium," Morgan repeated, pronouncing it carefully. "You're right: I've never heard of it." But he seemed reassured.

They drew closer. The hangar bay gaped to admit them. Its atmosphere screen was a field of gravitics-related force which held the air molecules inside while permitting the passage in and out of large solid objects like spacecraft at slow speeds. Moving at higher speeds, such objects were deflected with a force proportional to their kinetic energy.

Jason turned to Mondrago. "You're sure you were able to program the missiles' drives to—"

"Trust me. I worked with these missiles a lot in Shahinian's Irregulars. They can be powered down. But of course, like any rockets, they're going to continue to build up velocity as long as they continue to burn. And even at low power, it won't take them long at all to accelerate to a speed that will cause the atmosphere screen to send them screaming off into space."

"Which is why we have to get very close for this to work," Jason nodded.

"Quite right," said Morgan, who was getting better at following the nontechnical parts of Standard International English. "Close to push of pike, that's what I always say!"

"It's also why we're only going to have time to fire one missile from each of the two launchers," added Mondrago, unnecessarily. They had been over all this before, of course. They were talking simply to fill the air with something besides tension.

The opening now filled the entire viewscreen. They could clearly see the hangar bay's cavernous interior, lined with machinery and controls, partially filled with small craft.

Sweat filmed Mondrago's face as he watched instruments and calculated distances. "Not quite. . . ."

Without warning, Romain surged as far forward in his seat as his bonds would permit and thrust his head at the console, just barely striking it and activating the communicator. "*Open fire now!*" he roared in Teloi. "It's a trick! Destroy this—" His shout cut off abruptly as Zenobia struck him above the ear with the pommel of her knife, knocking him unconscious.

He knows we're not going to let him live, so he's got nothing to lose, Jason thought. *And he also knows we've reached the point where he'll die just as quickly as the rest of us.*

In a corner of the viewscreen, he saw a defensive laser turret begin to swing toward them. And he knew it had to be now or never.

Without further thought, and without waiting for Mondrago's signal, Jason jabbed a red button. In both the launchers, the Firebirds' plasma drives awoke in a blinding blue-white flare, and the two missiles roared away, straight ahead into the hangar bay...and through the atmosphere screen, he saw with a rush of relief.

At the same instant, Mondrago wrenched the Kestrel sideways and away with a force that would have broken all their bones without the inertial compensators. Even with them, Zenobia and Morgan both lost their footing and tumbled to the deck, and the others slewed in their couches.

It was just in time. As the Kestrel pulled away they caught sight of the hangar bay's interior as its dim electric lighting turned to something resembling the surface of the sun. Then, just barely astern of them, the atmosphere screen went down and a jet of superheated gas like a titanic blowtorch shot out of the bay into the space the Kestrel had occupied less than a second before.

Mondrago gave the photon drive full power and they shot away. Jason had worried that the battlestation might mount a tractor beam powerful enough to grip and hold the Kestrel against the power of its own drive. Evidently it didn't, or if it did the controls for such a beam had been wrecked...or, perhaps, its operators were in a state of shock at the thermonuclear evisceration of their great vessel's interior.

Not everything aboard the battlestation was paralyzed, however. A heavy laser weapon turret swiveled, seeking them out. It fired a bolt, but the Kestrel's wild maneuvers, at such short range, made any sort of targeting solution impossible. Mondrago flipped the Kestrel over and reversed direction, using the limited power of the grav repulsors to help overcome inertia and also to introduce a confusing wobble. With anti-ship laser bolts stabbing through space just astern of them, they shot past the battlestation, which was now beginning to show fissures of flame as secondary explosions rippled through its massive bulk. Jason just barely had time to launch two more missiles before they were away. The point-defense lasers that might have stopped those missiles even at this range were no longer functioning.

Mondrago switched the screen to view-aft just in time for them to see the last two missiles impact the receding battlestation. Then the secondary explosions began coming at closer intervals, rising to an almost stroboscopic crescendo and then seeming to merge together, suddenly coalescing into one great, sunlike glare that filled the screen and dazzled their eyes. Then that glow died down, revealing an expanding cloud of glowing gas and debris. The vacuum of space could not carry a shock wave, but the Kestrel shuddered when the wave front of superheated gas reached them.

Morgan hauled himself to his feet and stared at the screen. "Sweet Jesus!" he gasped.

CHAPTER TWENTY-SIX

"What are our orbital elements like?" Jason demanded anxiously.

"Believe it or not, I spared that a little bit of thought, there at the end," Mondrago assured him. He returned the viewscreen to view-forward, in which the great blue curve of Earth waxed.

Jason let out a sigh of relief. If they had been thrown into an outward orbital path, not even the technology at their command would have saved them from a long-drawn-out struggle back to Earth. And that was something they could not afford at the moment.

"So," said Morgan, staring at the screen, "we're on our way back. Maybe the fleet is out of the storm by now."

"Hopefully." Jason consulted his implant; it had only been a few hours. "We'll have no trouble finding them. Once we get in the same general area, I have . . . means by which I can locate my two men who're still aboard *Soledad*."

"And what a story we'll have to tell everyone!"

Morgan's eyes were alight. "They'll have to believe us—not even old John Mandeville himself would have dared make up such a lie. And they'll wet themselves when we appear from out of the sky in this flying ship!"

"Well, er...maybe." Once again, Jason found himself face to face with the impossible, unthinkable but inescapable fact that he was talking to Henry Morgan aboard a spaceship. *Now what the hell am I going to do?* he thought desperately. *I can't evade the issue any longer.*

"And," Morgan went on with oblivious happiness, "before you return to your own time...Jason, do you have any idea what we can do with this ship and its weapons? Why, nothing can stop us! All the treasures of the Spanish Main are ours for the taking. And India...and the Orient..." His eyes glazed over. He seemed to be going into an ecstasy of greed.

"For now, though," said Zenobia drily, "what about this offal?" She indicated Romain, who was groaning as he returned to consciousness.

"Oh." Morgan blinked as he returned to immediate practicalities. "I forgot about him. Shall I cut his throat now or later?"

"Later," said Jason, without quite knowing why. He could never be comfortable with cold-blooded killing, even of a creature like this.

He also wasn't entirely clear in his own mind on why he was so concerned with getting Nesbit and Grenfell back. In less than two weeks, their TRDs would automatically activate and they, along with Mondrago and himself, would be snatched back to the displacer stage in Australia in the late twenty-fourth century. All they had to do was stay alive until then. And that, of course, was the rub: it was Jason's job to keep them alive. And besides, he told himself, the transition would hit them quite unexpectedly without him there to give them a countdown. It had only happened a few times in the history of time travel, but the people involved had found it disturbing.

As they entered atmosphere and overflew the Caribbean, they could see that it was almost sunset and the tatters of the storm had moved on. At low altitude, Mondrago proceeded on grav repulsion alone. He also activated the refraction field, and they cruised over the still unsettled water, invisible and practically silent. Presently they began to sight the ships of Morgan's fleet, somewhat scattered but more or less on course through a mass of floating debris. *Soledad*, the biggest of the lot, was easy to spot. And . . .

"There's *Rolling-Calf*, not far away!" exclaimed Zenobia. "I've got to get back to her."

"All right," said Jason. His thoughts were raging. This was all going to have to be sheer improvisation . . . and at the back of his mind the seemingly insoluble problem of Morgan wouldn't go away. "All right," he repeated. "We'll come over them and hover. It's still daylight, so If we open the hatch of the cargo bay without the lights on, maybe no one will look up and notice. And we can use the tractor beam to lower ourselves down."

"Won't that look kind of funny?" Mondrago inquired. "Us drifting down from the sky? Besides which, the tractor beam requires an operator to remain here at the controls."

"Well . . . we'll drop down to really low altitude, just aft of the ships, and simply jump out. There's plenty of flotsam down there for us to grab hold of. Then we'll call out for rescue."

And then what? jibed Jason's inner critic. He was still evading his basic problems—not just the most important, which was, of course, Morgan, but also a relatively lesser one . . . He looked at Romain, who was now fully conscious.

That last, at least, has an obvious solution. Jason had heard somewhere that drowning was a decent way to die. (*Who, exactly, conveyed the information?* he couldn't help wondering.) He stood up, walked over to Romain's seat, grasped him by his bound arms and hauled him to his feet.

"As you've doubtless gathered, given the fact that you're still alive," he hissed in the Tranhumanist's ear, "your little attempt failed. We've destroyed the battlestation of your Teloi allies. Your plans have come to nothing. *You* have come to nothing. Now we're back in Earth's atmosphere, at low altitude over the Caribbean. And—God knows why—I'm going to make this as easy as possible."

Out of the corner of his eye, he saw Mondrago's resentful expression. "Let me—"

"No. We owe him nothing. But we owe it to ourselves. *We're* still human!" Jason gave Romain another jerk. "Come on!" He twisted the Transhumanist around to face aft, toward the cargo hold.

Morgan had obviously lost the thread of the Standard International English. "But," he objected, "aren't we going to—?"

"No, Captain," said Zenobia, and Jason could sense the subsonic undercurrent of her vocal implant. "It's going to be necessary to do it this way. Let's go."

With out-of-character passivity, Morgan followed her aft, from the cabin into the hold as Mondrago touched the button that caused the cargo hatch to slide open.

Mondrago, at the pilot's station, manipulated the controls. "All right. We're just behind *Rolling-Calf*, with Soledad off to the left, or port or whatever. We're not much above wavetop level, and lazing along, keeping pace with them."

"Good," said Jason abstractedly as he shoved Romain aft. Looking into the hold, he saw Zenobia and Morgan standing on the limited deck space surrounding the now-open cargo hatch, looking down into the water. The overriding concern was still preying on his mind: *What about Morgan?*

Then, suddenly, like an explosion in his brain, the solution came to him in all its blinding obviousness. *Why didn't I see it before?* The staggering realization wiped all else from his mind and caused him to relax his grip.

Which, of course, gave Romain his chance.

With the strength and speed of his genetic upgrades, Romain broke free, gave a desperate heave, and broke his bonds. Afterwards, Jason would conclude that earlier, while conscious, he had been inconspicuously rubbing them against some sharp protrusion of the copilot's seat, gradually fraying and weakening them. At the moment, though, he had no opportunity for such reflections. With that same adderlike speed, Romain gripped his left wrist with one viselike hand while the other simultaneously snatched the dagger from Jason's belt-rope and pressed it to his throat just hard enough to break the skin. Jason froze, knowing that any struggles would mean instant death.

Mondrago started to surge to his feet, and Zenobia and Morgan poised to lunge back into the cabin. "Stop right there, or he dies!" Romain shouted. They all stopped cold.

"Now, do exactly as I say," Romain ordered Mondrago. "Set in a course for Hispaniola—specifically, for the region of the Massif de la Selle, at the eastern base of the island's southern peninsula. That's where my men currently are. I'll keep you with me to handle the final approach." Romain, Jason thought, must not be a qualified pilot. "In exchange for which, I *may* decide to kill you quickly. Move!" he barked as Mondrago hesitated. Very slowly, the Corsican sat back down and began to manipulate controls.

"As for you, though," Romain hissed into Jason's ear, "I can't safely keep more than one of you aboard with me. So I can't take you back to Hispaniola with me, as much as I'd like to. Oh, yes, I'd devise something truly special there! But you'll have to stay here...with a long, freely bleeding cut. There are sharks in these waters." He was so close that Jason could smell his breath, which caused his gorge to rise, given what he remembered. With a sideways motion, Romain began to prod Jason aft along the short aisle toward the cargo hatch. "You two, jump out first!" he snapped at Morgan and Zenobia.

The buccaneer, one hand on his cutlass hilt, stood glaring for a moment. "Go ahead, Captain," Jason, told him, speaking carefully as the knife-edge pricked his Adam's apple. "I...think I may see you again."

Romain gave a derisive snort. Morgan hesitated another instant, then jumped over the edge. "Next you, bitch," said Romain. "I have to let you go now, but we'll keep looking for you in Jamaica, and eventually find you. Think about that. Think about what's going to happen afterwards."

"Maybe," said Zenobia with a lazy, feline smile that seemed strangely incongruous. "But there's one thing you're overlooking."

"What's that?"

She jerked her chin in the direction of the cabin, beyond him. "Mondrago is coming up behind you."

Romain barked laughter. "You silly cunt! That's the oldest, most childlike trick—"

Like a projectile propelled by bunched leg muscles, the Corsican crashed into Romain's back. At the same instant, with an unnatural quickness matching Romain's, Zenobia grabbed the wrist of his knife-hand, yanking it away from Jason's throat. They all fell in a tumble toward the edge of the yawning cargo hold. Zenobia lost her balance and toppled over the edge, still holding Romain's wrist, while Jason and Mondrago grappled with him. Then she lost her grip and fell.

They struggled at the edge of the hatch. For the barest instant, Jason found himself looking down over the edge, at the water below. He spotted Zenobia, swimming through the scattered flotsam toward *Rolling-Calf*. He also saw Morgan, clinging to a floating yardarm. Then Romain gave a superhuman heave and rolled him over. The Transhumanist was stronger than either of them. But together, Jason and Mondrago wrestled him down into a prone position, each grasping one of his arms. Jason put a knee on Romain's shoulder blade and pulled up and back on the arm with all his strength, breaking the shoulder. The Transhumanist's shriek of pain was instantly followed by another as Mondrago followed suit.

They hauled Romain to his feet, oblivious to his

cries as they grasped his broken arms, and marched him back toward the cabin. As they turned, Jason paused to look through the cargo hatch again. Zenobia was already being hauled aboard *Rolling-Calf* by her Maroons. But that wasn't what riveted Jason's attention.

Morgan was still holding onto the yardarm...but he was no longer alone. There was another man clinging to it with him.

Now who is that, *and where did* he *come from?* Jason wondered. Then the man turned around and looked up as though he knew what he would see in the sky.

For a frozen instant in time, Jason looked into that man's face. Two pairs of eyes locked.

So I was right about the solution, he thought, eerily calm, for it was all so clear now. Barely conscious of what he was doing, he mentally activated the recorder function of his brain implant.

Mondrago's voice ended the moment. "Uh...sir? Are you okay?"

"Oh, yes. Right." Jason shook himself and helped the Corsican haul the moaning Romain to his feet. As they turned to march the Transhumanist back into the cabin, Jason looked back one more time. The waves had swept the yardarm away, and the dark head beside Morgan's was now turned toward *Soledad*, which was coming about to effect a rescue. As they left the cargo hold, an obscure instinct caused Jason to slap a switch and turn off the hold's interior lighting.

In the cabin, they used belt-ropes to lash Romain to one of the passenger seats, and a strip torn from Mondrago's shirt to gag him. His eyes were molten with pain and hate as he glared at them.

"All right," said Jason. "Let's get off this ship."

"What?" Mondrago looked mutinous. "Sir, do you mean to say we're just going to leave him alive? After... Pauline?" He couldn't bring himself to elaborate.

"That's right. In fact, we're going to send him on his way... under autopilot, on the course you set in at his order." Jason held Mondrago's eyes for a moment. The Corsican's expression softened as understanding awoke.

"Oh—I see. Of course." Mondrago bestowed a charming smile on Romain, then went to the pilot station to set the autopilot.

Jason leaned over Romain with a smile of his own. "We're sending you straight to where you wanted to go: the Massif de la Selle in Hispaniola—where, in 1791, an expedition of ours is going to find a century-and-a-quarter-old wreck of a small spacecraft on a mountainside."

The pain and the hate fled from Romain's eyes, replaced by something else. He frantically tried to talk through his gag, producing only choking sounds.

"Okay," said Mondrago. "We have a minute to get off this ship."

They returned to the cargo hold, ignoring Romain's strangled noises, and jumped out into the water. Overhead, the cargo hatch closed and the arrowhead-shaped area of barely visible distortion swung around and headed north by northwest. In the middle distance, Jason saw Morgan and his companion being hauled aboard *Soledad*.

They didn't have to tread water long before *Rolling-Calf* picked them up.

Zenobia looked dissatisfied after Jason finished relating the story of their final disposition of Romain. "It was too easy for him."

"Life is unfair," Jason philosophized.

"So our rulers are always telling us, as though that platitude somehow excuses all their tyrannies and stupidities." Zenobia dismissed the subject with a toss of her head. "Well, we're about to separate from the fleet."

"You're not going back to Port Royal with Morgan?" asked Mondrago.

"No. We've already got our share of the loot aboard this ship. And Port Royal isn't the most comfortable place for my men; too many slave-catchers nosing around. We're going straight back to Morant Bay at the eastern end of Jamaica, not far from the Maroon settlements in the Blue Mountains. But first, I suppose you two will want to be put aboard *Soledad*."

Jason shook his head. "No. If we may, we'd like to come with you."

Zenobia and Mondrago both stared.

"But," Zenobia said, gesturing over the taffrail at the flagship across the water, "two of your men are still over there. Don't you want to—?"

"No," Jason repeated with a more emphatic head-shake. "It is vitally important that I not set foot aboard *Soledad*, and that I not encounter Henry Morgan again."

"Why?" they both demanded in unison.

Jason told them. A long, stunned silence followed.

"Of course you can come with us," Zenobia finally said.

By the time *Rolling-Calf* reached Jamaica, Jason and his party had only four days to go before retrieval. After the ketch's cramped quarters, the trek up into the Blue Mountains was positively refreshing.

While still at sea, Jason had been able to draw Zenobia out concerning the Transhumanist underground. She had been a mine of information, but—as he had more than half expected—she was unable to tell him the two things he most wanted to know. She had never been told when *The Day* was due to come; she was too low-ranking for that. And she couldn't venture to predict where the Transhumanists' compact temporal displacer would be located at any given time, for it was periodically disassembled and moved.

The voyage had also given Zenobia the opportunity to quiet the last terrors of her men, who had seen her floating up into the sky and disappearing into the storm. "I've explained that it was the work of the demons, and that I was able to escape by magic," she told Jason and Mondrago on May 20, as the digital countdown projected onto Jason's optic nerve ticked down, "They were able to accept it. Their belief system holds stranger things than that."

"Speaking of 'demons,'" said Jason, "Romain mentioned an 'advance party' of the *Tuova'Zhonglu* Teloi. Ahriman was the only one we ever saw. But it's possible that there are others still alive, on Hispaniola."

"If so, they're now stranded there permanently," said Mondrago with deep satisfaction.

"Still, they could cause some trouble, especially given their long lifespans."

"Which," said Zenobia, "is why it's important that I continue doing what I've been doing: creating a 'counter-cult' that will clearly identify them as demons—and humans who worship them as evil. Furthermore, I'm going to devote the rest of my life here to cutting those 'long lifespans' as short as possible! Their cult can't be eradicated at once, but with no supply of fresh Teloi it's bound to wither and die out over time if we can eliminate any that are already here. And as long as I'm alive, they'll have me for an enemy."

"I don't think I envy them," Mondrago remarked drily.

"Zenobia," said Jason, "we don't have much time. Let me ask you one thing. Henri Boyer told me how you feel about the Authority—no, about the entire society the Authority represents. But would you accept help from us if—and I can make no promises—we could sometimes send expeditions back here to your probable lifetime?"

"I think I might," she said with unwonted quietness. "You can't expect me to feel exactly the same way you do; there's too much history in the way. But I think I've changed my mind about a few things. To some extent you have Henri to thank for that." For an instant, she couldn't continue. But then she raised her head and met his eyes unflinchingly. "And besides, I've come to understand why your ancestors did what they did to mine—why they *had* to. Humanity must be kept human."

"That's our job in Special Ops."

"Keep on doing it—any way you have to." She extended a hand. Jason took it in a firm clasp.

Then the countdown reached zero, and neither of their hands was holding anything anymore.

CHAPTER TWENTY-SEVEN

After blinking the bright electric lighting of the displacer dome out of his eyes and overcoming the momentary dizziness of transition, the first thing Jason did was to look around and confirm that Nesbit and Grenfell were both on the stage with himself and Mondrago, and both alive.

The second thing he noticed was Kyle Rutherford, in his usual position to await a scheduled retrieval. The old man looked as though he had been struck in the chest as he stared at the stage with its four—not six—figures.

Rutherford hastened forward. "Where—?"

Jason pulled no punches. "Dr. Boyer and Inspector Da Cunha are dead, with no remains." He glanced around the floor of the displacer stage. A spot of wetness caught his eye—a puddle in which lay a tiny sphere with slimy strands of undersea life adhering to it. (Mondrago, in a moment of mordant humor, had wondered aloud if there would be a shark flopping about the stage with Boyer's TRD in its belly.) Elsewhere, he knew, would be another TRD, covered with ash and dirt. "You don't want to know how Pauline died."

"This is terrible!" gasped Rutherford. "What happened?"

"It's a long story, which I need to relate to you in private."

"Yes, at once. Come to my office."

"Right. But first..." Jason turned to Nesbit and Grenfell and shook hands vigorously with both of them. "I'm very glad—very, *very* glad—to see that you two made it. I hope it wasn't too difficult, there at the end."

They returned his handclasp, but their expressions said they felt there was something slightly odd about the intensity of his relief. "We had no great problems, Commander," said Nesbit. "We simply followed your instructions."

"My 'instructions'?" echoed Jason, puzzled.

"Why, yes, Commander. The instructions you gave us aboard *Soledad* before your departure. Everything went as you predicted. Oh, by the way...where *did* you go after that?"

Jason and Mondrago exchanged a blank look. Then Jason understood, and slowly smiled. It all fit.

Jason found himself wishing for some kill-devil by the time he had finished talking. In his preliminary oral report to Rutherford, he had left out only one thing—the most important thing.

So now Rutherford knew about the *Tuova'Zhonglu* Teloi, and the repulsive cult they and the Transhumanists had founded in seventeenth-century Hispaniola, and about Zenobia and her efforts to counter it. He also knew the origin of the spacecraft wreck Sam Asamoa had found. Finally, he knew about the destruction of the Teloi battlestation. Jason had dared hope to receive a pat on the head for that last. But it, and everything else, paled into insignificance beside the one other thing Rutherford now knew.

"So," Rutherford said in a hollow voice, "Henry Morgan returned to his fleet after learning about time travel, and going into space, and seeing modern technology in operation, and . . . and . . ." He couldn't continue, and his eyes went to the sword in his display case as he so often did at moments like this.

"At least," Jason reminded him, "Morgan *did* return to his fleet as history required."

"Yes. That's something." A shudder ran through Rutherford as he contemplated the alternative. "Nevertheless, he did so with knowledge that neither he nor anyone else of his century was supposed to possess. There's nothing in recorded history to suggest that anyone *did* possess it. But surely he talked about his adventures! The story would spread!" His face wore the look of a man peering over a precipice at whose bottom lurked the unthinkable.

"As you've observed," Jason said quietly, "history holds nothing to indicate that it happened. Which means it didn't happen—it must have been prevented. And . . . I believe I know how it was prevented. You see, there's one thing I haven't told you."

"Yes?"

"I haven't told you because I knew you wouldn't believe me without evidence."

"I realize we've had our differences, Jason, but I know you to be a man of your word."

"Nevertheless, you would have found this unacceptable. It was hard enough for *me* to accept. But there's no other answer. And something Nesbit said to me down there on the displacer stage confirmed it."

Rutherford's eyes narrowed. "You spoke of 'evidence.'"

"Right. Let's go and view the disc from my implant."

"There," said the technician as she put back in place the tiny flap of artificial skin that covered the slot in Jason's right temple. In her other hand was the retracting tool which now held an almost invisibly tiny computer disc.

The neurally interfaced brain implant was such a flagrant violation of the Human Integrity Act that the Authority had had to expend a fair amount of political capital to obtain a special exemption for it. They had gone to the trouble anyway because it had a large number of very useful functions. One of the most important—and the one which required the highest percentage of the implant's almost negligible volume—was that of recording what Jason saw and heard, by means of a direct splicing onto his optic and auditory nerves. It didn't do so continuously, because the disc's capacity, while considerable (two hours of footage per gigabyte), was not infinite. Instead, it was turned on and off by direct neural command, enabling Jason to ration his available time, recording only the significant sights and sounds.

"I am, of course, consumed with curiosity to see this Teloi battlestation," said Rutherford as the technician inserted the disc into the highly specialized projector it required.

"You will," Jason assured him. "As always, you'll view

the whole thing in the course of my formal debriefing. But right now there's just one thing I want to show you." He addressed the technician. "Fast-forward to almost the end. And we don't need audio."

It took only a few moments to zero in on the view from the Kestrel's cargo hold, with Mondrago and Romain at the edge of vision and the Caribbean visible a short distance below through the yawning cargo hatch. A yardarm floated on those unsettled waters, with two men clutching it. The one to the right was looking up, so that they were looking directly into his face.

"Freeze," Jason told the technician. "That's Henry Morgan on the left," he said to Rutherford. "But let's zoom in on that face to the right." The technician complied, and the face filled the screen.

At first, Rutherford looked blank. "What were you doing—?" he began . . . and then he remembered whose implant had recorded this image, and his breath caught.

Jason nodded. "Yes, that's right. I'm the first person in the history of time travel to catch a glimpse of myself."

Rutherford said nothing, for he had lost the power of speech. Even after he regained it, he was unable to form sentences, only managing false starts. "But . . . It can't . . . Impossible . . . How . . . ?"

"Now we know how the seeming paradox involving Morgan is going to be prevented. *I'm* going to go back and prevent it."

By a stroke of ill luck, Alistair Kung currently held the revolving chairmanship of the council's special ops oversight committee. Now the committee met in special session, with Jason, Rutherford and Irving Nesbit in attendance—the last at Kung's insistence. Kung spoke in a voice as heavy as the rest of him.

"So do I understand, Commander Thanou, that you want us to send back a party—"

"No, not a party. Just me. It's a matter of shaving with Occam's Razor. I'm the only one we *know* was involved." The committee members' expressions said they did indeed know it, having viewed the recording, and that knowing wasn't the same thing as being happy about it.

"I am gratified that you are adopting such an uncharacteristically conservative philosophy," said Kung ponderously.

"But," Helene de Tredville pointed out with prim severity, "the fact remains that we would be sending you to a period of time when you yourself were already present at an earlier point in the timeline of your personal consciousness. As you know, this flies in the face of one of the Authority's most fundamental guidelines. There must never be a possibility of a time traveler encountering himself."

"But," Jason reminded her, "I *didn't* 'encounter' myself. I merely *saw* myself. No harm done."

"But even that is unprecedented!" sputtered Alcide Martiletto, who looked as if he was experiencing heart palpitations at the thought. Everyone ignored him, as usual. Jason wondered how he had gotten onto the committee. He wasn't sure he wanted to know.

"Also," Jadoukh Kubischev said, hoisting his large frame up straighter in his chair, "there is the matter of the piece of equipment you want to take with you."

"That I *must* take with me if I'm to do what's

needful," Jason corrected him. "And prior to this meeting I've had a chance to consult with the experts. They assure me that the item I require can be miniaturized to the point of meeting the 'all-you-can-conveniently-carry' rule, at least if it's designed for a preset, one-shot application as this one would be. And it should be light enough for me to tread water with it. Disguising it as an in-period artifact would be difficult—but there's no need to do so."

"No need?" Rutherford sounded like a surgeon who had just heard someone say there was no need to sterilize the instruments.

"No, because after using it I'll simply let go of it and it will sink to the bottom of the Caribbean. Here's my plan. I'll go back to the precise moment after Morgan jumped into the sea. That moment will be easily ascertainable, since my implant automatically keeps time on the recorder imagery. The exact location will be a little trickier, but it can be inferred from the recorded data. I'll appear just over the water, fall in, join Morgan on the yardarm he was holding onto, and do what has to be done." Jason glanced at Nesbit. "There's something else I have to do, once Morgan and I are hauled aboard his flagship. After I've done that, I'll activate my TRD—one of the Special Ops 'controllable' versions, of course. It shouldn't be necessary to keep the stage clear for more than a few hours at most."

De Tredville looked alarmed. "You mean to say you're going to vanish from sight aboard a crowded sailing ship?"

"Don't worry, I won't do it in anyone's view. Thanks to conversations I've had recently with Mr. Nesbit and Dr. Grenfell, I know how I'm going to do it unobserved."

"So," Kubischev said slowly, "they've told you what you're going to do, because they've already experienced it . . ." He trailed off, shaking his head.

"This is all frightfully upsetting!" Martiletto fluted.

"An understatement," rumbled Kung. He puffed himself up, toadlike. "Commander Thanou, this is a perfect example of the kind of problems that I have predicted all along your Special Operations Section would cause with its departures from our traditional, tried-and-true guidelines. This entire fiasco of giving Henry Morgan a glimpse of the future—"

"—was the result of mischance and hostile action," Rutherford reminded him.

"Perhaps. But compounding the problem by taking Morgan into space was Commander Thanou's own unilateral, unauthorized decision. Entirely on his own initiative he went charging off and attacked the Teloi battlestation, at the urging of a primitive scalawag like Morgan."

"Thereby preventing the Transhumanist underground from obtaining Teloi military technology, which would have been a calamity of imponderable proportions."

"Er . . . that's beside the point, Kyle! Correct doctrine and proper procedure: those are the important things, not mere results!" Kung's tone suggested that there was something faintly vulgar about results, or at least about people who got them. "Furthermore, it is clear from Commander Thanou's report that he also committed other, lesser improprieties and indiscretions, including various gratuitous heroics. Fortunately, I had the foresight to insist that a person of sound attitudes accompany the expedition, to rein in Commander Thanou's enthusiasms if possible or, failing that, to report on them to the council." He shone the light of his countenance on Nesbit. "You were with Commander Thanou at all times, save for the very end. I now invite you to share with the committee your observations on his conduct—observations which I am confident will confirm my misgivings about the Special Operations Section in general and Commander Thanou in particular. You have the floor."

This is it, thought Jason with a sinking feeling. *He's heard his master's voice.*

Nesbit stood up. A few days hadn't sufficed to erase the effects of months of tropical sun and often inadequate food, and the rabbit semblance that had always struck Jason was somewhat in abeyance. His eyes made the circuit of the table, finally coming to rest to meet Jason's for an instant. Then he turned and faced Kung squarely.

"Yes, councilor, I accompanied Commander Thanou for the entire course of the expedition up to the storm off Maracaibo. During which time he saved my life, and the lives of other members of the expedition, repeatedly. And during which time he was forced to make numerous decisions, without any possibility of recourse to higher authority, entirely on his own. And those decisions were invariably the correct ones."

At first it didn't seem to register on Kung. Then he started to open his mouth, but Nesbit continued on without a break, overriding him.

"We all owe a debt of gratitude to Commander Thanou for his willingness to exercise an effectively independent command on the basis of the information available to him in the field, and without regard for any second-guessing he might encounter on his return. I fully endorse all his actions."

Kung now seemed to be experiencing difficulty breathing.

Well, well! thought Jason, awestruck. *Somewhere in the jungles of Hispaniola, he grew a backbone.*

"Furthermore," Nesbit went on, "we have no choice but to approve Commander Thanou's plan, simply because we *know* that he will in fact carry it out. We know this not only from the evidence of his visual recording, but also from the demonstrable fact that we live today in a world in which neither Henry Morgan nor anyone else in the seventeenth century disseminated knowledge of the future."

"Very true," said Rutherford gravely. "We like to say that 'reality protects itself.' In this case, an element of conscious human decision-making has been introduced into the process of its doing so. And yes, I am aware of the disturbing philosophical implications of all this for the concept of free will. But the fact remains that, as Mr. Nesbit put it, we have no choice."

None of them looked happy. But there really was no alternative. And Nesbit's testimony clearly made an impression on everyone, coming as it did from one generally regarded as Kung's lapdog. There was very little further discussion.

Afterwards, Jason stopped Nesbit in the hallway. "Irving . . . I hope you won't take this the wrong way, but you surprised the hell out of me."

Nesbit's expression was rueful. "I think I surprised a number of people—notably Councilor Kung."

"Yeah. I hope there won't be any adverse consequences for you." *The lapdog that stood up and barked*, Jason thought.

Nesbit shrugged, then smiled. "It will have been worth it. You see . . . I also surprised myself." He paused. "I suppose you'll be departing soon."

"Right. There's not much that needs to be done in the way of preparation. I've already got the language, and the bio cleansing is still current, and . . ." Jason rubbed his face, which he hadn't shaved since his return. "So it's just a matter of fabricating one piece of equipment."

"Of course." Nesbit hesitated. "Commander, I understood what you said about why this must be a one-man expedition by you. But . . . I wish I could be coming with you."

"I wouldn't mind having you along." To his amazement, Jason found he actually meant it.

They shook hands and Jason departed, leaving Nesbit looking wistful.

CHAPTER TWENTY-EIGHT

Jason was a seasoned veteran of numerous temporal displacements. But on all those occasions, he had arrived in the target milieu with solid ground under his feet. So, despite all his mental preparation, it was disorienting to abruptly find himself in midair a few feet above the waves.

For a split second he was in free fall, before striking the surface of the water and going under. At least the cold wasn't shocking, here in the tropics. Nevertheless, sheer startlement caused him to release his carefully held breath. He struggled back up, broke the surface, and spent a moment treading water, coughing salt water out of his lungs and taking deep gasps of the air of the seventeenth century. Only then did he have the leisure to look around him.

Yes! Not far away, Henry Morgan was swimming toward a floating yardarm. The complex calculations based on his recorder data had proven accurate. *But of course they were*, flashed through his mind. *They had to be.* He dismissed the matter, for there was no time for philosophical conundrums just now. He began swimming toward the yardarm which Morgan was now grasping. At this moment, Jason knew, Morgan was being glimpsed from above by what he decided to think of as "Jason Mark I," who was currently engaged in a struggle with Romain. But Jason was in no position to look skyward at the moment. He was too busy swimming—somewhat awkwardly, with the compact but by no means weightless device in the satchel that was strapped to his back.

A few strokes brought him to the yardarm, which he caught with his left hand. Morgan, to his left, turned to him with a grin. "Jason! You got off the flying ship after all! Where are the others?"

"They're fine, Captain, and we scuppered Romain," With his right hand, Jason slipped the strap of the satchel around the yardarm so as to leave both his hands free. "I'll tell you all about it later, after we've been picked up."

"Right," said Morgan. "It won't be long now. They've spotted us." He jerked his chin in the direction of *Soledad*, on whose deck small, waving figures could be seen. "And afterwards, you must tell me how we can go about retrieving the flying ship!" He called out and waved back.

With Morgan's attention thus diverted, Jason turned his head and looked upward. The unnatural rectangular hole in the sky that was the Kestrel's cargo hatch was overhead, and a face was peering down over its edge. For a brief instant of soul-shaking *wrongness*, Jason met the eyes of his own very slightly younger self. Then Jason Mark I was no longer visible, and the cargo hold's interior lights went off, rendering the hatch effectively invisible to anyone who didn't know where to look for it. And Jason Mark II knew he had only a moment before *Soledad* drew close enough for its crew to observe what he was about to do.

With his right hand, he reached behind his shoulder and pulled from the satchel an object shaped vaguely like a fat pistol, and clearly a product of a technology unknown to this century. At the same time, his left arm went around Morgan's throat in an unbreakable choke hold. The buccaneer admiral gagged, and his eyes bulged in shock, as Jason placed the "muzzle" of the pistollike device against his right temple.

"I'm truly sorry, Captain," Jason whispered. "But remember what you said about 'making a chaos of creation'? That can't be permitted." He squeezed with his left arm, applying pressure in a very precise way, and Morgan passed out momentarily. (For what was about to happen, the subject had to be unconscious, lest severe mental trauma result.) Then he put his finger to a stud . . . and, in spite of himself, hesitated for an instant.

Selective artificially induced partial amnesia—vulgarly called "mindwipe" to the tight-lipped disapproval of the medical profession—was held by many to violate the spirit if not the letter of the Human Integrity Act. For this reason it was normally restricted to use as a last-resort tool of mental therapy, as a means of removing intolerable memories. Jason had thought at one time that it might have to be used on Grenfell, but traditional methods had proven efficacious. There were persistent rumors—just as persistently denied—that intelligence agencies also found certain uses for it, such as excising highly sensitive knowledge from the minds of personnel who might be captured and interrogated under truth drugs. Either way, it generally required a bulky array of equipment—but most of that consisted of highly sophisticated scanners and their associated computers, for the delicate and complex task of identifying and isolating the particular memories to be erased. The actual generator of the very short-ranged neural beam that did the erasing was quite small . . . and when the objective was to simply eliminate *all* memories going back a preset length of time, that generator was just about all that was required. This was all the more so when the generator could be engineered for a single-shot pulse that would burn out its tiny energy cell.

Thus it was that when Jason pressed the stud, everything that had happened since the moment the storm had swept him, Jason and Mondrago overboard—a moment precisely ascertainable from the timer function of Jason's implant—vanished from Morgan's memory.

The technology wasn't infallible, for the effects did not reach down to the very bedrock of the subconscious. In the coming years Morgan's dreams might occasionally be troubled by glimpses of outlandish machines, unimagined celestial vistas, and weapons beyond the powers of pagan gods. But then he would awaken and attribute it to the rum, for manifestly it could be nothing else.

Jason released his grip on the device's handle and it fell into the water with a splash. Then he held onto Morgan and watched *Soledad* draw closer.

Morgan soon regained consciousness, wincing with the headache that always followed memory erasure, and looked around, bewildered. "Jason, it's you. But . . . the storm . . . ?"

"It's over, Captain. We fell over the side together. You must have hit your head on something; you've been out for a few hours. I got you to this yardarm. And here comes the flagship—they've sighted us."

"By God, Jason, you saved my life! I'll be damned and roasting in Hell before I forget it!" Morgan waved to the figures leaning over *Soledad*'s rail. "Ahoy, you lubbers! Throw us a line!"

As *Soledad* drew alongside, Jason glanced back over his shoulder. He fancied he could see two splashes in the distance, not far from *Rolling-Calf*: Mondrago and Jason Mark I, hitting the water. But he was looking into the setting sun and he couldn't be certain.

They were soon clambering aboard the flagship, surrounded by its vociferously welcoming crew. "What of the fleet?" Morgan demanded.

"All the ships came through the storm, Captain," someone declared. "Your good fortune must have rubbed off on all of us!" There was a chorus of profanely awestruck comments on this latest manifestation of Henry Morgan's famous luck.

"Here's my luck!" boomed Morgan, slapping Jason on the back. "If it weren't for Jason here I'd be shark shit! As it is, I've got the worst headache of my life. Let's get some rum!"

As the laughing throng moved away, Jason spotted Nesbit and Grenfell, both visibly relieved. After they'd all drunk enough kill-devil to be sociable, and dusk had fallen, Jason led the two away to where they could talk in relative privacy. The stars were starting to come out with tropical rapidity, and as he gazed up at them he smiled at the recollection of what had occurred out there just a short time ago.

"We were afraid you were lost, Commander," said Nesbit. "Is Alexandre . . . ?"

"He's all right. He's over there on *Rolling-Calf* with Zenobia." Which, Jason reflected, was the truth as far as it went; he just didn't mention who else was there. "I don't have much time, so listen carefully. I'm going to have to leave this ship—by which I mean jump over the side. It must appear to be a simple 'man overboard' situation, so I'll need your cooperation."

Nesbit looked understandably bewildered. "But . . . Commander, where are you going? And why?"

"I'm afraid, Irving, that you don't have a need to know that." Jason quirked a smile. "Yes, I recall your low opinion of that doctrine. But you're just going to have to live with it. You're also going to have to live with being on your own until your retrieval." Nesbit's stricken look awoke Jason's compassion. "It shouldn't be so bad. Remember, the retrieval date is May 20. By the time this ship gets back to Port Royal, you won't have long to wait."

"Yes!" Grenfell's eyes lit up. "I seem to recall, now: Morgan returned on May 16."

Roughly the same time Zenobia is going to get to Morant Bay with Jason Mark I, Jason reflected. "Right. So you'll only have to lay low in Port Royal for four days. It shouldn't be hard. Everybody in that town is going to be concentrating on having a colossal party, with Morgan's boys back ashore with a ton of loot to spend." Jason was almost sorry he was going to miss it. "Go back to the inn we stayed at before. If they can't accommodate you, just sleep outside like so many others do—but be sure to stand watches. It shouldn't be hard to maintain a low profile."

"But, Commander," Nesbit protested, "we won't have you to give us a countdown to our retrieval." He clearly didn't relish the prospect of having the world around him vanish without warning.

"No, you won't. But remember, it's going to be four days after your arrival at Port Royal. And, like all our retrievals, it's timed for shortly before local dawn, to minimize the chances of anyone observing us disappearing into thin air. So in the small hours of May 20, get somewhere private and hold yourselves in readiness so it won't be too much of a shock to the system."

They waited a while longer, until it was well and truly dark, before going inconspicuously to the forecastle. No one was about, under the tropical stars.

"Now," Jason explained, "I don't want any unexplained disappearance that will cause people to wonder. This will be a routine accident. Afterwards, tell everyone that I had too much to drink and fell over the side and drowned."

"I think Morgan will be genuinely regretful," Grenfell opined.

I think I might be too, Jason was honest enough to admit to himself.

"Very well, Commander, I'll give the alert as instructed." Nesbit's brow furrowed in the moonlight. "How, exactly, are you going to get to wherever it is you're going, after falling in the water?"

"'Need to know,' Irving," Jason reminded him with a grin. He shook hands with both of them. "I'll see you in twenty-fourth-century Australia soon." Then he hitched himself up on the rail and went over the side feet first, crossing his ankles and folding his arms to make himself a projectile entering the water with minimal resistance.

He heard Nesbit's shout of "Man overboard!" a split second before he hit the water and went under. Then, while holding his breath, he thought a command. There was the usual indescribable moment of *wrongness*, and then he collapsed in a soaking heap on the displacer stage.

CHAPTER TWENTY-NINE

"Yes," said Roderick Grenfell, "Esquemeling's *The Buccaneers of America*, our primary source, says Morgan's fleet encountered a severe storm the day after departing from Maracaibo. It says nothing about Morgan himself being washed overboard. But there is nothing about Morgan being separated from the rest of the fleet for a few hours that is incompatible with the account, which at any rate is very brief and sketchy."

"Good!" Kyle Rutherford's relief was palpable.

Along with Grenfell and Rutherford, the latter's private office held Jason and Mondrago. Chantal Frey was also there, for this involved the Transhumanist underground. She had, from the first, been fascinated by Zenobia. At the moment, though, she was occupied with another question.

"I still don't quite understand why Asamoa's expedition in 1791 found the wreck of the Kestrel. After all, the Transhumanists had temporally displaced it, so I assume it had its own TRD. Why didn't it just snap back to their linear present when..." Her brow furrowed. "Oh. I see. The thing was smashed to fragments—including the fragment that contained the TRD. So only that particular fragment was retrieved."

"That's one possibility," Jason nodded. "Another is that it had no TRD at all. Romain mentioned that they were thinking of leaving it in the seventeenth century and making their Teloi allies a present of it."

"Either way," stated Rutherford with subject-closing firmness, "it is a fact. So it seems as though we have tied all the loose ends together, as people say."

"Not quite," said Jason. "There's a rather large loose end in the form of the *Tuova'Zhonglu* Teloi."

"But Jason, you destroyed their battlestation."

"Yes—*one* battlestation," Jason countered. "How do we know there aren't more of them, still around today, roaming the spacelanes in the manner Ahriman described?"

Rutherford's color didn't look particularly good. "We've never found any evidence of surviving Teloi in today's galaxy."

"How much of the galaxy have we explored? Practically none of it. All our colonies are within fifty light-years of Sol. In 1669 they had been wandering the galaxy for a long time, with the patience of lifespans in years best expressed in powers of ten. And you should abandon all your previous ideas about the Teloi character, which are based on the *Oratioi'Zhonglu* I encountered in ancient Greece. *These* Teloi are *really* nasty."

"And," Mondrago put in, "we have absolutely no idea of where their base planet is. And..." He came to a halt of horrified realization.

"Go ahead, Alexandre," Jason urged.

"Well, sir . . . this is just speculation. But I can't help wondering. What if the Trahshumanist underground knows how to get in touch with them, and does so—or *has* done so, or *will* do so—at some point in time? Remember, the Transhumanist equivalent of our temporal displacer is relatively small and compact and, therefore, portable. I know it can only work within, and in relation to, a planetary gravitational field. But there's no reason that planet has to be Earth."

For a moment, they all stared nightmare in the face.

"We've always been told that nothing can change recorded history," said Grenfell, speaking at least half to himself. "But *whose* history? If there are in fact surviving Teloi today, presumably they keep written records."

"Well," said Rutherford briskly, "it is obvious that from now on our interstellar exploration vessels are going to have to be constantly on the alert for evidence of Teloi survivals." His briskness did not deceive Jason. Underneath it lay an old man's dreary realization that the assumed truths on which his life had been built were slipping away into the dim and dusty realm of aging memory, as though they had never really been, leaving him to wonder what his life had really meant.

"In fact," said Mondrago, unintentionally deepening Rutherford's depression, "all exploratory expeditions from now on probably ought to have armed escorts."

"That's not the half of it," Jason added. "We're going to need to institute a whole new survey program, moving outward much faster than the kind of leisurely in-depth exploration we've done so far because it will be a very narrowly focused Teloi hunt."

"*Those* ships will definitely have to travel in armed convoys," Mondrago nodded.

Rutherford turned brisk again. "Well, that's outside our purview, although I will of course pass these observations on to the appropriate authorities. That, and the fact that law enforcement agencies must redouble their efforts to root out the Transhumanist underground in the present day—and, most especially, find their temporal displacer. But for the present, our own job is done, thanks to you, Jason." His eyes narrowed as he studied the younger man. "And yet I can't avoid the impression that something about this mission is still bothering you."

"What? Oh, nothing, really. It's just..." Jason flashed a self-deprecating smile. "Silly of me, but I still can't help thinking it was a rotten trick to play on Morgan. It was like killing—or at least stealing—a part of his life."

Chantal gave him an appraising look. "You liked him, didn't you?"

"On a certain level, yes, I admit it. He was a... character."

Rutherford raised one primly disapproving eyebrow. "He was also a wicked cutthroat."

"Well, nobody's perfect." Jason chuckled. "Alexandre, do you remember what he said to us after we went along with his idea of going after the Teloi battlestation?"

"Yeah," Modrago grinned. "He said you and I were buccaneers at heart."

Chantal looked from one of them to the other and smiled. "I think he may have had a point."

Rutherford did not smile. "I'm inclined to agree. And... I believe that in the times ahead, that may be exactly what we need, and what we'll be grateful to still have." He blinked, as though surprised at himself, and hastily wrapped around himself the persona that was expected of him, dismissing the meeting with a few dry, meaningless words.

Jason was departing along the corridor when he heard a hesitant voice call his name behind him. He stopped and turned around.

"Yes, Chantal?"

"If you have moment . . . I wanted to ask you something about Zenobia."

"Yes, I couldn't help noticing your interest in her."

"I recall you mentioning that you had suggested to her the possibility of subsequent expeditions to give her aid in combatting the Transhumanist cult and any stranded *Tuova'Zhonglu* Teloi that might be assisting it."

Yes, thought Jason, *come to think of it, your eyes did light up on hearing that.* "Yes. I wanted to make sure she'd be willing to accept such help. But, as you'll recall me saying, I made no promises to her. That would have exceeded my authority. And besides, I have to rate the likelihood of it actually happening as very low, given the cost—at least given the technology available to our side—of temporal displacements."

"Still, if you lend your support to the idea . . ."

"Maybe. Tell me: why are you so interested?"

Chantal blushed slightly. "Well . . . I *am*, after all, sort of the resident expert on the Transhumanists, and she *is* working against them, and . . . well . . ." She sought for words and failed.

But further words were unnecessary, for Jason finally understood. She was cherishing a hope that, at some point, the Authority would trust her sufficiently to send her back in time again, to meet the formidable female Transhumanist renegade.

"Hey," he told her with a grin, "maybe Alexandre and I aren't the only ones around here who are buccaneers at heart!"

Leaving her spluttering in search of a response, he turned and departed with a jaunty wave, whistling the tune of a sea shanty he had learned under the Caribbean stars.

AUTHOR'S NOTE

It would be dishonest to deny our continued fascination with the pirates of the Caribbean, even though it probably says something about us that we would rather not hear.

Some readers may feel that my depiction of Port Royal, Jamaica, a.k.a. "the Sodom of the New World" in its piratical heyday of the 1660s must be just a mite exaggerated. They may be assured that everything I have written about the place is fully supported by contemporary sources. If it were still in business today it would be a favorite destination for Spring Break.

Likewise, Henry Morgan's 1669 expedition to Maracaibo and subsequent getaway, which reads like something out of an over-the-top Hollywood pirate movie, is absolutely factual—and, as far as we know, accomplished without assistance from time travelers. Equally factual, for that matter, is Morgan's later taking of Panama with a two-thousand-man pirate army he led across the isthmus in a march of incredible privations to fight and win a pitched battle against two-to-one odds. Think about that for a moment. Try to imagine forging a disciplined army out of two thousand Jack Sparrows. The man's leadership ability must have been off the charts. Indeed, the entire career of this remarkable (if deplorable) figure is proof of the old chestnut that truth is stranger than fiction. It seems safe to say, as the Jamaicans still do, that his was a very powerful duppy. And it is eminently appropriate that a brand of rum is named after him.

Zenobia aside, all the pirate captains I have named as associates of Morgan are factual, and commanded the ships I have assigned to them. I know of no evidence that Roche Braziliano (roughly translatable as "The Brazilian Rock," which sounds like the professional wrestler he would probably be if he were around today) was with Morgan at Maracaibo. But since he did not disappear from history until 1671, it is not impossible that he could have been. I challenge anyone to prove he wasn't.

Don Alonzo de Campos y Espinosa is also a true-life portrait. On his return to Spain he was court-martialed for the Maracaibo fiasco by the War Tribunal of the Council of the Indies, but his conviction was voided. The feeling seems to have been that it wasn't his fault that he had been up against a genius of sorts.

I couldn't make up the names of the Port Royal whores if I tried. They are authentic, although I can't prove that all the ladies named herein were practicing their profession at the time of the story.

There seems to be some disagreement on how far back the word "privateer" goes. It may not have been coined until the eighteenth century. But the people of the seventeenth century were nothing if not familiar with the concept, so even if the word itself is an anachronism I consider it a permissible one in the interest of clarity. And "pirate" was a fighting word—especially among privateers. Henry Morgan's sensibilities were deeply wounded whenever anyone called him a pirate. You didn't want to wound Morgan's sensibilities. You really didn't.

Dates in the historical sources are often imprecise, and the course of events immediately preceding the captains' council off Cow Island is especially unclear. One account seems to suggest that HMS *Oxford* joined Morgan there and arrested *Le Cerf Volant*, only becoming Morgan's flagship afterwards. I find this impossible to believe. Without the instantaneous global communications we take for granted today, her captain would have had no way of knowing Morgan and his fleet were going to be rendezvousing there and therefore no reason for going to that particular speck of land. I have accepted the other version, which is that *Oxford* reported to Governor Modyford at Port Royal, and that Morgan subsequently took her to Cow Island. This involves a certain amount of "random motion," but the math works. Incidentally, Morgan actually had a total of twelve ships there before the *Oxford* disaster, and eight for his descent on Maracaibo. I have added one: the *Rolling-Calf*, which is imaginary, as is her set-to with the equally fictional *L'Enfer*.

Likewise fictional (needless to say) is my version of the *Oxford* explosion's cause, although everything else about it is supported by contemporary accounts. These accounts sometimes contradict each other; I have picked and chosen, taking the elements that seem most plausible and rejecting things like the mainmast falling across Morgan's dinner table. The mere fact that he survived at all was so extraordinary that it seems to have lent itself to embellishment.

The Afro-Caribbean syncretic religions are a complex and fascinating subject to which I have endeavored to do accurate and respectful justice. The same goes for Jamaican folkways, but our information on these goes back only to much later periods. I have used aspects of the "Nine Night" funeral ceremonies and of the "Koo-min-ah" as it was witnessed among the Maroons as recently as the 1930s, and have attempted to "reverse-engineer" these practices back to the seventeenth century, with reference to their West African origins. The resulting synthesis should be considered, in its totality, a product of the author's imagination. But the elements from which it is synthesized are authentic—except, of course, for the innovations introduced by Zenobia, which needless to say are entirely imaginary. In the same manner, the fictional rites in Chapter Sixteen—aside from the participation of a Teloi—are cobbled together out of actual practices of the *Secte Rouge* that were attested to in the same period of the 1930s. In all of these matters, I make a point of acknowledging my indebtedness to Zora Neale Hurston's *Tell My Horse*.

The buccaneers' articles of agreement described in Chapter Thirteen are also something of a composite, incorporating some provisions drawn from similar articles dating from the early eighteenth century. I doubt if these things changed much in fifty years or so.

There is really no meaningful way to compare currencies across the centuries, but it has been estimated that a piece of eight was the equivalent in purchasing power of a little over fifty turn-of-the-twenty-first-century U.S. dollars. An English pound was worth about four pieces of eight. To put it in perspective: under the provisions of typical articles like those described herein, a buccaneer who lost his right arm on a successful expedition got something over $30,000 in "disability compensation."

The following is an excerpt from:

GHOSTS OF TIME

STEVE WHITE

Available from Baen Books
July 2014
trade paperback

CHAPTER ONE

It might almost have been the Caribbean.

Not really, of course. The Caribbean was far away indeed, across the unthinkable gulf of forty-eight and a half light years, no mean journey even in these days of the negative mass drive. And the afternoon sunlight that sparkled eye-wateringly on these tropical waters was that of Psi 5 Aurigae, a G0v star slightly more massive than Sol and perhaps half a billion years younger. And the vegetation that clothed these islands was not the wild, rank jungle that Jason Thanou remembered. This world of Hesperia, colonized only three generations ago, was still incompletely terraformed. Even in areas like this where biotech and nanotech had transformed the original naked rock and sand into soil, the scientifically selected, carefully nurtured terrestrial flora still stood in regimented rows. Only later, with the passage of time and the introduction of additional species, would it rebel, diversifying and efflorescing into something like what Jason had struggled through on Hispaniola.

And yet in spite of everything, as Jason flew his aircar westward over the Verdant Sea and gazed to his right at the mountainous islands that marked the boundary of the Cerulean Ocean to the north, he could almost imagine that those islands were the Greater Antilles, and that those peaks rearing above the orderly forest were the Blue Mountains of Jamaica, in whose shadow Port Royal had flourished in all its gaudy and unabashed sinfulness.

Port Royal had vanished almost seven centuries before, in 1692. But Jason had seen it with his own eyes, for he was head of the Special Operations Section of the Temporal Service, enforcement arm of the Temporal Regulatory Authority which held exclusive jurisdiction over all time travel. Only a couple of months before, in terms of his own consciousness, he had sailed those seas beside that preposterously engaging scoundrel Henry Morgan...and a certain she-pirate who was very difficult to forget.

He shook his head. Hesperia, his homeworld to which he had returned on a much-overdue leave, would never be mistaken for Earth, even though the two planets were near-twins in all physical parameters, and not just because of the newness of this world's imported ecology. Earth's aura of age went deeper than biology, into psychic realms that could not be measured or detected but which all but the most insensitive outworlders could feel in their souls as they walked through history-littered landscapes suffused with the memory of thousands of years of human experience in all its fervor and urgency.

Presently Jason flew over the continental shelf, and the shallow water below took on the greenness that gave the sea its name, courtesy of masses of the seaweed-like aquatic vegetation that was one of the highest expressions of Hesperia's mostly microbial indigenous life. Ahead lay the continent of Darcy's Land. A long beach backed by sandy bluffs extended as far as the eye could see to the south, but a few miles to the north the bluffs rose into a range of low hills extending down to cliff-faces at the sea. Lines of white surf rolled up and down the sand as the tide came in. (Hesperia's moon, believed to be a captured asteroid, was smaller than Earth's but orbited more closely, hurtling around the planet so swiftly that its motion was clearly visible at night. So the tides were at least equal in strength to the mother planet's, and more irregular. Sand erosion was a problem.) Low-built, light-tinted villas lined the crest of the bluffs, and it was toward one of these that Jason steered his aircar. It settled to the ground with a hum of grav repulsion and a swirl of dust from its ground-pressure effect.

The canopy clamshelled open and Jason stepped out into the hot sunlight. As always on visits home from Earth, he couldn't avoid the feeling that Hesperia's 0.97 G gravitation somehow seemed lighter than that, as though Earth's burden of history somehow added to the planet's mass. He yawned, having still not completely readjusted to his homeworld's rotation period of 27.3 standard hours. Then he smiled and waved as a handsome woman wearing a loose flowing gown emerged from the villa and walked along a palm-shaded walkway toward the landing stage, smiling in return at her son.

Helena Jankovic-Thanou was eighty-one standard years old (a little over seventy-nine in Hesperia's slightly longer years), but that was a less advanced age in this era than it had once been. She still walked with a sprightly step, and her hair was a dark iron-gray. Her straight features, light-olive skin and dark-brown eyes were those of her son, but when she gave Jason a quick kiss on the cheek she didn't have to reach up to do it. At five feet eleven, he was below average height for human males from Earth and other approximately one-gee planets in this day and age. It was a useful attribute for one whose work required him to pass inconspicuously in earlier, less well-nourished epochs. He inherited his relative shortness and solid muscularity from his father, who had been noticeably shorter than the willowy Helena, and positively stocky. When

Paul Thanou had died in a storm at sea, his widow had bought this small villa in the tropics.

"How is Daphne doing, dear?" she inquired.

"Fine. She sends her love." Jason had been visiting his older sister in one of the archipelagoes in the eastern reaches of the Verdant Sea, where she followed in their father's footsteps by working on one of the terraforming projects. Their mother had always been more comfortable with that than with her son's somewhat unorthodox career choices. It hadn't been so bad when he had joined the Hesperian Colonial Rangers, a paramilitary constabulary whose functions included suppression of the lawless elements that had sprung up on the frontiers of the terraformed regions as a kind of toxic sociological byproduct. But when he had accepted an (admittedly extremely well-paying) offer from the Temporal Regulatory Authority...!

"Good. Oh, by the way," Helena added as an afterthought, "there's a gentleman here to see you."

"Oh?" Jason was puzzled, having already touched bases with all his old friends and acquaintances.

"Yes. He just came down here from the Port Marshak spaceport. He's waiting in the study."

All at once, Jason's danger-tendrils tingled. Despite many attempts over the centuries to exploit quantum entanglement, there was still no such thing as instantaneous "interstellar radio."

Messages had to be carried by shipborne courier. It was one of the reasons for the effective political independence the colonies all enjoyed, however vociferous their protestations of loyalty to Mother Earth. At the same time, when Earth found it necessary to go to the expense of sending such a courier....

"Tell me, Mother: does this gentleman by any chance have the kind of features—plump cheeks, receding chin, slightly buck teeth—that vaguely suggest a rabbit?"

"Well, er, I wouldn't exactly have put it that way, dear. But now that you mention it..."

"Uh *huh!*" nodded Jason with the dourness of confirmed pessimism. He stalked to the villa and proceeded down an airy gallery where the afternoon sunlight was filtered through hanging ferns, to a vaulted room. The visitor rose to his feet from a recliner.

Irving Nesbit didn't really resemble a rabbit nearly as much as he once had. He had accompanied Jason's party to the seventeenth-century Caribbean, and to Jason's amazement had come out of that crucible of horrors and hardships with some of the physical and mental softness melted away. "Commander Thanou!" he beamed. "It is a pleasure to see you again."

"And it's something of a *surprise* to see you, Irving," said Jason, accepting Nesbit's extended hand. "After...what happened following your retrieval, I was worried that the Authority wouldn't be requiring your services for jobs like this. Or for anything else."

Nesbit looked rueful. His presence on the Caribbean expedition—to the despair of Jason, who had always regarded him as enough to give spineless bureaucrats a bad name—had been the work of Alastair Kung, a powerful member of the Authority's governing council who regarded the often unorthodox Special Operations Section as a necessary evil of whose necessity he was not totally convinced. In effect, Kung had sought to use his lap dog as a watchdog, keeping Jason on the straight and narrow path of the Authority's sacrosanct operational guidelines. Instead, on their return Nesbit had excelled himself and floored everyone by vehemently defending Jason's flagrant irregularities—surely at the price of his career, Jason had been certain.

"It's true that I was in bad odor with Councilor Kung for a while," Nesbit acknowledged. "But in the end even he was forced to admit that you had no choice but to take the actions you did, and indeed that your boldness may well have averted disaster."

Jason nodded. He knew what Nesbit meant, and that "disaster" might well be too weak a word.

On an earlier expedition to Bronze Age Greece, Jason had discovered the Teloi aliens who had once been worshipped as gods by the human race that they themselves had created by genetic manipulation of *homo erectus*. He and his companions had seriously weakened them, and by the time he had gone back to 490 B.C. to investigate their possible survival they had been a shadow of their former selves. But on that expedition he had uncovered something in its own way even more appalling. He had discovered that the Authority's carefully regulated time travelers were not the only interlopers in the human past.

A little over a century before, Earth (with the help of its returning extrasolar colonists) had freed itself from the Transhuman Dispensation and its twisted dream of distorting the natural human genotype into a grotesque hierarchy of gods and monsters. It had taken a torrent of blood to wash the motherworld clean of the Transhumanist abominations, but at least the job had been done...or so it had been generally believed. But, as Jason had discovered, surviving Transhumanist remnants had gone deep underground, licking their wounds and recovering their strength...and stealing Weintraub's work that had led to the invention of the Fujiwara-Weintraub Temporal Displacer. But they had avoided some flaw in Fujiwara's mathematics, as a result of which *their* temporal displacer was far more efficient and compact than the Authority's town-sized installation, and could be concealed. And they were using it to subvert the past. They could not change recorded history—the poorly understood "Observer Effect" saw to that. But they were filling the past's "blank spaces" with a secret history of conspiracies, genetically-engineered plagues, sociologically-engineered cults and delayed-action nanotechnological viruses that would all culminate in a Transhumanist triumph on *The Day*—a date somewhen in Jason's future which the Authority devoutly wished to learn.

It was to combat the Transhuman underground that the Special Operations Section had been formed, and granted a degree of latitude which gave Kung and his conservative ilk attacks of the vapors. And it was for this purpose that Jason had led an expedition—with Nesbit in tow—back to the seventeenth century, when the Teloi on Earth were all long dead and consigned to the realms of myth. But the Transhumanists were only too active—and the Teloi had returned, in a new and virulent form. An interstellar war had left their race extinct save for a hard core of military fanatics, the *Tuova'Zhonglu*, who for thousands of years had skulked about the galaxy, stewing in their own megalomania and grimly determined to reassert their dominance when the time was right. And the Transhumanists had tricked them into an alliance which had nearly culminated in the acquisition by the Transhumanists of Teloi military technology. To forestall that nightmare possibility, Jason had gone into space with his companions—including Captain Morgan, who had no business being there three centuries before Yuri Gagarin. That, in turn, had forced Jason to go back to the same time period as his own slightly younger self and restore the rightness of history by wiping the impermissible parts of Morgan's memory. For Kung, that had been the final straw. It was only Nesbit's unexpected support that had made it possible, and Jason had been properly grateful.

Now, however. . . .

"Well, Irving, I'm glad you're back in favor. Although come to think of it, sending you here may have been intended as a form of punishment, given the way Kung feels about the outworlds." *And their inhabitants*, Jason mentally added. *Especially me.*

Nesbit looked slightly ill at ease. "Actually, it was Director Rutherford who sent me."

"I had a feeling it might be coming to that," Jason sighed. Kyle Rutherford was the Authority's operations director, possessed of wide powers but subject to the council's oversight. Over the years, he and Jason had had their ups and downs. Some of the downs had resulted from Rutherford's occasionally cavalier attitude toward leaves of absence. "So, Irving," Jason continued in what Nesbit by now recognized as a deceptively mild tone of voice, "do I gather that you're back in your old job as Rutherford's bearer of ill tidings?"

"Well . . . er. . . ."

"What deliberately inconspicuous 'special circumstances' or 'emergency contingency' clause is it this time, Irving?" Jason's voice grew even milder. "I know from experience that you can quote me Part, Article, Paragraph and Subparagraph."

"Director Rutherford thought that, in this instance, perhaps you would want to voluntarily cut your leave short."

"Did he indeed?"

"Yes. You see, the matter at hand concerns your next-to-last mission."

"What?" Jason blinked with surprise. "You mean the one to April, 1865?" Jason had only just brought a Special Ops team back from the final cataclysm of the Confederate States of America, where he had foiled a Transhumanist plot while Richmond burned, and departed for Hesperia on leave when Nesbit had been sent to summon him back to Earth for the seventeenth-century Caribbean expedition.

"The same. I'm not privy to the details—'need to know' and all that sort of thing—but it seems that evidence had come to light suggesting that at some point in our own near future the Transhumanists will launch an expedition back to a point in time earlier in 1865 than their previous expedition, in an effort to undo your work."

Jason stared. "Irving, do you realize what this means? This was one of their nanotech time bombs, deigned to disable technologically advanced equipment! On The Day it would have sent much of North America back to the nineteenth century—only worse, because people in the nineteenth century knew how to cope with such conditions."

"This is precisely why the Authority views the matter with such seriousness. You must be on hand in that time period, in the latter phases of the American Civil War, to counter this new attempt to put their nefarious plan into effect."

"Why me, in particular?"

"It is obviously a job for the Special Operations Section. And Director Rutherford feels that you, as leader of the previous expedition, will be in the best position to deal with this threat. After all, you have already received orientation in the period, including language and—"

"All well and good. But has it occurred to anyone that—depending on the exact dates to which I'm temporally displaced—this might result in me being present in the same area and time-frame as myself? That's only happened once in the history of the Authority, and you of all people ought to remember what a flap *that* caused."

"I certainly do." Nesbit suddenly took on a look of crafty calculation. "Councilor Kung will no doubt be absolutely livid."

Jason's face lit up. "Yes, he will, won't he?"

"In fact," Nesbit continued with careful expressionlessness, "he might even have a stroke."

"That *could* be a danger, couldn't it?" Jason brightened still further. "Especially considering how overweight he is."

"I would be deeply concerned for his health," said Nesbit solemnly.

"As should we all," Jason intoned with equal solemnity.

"He would be a great loss."

"I couldn't agree more." Jason was smiling broadly now. He walked over to a side table which held a cut-glass decanter filled with Hesperian rum from the easternmost islands of the Verdant Sea, where sugarcane had successfully taken root. It wasn't competitive with the mellow products of Earth's present-day West Indies, but it was a considerably smoother article than the ferocious kill-devil the two of them had somehow survived drinking in their days among the buccaneers of the Spanish Main. He opened the decanter and poured two glasses.

"I believe the sun is over the yardarm, Irving. Now, tell me more about this mission."

—end excerpt—

from *Ghosts of Time*
available in trade paperback,
July 2014, from Baen Books

Andre Norton

"The sky's no limit to Andre Norton's imagination…a superb storyteller." —The New York Times

---

Time Traders   0-671-31829-2 ★ $7.99 PB

"This is nothing less than class swashbuckling adventure—the very definition of space opera." —*Starlog*

Time Traders II   0-671-31968-X ★ $19.00

Previously published in parts as *The Defiant Agents* and *Key Out of Time*.

Janus   0-7434-7180-6 ★ $6.99 PB

Two novels. On the jungle world of Janus, one man seeks to find his alien heritage and joins a battle against aliens despoiling his world.

Darkness & Dawn   0-7434-8831-8 ★ $7.99 PB

Two novels: *Daybreak: 2250* and *No Night Without Stars*.

Gods & Androids   0-7434-8817-2 ★ $24.00 HC

Two novels: *Androids at Arms* and *Wraiths of Time*.

Dark Companion   1-4165-2119-4 ★ $7.99 PB

Two complete novels of very different heroes fighting to protect the helpless in worlds wondrous, terrifying, and utterly alien.

Star Soldiers   0-7434-3554-0 ★ $6.99 PB

Two novels: *Star Guard* and *Star Rangers*.

Moonsinger   1-4165-5517-X ★ $7.99 PB

Two novels: *Moon of Three Rings* and *Exiles of the Stars*.

From the Sea to the Stars   1-4165-2122-4 ★ $15.00 TPB

Two novels: *Star Gate* and *Sea Siege*.

Star Flight   1-4165-5506-4 ★ $7.99 PB

Two novels: *The Stars Are Ours* and *Star Born*.

Crosstime   1-4165-5529-3 ★ $23.00 HC

Two novels: *The Crossroads of Time* and *Quest Crosstime*.

Deadly Dreams   978-1-4391-3444-3 ★ $7.99 PB

Two novels: *Knave of Dreams* and *Perilous Dreams*.